Val McDermid comes from Kirkcaldy, Fife and was educated at St Hilda's College, Oxford, where she was the first student from a state school in Scotland. After graduation she became a journalist and worked briefly as a dramatist for BBC Radio, before embarking upon her career as a writer. She is now a No. 1 bestseller whose novels have been translated into more than thirty languages and have sold over fifteen million copies. Val has won many awards internationally, including the CWA Gold Dagger for best crime novel of the year, and the *LA Times* Book of the Year Award. She was inducted into the ITV3 Crime Thriller Awards Hall of Fame in 2009, was the recipient of the CWA Cartier Diamond Dagger in 2010, and received the Lambda Literary Foundation Pioneer Award in 2011. In 2016, Val received the Outstanding Contribution to Crime Fiction Award at the Theakston Old Peculier Crime Writing Festival. She writes full time and lives in Cheshire and Edinburgh.

You can discover more about the author at www.valmcdermid.com

BROKEN GROUND

When a body is discovered in the remote depths of the Highlands, DCI Karen Pirie finds herself in the right place at the right time. Unearthed with someone's long-buried inheritance, the victim seems to belong to the distant past — until new evidence suggests otherwise, and Karen is called in to unravel a mystery where nothing is as it seems. It's not long before an overheard conversation draws her into the heart of a different case, however — a shocking crime she thought she'd already prevented. As she inches closer to the twisted truths at the centre of these murders, it becomes clear that she's dealing with a version of justice terrifyingly different to her own . . .

Books by Val McDermid
Published by Ulverscroft:

THE GRAVE TATTOO
BENEATH THE BLEEDING
FEVER OF THE BONE
TRICK OF THE DARK
THE RETRIBUTION
THE VANISHING POINT
CROSS AND BURN
NORTHANGER ABBEY
THE SKELETON ROAD
SPLINTER THE SILENCE
OUT OF BOUNDS
INSIDIOUS INTENT

VAL McDERMID

BROKEN GROUND

Complete and Unabridged

CHARNWOOD
Leicester

First published in Great Britain in 2018 by
Little, Brown
An imprint of Little, Brown Book Group
London

First Charnwood Edition
published 2019
by arrangement with
Little, Brown Book Group
An Hachette UK Company
London

A catalogue record for this book is available
from the British Library.

ISBN 978–1–4448–4057–5

Published by
F. A. Thorpe (Publishing)
Anstey, Leicestershire

Set by Words & Graphics Ltd.
Anstey, Leicestershire
Printed and bound in Great Britain by
T. J. International Ltd., Padstow, Cornwall

This book is printed on acid-free paper

This book started with a bookseller telling me a story. And so it's dedicated to all the booksellers who love stories and thrust them into our hands and make addicts of us.

Three may keep a secret, if two of them are dead.

Benjamin Franklin,
Poor Richard's Almanack

1

1944 — Wester Ross, Scotland

The slap of spades in dense peat was an unmistakable sound. They slipped in and out of rhythm; overlapping, separating, cascading, then coming together again, much like the men's heavy breathing. The older of the pair paused for a moment, leaning on the handle, letting the cool night air wick the sweat from the back of his neck. He felt a new respect for gravediggers who had to do this every working day. When all of this was over, you wouldn't catch him doing that for a living.

'Come on, you old git,' his companion called softly. 'We ain't got time for tea breaks.'

The resting man knew that. They'd got into this together and he didn't want to let his friend down. But his breath was tight in his chest. He stifled a cough and bent to his task again.

At least they'd picked the right night for it. Clear skies with a half-moon that gave barely enough light for them to work by. True, they'd be visible to anyone who came up the track past the croft. But there was no reason for anyone to be out and about in the middle of the night. No patrols ventured this far up the glen, and the moonlight meant they didn't have to show a light that might attract attention. They were confident of not being discovered. Their training, after all, had made clandestine operations second nature.

A light breeze from the sea loch carried the low-tide tang of seaweed and the soft surge of the waves against the rocks. Occasionally a night bird neither could identify uttered a desolate cry, startling them every time. But the deeper the hole grew, the less the outside world impinged. At last, they could no longer see over the lip of the pit. Neither suffered from claustrophobia, but being that enclosed was discomfiting.

'Enough.' The older man set the ladder against the side and climbed slowly back into the world, relieved to feel the air move around him again. A couple of sheep stirred on the opposite side of the glen and in the distance, a fox barked. But there was still no sign of another human being. He headed for the trailer a dozen yards away, where a tarpaulin covered a large rectangular shape.

Together they drew back the canvas shroud to reveal the two wooden crates they'd built earlier. They looked like a pair of crude coffins standing on their sides. The men shaped up to the first crate, grabbing the ropes that secured it, and eased it off the bed of the trailer. Grunting and swearing with the effort, they walked it to the edge of the pit and carefully lowered it.

'Shit!' the younger man exclaimed when the rope ran too fast through one palm, burning the skin.

'Put a bleeding sock in it. You'll wake up the whole bloody glen.' He stamped back to the trailer, looking over his shoulder to check the other was behind him. They repeated the exercise, slower

2

and clumsier now, their exertions catching up with them.

Then it was time to fill the hole. They worked in grim silence, shovelling as fast as they could. As the night began to fade along the line of the mountains in the east, they attacked the last phase of their task, stamping the top layer of peat divots back in place. They were filthy, stinking and exhausted. But the job was done. One day, some way hence, it would be worth it.

Before they dragged themselves back into the cab, they shook hands then pulled each other into a rough embrace. 'We did it,' the older man said between coughs, pulling himself up into the driver's seat. 'We fucking did it.'

Even as he spoke, the *Mycobacterium tuberculosis* organisms were creeping through his lungs, destroying tissue, carving out holes, blocking airways. Within two years, he'd be forever beyond the consequences of his actions.

2

2018 — Edinburgh

The snell north wind at her back propelled Detective Chief Inspector Karen Pirie up the steady incline of Leith Walk towards her office. Her ears were tingling from the wind and tormented by the grinding, drilling and crashing from the massive demolition site that dominated the top end of the street. The promised development, with its luxury flats, high-end shops and expensive restaurants, might boost Edinburgh's economy, but Karen didn't think she'd be spending much time or money there. It would be nice, she thought, if the city council came up with ideas that benefited its citizens more than its visitors.

'Grumpy old bag,' she muttered to herself as she turned into Gayfield Square and made for the squat concrete boxes that housed the police station. More than a year on from the bereavement that had left her unmoored, Karen was making a conscious effort to breach the gloom that had fallen across her life like a curtain. She had to admit that, even on a good day, she still had a fair distance to go. But she was trying.

She nodded a greeting to the uniform on the front counter, stabbed the keypad with a gloved finger and marched down the long corridor to an office tacked on at the back like a grudging afterthought. Karen opened the door and stopped short on the threshold. A stranger was sitting at the usually unoccupied third desk in the room, feet on the wastepaper bin, the *Daily Record* open in his lap, in one hand a floury roll trailing bacon.

Karen made a theatrical show of stepping back and staring at the door plaque that read 'Historic Cases Unit'. When she turned back, the scrappy little guy's face still pointed at the paper but his eyes were on her, wary, ready to slide back to the newsprint with full deniability. 'I don't know who you are, or what you think you're doing here, pal,' she said, moving inside. 'But I know one thing. You've left it way too late to make a good first impression.'

Unhurried, he shifted his feet from the bin to the floor. Before he could say or do more, Karen heard familiar heavy footsteps in the hall behind her. She glanced over her shoulder to see Detective Constable Jason 'the Mint' Murray bearing down on her, trying to balance three cups of Valvona & Crolla coffee on top of each other. *Three* cups?

'Hi, boss, I'd have waited for you to get in but DS McCartney, he was gagging for a coffee so I thought I'd just . . . ' He registered the frost in her eyes and gave a weak smile.

Karen crossed the room to her desk, the only one with anything approximating a view. An insult of a window looked out across an alley on to a blank wall. She stared at it for a moment then fixed the presumed DS McCartney with a thin smile. He'd had the good sense to close his paper but not to straighten up in his seat. Jason gingerly stretched at full length to place Karen's coffee in front of her without getting too close. 'DS McCartney?' She gave it the full measure of disdain.

'That's right.' Two words was enough to nail his origins: Glasgow. She should have guessed from his gallus swagger. 'Detective Sergeant Gerry McCartney.' He grinned, either oblivious or indifferent. 'I'm your new pair of hands.'

'Since when?'

He shrugged. 'Since the ACC decided you needed one. Obviously she thinks you need a boy that knows what he's about. And that would be me.' His smile soured slightly. 'Hotfoot from the Major Incident Team.'

The new Assistant Chief Constable. Of course she was behind this. Karen had hoped her working life would have changed for the better when her previous boss had been caught up in the crossfire of a high-level corruption scandal and swept out with the rubbish. She'd never fitted his image of what a woman should be — obsequious, obedient and ornamental — and he'd always tried unsuccessfully to sniff out the slightest improprieties in her inquiries. Karen had wasted too much energy over the years keeping his nose out of the detail of her investigations.

When Ann Markie had won the promotion that brought the HCU under her aegis, Karen had hoped for a less complicated relationship with her boss. What she got was differently complicated. Ann Markie and Karen shared a gender and a formidable intelligence. But that was the limit of their congruence. Markie turned up for work every day camera-ready and box-fresh. She was the glamorous face of Police Scotland. And she made it clear at their first meeting that she was 110 per cent behind the Historic Cases Unit as long as Karen and Jason cracked cases that made Police Scotland look modern, committed and caring. As opposed to the sort of idiots who could spend a month searching for a man reported missing who was lying dead in his own home. Ann Markie was devoted to the kind of justice that let her craft sound bites for the evening news.

Markie had mentioned that the budget might stretch to an extra body in HCU. Karen had been hoping for a civilian who could devote themselves to admin and basic digital searches, leaving her and Jason to get on with the sharp end. Well, maybe sharp was the wrong word where Jason was concerned. But although he might not be the brightest, the Mint had a warmth that tempered Karen's occasional impatience. They made a good team. What they needed was backroom support, not some strutting Glasgow keelie who thought he'd been sent to be their saviour.

She gave him her best hard stare. 'From MIT to HCU? Whose chips did you piss on?'

A momentary frown, then McCartney recovered himself. 'Is this not your idea of a reward, then?' His lower jaw inched forward.

'My ideas don't always coincide with those of

7

my colleagues.' She picked the lid off her coffee and took a sip. 'As long as you don't think it's a holiday.'

'Naw, no way,' he said. Now he straightened up in his seat and looked alert. 'You get a lot of respect from the MIT,' he added hastily.

Karen kept her face straight. Now she'd learned one useful thing about Gerry McCartney — he was a good liar. She knew exactly how much respect her unit had with detectives who wrestled with intractable crimes in real time. They thought HCU was a doddle. If she nailed a historic perpetrator, she was a media hero for a day. If she failed? Well, nobody had their beady eyes looking over her shoulder, did they? 'Jason's working his way through a list of people who owned a red Rover 214 in 1986. You can give him a hand with that.'

McCartney's lip twitched in faint disgust. 'What for?'

'A series of violent rapes,' Jason said. 'He beat the last lassie so badly she ended up brain damaged in a wheelchair. She died only a couple of weeks ago.'

'Which is why our new evidence turned up. A former street girl saw the story in the paper. She didn't come forward at the time because she was still using and she didn't want to get on the wrong side of her dealer. But she had a wee notebook where she used to write down the cars that other women got into. Amazingly, she still had it, tucked away in an old handbag. The red Rover was around on all of the nights when the rapes took place.'

McCartney raised his eyebrows and sighed. 'But she couldn't manage to get the number. Is that not typical of your average whore?'

Jason looked apprehensive.

'Something you might like to take on board, Sergeant? We prefer the term 'sex worker' in this unit,' Karen said. It wasn't a tone of voice people argued with. Gerry sniffed but said nothing.

'She did get the number,' Jason said brightly. 'But the bag was in the attic where she lives now and the mice have been at it. The edges of the pages have all been chewed away. All we've got is the first letter: B.'

Karen smiled. 'So you guys have got the fun job of going through the DVLA records and tracking down the owners from thirty years ago. Some clerk in the driving licence office is going to love you. On the plus side, the lab at Gartcosh have managed to extract DNA from the evidence that's been sitting in a box all these years. So if we find a likely lad, we could get a nice neat result.' She finished her coffee and binned the cup. 'Good luck with that.'

'OK, boss,' Jason mumbled, already focused on the task. Setting a good example, Karen thought. The boy was learning. Slowly but surely, he was learning.

'Where are you heading?' McCartney asked as she made for the door.

She wanted to say, 'None of your business,' but she decided it was probably worth trying to keep him more or less on side. For now, at least. Till she had the full measure of him and the closeness of his connection to Ann Markie. 'I'm off to Granton to talk to one of the conservators who thinks she might have seen a stolen painting in a private collection.'

Again that slight twitch of the lip. 'I didn't think that was our thing. Stolen paintings.'

'It is when a security guard got a face full of shotgun pellets in the course of the theft. Eight years ago, and this is the first sniff we've had of where the painting might have ended up.' And she was gone, already planning the route in her head. One of the many things she loved about Edinburgh was that it was easier to get places on the bus and on foot than it was to wrangle a pool car out of the division. Anything that avoided the petty exercise of petty power was a plus in Karen's book. 'Number sixteen,' she muttered as she headed for the bus stops on Leith Walk. 'That'll do nicely.'

3

2018 — Wester Ross

Alice Somerville struggled out of the driver's seat of her Ford Focus with the supple grace of a woman forty years her senior. She groaned as she stretched her limbs, shivering in the cool breeze drifting in from the sea loch at the foot of the slope. 'I'd forgotten it's such a long way up,' she grumbled. 'That last hour from Ullapool seemed to go on for ever.'

Her husband unfolded himself from the passenger seat. 'And you were the one who objected when I insisted we stop in Glasgow last night.' He rolled his shoulders and arched his spine. 'If I'd listened to you, I'd have suffered irreversible spinal damage.' He grinned at her, oblivious to the goofy cast it gave his features. 'Scotland always goes on further than you expect it to.' He waggled each leg, trying to force his skinny jeans down to meet his brown leather lace-ups.

Alice pulled the scrunchie from her ponytail and shook her dark hair loose. As it fell around her face, it softened the sharpness of her features and emphasised her straight brows and high cheekbones. She popped the boot and took out her backpack. 'We were so excited last year, we didn't notice the distance so much. It is lovely, though. Look at those mountains, the way they

11

almost seem to fold into each other. And the sea, those big waves rolling in. It's hard to believe this is the same country as Hertfordshire.'

She rolled her shoulders then leaned back inside the car to retrieve a sheet of paper she'd printed out before they set off. 'This is definitely the place,' she said, comparing the photograph on the page to the long low building they'd parked in front of. It was a graceless huddle of stone crouching against the hillside, but it had clearly been recently renovated with an eye on its original lines. The pointing between the stones was still relatively uncolonised by moss and lichen, the window frames sturdy and true, their paintwork unblemished by the weather.

Will swung round and pointed to a two-storey white-washed cottage across the glen. 'And that must be Hamish's place. It looks pretty smart for the back end of beyond.'

'It's no wonder we didn't work it all out last year. According to Granto's map, this place was no more than a ruin. A pile of stone that used to be a byre. And there's no sign of the sheepfold he had down as the key landmark from the road.' Alice harrumphed. She pointed at the hillside where dozens of sheep nibbled at grass that looked already well cropped. 'Wherever they get folded, it's not on that hill any more.'

'Well, we're here now. Thanks to Hamish.' Will unloaded a large holdall. 'Let's get settled in.'

Alice gazed across the glen. The white cottage looked tantalisingly near, but Hamish had warned them that a treacherous peat bog lay between them. It certainly didn't look anything

12

like the manicured countryside near their home. *Don't even think about crossing it*, he'd cautioned in the email he'd sent with detailed explanations and directions. It was the best part of a mile by the uneven single-track road but at least they'd arrive safe and dry. 'It's not that far. I reckon it wouldn't take more than half an hour, tops. We could always pop over and say hello now? It'd be nice to stretch our legs.'

'We told Hamish, tomorrow, Alice. I don't want to start off on the wrong foot. Let's not forget, he's the one doing us a favour. Plus we need to get the dinner on. I'm starving already. Whatever's waiting for us up at Clashstronach will still be there in the morning.' The place-name was clumsy in his mouth. He drew her to him in a one-armed hug. 'You're always so impatient.'

Alice harrumphed, but she stood on tiptoe to kiss his cheek. Then she headed up the flagstone path to the rented cottage Hamish had recommended to them. She checked the paper again and typed a code into the secure lockbox. It swung open, revealing two sets of keys on a hook. Will paused to check his look in the wing mirror — dark blond quiff in place, goatee neat, no black-pudding detritus from lunch between his teeth — before he followed her.

The door opened on a small hall, an open door off to one side revealing the main room of the cottage. One end was laid out as a galley kitchen, complete with fridge freezer and gas stove. Next to it, a rustic pine dining table with four cane-backed chairs, comfy-looking cushion pads tied in place. A vase of sweet peas sat in the middle of the table. Alice assumed they were artificial, given the climate and the time of year, but they looked like the real thing and they added a touch of homeliness.

At the other end of the room, a well-stuffed sofa faced a wall-mounted flat-screen TV hanging above a stone fireplace with a solid fuel burner, peat bricks stacked neatly on either side. A pair of armchairs flanked the fireplace. 'Looks all right,' Will said.

'A bit spartan.' Alice dumped her backpack on one of the kitchen chairs. 'Even with those pictures on the walls.' She waved at the photographs of wild seascapes and rocks.

'Hamish said they'd only finished the work a few weeks ago,' he reminded her, crossing towards the two doors on the far side of the room. He opened the one on the left, which led to a smartly tiled bathroom with a long picture window that looked out on the sea loch. 'Wow,' he said. 'Helluva view when you're in the bath or the shower.'

Alice looked over his shoulder. 'At least the toilet's behind a modesty screen,' she said.

'So bourgeois,' he teased.

Alice, who generally gave as good as she got, dug him gently in the ribs and said, 'I just don't want to provide anyone with an image they can't un-see.'

The other door led to a bedroom, plainly furnished with a king-sized bed and a suite of matching pine furniture that had clearly come from a flat-pack superstore. The star of the show

14

was another picture window with a stunning view of the sea and blue-grey mountains that folded into each other on the horizon. 'This will do nicely,' Alice said.

Will dumped the holdall on the bed. 'It's a lot more comfortable than what Long John Silver and Jim Hawkins ended up with on their treasure hunt. I'll go and bring the shopping in.'

As he turned, Alice stepped close and reached round him, hands on his buttocks, pulling him to her. 'Plenty of time for that,' she murmured, running her lips along his neck, her breath warm and teasing against his skin. 'This is really exciting, Will. I feel like we're on the brink of uncovering Granto's real legacy.'

There was, Will thought, something to be said for a treasure hunt. Three years into their marriage, Alice's enthusiasm for sex bubbled up less frequently. But preparing for this expedition and imagining what it might bring had sparked an excitement in her that he was all too happy to exploit to the full. 'I'm not going to argue with that,' he said, wrapping his arms around her, gratified that it still took so little encouragement from her for his body to respond. He let himself fall backwards.

She kissed him again, this time on his mouth, shifting her body so she had him pinned to the bed. She slipped one hand between them. 'Mmm, I can tell.'

'We should come treasure-hunting more often.' And then the time for conversation was past.

4

2018 — Edinburgh

The women locked in conversation at the table behind Karen couldn't have been more out of place. She could see them in the mirror on the wall of Café Aleppo and if she concentrated, she could hear every word of their conversation. Ironically, she'd have paid no attention if they'd been in their natural habitat — Bruntsfield or Morningside, at a guess, sipping a Viennese filter coffee in the German Konditorei or a flat white in an artisanal hipster café. But there had to be a reason for white, middle-class women of a deliberately indeterminate age to be down at the bottom of Leith Walk hunched over small glasses of Miran's intense cardamom coffee.

Karen was the only other person in the café who wasn't from the Middle East and she had her own reasons for being there. For one thing, it was more or less halfway between the storage facility and her office, and she'd needed a coffee to restore her after an hour of artistic dithering down in Granton. For another, she needed to work out what having Ann Markie's placeman foisted on her meant. She could take time out to consider how to deal with DS Gerry McCartney because she knew with absolute certainty that none of her colleagues would accidentally bump into her here. A social enterprise run by a bunch

16

of Syrian refugees wasn't the kind of place most police officers would choose for their refreshment break.

That wasn't her only reason for coming. Karen had first encountered Miran and his fellow Syrians on her nocturnal ramblings round the city. They'd been huddled round a makeshift brazier under a bridge because they had nowhere else to meet. Karen had felt a strange kinship with them and had helped them make the connections that had led to the setting up of the social enterprise café. Every time, it embarrassed her that, as a result, her money was no good there. In her mind she'd been repaying a debt rather than going out of her way to hold out a helping hand. They thought otherwise and consistently refused to let her pay. She'd protested that to an observer, it might look as if they were trying to bribe a Detective Chief Inspector. Miran had laughed. 'I think nobody who knows you would be so stupid,' he said.

And so she always calculated the cost of what she ate and drank and dropped an appropriate amount in the collection box for the charity that supported the people who hadn't been lucky enough to escape the hell that Syria had become. Miran's wife Amena had caught her eye once and inclined her head in a small nod of approval. If Karen belonged anywhere in Edinburgh, she thought it might be Aleppo.

But those two women with their expertly coloured hair, their understated gold earrings and their cashmere wraps absolutely didn't fit in. There was usually no shortage of Scottish customers in Aleppo but those were Leithers — locals who came in for the authentic Middle Eastern food and the ferociously strong coffee. Nothing like these women. So because she never quite managed to be off duty, Karen gave her full attention to a conversation that probably wasn't meant to be overheard.

The blonde-with-lowlights nodded sympathetically to the brunette-with-highlights. 'We were all shocked,' she said. Well-modulated Edinburgh, vibrant and low. 'I mean, obviously we were absolutely appalled when you told us he'd tried to strangle you, but it was just mind-boggling that he barged into the middle of a dinner party and confessed to it.' Now Karen was well and truly snared. Whatever she'd expected to hear, it wasn't this.

'He was trying to get himself off the hook.' The other voice had subtly different vowels. Perthshire, maybe? 'Showing remorse. So you'd all feel sorry for poor Logan and blame me. He didn't realise it was too late. That I'd already gone to the police.'

'He knows that now, though?'

The brunette scoffed. 'Damn right he does. He's being formally interviewed next week.' Karen relaxed a little. At least the woman had been taken seriously. Though that might be a class thing too. It was regrettable, but a woman like this making such an allegation would always command more attention than someone further down the social scale.

The soft clink of glass on saucer. An indrawn breath. Then, cautiously, feeling her way, the blonde said, 'You don't think that maybe, with that hanging over him, this wouldn't be the best time for you to move back into the house?'

No kidding, thought Karen.

'He needs to move out.' Firm. Calm. A woman who had made her mind up. 'I need to be back in the house with the kids. It's crazy that we're camped out in Fiona's granny flat while he's in the family home. He's the one who hasn't been paying the mortgage. He's the one who's lost half a million pounds of our money betting on sports he knows nothing about. He's the one who had the affair. He's the one who put his hands round my throat and tried to strangle me.' Her voice was calm, almost robotic. Karen sneaked another look in the mirror. The speaker looked as relaxed as if she was discussing her weekly Waitrose shopping order. There was something stagey about this, almost as if it was a performance with a purpose. But then, Karen acknowledged she had a naturally suspicious mind.

'All of that's true, Willow. But what will you do if he refuses to go?'

Willow sighed. 'I'll just have to make sure he sees sense, Dandy. Because Fiona's goodwill is running out. I'll appeal to his love for the children.'

'You can't go to the house by yourself. You can't confront a man who's tried to strangle you without back-up. I'll get Ed to come with you.'

Willow gave a laugh that Karen suspected would be described in a certain kind of magazine as a tinkle. 'I'm trying to take the heat out of the situation. Ed's about four inches taller and six inches broader than Logan. That'll only make things worse. Look, he's learned his lesson. He's got the police on his back already. He's not going to make things worse.'

Dandy — *Dandy? Who named their kid after a comic?* — sighed. 'I think you're reading this all wrong. He's got nothing left to lose, Willow. He's got no money, no job. After the police have finished with him and he's got a record for domestic abuse, the family courts won't let him near the children on his own. If you throw him out, to add to all that, he'll be homeless because, after what we know now, none of us will take him in.'

'Serves him right.' Willow's voice was curiously flat and cold.

A long pause. Long enough for Karen to twist the kaleidoscope and come up with another picture.

'I'm not saying he doesn't deserve all of that and more. But think about it from his perspective for a moment, Willow,' Dandy continued. 'Right now, the roof over his head is the only thing he's got left. If you try to take that from him . . . well, who knows how he'll react?'

Karen shrugged into her coat and stood up. She moved to the side of their table, aware of the baffled surprise on their faces as they took in her presence. 'I'm sorry to interrupt, ladies,' she said. 'But I couldn't help overhearing your conversation.' She gave them her best warm smile. They were polite; they couldn't resist returning it. 'I'm a police officer.' That wiped the smiles off. 'I simply wanted to say that in my experience when you back someone into a corner who has nothing left to lose, someone who's already had his hands round your throat? That's when women end up dead.'

Dandy pushed her chair back, recoiling from this harsh truth, shock rearranging her face. But Willow became still as a cat watching prey. 'Logan would never kill Willow,' Dandy protested.

'Best to avoid that possibility. Best to avoid a showdown between the two of you. Especially in a kitchen equipped with sharp knives,' Karen said.

'This is ridiculous. I don't have to listen to this.' Willow stood up, drawing her wrap around her. 'I'm going to the loo, Dandy, then I'm getting the check. I'll see you outside.'

Karen watched her leave then turned back to Dandy, who was still frozen in affront. 'There's something else I want to say, Dandy. I have a suspicious mind. It comes with the territory. And listening to your pal just now, seeing how composed she was, I couldn't help wondering what's really going on here. Is she actually afraid of him? Or is she preparing the ground for something completely different? The courts are very sympathetic these days to women who defend themselves when they're in immediate fear of their lives from men who have already been demonstrably violent towards them.'

Now Dandy was on her feet. 'How dare you!'

Karen shrugged. 'I dare because it's my job to protect Logan as much as it is to protect Willow.

Are you sure you're not being set up as a defence witness? Conveniently able to confirm your friend's version of events?'

'That is outrageous! What's your name? I'm going to report you,' Dandy shouted, drawing the eyes of all the other customers.

Karen took a couple of steps towards the door then turned back. 'I'll be keeping a close eye on the news, Dandy. I only hope I don't ever have to see you or your pal Willow again.' She dropped a handful of coins in the collection box on the way out, wondering whether she'd just made a complete fool of herself or saved someone's life.

5

2018 — Edinburgh

Later that evening, when she told DCI Jimmy Hutton about the encounter, Karen was gratified to hear he thought she hadn't overreacted. They sat inside her waterfront flat, the lights down low not for any romantic reason but because they both enjoyed the dramatic view of the Firth of Forth from the picture window of the living room. Every week it was different, depending on the weather, the season and the traffic on the wide estuary.

'For what it's worth, I think you did the right thing, Karen,' Jimmy said, reaching for the ice-bucket to add another cube to his Strathearn Rose gin. This had become their ritual. It had started out as a regular Monday evening session but pressures of work meant these days it was a moveable feast. Karen's flat; an assortment of gins; and the appropriate accompaniments. Which were becoming more and more baroque with every passing month. They had, however, drawn the line at the one that demanded an obscure artisanal tonic water plus a special infusion of seaweed and a slice of pink grapefruit.

'It's a gin and tonic I want, not a Japanese tea ceremony,' Karen had complained. 'And besides, have you seen the price of the seaweed water?'

Gin Nights had started as a mutual support group after the death of Phil Parhatka, Karen's lover. A fellow police officer, he'd been killed in the line of duty. Karen had thought she understood the effect of sudden violent death on those left behind. Until she experienced it herself, she hadn't realised the way it carved a line through your life. She felt the ties between herself and the rest of her life had been severed. At first, she couldn't bear to talk to anyone about what had happened and what it meant because nobody else could share her particular knowledge.

Then Jimmy, who had been Phil's boss, had turned up at her flat one Monday night with a bottle of gin and Karen instinctively knew he was having the same struggle as she was. It took them both a while — long evenings of talking about work, Scottish politics and the foibles of their colleagues — but eventually they broke their silence and shared their grief.

Now it had become an institution. Jimmy's wife had told Karen at his team's Christmas party that the gin was cheaper than a therapist and it was doing her man good. It was a sort of permission, a way of saying she saw Karen as no threat to her marriage. But then Karen had never seen herself as a threat to anybody's marriage. She was, she knew, the kind of woman men either dismissed or treated like the sister they were slightly intimidated by. Only Phil had ever seen past that. Only Phil had ever truly seen her.

'I was sitting there listening to those women, and I couldn't help thinking about you and Phil and the rest of your squad. If I'd been on the

Murder Prevention Team, could I have sat there and said nothing? The answer was obvious,' Karen said.

'You'd never forgive yourself if you'd kept your mouth shut and something terrible was to happen.'

Karen gave a soft chuckle. 'I know. But I also wondered if I'm turning into the Mint.'

'How so?'

She sighed and stared into her drink. 'He told me his new motto is, 'What would Phil do?' Which left me no choice but to speak in Aleppo because Phil would have been right in there.'

'That's good, isn't it? That Jason's thinking that way?'

Karen twisted her mouth in a sardonic smile. 'Of course it is. He's learning how to be a better polis. But it freaks me out a bit to see that frown on his face and know he's trying to channel a man he'll never match.'

'Aye well, the Mint's not the only one.'

'And speaking of never living up to Phil — bloody Ann Markie has sent me another body.'

Jimmy's smile was wry. 'I take it you're not impressed.'

'I wanted someone who could tackle the backroom stuff to free me and Jason up for actual investigations. I was thinking maybe somebody heading for retirement and looking to get off the streets but still hanging on to a bit of enthusiasm for caging the bad guys. And what did she send me? A wee Glasgow nyaff so full of himself I'm surprised he's got room to draw breath.'

Jimmy couldn't hold back a chuckle. 'I'm sorry, I shouldn't laugh, but the Dog Biscuit's really got your number. She knows exactly how to push your buttons.'

Karen stopped short, headed off at the pass by a tag she hadn't heard before. Cops — and journalists, she'd heard — always found nicknames for their colleagues and bosses. The more obscure the better, in case of unauthorised eavesdroppers. Hence the Mint, so-called because there was a brand of confectionery called Murray Mints. More than that, their slogan was 'Too good to hurry mints', a perfect fit for a polis who wasn't the quickest on the uptake. Karen didn't know what her own AKA was and she was happy for it to stay that way. She had a feeling it would only feel like an affront. ' 'Dog Biscuit?' ' she repeated.

Jimmy was grinning now, delighted to know something his pal didn't. 'You know those dog biscuits that are meant to look like marrow bones, but instead, they look like wee sausage rolls? They're called Markies.'

Karen got it. 'Nice one.'

'Aye. A few of the guys tried calling her Sparks, after Marks and Spencer, but it didn't catch on.'

'Too cosy,' Karen said. 'I like Dog Biscuit. Just the right level of disrespect. Anyway, this guy she's landed me with, a sergeant called McCartney, he says he's come from the Major Incident Team. Which makes no sense to me unless he's been a very bad boy. Nobody with any ambition chooses the HCU.'

'You did.'

Karen shook her head. 'Different kind of ambition. I've got no desire to struggle up the down escalator that is Police Scotland promotion. My ambition is to clear cases that everybody else has given up on. To give answers to people that have been waiting way too long to find out who blew a hole in their lives and why.'

'Fair point. You think the Dog Biscuit's put him there to keep tabs on you?'

'I don't know. I sailed pretty close to the wind on that Gabriel Abbott business. If the Macaroon hadn't got the bullet, I might have been in deep shit. I can't help wondering whether I've swapped one boss who wanted to hang me out to dry for another.'

'So what are you doing to keep the new boy occupied?'

'I've got him tracking down the owners of red Rover 214s from the 1980s.' A wicked smile curled round her lips.

'Half of them will be dead. Was it not compulsory to be in possession of a pension book and a wee tweed hat with a feather in it before you were allowed to buy one of them?'

'That, or else you worked for an outfit whose fleet buyer hated everybody that got a company car. Still, some of them'll be kicking around yet. There's a slim chance it might not be a dead end. That's the thing with cold cases. Sometimes it's the least promising loose end that makes the whole thing unravel.'

'You want me to see what I can find out about this McCartney?'

Karen reached for the Strathearn and topped

up her glass. 'Well, you are a damn sight closer to the beating heart of Police Scotland than me. Don't put yourself out, but if you were to hear something . . . ' She pushed the bottle towards him.

'No bother. Consider it done.'

'And till I hear back from you, I'll just treat McCartney as the Dog Biscuit's lapdog.'

6

2018 — Wester Ross

If Alice had constructed a fantasy Highland crofter, he'd have looked a lot like the man who opened the door of the white cottage as their car pulled up next to a seven-year-old Toyota Landcruiser, its wheel arches caked with a layer of mud so dense it resembled fibreglass insulation.

He was a fraction under two metres tall. His hair, the same shades as the peat bricks piled in their living room, fell to his shoulders in unruly waves. His luxuriant beard looked so soft she wanted to bury her face in it. He wore a baggy hand-knitted jumper the colour of fruits of the forest over a kilt that emphasised narrow hips and muscular calves. Thick wool socks pooled over the top of a pair of battered construction boots. He wasn't exactly handsome. Just magnificent. Either this was Hamish Mackenzie, she thought, or a minor royal from *Game of Thrones*.

He stepped out of the doorway, a welcoming smile on his face. 'Alice,' he said as she got out of the car. 'And Will. It's great to meet you. I'm Hamish.' He seized her hand in a warm grip. His skin felt dry and calloused. Alice was suddenly aware of Will's soft fingers spread across the small of her back as he reached out with his other hand to accept Hamish's handshake.

'Come away in, we'll have a coffee and take another look at the maps in the flesh, so to speak.' His voice was deep and seemed to carry a faint note of amusement below the surface.

They followed him into a kitchen that felt indefinably masculine. Stainless steel and oak buffed to a soft sheen, the sort of appliances Alice had only ever seen on cheffy TV shows, framed monochrome prints of fruit and veg from peculiar angles. 'Grab a seat.' Hamish waved them towards a breakfast bar while he approached a coffee machine that looked complicated enough to underpin the next mission to Mars. 'Espresso? Flat white?' A pause, and then, his voice a couple of tones deeper, 'Latte?'

'Flat white's great,' Alice said.

Will frowned. 'I'll have a latte.'

'I like a flat white for a change.' She tried not to sound defensive.

There was no possibility of conversation while the machine grunted and whizzed and spat and exhaled, but Hamish had left an array of maps on the breakfast bar which Alice fell on eagerly. 'That's my Granto's map,' she said absently, pushing it aside to study the two maps she assumed Hamish had drawn. One showed the croft and its features as it was now, including the holiday cottage. The one below it had a note across the top: *Cobbled together from old Ordnance Survey maps, parish maps and one from the library at Inverness. It would have looked something like this in 1944.* His handwriting was neat and legible, the maps clearly and carefully drawn.

''Granto?'' Hamish asked.

'That's what we called my grandfather.'

Hamish brought over the mugs, dwarfed in his big hands. 'It's easy to see how you missed it when you were on the prowl last summer. Hardly a landmark still standing. Or at least, standing in any recognisable configuration.' He handed them their drinks and pointed to the cottage where they were staying. 'Back in the mists of time, that was a byre. Packed full of cows in the winter. But we gave up on cows a few generations ago and the place fell to rack and ruin over the years. It probably looked like a pile of random rubble in your granddad's day.' He pointed to her grandfather's sketch of the glen. 'And this sheepfold here's long gone. We've got a proper pen now, just over the brow of the hill.'

'I see now how it fits,' Alice said, an undercurrent of excitement vibrating in her voice.

'I'm amazed you recognised it, Hamish,' Will said. 'I don't know that I would have done.'

Hamish shrugged. 'I've known this land since I was a wee boy. When you posted your grand-dad's map on our local Facebook page . . . ' He lifted one shoulder in a casual shrug. 'I saw the similarities. And I wondered.'

He'd wondered enough to respond to Alice's post, asking if she knew where it was her grandfather had been stationed in 1944. When she'd revealed it was Clachtorr Lodge, a mere couple of miles down the road, that had clinched it.

'Once you know what you're looking at, it's obvious,' Will said, leaning back with a proprietary air, as if the discovery had somehow attached itself to him. 'So, what's the plan of action?'

'Hamish, this is a fabulous cup of coffee.' Alice interrupted. 'Wow.'

'Thank you, I like to think I know what I'm doing when it comes to making a decent cup of coffee.' The big man smiled, dipping his chin in satisfied acknowledgement.

Will grudgingly tasted his latte. 'Pretty good,' he conceded. 'As I was saying, what's the plan of action?'

Hamish perched on a bar stool across the table from them, his expression a little shame-faced. 'I have a confession to make,' he said. 'Once we'd agreed this was more than likely where your granddad buried his treasure, I borrowed a metal detector and had a wee howk about to see whether there was anything doing.'

'Wow,' Alice said again. 'And did you find anything?'

'I did. There were a couple of areas where it went off like a siren. Right next to each other, and in the general area where your X marks the spot.'

'Amazing,' Alice said, beaming.

'Tell me you didn't start digging.' Will's smile was fake as a Christmas cracker engagement ring.

'Of course I didn't. This is your deal, Alice. No way was I going to spoil it for you. All I did was mark out the area with some baler twine and a couple of iron stakes, just to make it a wee bit easier on the day.' Hamish was more amused than indignant, which Alice thought he had every right to be.

'Not everyone's as impatient as me, Will,' she scolded him. 'Thank you, Hamish. That's so kind of you.'

Hamish knocked back his tiny espresso and grinned. 'Not really, I was intrigued. Believe me, this is the most exciting thing to happen round here since Willie Macleod's bull fell off the headland and got stuck on the rocks with the tide coming in.'

She wasn't sure whether he was telling the truth or playing up to their imagined expectations of a simple Highland crofter, but she chuckled anyway. 'Well, it's exciting for me too. Granto talked about his Highland adventures in the war so many times, I almost feel like I was there myself.'

'So how do we go about this?' Will asked: the broken record jumping and clicking in the background.

Hamish stood up and put his cup in the dishwasher. 'I thought the easiest plan would be to use the wee digger to clear the top layers of the peat, maybe down to about three feet or so? Then, I'm afraid, it's going to be a bit of hard labour for us.' He looked them up and down. 'You're not really dressed for it, are you?'

'We've got wellies in the car,' Alice said.

'That's something, I suppose,' Hamish said dubiously. 'I've a spare set of overalls would maybe fit you, Will. They'll be a bit big but you can tuck them in your wellies.' He frowned, his mouth pursing. Then his face cleared. 'I think there might be some old dungies out the back in the shed. From when I was growing up. My gran never threw anything out that might come in handy. Give me a minute.' He strode out of the room and they heard a door open and close.

'What a nice guy,' Alice said.

'Well, you obviously think so.' Will couldn't keep the sourness from his tone. He usually managed to camouflage his jealous streak behind a line of banter, but something about Hamish Mackenzie had clearly infiltrated his defences.

'He's really putting himself out for us. I'm grateful, that's all. He didn't have to get involved with us in the first place, never mind research old maps and make us the best cup of coffee I've had in weeks.' She drained her mug and got up to put it in the dishwasher.

'All of that is true,' Will said. 'But it doesn't mean you have to come off like some goofy teenager. 'Wow,' every other sentence.'

She came up behind him and hugged him. 'Stupid boy,' she whispered in his ear. 'As if I'd look at another man when I've got your ring on my finger.'

He grunted. She knew it was the best she'd get and decided to let it lie. 'I quite fancy the idea of you in overalls.' An olive branch.

'Huh. If they're made for Iron Man there, I'll look like a complete dick.' He squirmed round and planted a firm kiss on her mouth. 'But who cares, as long as it gets us what we came for.'

34

7

2018 — Wester Ross

They made an odd-looking trio walking up the track from the croft house. More Hollywood comedy mismatch than serious business — Hamish, tall and broad, hair now pulled back in a short ponytail, well-fitting forest green overalls tucked into scuffed black wellies; Will, shorter and slighter, diminished even further by tan overalls at least two sizes too big, flopping over a pair of Hunters that had looked as if they'd never been worn anywhere more demanding than the local Waitrose; and Alice, squeezed into a set of blue dungarees, at odds with the rubber boots patterned with liquorice allsorts. 'We might as well walk up,' Hamish had said. 'It's only half a mile or so, and I've already moved the digger and the tools up there. And it's a braw morning for it.'

Alice looked around eagerly as they went. 'It's funny to think of my Granto here in this identical landscape all those years ago. The war raging right across the world and here he was, in this peaceful, timeless place.'

'Obviously not identical,' Will muttered. 'Or we'd have found it ourselves last year.'

Hamish chuckled. 'Aye. And I hate to disillusion you, Alice, but it's only timeless if you measure time in a relatively short span. People think of the Highlands as a wilderness. A kind of playground for people who want to go hunting, shooting, fishing and hiking. But it's as much a man-made environment as the big cities you leave behind you.'

'What do you mean?' Alice paused and looked around her at the heather and the hills, the rocky outcroppings pushing through the soil, their surfaces stained with lichen and moss. 'This looks pretty natural to me.'

'And that's because nature's had time to reclaim what we'd previously colonised. Go back three hundred years or so, and this glen would have been busy with people working the land. Just picture it. Smoke rising from somewhere between a dozen and twenty chimneys. A few cattle here and there on the common grazing. Crops growing in run rigs, every croft farming its own five acres.' Hamish pointed towards the sparkle of the sea loch beyond the margin of the machair. 'Down on the shore, a few small boats, their fishing nets spread out for drying and mending.'

'So what happened?' Will chipped in.

Hamish grimaced. 'The Highland clearances. Crofting was subsistence farming at best. There wasn't much in the way of profit, so it was never easy to pay the rent. And the aristos who owned the land were greedy bastards. They wanted a higher return on their inheritances to pay off the debts they ran up with their high living. Then along came organised sheep farming. Enclose the land, fill it with sheep, and you hardly need any labour. See that hill on the other side of the glen? That's my sheep. I've got nearly five hundred Cheviots, and most of the work of running them gets done by Teegan and Donny. Throw shooting parties into the mix and you've got a whole new economy that only needs a handful of skilled people and an imported pool of seasonal labour to make it work.'

'So where did all the people go?' Alice asked.

'Well, duh,' Will said. 'How do you think Canada ended up full of people with Scottish names?'

'Canada, and New Zealand, and the Carolinas, and India and pretty much everywhere else the British Empire needed willing bodies,' Hamish said, his tone less blunt. 'Right now, there are far more descendants of the Scottish diaspora scattered around the world than there are living in Scotland.'

'Wow, I so didn't know that.' Alice surveyed the landscape, trying to imagine what Hamish had described. 'Was that even legal?'

Hamish shook his head. 'They didn't have secure tenancies back then.'

'But couldn't they protest? Put up a fight?'

Hamish gave her a long, hard look. 'There's not much you can do about it when they set fire to your house in the middle of the night because you want to stand up for yourself.'

'That's terrible.' Alice's eyes were wide.

'So, how long have your family been farming here?' Will asked before she could say anything more.

'The parish records go back to 1659, and we were here then. My grandparents thought they would be the last of the line because my mum moved away to Edinburgh to become a doctor and my uncle joined the army and married a German woman and settled over there. But I've been coming here every chance I get since I was wee, and I learned from them how to manage the land. So they left the tenancy to me.' He grinned at them. 'How lucky am I?'

Alice looked dubious. 'Does it not get lonely?'

Hamish shook his head. 'Plenty going on around here.'

'The winters must be very bloody bleak.' Will's expression was sour.

'I kinda like bleak. And it's a contrast with now. I mean, look at it. With the sun out, you could be in Greece. The sparkle of sea, all turquoise like the Med. And the landscape, it's not that different from Crete.'

'Apart from the temperature being about fifteen degrees lower.' Will again, his resentment getting the better of him.

And then they breasted a gentle rise in the road and right ahead of them a yellow mini-digger squatted by the side of the road. A small cab with a flimsy roof perched on top of a pair of caterpillar treads, its toothed bucket tucked under its folded arm like some sleeping mechanical bird. The paintwork was faded and the dents and scratches had been repainted in a not-quite-matching shade. 'It's not exactly a new bit of kit,' Hamish admitted. 'But we look after stuff round here — it has to last a long time before it starts to earn its keep.'

He swung himself easily into the cab, where he looked like an adult in an over-indulged child's toy. 'Let's get started.' The engine caught at the first attempt. 'Will, can you grab those spades and the crowbar?' He pointed towards the crooked tree on the far side of the digger, then set off across the boggy heathland.

'Where's he going?' Will said, struggling to manage three spades and a substantial crowbar.

'Give me that.' Alice reached for the crowbar. 'Wow, that's heavy. He said he'd marked the spot, remember? I'm assuming he knows what direction he's going in. I mean, he's not going to go off at random, is he? It might look like a wilderness to us, but he probably knows it like the back of his hand.'

Will hung back. 'Alice? How much do we know about this guy? I mean, we're out here in the middle of nowhere. Not another human being in sight. He's got a digger and a bloody heavy crowbar. He could be some kind of mad Highland serial killer for all we know.'

Alice's mouth fell open momentarily, then she burst into a fit of giggles. 'You had me there for a nanosecond, you bad, bad boy. Mad Highland serial killer.' She snorted with laughter. 'Come on, you lazy sod. Let's go and make our fortune.'

8

2018 — Wester Ross

It was immediately apparent that Hamish knew what he was doing with the digger. He positioned the bucket on the far side of the staked-out area and lowered it with surprisingly smooth delicacy towards the surface of the rough bogland. The teeth bit through the coarse grasses and scrubby heather, digging into the peaty soil. They scraped a long scar across the surface, then Hamish manoeuvred the bucket up and across, depositing the contents outside the baler twine he'd positioned as a guide.

Alice couldn't help herself. She gave a whoop of delight as the claggy peat slid out in a glistening pile. Hamish caught her enthusiasm and grinned back at her then returned to his task. He stripped an area about two and a half metres by a metre. Then, painstakingly, he cleared the layers of peat until, without warning, the soft sucking of the peat gave way to a faint scraping. Frantic, Will waved his arms, convinced Hamish couldn't hear the change of note over the digger's engine.

But Hamish had already disengaged the bucket; years of working the land had sensitised him to the shift in vibration as the digger hit a different density. He jumped down and joined Alice and Will, who were peering into the hole. It

40

was over a metre deep, the brown water seeping from the edges making it hard to distinguish anything. 'What is it?' Alice asked.

Hamish took a torch from his pocket, playing a thin beam of light over the surface below. 'I'm not sure. Could be wood, could be stone,' he said. 'Only one way to find out.' He crouched at the edge and let himself slide down into the hole. His boots squelched on soft peat but he could feel something substantial underfoot. He hunkered down and rubbed his fingers cautiously through the muck. Definitely something solid. 'Chuck me down one of the spades,' he said.

'I'm coming down,' Alice said, her voice shrill with excitement.

'Wait, no!' Will sounded cross but it had no impact on his wife. She jumped down regardless, staggering into Hamish as she landed and almost sending him sprawling.

He laughed and shook his head in faint exasperation. 'Better make that two spades, Will.'

★ ★ ★

Clearing the surface was tedious work, but half an hour later they'd exposed a series of planks stained the same dark brown as the peat walls of the hole. 'It looks like a coffin,' Alice said.

'Wrong shape,' Hamish grunted, scraping the last of the peat from the far end of the wood.

'Do you want the crowbar now?' Will asked.

Hamish nodded, wiping the sweat from his brow and leaving a dark smear on his skin. 'Aye, let's see if we can get inside.'

Alice reached up and grabbed the end of the crowbar as Will lowered it. 'This is so exciting,' she said. 'I can't wait.'

'There are no guarantees,' Hamish cautioned her. 'There's no knowing what state your inheritance is going to be in. It's been down here a long time.'

'Yeah, but it's a peat bog, right?' Will chipped in. 'I mean, I've read about bodies being preserved in peat bogs for hundreds of years.'

'Bodies are one thing. I've no idea what happens to metal if the water gets to it down here. I'm no chemist, but it's really acidic and I'm guessing it's not very kind to metal and rubber.' Seeing Alice's downcast expression, he shrugged. 'Fingers crossed, though. Come on, let's see if we can get a look inside.'

Hamish stood on the furthest side and jammed the claw of the crowbar into the narrow gap he'd cleared between the planks. Grunting with effort, he struggled to raise the furthermost board. For a long moment, nothing happened. Then a creak; a groan; and finally a toe-curling screech as the long-sealed gap succumbed to Hamish's weight. Freed, the plank tipped sideways against the peat wall. 'Bloody hell,' Hamish gasped.

Alice paid no heed, leaning past him and snatching the torch up from where he'd put it down earlier. 'There's definitely something there,' she shouted. 'Will, I can see something.'

'What sort of something?' Will demanded.

'It's impossible to tell. We need to get the other boards up,' Hamish said. He attacked the next plank over, which shifted more readily now it had somewhere to go. A third followed it, and that cleared enough of a space for them to get a sense of what lay beneath. It was a shapeless bulk, stained dark brown from the peaty water that had seeped into the crate over the years. 'Looks like a tarpaulin,' he said.

'Christ,' Will exploded. 'Is it waterproof? Or are we just going to find a bag of rust?'

'How should I know?' Hamish's tone was mild but Alice caught the look of irritation that tightened his mouth and furrowed his brow.

'What do we need to do, Hamish?' Her voice had a sweet warmth that Will recognised. But he didn't resent it; rather, he recognised it as step one on Alice's regular route to getting her own way.

'We need to get the rest of these boards lifted and then get a rope round the tarp. I can fasten that on to the digger arm, then we'll be able to lift it clear.' Hamish picked up one of the loose boards and thrust it upwards towards Will. 'There you go, do something useful and put that out the road.'

Alice put a hand on Hamish's shoulder. 'I bet all that's easier said than done,' she said. 'You're amazing, Hamish. I can't believe you're putting yourself out like this for a pair of strangers.'

'That's Highland hospitality for you.' It was impossible to miss the thread of sarcasm in his voice but he carried on with the backbreaking filthy task he'd outlined. After he prised another plank free, Hamish persuaded Alice to accept a leg-up out of the hole to give him space to finish the job. 'It's easier to manage by myself.' The implication was clear; neither Alice nor Will had enough of a clue to be any use in the practical matter of unearthing their own inheritance.

'You're so strong,' Alice said as she scrambled out of the way. 'It's amazing, watching you work.'

He chuckled. 'There's a dozen like me in the local pub. So much of the land around here is impossible to cultivate with conventional machinery. You work this land, you can't avoid building muscle.'

'All the same . . . ' She gave him a dreamy look.

Will caught it and scowled. 'Yeah, well, horses for courses. I bet Hamish wouldn't feel so confident preparing a costing proposal for replacement windows.'

Hamish shook his head and continued with the back-breaking work. It took a while, and attaching the rope to the tarpaulin was difficult and treacherous, but finally, he clambered back to the surface, the rope wound round his body. He undid it and attached it to the arm of the digger, above the bucket. Then centimetre by slow centimetre, the mahogany-stained bundle emerged from the boggy hole, dripping with sludge and clarted with muck. The tarpaulin rendered its contents entirely amorphous.

Hamish gently lowered it to the ground. Eyes wide, Alice and Will drew close, one step at a time, both apparently struck at last by how amazing an achievement this was. 'Wow,' Alice breathed as Hamish jumped down and joined them. He unzipped a breast pocket and took out a large clasp knife, opened the blade and handed it haft first to Alice. She looked startled.

'Go on,' Hamish said. 'It was your granddad that buried it, it's only right that you should be the one to open it up.'

'How? Where do I . . . ?'

'I don't think it matters. Grab the tarp with one hand and stick the knife in. It's sharp, it'll do the work for you.'

They all held their breath. Almost overwhelmed with the mixture of trepidation and anticipation, Alice did her best to grip the slimy unyielding canvas.

'Up a bit,' Hamish said. 'Look, it's like a seam. I think somebody's taped it down to make it watertight.'

Alice peered down. It took the best part of a minute, but she eventually made out what Hamish had noticed. Gingerly, she stuck the knife in and wiggled it about. For a moment, nothing happened. Then the blade found a weakness and sliced cleanly along the barely visible seam. Alice let out a low scream of delight, almost capering along the side of the tarpaulin, splitting it open like a giant banana peel.

The canvas slid away, revealing a second protective sheath. 'Oilskin,' Hamish said. 'Whoever did this, they knew their business. Go on, Alice, you're nearly there.'

A second cut, and this time, nobody spoke. The buried treasure emerged from its covering like a moth from a chrysalis. Painted in khaki drab, complete with twin leather panniers, as clean as the day it was cocooned: a 1944 Indian 741 motorcycle.

'Fuck me,' Hamish breathed. 'Now that's what I call a miracle.'

9

2018 — Edinburgh

If Gerry McCartney really was the Dog Biscuit's lapdog, Karen decided she'd better not offer herself up on a plate to the ACC. There was an argument that said senior officers shouldn't dirty their hands with the scut work. But the Historic Cases Unit was so tiny, Karen had grown accustomed to mucking in when she had nothing more pressing to occupy her. So as she'd walked up the hill the next morning, hunched against a steady drizzle blowing in from the North Sea, she'd decided to roll up her sleeves and show McCartney how they did things on her team.

There was no sign of the new boy but Jason was already at his desk, his ginger hair darkened to auburn by the rain that had plastered it to his head. He'd recently moved into a cramped one-bedroom flat on the fifth floor of a tenement building in one of the side streets near the bottom of Leith Walk. He'd explained to Karen that parking spots were at such a premium, he only moved the car if he absolutely had to. Getting soaked on the fifteen-minute walk to work was better than a twenty-minute hunt at the end of the day for somewhere to park. It was a familiar complaint in the city; the council sold far more parking permits than there were available spaces. It had been one of the reasons

Karen had opted for a modern block with dedicated underground parking.

'You need to invest in a hat.' Karen shook out her umbrella and hung up her coat.

'I look stupid in a hat.'

'You don't look that smart without one.' McCartney had arrived. Dry as a bone. 'Am I the only one that knows what a car's for?'

Jason flushed and frowned at his screen. Irritated, Karen produced an insincere smile and said, 'Well, Gerry, since you're the only one that's not already drookit, you can go and get the coffees. Mine's a flat white with an extra shot. From Valvona and Crolla, across the road on Elm Row.'

McCartney stopped halfway through taking off his overcoat. 'That makes no sense. Jason's already wet, it's no skin off his nose to go back out in the rain.'

'Jason's already stuck in at his work, Gerry. I don't want to interrupt that. Last in . . . '

He muttered something unintelligible through tight lips and shrugged his coat back on. 'Fine,' he snapped. 'What does the ginger ninja want?' Jason flicked a quick glance at the sergeant, but said nothing. McCartney caught Karen's eyes narrowing and blustered. 'What? This is a cop shop. Everybody's got a nickname.'

'Aye. And Jason's is the Mint.' The final 't' was percussive and dismissive. 'I've heard what they call you, Gerry. If you're lucky, we'll not use it.' Karen turned away and wakened her computer screen. 'At least, not to your face.'

The door shut with a sharp snick, the nearest

it was possible to get to a slam thanks to its slightly warped frame. There was a long moment of silence, then Jason said, 'What is his nickname, boss?'

Karen chuckled. 'I neither know nor care. But he obviously does.' She swung round in her chair. 'So where are we up to with the red Rovers?'

'Well, it's not quite as bad as I thought it was going to be. According to DVLA's records, there were only sixteen red Rovers registered in Scotland in 1986 with a first letter B in the reg. They pinged the details across late yesterday morning and we were doing our best to track down the owners.'

' "We?" '

Jason's eyes slid to the side, as if he was checking something on his screen. 'Well, mostly me. DS McCartney had some calls to make. You know how it is?'

Karen shook her head. 'Don't let him make you his drudge, Jason. If he's dodging, you need to tell me, OK? He's here to do a job, same as you.'

Jason sighed, but he nodded weakly. 'So, I wasn't getting very far and then I had a thought.' He gave her a wary look, half-expecting incredulity.

'Always a good start,' Karen said, her tone neutral.

'I went back to DVLA, because I figured if somebody was the registered owner of a motor, chances were they had a driving licence as well. So I asked them if it was possible to run the

49

drivers' details that corresponded to the registered owners. The lassie I spoke to was really helpful, for once. So when I came in this morning, she'd sent me current addresses for thirteen of them. I think the other three are dead or abroad because they all drop off the records between six months and five years ago, according to the DVLA lassie. Kayleigh, her name is.'

'I'm impressed.' Karen tried not to sound surprised, but she was. As Jason grew in confidence, he was starting to confound her expectations. Maybe choosing, 'What would Phil do?' as a mantra was paying off. How weird would that be? Phil's ghostly presence improving her working life — she'd better not tell Jimmy or he'd be sending for the guys with the jackets that fasten up the back. 'Let's have a look.'

Jason nodded and set the printer wheezing into action. It spat out a couple of sheets of paper, which he passed across. Names, addresses, dates of birth. She grinned. 'This is a great start. I really didn't think we'd get anywhere with something so slender.'

'How're we going to tackle it?'

Karen pored over the list, mentally dividing it by location, age and gender. She marked four with a cross, six with an asterisk and three with a horizontal line. 'Those four are guys in the Central Belt. All mid-fifties upwards. Gerry's the best fit for them. These six are all older women, from Edinburgh to Stonehaven. That's your slice of the action, Jason. Little old ladies love you. And I'll take these last three. Women in their fifties. That's about my speed. We'll crack on

50

with the interviews today.'

As she spoke, the door opened and McCartney almost fell into the office. 'Opening the door with your elbow's never a good look,' Karen said.

'You try balancing three cups and a bag of bomboloni,' he grumbled.

'Bomboloni? Jings, is it somebody's birthday or are you trying to bribe me into keeping your nickname secret?' Karen took two of the coffees from him so he could put down the rest.

'Just trying to be nice, for fuck's sake.' He shrugged off his coat and draped it over the back of his chair then ripped open the paper bag to reveal three sugar-coated Italian doughnuts. He pushed them across the desk towards Karen, who didn't need to be asked twice. One of the reasons she always sent Jason for the coffees was because she was incapable of resisting the pastries.

McCartney waited till she had taken her first bite, then said, 'Crack on with what interviews today?'

'Mmm,' Karen moaned. 'Bloody hell, somebody must have sold their soul to the devil for the recipe for these.' She cleared her throat. 'Sorry. Interviews. Tell him, Jason.'

Jason swallowed a chunk of bombolone in a gulp. 'I got the DVLA to cross-reference the registered keepers with their driving licences and managed to get current addresses for most of them.'

McCartney's eyebrows did a slow rise to amazement. 'Nice one. Any chance they've all bothered to tell the DVLA the last time they flitted?'

'It's a place to start,' Karen said firmly. 'You're

down for four guys — Edinburgh, Camelon, East Kilbride and Portpatrick.'

'Portpatrick? Jeez. That's a helluva drive just to end up in God's waiting room. How many's he doing?' He stabbed a finger at Jason.

'Six,' Jason said. 'All the way from here to the Highlands.'

'And I've got the last three. Melrose, Elgin and Dunfermline. Horses for courses, Gerry.'

'So what exactly is the point of this?' He affected a camp accent. ' "Excuse me, sir, but do you have an alibi for a Tuesday night in May in 1986?' That's really going to work.'

Karen dropped the remains of her bombolone in the bin. McCartney had been too quick to spot her Achilles heel and she'd been too easily suckered. She needed to assert herself before he decided he could get away with the kind of antics nobody tolerated in the MIT. 'That's exactly where we're going to start. And then when we get nowhere, we ask for the DNA sample.'

McCartney lazily reached over for the list. 'Why are we bothering with women? It wasn't a woman that raped and murdered a hooker on an Edinburgh street.'

'Because women have husbands and sons that borrow their cars,' Jason said. 'We've nailed killers on familial DNA before.'

'Familial DNA's not going to nail anybody's husband,' McCartney sneered.

'We pursue every avenue,' Karen said. Even McCartney recognised it wasn't a tone of voice to debate. 'So let's get our coffee drunk and get on the road.'

'Are we not going to phone ahead? Port-patrick's a helluva drive if there's nobody home,' McCartney muttered, stirring two sachets of sugar into his coffee.

'We hit them cold,' Karen said. 'There's more than one reason why these are called cold cases.' The look he gave her was appropriately chilly. 'I don't care whether you like the way I do things, Sergeant. Our record speaks for itself in this unit. And while you're here, you'll play by our rules.'

McCartney shrugged one shoulder. 'You're the boss,' he said, the mildness of his tone at odds with the tightness of his jaw.

At that moment, the last thing Karen felt was in control. She needed a strategy to neutralise whatever Ann Markie had in mind for her. And right then, locking eyes with Gerry McCartney, she was coming up empty.

10

2018 — Wester Ross

The excitement at the successful disinterment of the Indian fuelled a desire in all three of them to crack on and recover the second bike. Any notion of stopping for lunch had fizzled out with the prospect of another dramatic discovery. Hamish had found his second wind and he was as eager to carry on as Alice and Will. He folded himself back into the cab and started up the digger again, repeating the same procedure a couple of feet to the left of where he'd excavated before, leaving a narrow wall of peat between the two holes.

For the first metre or so, nothing was different. And then it was.

The teeth of the bucket snagged on something and before Hamish could react, a chunk of wood snapped off and flew through the air, making Will yelp as he jumped aside to avoid it. 'What the *fuck*?' he yelled. But Hamish had already cut the engine and emerged from the cab, joining Alice at the side of the hole.

There wasn't much to see. A claggy bed of peat, puddled with water, a jagged edge of wood sticking out of it. 'I don't understand,' Alice said. 'What happened?'

Hamish frowned. 'I'm not sure.'

'Maybe this crate wasn't buried so deep and

the bucket caught the end of a board?' Will peered down, trying to make sense of what he was looking at. 'That would work, wouldn't it?'

'Possibly.' Hamish slid down into the hole. 'Pass me a spade.'

Alice did as he asked then glanced at Will. 'Maybe you could give Hamish a hand?'

Will did not appear enthusiastic. 'Wouldn't I just be in the way?'

Hamish's wry smile mirrored Alice's disappointment at her husband's unwillingness to help. 'Probably,' he said, starting to dig around the broken plank. It was soon plain that the board was buried at an angle, rather than forming part of the top of a second crate.

'That's weird,' Alice said.

'Maybe the crate was damaged when they buried it?' Will offered, determined to be part of the conversation if not the work.

'We'll soon see.' Hamish carried on shovelling slices of heavy peat to one side of the hole. Time crawled past for Alice and Will, consigned to the most minor roles in the drama.

Eventually, Hamish paused. 'There's two more boards here. One kind of crossing over the other. It looks to me like the second crate's been disturbed.'

'Could someone have got here before us?' Will asked, turning to Alice.

She shook her head, dubious. 'I suppose, in theory. Granto buried the bikes with his mate Kenny, but Kenny died from TB not long afterwards. As far as Granto knew, the secret died with him. Nobody ever got in touch with him about it. I don't see how anybody could have found the location without talking to him. I mean, look how much trouble we had finding it, and we knew the general area we were looking in.'

Hamish moved the exposed boards and returned to his task, sweat streaking his hair with dark tramlines. The pile of peat grew higher, his digging grew slower till all at once the ground gave way beneath him and he was floundering waist deep in peat, unable to find secure footing. 'Fucking hell,' he exploded, desperately struggling to stay upright. 'Whatever's down here, it's slippery as hell.'

'Will, do something!' Alice pushed him forward and reluctantly, Will slid cautiously into the main hole at the opposite end to Hamish's flailing arms.

'What do you need me to do?' Will asked.

'Clear a space around me so I can get out.' Hamish wasn't hiding his exasperation any longer. 'Dig the bloody peat out from in front of me, I'll be able to pull myself clear.'

Gingerly Will grasped the spade and started to shift the muck in noticeably smaller amounts than Hamish. 'Oh, come on, Will, put your back into it,' Alice said. 'You need to get Hamish out of there.'

'I'm doing my best,' he grunted. 'I don't spend my days running up mountains with a sheep under each arm.'

Hamish laughed. 'That's right. Give the boy a break, Alice. I'm not in any danger now, I've just about found my feet. I don't think I've got further to fall.'

To Alice, it seemed to take an unconscionable length of time for Will to create an escape route for Hamish. In reality, it was barely half an hour of messy slog before Hamish was able to drag himself clear with a horrible sucking sound and an impressive repertoire of swearing. Exhausted, he crouched against the wall of the hole, breathing heavily. Will meanwhile had edged closer to where Hamish had been trapped.

His voice rose in excitement. 'I think there's another tarpaulin down here,' he cried. 'Look, Hamish, that's why you were struggling to stand up. You were trying to balance on top of the second Indian.'

Hamish dragged himself upright and joined Will. 'Right enough.' He groaned. 'I don't know what's happened to the top of the crate but we'll need to clear a bit more peat so we can get a rope round the bike. Chuck down the other spade, Alice, we'll soon get it done with two of us.'

They worked in silence, apart from the grunting and heavy breathing that accompanied their effort. Gradually the tarpaulin emerged. Hamish thought it seemed looser than the first one, but said nothing because he couldn't be sure.

Then, with half the hole dug clear, Will leaped back with a startled yell. 'What the fuck is that?' He pointed dramatically to what had been revealed by his last spadeful of peat, trying to turn what he was seeing into something different.

Hamish paused and shifted for a better view.

He drew his breath in sharply, recoiling from the sight that had so shocked Will. 'I was right,' he said. 'Somebody has been here before us. And he's still here.'

11

2018 — Dundee

Dr River Wilde had clicked on her last PowerPoint slide when she felt her phone vibrate against her hip. Whoever it was would have to wait until she'd finished running through the week's reading list for her second-year forensic anthropology students. The undergraduates could find the details of the required texts at the end of her online lecture notes, but River always liked to end the lecture with a quick run-through. That way nobody could claim they didn't know what they were supposed to have covered before their next session in the dissection room.

She zipped through the list at top speed then gathered her scant notes and turned her back on the exiting students to check her phone. As she suspected, the missed call was from a withheld number. But there was a voicemail. River would have put money on it being from a police officer. Colleagues would know she was lecturing; friends rang in the evenings when she was less likely to be up to her elbows in cadavers; and because her partner was a senior cop, they generally texted first to arrange their calls.

Aware that a handful of students were still hanging around near the podium, River tucked her phone back into the pocket of her jeans and

59

faced them. 'Was there something?' she asked. Polite, but brisk enough to discourage the trivial questions that one or two students seemed impelled to put to her at the end of every lecture.

She fielded a couple of inquiries about dates by which assessments were due, refraining from pointing out that they were easily discoverable on the course website, then disengaged, taking the stairs at a jog. When the police called her, it was always a matter of life and death. Literally, not metaphorically. For a forensic anthropologist like River, the death was invariably in the past, the life something to be teased from what the corruption of the expedient grave had left behind. So while she didn't like to keep the police waiting, she'd never felt the need for the performance of urgency and self-aggrandisement that she'd witnessed in some of her colleagues. You didn't serve the dead by being self-serving.

The nearest private space was the mortuary. River used her keycard to enter the secure corridor then turned into the cool space where the cadavers were prepared for dissection. Visitors were always surprised when they walked through the doors. They expected to see bodies on slabs being pumped with embalming fluids. But here there was nothing visible to show that this was a place where bodies were stored. The main part of the room was occupied by large stainless steel tanks. Each was about the size of an American-style fridge freezer lying on its back, and the tanks were stacked two deep. Each had a serial number slotted into a holder. It could have been some arcane industrial food processing plant — a hydroponic system, or a vessel for growing mycoprotein. The reality was at once more extraordinary and more mundane.

Each tank held a preservative solution and a body. Over a period of months, the bodies would effectively be cured by the salts in the solution. By the end, they would still be soft and flexible so that student anthropologists, dentists and surgeons could learn their trade on something that closely approximated a live body. River's technicians had even worked out how to simulate blood flow in the cadavers. In her dissecting room, when a trainee surgeon nicked a blood vessel, there was no hiding place.

That afternoon, there was nothing visible to even hint at what went on there. River leaned against the nearest tank and pulled out her phone, summoning her voicemail. A man's voice spoke clearly and decisively. 'Dr Wilde? This is Inspector Walter Wilson from N Division, based at Ullapool. We've got a matter we need to consult you on. I'd appreciate it if you could call me back as soon as you get this. Thank you.' He finished with a mobile phone number. River scrambled in her lecture folder for a pen and played the message again so she could catch the number.

'A matter' meant human remains. Not a warm body, never that. Those were for the pathologists. When they called for River, it was because they needed someone who could find answers in teeth and bones, hair and nails. Unpicking a life — and often a death — from what was left was her stock in trade. The university website cut straight to the heart of it: *Forensic Anthropology is best described as the analysis of human remains for the medicolegal purposes of establishing identity, investigating suspicious deaths and identifying victims of mass disasters. It is a specialised area of forensic science that requires detailed anatomical and osteological training. Being able to assign a name to the deceased is critical to the successful outcome of all legal investigations.* The squeamish thought there was something creepy about her work. Not River. Bringing the dead home. That was how she thought of her trade.

River tapped in Inspector Walter Wilson's number. He answered on the second ring. 'This is Dr River Wilde,' she said. All these years in the job and still, every time she spoke to a cop for the first time, she inwardly cursed her hippie parents. 'You left a message for me.'

'Thanks for getting back to me, Doc.' His voice was deep and gravelly, the Aberdeen accent still clear in spite of having had the corners knocked off by time and seniority. 'We've got a body we need your input on. It turned up in a peat bog in Wester Ross earlier this afternoon. Based on the information we've got from the witnesses, we think it likely dates back to 1944.'

'And you want me to confirm that?'

'Ideally, aye. We could use your help in trying for an ID as well.'

'When would you like me on site?'

'Well, we've got it taped and tented, so it's reasonably protected. If you could get here for tomorrow morning, that would be good.'

'Where exactly are you?'

'A wee place called Clashstronach. It's about an hour north of Ullapool, just this side of the boundary with Sutherland.'

River thought for a moment. It was a long drive, but she could set off within a couple of hours. She was due to take a class in the dissection room in the morning but one of her post-docs could handle it. Cecile had specialised in the spinal work they'd be doing; she'd enjoy the opportunity to strut her stuff. 'Can you book me a hotel room for tonight?'

'No bother,' Wilson said. 'I'll get you something sorted in Ullapool, that's handy for our office and there's a couple of decent places to stay. I'll send you a text, will I?'

Two hours later, she was on the road. Four hours should do it, she reckoned. Dundee to Perth, then there would be clots of traffic as she left the city and struck out up the A9, with its average speed cameras and long stretches where overtaking was damn near impossible. But this wasn't summer, and there would be few tourists and no caravans so once she'd passed Pitlochry it would be an easy run to Inverness, then a final hour or so with added twists and turns as the road snaked across the Highlands to the west coast. She plugged her phone into the car's sound system and let rip with her driving music, an eclectic mix that spanned the past thirty years of female rockers. It was one of the few things that she and her partner disagreed about. Detective Chief Inspector Ewan Rigston liked torch singers who delivered big ballads — Adele,

Emeli Sandé, Ren Harvieu. Once she'd even caught him listening to Shirley Bassey. River reckoned that was all the blackmail capital she'd ever need with his CID team.

Amy Winehouse finished belting out her version of 'Valerie' somewhere north of Dalwhinnie and River decided she needed some conversation. She cut the music and rang the number of her best friend. She thought it was going to shunt straight to voicemail, but at the last second, Karen Pirie's voice filled the car. 'Hey, River, how's tricks?' It sounded like they were doing the same thing — driving on a fast road at speed.

'I'm good. I'm heading up the A9.'

Karen laughed. 'You're kidding?'

'I wish I was. This is — '

Karen interrupted with a bad Chris Rea impersonation: ' — the road to hell.' Both women laughed. 'Funny thing is, so am I.'

'Really? Where are you headed?'

'Elgin. I need to interview a woman who owned a red Rover 214 in 1986.'

River snorted. 'Has that been reclassified as a crime?'

'Only when Jeremy Clarkson rules the world. No, we've got a lead on a car that might be implicated in a series of brutal rapes from the eighties. I'm checking out the possibilities.'

'Is that not what you've got Jason for?'

'There's quite a few possibilities and I've nothing else pressing. Plus . . . ' She paused. 'Ann Markie has landed me with another body. A Weegie refugee from the MIT through in the west.'

'MIT? Whose toes did he stamp on to end up with HCU? Not that I see that as a demotion, obviously.'

'That's because you get it. The work we do, what it means. Jimmy Hutton's doing some digging to see what he can find out. I wonder whether it's as simple as the Dog Biscuit trying to keep me in line.'

'The Dog Biscuit?' River knew there would be an explanation.

'Markies are apparently a kind of dog treat. According to Jimmy. Anyway, I think what she really wants is a spy to see what rules I'm breaking. Like Leonard Cohen says, 'The rich have got their channels in the bedrooms of the poor.''

'I thought you'd given up listening to that miserable old man? Are you slipping back into the depths? Phil so wouldn't approve.'

Karen chuckled. 'Field Commander Cohen was wise as well as miserable. Anyway, enough of me. What's dragging you up the A9?'

'Inspector Walter Wilson. You ever come across him?'

'No, is he with Highland?'

'Yes. Specifically, Ullapool. He's got a bog body for me.'

'Ooh. Anything for me?'

River chuckled. 'You're a glutton for punishment. But no, not this time. Inspector Wilson's information is that it probably dates back to 1944. So even if we're looking at foul play, it's well outside your seventy-year limit. No reprieve from the red Rovers for you.'

'So it goes. Good luck with it anyway. I look forward to hearing all about it.'

'Always interesting, a bog body. Up there in Wester Ross, there should be a high level of preservation, given the levels of sphagnum moss in the peat. We might even get fingerprints.'

'Aye, but what are the chances of meaningful fingerprints from 1944? We didn't even finger-print the army back then in case it put people off joining up.'

'I know. But I still enjoy the challenge.'

'I know what you mean. Like me and my red Rovers. Anyway, if you can squeeze your bog body under the seventy-year rule, I'll only be a couple of hours away in the morning.'

'I'll bear that in mind. But don't hold your breath.'

12

2018 — Wester Ross

River had barely made a start on her first cup of coffee of the morning when a stocky man with a shock of white hair and a weathered face appeared across the table from her. He gripped the back of the chair opposite hers and peered at her from beneath eyebrows that jutted like a pair of awnings over bright blue eyes. The black quilted anorak over the black crew-neck sweater on top of a white dress shirt with the knot of a black tie peeping out was the equivalent of walking in with a blue flashing light strapped to his head. 'You'll be Dr Wilde,' he said.

She recognised the voice. 'Inspector Wilson.' She gestured towards the chair. 'Join me?'

'Thanks, I will.' He pulled out the chair, half-turning to wave the waitress across. 'I'll have a coffee, pet,' he said as she approached. He sat and gave River a tight smile. 'You had a comfortable night?'

'I did, thanks.'

He nodded, with an air of satisfaction that seemed to suggest he was somehow responsible for that. 'They're good here at the Ceilidh Place. Very reliable.'

'Thanks for sorting it out for me.'

He dipped his head. 'All part of the service. We pride ourselves on treating our visitors well up here. I thought you might like to follow me up to the locus after you've had your breakfast. It's not the easiest place to find if you're a stranger.'

'That's kind.' It was the level of task that would usually fall to a more junior officer. She wondered whether Wilson was one of those who enjoyed micro-managing their officers. She hoped he wouldn't make the mistake of trying that on her.

'It's an interesting case,' Wilson said, leaning forward conspiratorially over his coffee. 'Very unusual set of circumstances.'

Clearly he wanted her to prompt him for more information. River took advantage of the arrival of her breakfast of scrambled eggs and sausages to make him do the work himself.

'It seems this married couple, Alice and Will Somerville, came up here looking for a couple of motorbikes that her grandfather buried at the end of the Second World War. I know that probably sounds completely daft to you' — he raised one caterpillar eyebrow, daring her to exclaim — 'but there were all sorts of things going on in these parts at that time, so up here, it doesn't strike us as entirely crazy. That's why we think the body dates back beyond the seventy-year limit, by the way.'

'Fair enough.' River carried on with her breakfast.

'They recruited a local crofter, Hamish Mackenzie, to help them. The three of them excavated one of the bikes without incident, but when they came to the second one, it seemed it had been interfered with. When they investigated further, they got a hell of a shock. They unearthed a man's arm. Thankfully they stopped then and there and called us in. My lads took a closer look — '

'Tell me they didn't clear away the rest of the peat.' River's tone was stern.

'Well, they had to check out what was there.' Defensive indignation lurked in Wilson's response.

'Did they at least keep separate the peat they dug out?' Almost a growl. But not quite.

'It's all on site. We're not bumpkins. They were very careful. Anyway, it's definitely a body. A gey big chap too. When they called me from the locus, I knew we needed an expert. And that's why I called you.'

River cut a sausage into precise bite-sized chunks. 'How well preserved is he?' She tucked in without waiting for a reply.

Wilson cleared his throat. 'I was in Inverness yesterday. I didn't get back till early evening, so haven't actually seen him myself, but I'm told it's quite a remarkable sight. He's very well-preserved, apparently. Right down to the eyelashes, one of our boys tells me.'

'That should make my job a bit easier. Just let me finish this and I'll be with you.'

Fifteen minutes later, River was following Wilson's police Land Rover north out of Ullapool. In a matter of minutes, the town was behind them and the landscape so wild it was almost impossible to believe a modern settlement was close at hand. The land swept upwards to peaks and ridges, some rounded and gentle, others jagged and savage. Sheep dotted the grasses and the machair, flocking together in seemingly random areas, since there were no visible fences or walls to confine them. Occasional patches of conifers were contained by deer fences, marching up the hillsides in orderly rows. From time to time, a roadside sign would direct passers-by to a smoke-house, a pottery or a tearoom, the destination often invisible from the road. And then there were the mountains. Every one rising from the plateau to make its own abrupt statement. The steep porcupine pinnacle of Stac Pollaidh; the isolated cone of Canisp; and the big daddy of them all, the blunt thumb of Suilven's barrel buttress.

River found the drive almost hypnotic. Usually when she was on her way to an investigation, she felt tensed for action, her mind racing over the possible scenarios that awaited her. But that morning, she was curiously soothed by the panoramas that altered subtly every couple of miles. She resolved to bring Ewan up here to share the magic. He thought nothing compared to his beloved Lake District but she had a feeling this might shake his certainty. They might not get weather like this — crisp blue sky with tattered shreds of cloud that made every colour more vivid — but she suspected this landscape would have a distinct beauty in all weathers.

The best part of an hour passed easily, then at last they turned off the main road on to a narrow strip of tarmac that ran between rough ground where sheep grazed oblivious to their passing. Soon she caught sight of a white two-storey croft house nestled against the hillside, and beyond that, two more police 4x4s and an unmarked van that she surmised would belong to the forensic technicians who would be getting on with whatever they thought was worthwhile until she'd done what she could at the site.

The tarmac gave way to an unpaved track as they turned down past the croft house. The sound of their approach brought a man to the door. Tall and broad, dressed in overalls and wellies, he put one hand possessively on the door jamb and raised the other in acknowledgement. As she pulled in behind the other vehicles, River caught a glimpse of him in her rear-view mirror, striding purposefully down the track towards them.

She went round to the rear of her own Land Rover and put a vinyl mat on the ground. She took off her walking boots and battered waxed jacket then pulled on a white Tyvek suit over her jeans and T-shirt. She was shoving her feet into her rubber boots when Wilson appeared with a uniformed sergeant in a hi-vis jacket. He had a face like an unsuccessful prize fighter. Wilson gestured at him with his thumb. 'Dr Wilde, this is Sergeant Slater. He was first on the scene yesterday.'

River smiled up at the tall burly man as she double-gloved her hands in blue nitrile. 'Hi, Sergeant. I understand you've cleared the peat from the body?'

'It was a bit of a dilemma, Doctor. It was hard to tell whether we were looking at a body or just an arm. Either way, we were told the crates had been in the ground since 1944, so obviously there wasn't an issue of damaging or disturbing evidence from a live case.' He sounded like a stranger to doubt. 'If you'd like to follow me, you can get started.'

'Can you carry one of these?' River pointed to the two hard plastic boxes that contained most of her scene kit.

Slater turned away. 'Hector,' he shouted. 'Get over here and carry Dr Wilde's kit.' He gave her a condescending smile. 'The boys like to make themselves useful. Leave them both there, we'll head over to the excavation.'

She was about to follow him when the man from the croft arrived. 'I'm Hamish Mackenzie,' he said, thrusting out a large calloused hand towards her. 'This is my land.'

River shook his hand. She couldn't help noticing he was definitely worth a second look. Just because you were happily committed to one man didn't mean you had to pretend not to notice striking. 'Dr River Wilde. Sorry for the inconvenience,' she said.

'Is it OK if I come over and watch?'

'It's fine by me. So long as you don't interfere,' River said.

'Where are Mr and Mrs Somerville?' Wilson asked.

Hamish pointed to a low stone cottage across the glen. 'That's where they're staying. I told Will it might be best if they kept out of the way this morning. Alice is pretty much in a state of shock. This was supposed to be a happy, fun kind of thing, getting their hands on her inheritance.

72

Now she's wondering whether she knew her granddad at all. That sweet old man she thought was her best friend when she was wee? Was he really a killer? Did he get rid of his mate so he didn't have to share the treasure?' He shrugged, spreading his hands expressively. 'It's a lot to get your head round.'

'We will be talking to Mrs Somerville in due course,' Wilson said repressively. 'But right now, we need to take a look at what you people dug up. Somebody put that body down there and I intend to find out who. And why.'

13

2018 — Elgin

Karen sipped her breakfast coffee and did the sums in her head. Louise Macfarlane was fifty-nine, which meant she had been twenty-seven in 1986 when she'd been the registered keeper of a red Rover 214. Like the other two women she'd interviewed thus far, Louise had bucked the demographic trend of drivers of that make and model. Already, one of Karen's interviewees had confessed that she thought the Rover was an old man's car, but she hadn't been able to say no when her granddad had died and her mum had said she could have the car. It was that or nothing.

Louise was the school secretary of a primary school on the outskirts of Elgin. She'd asked Karen to come to the school at ten, after the morning rush of dealing with registers and issues raised by parents dropping off their children. The late start was fine by Karen. The difficulties she'd had with sleeping since her beloved Phil had been killed were gradually diminishing, but she still often found she needed a late-night walk to reach a point of exhaustion where sleep would hold her captive. So after she'd checked in, she'd found a decent fish and chip shop then threaded her way through Elgin, discovering the network of paths along the River Lossie before cutting back through the town. What, she couldn't help wondering, would Phil have made of the woman she had become? He'd always insisted he loved her exactly as she was, that he didn't want to live with some diet-obsessed stick insect. But the weight she'd unintentionally lost due to a combination of lack of appetite and the endless route-marching through the night streets of Edinburgh had changed the way she looked. 'Fat bastard' was no longer the first insult of choice from those she crossed swords with. She liked feeling fitter too. She used to struggle with the flights of stairs in high-rise blocks and tenements. Now she took them steadily, literally in her stride.

Those were the upsides of her loss that she forced herself to embrace. Finding an upside to the insomnia itself was harder. She'd never had trouble sleeping. Even when she'd first got together with Phil, there had been no period of adjustment to sharing a bed. When Karen used to switch the light off, it was as if she'd switched herself off too. Losing Phil had destroyed that facility and at first she'd struggled to accept that easy sleep had abandoned her. Walking had been a last desperate resort to stop her climbing the walls in frustration. It wasn't as if they'd been one of those couples who took to the hills at weekends. Not like Theresa May and her man, striding out for the cameras in identical walking gear like a skinny Tweedledum and Tweedledee. Going for a walk in the middle of the night would have been as alien to Phil as attending a poetry slam.

But somehow it had worked for her. The rhythm of her steps calmed her ragged heart. It helped her to order her thoughts about cases and create her own mental map of the city she now inhabited. In strange places like Elgin, she found her feet by night wandering. It was well after midnight when she returned to the hotel, but her sleep was still restless and broken. It was especially frustrating since for once she didn't have an early start. When she conceded she would sleep no more she had time yet for a leisurely hotel breakfast.

On the dot of ten, Karen arrived at Lossie Primary. She was about to buzz the intercom when a woman appeared on the other side of the glass door, waving a greeting. She released the door and gave Karen a generous smile. 'You must be Detective Chief Inspector Pirie. I'm Louise Macfarlane, come away in.'

Obviously the concept of stranger danger hadn't made it to Lossie Primary. Karen followed Louise down the hall and through the door marked 'School Office'. A quick glance convinced Karen that Louise was one of those whose motto could be, 'a place for everything and everything in its place.' Louise herself was equally neat, Karen noticed. Navy slacks — oh yes, definitely slacks, not trousers — and a plain white blouse without smudge or stain, grey hair in an immaculate twisted bun and perfectly manicured pale pink nails all added up to the sort of look Karen's mother would have loved her daughter to achieve. Or even aspire to, Karen thought wryly.

Louise's face matched the rest of her. Small features in an oval face, eyes that were somewhere between blue and grey, perfectly applied lipstick the same shade as her nails. The only flaw was a slight overbite. She smiled at Karen again, waving her to a seat on the opposite side of the desk. 'Your call was very intriguing. When you asked about my Rover, I thought at first you were one of those annoying people who call up pretending you've had an accident. But of course, I realised almost immediately that couldn't possibly be right, not after all these years.'

'Nothing like that,' Karen said. 'As I explained, I head up the Historic Case Unit. Information sometimes comes to us a long time after the fact and we have to do our best to use it to achieve a successful outcome in cases that weren't resolved at the time.'

Louise nodded vigorously. 'It's just like *Waking the Dead*, isn't it? So I suppose that makes you Trevor Eve.'

'Aye. But a bit less shouty,' Karen acknowledged. 'Thanks for agreeing to see me.'

'I'm intrigued, I won't deny it. I can't imagine how my old Rover has come up in a criminal investigation. I never even got a parking ticket in it.' She giggled, as if she'd said something funny.

'A witness has come forward, placing a car like yours at the scene of a serious crime in 1986. Nobody imagines for a moment that you had anything to do with it, but we have to go through the motions of eliminating all the possibilities.'

'Like Sherlock Holmes.' She made quote marks in the air with her fingers. ' "Once you

77

have eliminated the impossible, whatever remains, however improbable, must be the truth.' I can assure you, Chief Inspector, that I'm going to be one of your impossibles.'

On her present showing, Karen thought Louise a more likely victim than villain. 'I need to confirm that you were the driver of the car, not simply the registered keeper.'

'Oh yes, it was my car. I bought it from the dealership in 1984. It was an ex-demonstration model so I negotiated quite a substantial discount. I had it for almost ten years. It was very reliable.'

Karen scribbled a note in her pad. 'Can you tell me where you were living in 1986?'

'I can. I was living in a flat in Mastrick in Aberdeen. I was an advertising sales rep for the *Press and Journal*. I qualified for a company car because I had to go all over the area keeping our advertisers happy and securing new business. But I chose to use my own car because the mileage rates were very favourable. Even when you factored in depreciation and wear and tear, I reckoned I still came out ahead.'

'Did you live alone?'

Louise shook her head. 'I shared with the picture desk secretary, Fidelma McConachie. We were flatmates for four years, then in 1988 my mother took ill with cancer and I had to move back to Elgin. I've been here ever since.' She gave a dry little laugh. 'Still keeping house for my father. I never married, you see. My sister was the lucky one. She got herself a husband before my mother died, and that left me to be the dutiful daughter.'

Karen couldn't think of any twenty-first-century response to that. 'Did you ever take the car down to Edinburgh?'

Louise's eyes widened. If Karen had asked whether she'd participated in the Paris — Dakar rally, the woman couldn't have looked more shocked. 'Good heavens, no! I wouldn't dream of it. It's bad enough trying to navigate round Inverness without attempting Edinburgh. Not to mention the price of parking. If you can even find a parking space. Oh no. When I go to Edinburgh, which I don't do very often, to be honest, especially now Inverness is so good for shopping, I take the train. Much less stressful. I don't know how you can bear it, battling the city traffic day after day.'

Karen shrugged. 'I walk whenever I can. Or take the bus. So in May 1986, there is no possibility that you drove your car to Edinburgh?'

'None whatsoever, I can assure you.' Louise sounded affronted at the very idea.

'Did anybody else ever drive the car?'

'Oh no. I'm very particular about that sort of thing. I don't even like it when the garage mechanics drive it round to the service bay, even when they put those polythene covers on the seats.' She shook her head in despair at the trials of her life.

'Not even a colleague, perhaps? Maybe their car was in the garage and they needed to borrow yours?'

A firm shake of the head. 'Oh no. If their own car was off the road, they'd have had to make their own arrangements. I never even let Fidelma borrow it, and if I trusted anybody to look after it, it would have been her.'

This was the deadest of dead ends, Karen thought. But at least her trip hadn't been a waste of time. She could cross Louise Macfarlane's name off her list, which was more than Gerry McCartney had been able to do in Portpatrick. He'd driven all the way down there only to discover that, according to a neighbour, his target was sunning himself by the pool of the apartment complex in Spain where he and his wife spent half of their time. McCartney had however discovered they were due back at the weekend for a family wedding.

'You'll be there to meet them when they get home, then,' she'd said crisply. She was fairly sure she'd heard a muttered, 'Oh, for fuck's sake,' but she didn't care. When they were chasing a solid lead, weekends didn't matter. There were plenty of slack weeks when they could catch up with time off in lieu. Some officers thought there was no rush about cold cases, that you could dawdle through the work at a leisurely pace. Karen thought differently. Every day that she could whittle off a family's wait for answers about the fate of their loved one was worth saving. Jason shared that mindset these days. The only person who would suffer if McCartney couldn't learn to like it would be the sergeant himself. Better to submit than to live in a state of constant chafing.

Karen put her notebook back in her shoulder bag and was about to thank Louise Macfarlane for her time when her mobile rang. A quick glance told her she couldn't ignore this call. She held up a finger to signal she needed a moment, then answered. 'Hi there. What's up?'

From the other side of the Highlands, River's voice was a clear as if she were standing in the room. 'Are you still in Elgin?'

'I am. Why?'

'I need you over here. This body that's supposed to have been in the ground for seventy-four years? He's wearing a pair of Nikes. By my reckoning that makes him one of yours.'

14

2018 — Wester Ross

'That'll teach you to up your sartorial game,' Karen muttered under her breath as she walked back to her car. Ann Markie's accession to the boss's chair had provoked Karen into hitting the sales at John Lewis and refreshing her wardrobe with three much-needed new suits. The weight that grief had stripped from her bones meant that most of her clothes hung where once they'd clung but it had taken the sting of the Dog Biscuit's perfect grooming to push her into action. Anything to stop being put on the back foot before a word was uttered.

Which was all well and good if you weren't planning on spending your day ploutering around in a peat bog.

At least these days, the advantage of vast out-of-town supermarkets meant she could fix the problem without too much of a detour. When she crossed the Kessock Bridge heading north from Inverness, Karen was dressed in jeans, T-shirt, fleece-lined hoodie and two pairs of thick socks, and all for less than twenty-five quid. Add the kagoule and the wellies that had already been in the boot and she almost looked like she'd been planning a field trip.

Once she'd turned off the A9 and the traffic became less fraught, she called River. 'Sorry I couldn't say much before,' she said. 'I was with a witness.'

'No worries. Trust me, I've got plenty to be going on with here.'

'So what can you tell me that makes sense of a supposed seventy-odd-year-old burial that turns out to be well within my frame of reference?'

'Obviously you'll be getting the full SP from the happy band who carried out the excavation. The one-minute version goes like this. Alice's granddad was involved in stealing and caching two valuable motorbikes at the end of the war. He never went back to get them. When he died, Alice found the map among his things and decided to collect on her inheritance. She enlisted the crofter who owns the land. They dug up the first bike no trouble, but when they went for the second one, the crate had been disturbed and then they uncovered an arm. Sudden collapse of stout parties.' River drew in breath theatrically after her gallop through the back story.

'But it's a whole body, yeah? Not just an arm and a Nike?'

'A beautifully preserved bog body.' River tutted. 'Of course, the local tackety boot boys couldn't wait for somebody who knew what they were doing and cleared all the peat away from the body so they could get a better look. God knows what we've lost as a result.'

Karen could picture her friend's pugnacious expression. Redheads always looked fiercer than everybody else when they were riled. 'But presumably what we've gained is the realisation that it's not been in the ground for all those years?'

'That's the one positive I can find in what they did.' Karen could tell it killed River to admit that much. 'Our cadaver is wearing a pair of Nikes. So unless he's a time traveller, he's not been there since the end of the Second World War.'

'What kind of Nikes?'

River snorted. 'Cut to the chase, why don't you? Some kind of Air Nikes. I've taken pics and sent them off to grumpy John Iverson. You remember him? The weirdo who catalogues trainers?'

Karen remembered him. A man who knew all there was to know about trainers and who pretty much despised anybody who didn't. Rather than evangelise the ignorant, he preferred to castigate them for their failures. 'Well, if anybody can ID the shoes, it's probably him. I'll let you handle that side of things. What else can you tell me?'

A pause. 'I can tell you that this is definitely one for you. Our man has what looks like a small-calibre bullet wound in his neck. And maybe a second one in his chest. But that's harder to be sure of while he's still dressed. Either way, I'd say the chances are this was not a natural death.'

Karen let that sink in. 'What's he wearing?'

'Denim jeans. A leather belt. The buckle has quite a distinctive Celtic knot design. Sports socks and the Nike trainers. He was bare-chested, so chances are he didn't go in the ground in the dead of winter.'

'Have you checked his pockets?'

'There's a key on a plastic fob but there's no indication of what it might open. It doesn't appear to have any markings on it. It's probably a copy that's been cut from the original. But that's all. No ID, no wallet, no loose change. They also found a completely undistinguished clasp knife with a wooden riveted handle.'

'And the bike's still there?'

'It is. He was partly trapped underneath it.' She tutted again. 'The tackety boot boys shifted it off him. At least they took pics before they fucked up the scene completely.'

'So whatever was going on, it wasn't about stealing the bikes.' Karen spoke slowly, turning the thought over in her mind. It made no sense. Yet.

'Apparently not.'

'Anything else strike you?'

'Hang on . . . ' The sound altered, as if a hand was covering the phone. Karen heard an indistinguishable exchange, then River was back. 'Sorry, need to get back to work. One other thing I should mention — he's really huge, our boy. He's well over six feet and thanks to the preservative qualities of the peat, I can tell you he's very heavily muscled. Like a weight-lifter. Gotta go, see you later.'

The line died. Karen considered what River had told her and what she knew about those preservative powers of peat. Bodies survived for thousands of years in bogs if the conditions were right. On that scale, this body had barely taken up residence. There was every chance that most of the soft tissue would still be intact; they

85

should be able to come up with a photoshopped pic that wouldn't frighten the horses. It also sounded as if the dead man's appearance was distinctive. That should make it easier to identify him. If he was as bulked up as River had suggested, he'd almost certainly have worked out in a gym and that meant there were probably still people out there who'd recognise him.

As soon as she'd explained to the local big cheese why they needed to let her run the case, she'd have to get those actions under way. In fairness, most officers were delighted to hand over cold cases without a protest. They understood how time-consuming they were and how seldom they produced the headline-grabbing results that the public now believed should be routine.

However it turned out, she couldn't conduct a case on this scale single-handed. She didn't want to abandon the red Rover inquiries, but equally she needed another pair of hands up here. She was pretty sure the Dog Biscuit would want her to draft in Gerry McCartney. In Karen's head, that was reason enough not to do it. She didn't trust Markie looking over her shoulder, not even at one remove. But she knew she could also make a good operational case for it. It was better to leave the more experienced officer in charge of the red Rover inquiry and allow Jason to continue his education in the field. And in practical terms, McCartney was a good five or six hours drive away. Whereas, if the Mint was pursuing his witnesses in the order he'd committed to, he'd already be on the road to

Stonehaven. He could be with her early in the afternoon. She wouldn't put it past him to stick his magnetic flasher on the roof and cross the country like a mobile disco in his eagerness to be of use.

Karen called him. 'Morning, boss,' he shouted. He was the only person under fifty she knew who still thought you had to yell into a mobile.

'Morning, Jason. Where are you?'

A long moment. 'Between Forfar and Kirriemuir. I think.'

'OK. I need you to forget the red Rover for now and reset your satnav for a place called Clashstronach.'

'What?' Panic infused the single syllable.

'Just do 'Ullapool' for now. I'll text you the details.'

'OK, boss. What's happened? Did you find the driver?'

'No. This is a new case. A body in a peat bog in Wester Ross. The lads who found it assumed it was from the Second World War but as soon as River took a look at it, she knew it was one for us.'

'She's amazing, Dr Wilde. The things she can tell just by looking at a body.'

Karen chuckled. 'I think even we could have worked this one out, Jason. The body's wearing a pair of Air Nikes.'

A moment of silence. Then light dawned. 'They didnae have them back in the war, right?'

'Right. So, I'll text you the directions and I'll see you there soon as you like. And when you get a minute, ping the two outstanding red Rover witnesses over to Sergeant McCartney.' Karen ended the call. That had been the easy one. She allowed herself five minutes of enjoying the grey and green grandeur around her before she tackled the more demanding conversation.

'Sergeant,' she began breezily. 'How are you doing this fine morning?'

'It's raining in Gourock. But apart from that, not bad. I've knocked off another witness this morning. Our guy's been registered disabled since 1982. He had his Rover converted to hand controls because he could hardly get in and out of the car. The wife backs him up.'

'You happy with that?'

'I'll check with his doctor. Trust but verify, that's what ACC Markie always says.'

Not exactly an original sentiment. 'Good idea. You're making good progress with your witnesses. And I'm afraid I'm going to be adding to your burden. Jason's got a couple of outstanding inquiries on his witnesses and I'm going to need you to take them over.'

McCartney gave a snide little laugh. 'The Mint not up to nailing them? No surprises there.'

'Quite the opposite. Something else has come up and I need Jason with me.'

'Really? What kind of something?'

It was insolent but Karen decided to keep her powder dry. 'A body's turned up in Wester Ross. Looks like a murder.'

'A murrdurr?' He rolled the 'r's for full dramatic effect. 'How come it's HCU from the off and not N Division's CID?'

'Because the body's been in a peat bog. It's historic.'

'I could come up and lend a hand.'

'That's good of you, Sergeant. But I don't want to abandon the red Rover inquiries. And you're a safe pair of hands, with all your experience in MIT. You'd be wasted up here on all these routine inquiries. Give me a ring tonight, let me know how you're getting on.' She cut the call off before he could protest further. She was sure she'd done the right thing, even if it was for the wrong reasons. Somehow, she didn't think Gerry McCartney would see it that way.

Tough.

15

2018 — Wester Ross

Karen parked at the tail of the line of vehicles beside the track, hoping the verge wasn't as soft as it looked. She'd barely cut the engine when a uniformed constable with a hi-vis jacket and a clipboard loomed alongside. She opened the door, forcing him to step back awkwardly. 'Are you DCI Pirie?' he asked, consulting his clipboard.

'That's right. Inspector Wilson's expecting me.'

The constable nodded. 'He told me to ask you to wait here. I've to go and get him.'

Karen frowned. Did Wilson think she didn't know how to behave in a crime scene? That was rich, coming from a man whose officers had, according to River, comprehensively corrupted the body disposal site. 'Better go and do what you've been told then, Constable.'

He headed off across the bog at an unhurried pace. That's what she got for setting off on River's say-so, Karen thought. Wilson had called her about half an hour out from the croft, firmly standing on his dignity. He couldn't dispute Karen's claim to the case, but he made it clear that he thought River should have gone through him.

'In normal circumstances, that's exactly what

she'd have done,' Karen had said in her best placatory tone. 'But Dr Wilde knew I was in Elgin on another case and she was only trying to avoid me driving halfway down the A9 only to have to turn round and head back north.' For a spur-of-the-moment improvisation it wasn't bad. Hopefully it would be enough to soothe Wilson's *amour propre*. Huffy she could handle; hostile screwed things up.

'All the same, there's no excuse for not following protocol. Things are the way they are for a reason,' he'd grumbled.

'Well, there's no harm done. And I'll be with you in no time at all. Maybe you can bring me up to speed when I arrive?'

Gracelessly, he conceded that would be possible. And now he was flexing his muscles by keeping her hanging around on the fringes of what was still technically his crime scene. Karen blew out a frustrated puff of breath and walked round to the boot to change into her wellies. When she slammed the lid shut, she was startled to find a man standing next to her car who was very definitely neither a cop nor a crime scene tech. His overalls were dark green, the occasional oil stain and mud spatter revealing they were functional rather than fashionable. And the wavy dark hair that fell to his shoulders was about as far from a standard police cut as it was possible to get. The full beard wouldn't have met with approval in the labs either.

When he smiled, laughter lines creased his eyes and dimpled his cheeks. That was a look that didn't happen by accident, she thought.

Before she could speak, he seized the initiative. 'I'm Hamish Mackenzie,' he said. The voice matched the look. 'This is my croft. Are you with the police?'

'I'm Detective Chief Inspector Karen Pirie of the Historic Cases Unit. Very soon this will be my case,' she said, toes curling at her pomposity.

He seemed not to have noticed. 'Have you driven far?'

'I'm based in Edinburgh, but I was in Elgin last night on another matter, so it wasn't too bad a drive.'

'I bet you'd like a coffee,' he said.

'Are you trying to torture me?' Karen spread her arms, encompassing the wild and empty peat bog, the distant hill and the sky.

He laughed. 'Far from it. I brought a couple of flasks up for the workers ten minutes ago. There's still some left. Do you take milk?'

'Please. You may have saved my life.'

'I understand that feeling. I'll be right back.' He walked back up the track, disappearing behind a white van, leaving Karen to wonder whether she'd imagined the improbable encounter.

Much less improbable was the middle-aged man rounding the back of the white van on the bog side of the road. He'd pushed back the hood of his well-filled Tyvek suit and his white hair stood out in a halo like a red-faced Albert Einstein. 'DCI Pirie, I presume?' he demanded, thrusting his head forward like a farmyard rooster staking out his hens.

'Inspector Wilson? Pleased to meet you. Looks

92

like you've got the scene well organised.'

'We might not get many murders up here, but I like to think we know what we're doing. Now, what can I tell you?'

'Right now, what I want is to see the body and the crime scene,' Karen said firmly. 'I'm planning to interview the Somervilles and Mr Mackenzie when my bagman gets here in a couple of hours. And I'll need somewhere local to use as a base. Is there a room you can give me at the station in Ullapool?'

Hamish Mackenzie reappeared at her shoulder in time to hear the end of Karen's words. He handed her a steaming mug of coffee that smelled as improbably good as its provider looked. 'Sorry, I wasn't eavesdropping,' he said. 'But I couldn't help overhearing. We've got a brand-new straw-bale yurt half a mile down the track, just round the bend. It's a holiday let but our first bookings are not for a couple of weeks yet.' He shrugged. 'We didn't expect to get it finished as soon as we did. You'd be very welcome to use it. Without charge, obviously. Think of it as a snagging operation.'

'Straw-bale?' Karen looked dubious.

'It's all the rage now,' Wilson said, his disdain barely hidden. 'Solar powered, carbon neutral, supposedly. Bloody hobbit houses all over the landscape.'

Hamish rolled his eyes. 'I bet people said the same thing when they replaced thatch with corrugated tin roofs.'

'They had a point,' Karen said. 'Has it got electricity?'

'Solar panels and its own wind turbine. And satellite Wi-Fi. The bathroom uses rainwater capture, and there's a body dryer instead of towels. There's a peat stove as well.'

Wilson harrumphed. 'Or you could opt for civilisation. We can find you a room in Ullapool.'

Hamish smiled pleasantly. 'Up to you, Chief Inspector. But it's the best part of an hour's drive to Ullapool. I don't know how long you're going to be here, but that soon adds up . . . '

'Is it just the one bedroom?' Karen asked. Now she was stalling for time, weighing up why Hamish Mackenzie was being so helpful. Was he simply a generous man or was there something more hiding behind the charming exterior?

'A double room and a single.'

'That works for us,' she said. 'At least for tonight. Thanks, Mr Mackenzie.'

He dipped his head in acknowledgement. 'I'll see you later, then. I'd better take the flasks back so I can bring up another brew in a bit.' He strode off with a brief waggle of his fingers in a casual farewell.

'He seems very obliging,' Karen said. All her natural instincts told her to beware of Greeks, especially when bearing gifts. Her job had inoculated her against the easy charm of the beautiful. On balance, she thought she could gain more from accepting his offer, both practically and investigatively. If Hamish Mackenzie thought being kind to her would do him any favours if he'd broken the law, he'd be sorely disappointed. He was dealing with a woman who'd been accustomed to being passed over from the days of teenage discos. Karen had no illusions about her prosaic charms.

'Are you sure it's a good idea to be under an obligation to the man whose land this body was found on?' Wilson's mouth was as sulky as a toddler's.

'I think so. Keeping your friends close but your enemies closer cuts both ways, Inspector.' She smiled sweetly. 'Shall we go and take a look at this body, then?'

16

1944 — Antwerp

When Arnie Burke walked in on Oberstleutnant Gisbert Falk, the German was emptying his safe, shovelling folders and black velvet bags into a capacious leather satchel. Falk turned, hand on his pistol. When he saw who it was, he relaxed. Falk thought the man who was closing the door behind him was a trusted ally, a collaborator who had been supplying him with valuable intelligence for years. Not to mention the fine cigars that were beyond even the black market in Antwerp, a port where there was little that couldn't be bought if you had enough cash. Reassured, Falk went back to his task.

It was a misapprehension he wouldn't live long enough to regret. In two swift silent steps Burke crossed the office, drawing his own silenced CZ1927 pistol and firing two quick shots into the back of Falk's grizzled crewcut head. The German fell like a dropped sack of coal, clattering to the floor.

Burke worked fast. He grabbed the folders and stacked them back in the safe, closing the door and spinning the combination wheel to lock it. He collected the small black velvet bags and zipped them into a concealed body belt that circled his waist and sat unobtrusively on his hips beneath the heavy serge workman's trousers he always wore. If Falk was discovered by any of his Wehrmacht colleagues, the intact safe meant nobody would consider robbery as a motive. There were plenty of people who hated Falk enough to take the opportunity of the approaching Canadian Army to get their own back.

Burke replaced his gun in its soft leather shoulder holster and straightened his jacket before he left the second-floor office. He passed a cleaner sweeping the stairs on the way down, but the man didn't even raise his eyes. Even if the cleaner had heard the soft popping of the shots, there was no prospect of him talking. The poor fuckers who'd had to work for the German officers over the past few years had learned that being blind, deaf and mute were required survival strategies.

And what was one murder in the middle of a war, especially since the invading Canadians were fast approaching? Burke knew all about the exigencies of war. Falk wouldn't be the only German officer on the wrong end of an execution in the coming days.

He emerged into a busy street, crowded with people hurrying home at the end of the day. Fear was no stranger to the citizenry of Antwerp, but this evening there was an almost electrical hum of tension in the air. Everybody believed the end was close for the German occupiers. Even the soldiers in their field grey uniforms were infected with anxiety, nervous where usually they were full of bullying bluster. Burke kept his head down and hurried through the streets. He wasn't going home to the tiny apartment in the eaves of

97

a medieval building by the Scheldt. It was time to pull out. Time to stop pretending to be a dyed-in-the-wool supporter of the Vlaams Nationaal Verbond.

He'd known this moment would come and he was prepared. His exit strategy had been the first thing his OSS bosses had imprinted on his brain before they'd let him loose. But the secret of surviving undercover behind enemy lines was to make yourself truly believe in your fake life. He'd been acting the fascist for so long he'd almost forgotten what being Arnie Burke from Saginaw felt like. One thing he knew for sure. He wasn't going back to some shitty Midwestern life in a car plant. The contents of those black velvet bags were his ticket to a better life. Living a double life on the constant knife-edge of fear, he'd fucking earned that at least.

Burke walked the streets until darkness blanketed what remained of the warren of lanes behind the cathedral. He ducked into a narrow alleyway between a pair of crooked houses whose upper storeys almost touched. He unlocked the unassuming wooden door at the end and stepped into a tiny backyard. He crouched down and counted three bricks along and two up from the far corner. He scraped the dirt away with his clasp knife and eased the brick out. It was a con, like him. Only skin deep.

Behind the cover was a package wrapped tightly in oilskin. US identity papers, a passport, dollars. Burke pocketed the parcel and replaced it with the black velvet bags. It was a tight fit, but he managed it. He replaced the brick and smudged the seams around it with dirt. They'd search him when he returned to the US Army fold and he wasn't going to risk losing what he'd worked so hard to gain. The war in Belgium wasn't going to last much longer; Burke would find an excuse to come back to Antwerp and retrieve his treasure.

And then, look out world. Arnie Burke was on the up.

17

2018 — Wester Ross

Working cold cases, as she'd been doing for most of her career, Karen didn't often come across crime scenes with the bodies still in situ. Generally, she worked from photographs that had been taken a long time before, with all the limitations that implied. She followed Wilson, picking her way across the bog from tussock to tussock, avoiding the soft damp treacherous patches that would swallow her foot to the ankle and beyond.

The excavation area was protected by a white tent which was surrounded in turn by police tape. Not that there were any rubberneckers to keep at bay. If the news had reached what passed for locals around here, it hadn't been intriguing enough to drag them away from their routine tasks. Karen ducked under the tape and Wilson handed her a white suit from a box sitting by the tent entrance. Karen struggled into the overall, slipping out of her boots one at a time and trying to avoid standing on the wet ground with an exposed sock. At least the uncomfortable suits fitted her a bit better these days. Not much compensation for the reason behind her weight loss, but you had to rescue what you could from disaster.

The first thing she took in when she entered

the tent was River's bowed head sticking out of a hole in the ground. Karen took a deep breath and followed the marked path the few yards to the edge of the pit. River caught the movement out of the corner of her eye and straightened up. 'Karen,' she said. 'Good to see you.'

'Not the circumstances I'd have chosen, but yes, it's good to see you too. So, what have we got here?'

They both knew it was a superfluous question. All Karen had to do was look down past her feet into what was effectively a grave. What appeared to be a crude sculpture of a motorbike had been propped upright on one side of the hole, looking like a potential entrant for the Turner Prize. Beside it, his torso twisted at the waist, making an awkward angle to his legs, lay their victim. The peat had stained his skin the colour of weak coffee, but apart from that, he was as perfectly preserved as a shop window mannequin. Short dark hair, well-shaped brows, long eyelashes — they were all clearly visible now River had carefully cleared the peat debris from his head. The strong line of a square jaw and a small nose completed what was still a distinctively hand-some face. Hard to believe he hadn't been missed.

'You can see how well-developed his muscula-ture is,' River pointed out. 'He's a real he-man.'

'Gym bunny or working muscles?' Karen asked.

'I won't swear to it till I get him in the dissecting room, but I'd say these are from working out. Working out hard, over a long period of time. The thing with occupational muscles is that they're never symmetrical. You do the same task again and again and some muscles become disproportionately developed. Our man here looks as if his bulk has been built in a more balanced way.' River leaned forward and indicated two small circular marks, each a darker shade than the surrounding skin. 'And these are what killed him. A bullet to the chest, probably a bit to the right of the heart. But the real damage would have come from this one.' She laid a finger against the hole in his neck. 'All sorts of structures in here that could take major damage from a small projectile tumbling around inside. Major blood vessels, the spinal column. It could even end up bouncing around in the brain. No exit wound, you see?'

Karen understood. A small-calibre bullet, probably a .22 or something similar. Not enough power behind it to pass straight through a body, especially if it had an upward trajectory that took it inside the strong cage of the skull. But it would bounce and tunnel through every piece of soft tissue, every fragile blood vessel in its path. The dead man would have been beyond fear and pain in a matter of seconds. 'So now you've had a good look at him, any estimates as to how long he's been here?'

River shook her head. 'I won't know that for sure till I can do the lab tests. When John Iverson gets back to me, we'll at least have an end point.'

'If I pushed you?'

'I'd still say the same thing. You'll have somewhere to start soon enough, and with this degree of preservation, we'll be able to give you a good photographic likeness you can put out there. Anybody who knew him is going to recognise that face. And look.' She traced an outline on his forearm. 'He's got a tattoo. You can't see the colours because of the peat staining, but the dyes will have been taken up by his lymph nodes. We'll be able to enhance the design in the lab and tell you what the colours were.'

Karen grinned. 'You're a witch. Have I mentioned that?'

'Luckily we're not in the sixteenth century. I think I've done just about all I can do here. The crime scene techs have still got a shedload of work to do but they've taken their pix and vids, so as soon as the undertakers have bagged up the body for the drive back to Dundee, I'll be done here.' River moved to the end of the pit and climbed out.

'You're taking the body to Dundee?' It was the first thing Wilson had said since they'd entered the tent. Karen had hoped the presence of the body had been enough to silence him.

River shrugged. 'It's where my lab is. There's a whole battery of tests we need to do on this body and that's the best place to do them. We've got an accredited pathologist at our disposal for the post-mortem, and then we can proceed to a more detailed exploration of the victim's body.'

'It's the same jurisdiction,' Karen reminded him. 'We're all Police Scotland these days.'

'Still. This is a crime that's taken place on my patch. I'm not comfortable with letting the body disappear down the road where we've got no input into what's going on.' Wilson's prickles were fully extended again.

'Call your superintendent. I'm sure he'll confirm it's my case now.' Karen was tired of deferring to Wilson's swiftness to take umbrage. She knew his boss would be more than happy to hand off a complex and potentially budget-busting case like this. 'The most important thing at this stage is identification. And Dr Wilde's lab is all about ID. That's where the body needs to go. It's not up for discussion.' She moved across the tent to where the crime scene technicians were patiently working through the pile of peat that Wilson's officers had removed from the hole. She introduced herself and asked for the crime scene images to be sent to her. 'Make it a priority, please. We need to identify this man. Somebody somewhere is living with the pain of not knowing what happened to him. We get the chance to put a stop to that.'

By the time she turned back, Wilson had gone. River gave her a rueful smile. 'Another name to add to the Christmas card list.'

Karen pulled a face. 'I'm not here to make friends. I can't be doing with all that pissing up lampposts business. Murder isn't territorial. You going back tonight?'

'If the undertaker gets here soon, yes. You?'

'I'll be here a while yet. I have interviews to conduct. But Hamish the hunk has offered me a holiday let down the road. An eco-yurt, would you believe?'

River raised her eyebrows, a cheeky little smile

twitching her lips. 'Some girls have all the luck.'

'Aye. A night in an eco-yurt with the Mint. Be still my beating heart.'

'Jason's on his way?'

Karen checked her watch. 'Should be here within the hour. And then the real fun begins.'

18

2018 — Wester Ross

There was no doorbell on the low stone building Hamish had directed them to. Just a heavy iron door knocker in the shape of a Celtic knot. Karen nodded to it and Jason dutifully raised it and let it fall. Jason, who had arrived scant minutes before, said, 'So what's going on here, boss?'

'Good question. And what do we do when we don't know what's going on?'

He looked pained. 'We pretend,' he said, doom-laden. Pretending was not Jason's strong suit.

As he spoke, the door opened on a young man who looked like he'd spent much of his life in front of a mirror. His hair was immaculately shaped, held in place by the kind of product urban barbershops made their profits from. His goatee was trimmed and groomed with the same precision. Skinny jeans and a red-and-black plaid shirt that still had the creases from the packaging. Karen struggled to imagine him getting his hands dirty in a peat bog. 'Are you the police?' he said, an uncertain frown creasing his forehead. If he'd known how it betrayed his age, Karen thought, he'd never have let his face do that.

'We are. I'm Detective Chief Inspector Pirie of Police Scotland's Historic Cases Unit.' Sometimes she liked to roll out the full title. It distracted people from the depressing reality that she and Jason — and now, she supposed, Gerry McCartney — were the entirety of the Historic Cases Unit, 'And this is Detective Constable Murray. Mr Somerville, is it?'

He nodded. 'You'd better come in. It's all been a bit of a shock. Welcome to Scotland, dead bodies our speciality.' His yappy Estuary English voice was already setting Karen's teeth on edge.

'To be fair, they're not exactly a common occurrence,' Jason grunted as he followed Karen into the small square hallway.

Will Somerville opened the door on the left and led them into a spacious room that occupied about half of the building. With one sweeping look, Karen took in a compact galley kitchen at one end, separated from the sitting area by a pale wood dining table and four chairs; and exposed stone walls decorated with large framed photographs of the wild western coastline. In one corner of a tweed-covered sofa a woman was huddled, legs tucked under herself. Her dark hair was pulled back in a loose ponytail, from which a few untidy strands had escaped. Anxiety had sharpened the bones of her face, making her look like a small frightened animal. 'This is my wife, Alice,' Will said. 'Alice, it's the police. Finally.'

He dropped on to the sofa next to her and put an arm round her shoulders. 'We've had no information at all about what's been going on,' he added, trying for stern and achieving only sulky.

'We prefer to wait until we have something to

report,' Karen said, mild and calm. 'Now, I know you had a chat with the local officers earlier, but my team has taken over the case because it's clear that this is not a recent incident. And I'm afraid that means we'll have to go through the whole thing with you again.'

Will sighed, but Alice patted his knee. 'We understand. We want to get to the bottom of this, the same as you do. Please, sit down.' She waved at the pair of armchairs at an angle to the sofa.

Jason took the further chair, angling his body away from the couple and taking out his notebook only after Karen had started speaking. The lad was definitely getting better. 'Let's go right back to the beginning. I've got your address down south here.' She read it out. 'Is that correct?'

Alice nodded. 'Yes.'

'So can you tell me why you're here?'

They exchanged a quick glance. 'It's a long story,' she said.

'We weren't doing anything wrong,' Will added hastily.

The perennial cry of the guilty conscience, Karen thought. 'We're in no hurry.' She smiled. 'Tell me the story.'

Alice untucked her feet and sat up straight, planting her pink woolly socks firmly on the floor. 'In the Second World War, my grandfather was stationed near here at Clachtorr Lodge. You must have passed it on the way here, it's that big pile a couple of miles down the road. He was always very cagey about what he did then, but when all these stories started coming out about

Bletchley Park and the undercover spies we sent in to Europe, he finally started talking about it. He was employed as an instructor training SOE operatives in survival skills. You know what SOE was, right?'

Karen had a hazy idea. 'Secret service?'

'Not quite. It was Churchill's brainchild. The Special Operations Executive. They were set up to carry out stuff behind enemy lines. Espionage, reconnaissance and sabotage mainly. They did amazing things. And they were all trained up here in the Highlands.'

'I didn't know that,' Karen said.

'The Highlands was a restricted area in the Second World War,' Jason piped up. 'You had to have a pass to go north of the Great Glen. And even if you lived here, you had to have written permission to go more than twenty miles from your home. You could end up in jail if you didnae have the right paperwork.' He caught Karen's look of surprise. 'We had a history teacher who went on about how it was like a military coup, how the English treated Scotland like their own personal backyard.' He gave a slightly embarrassed smile.

'Thank you, DC Murray. So, Mrs Somerville, your grandfather was up here teaching spies how to live off the land?'

'More or less. Anyway, when the war ended, they had to withdraw from the area. Apparently, it was more trouble than it was worth to ship a lot of the kit back to wherever it came from, so the instructors and the staff were told to burn everything that was left. That, or bury it.'

'What? Just dump it?' Karen's thrifty soul was outraged.

'I know, it seems mad. But that's how it was. Anyway, a couple of weeks before the order came down, they'd taken delivery of two motorbikes from the US Army. Indian Scouts, they were called.'

'They're collectors' items now,' Will interrupted.

'Granto — my grandfather — and his mate Kenny fell in love with the bikes. He said they were beautiful examples of engineering. And they couldn't bring themselves to destroy them. So they came up with a plan. They decided to bury the bikes and come back for them later after everybody had forgotten all about them.' Alice paused, staring at Karen as if daring her to criticise.

'That was enterprising,' Karen said. 'If marginally illegal.'

'They weren't the only ones, according to Alice's granddad. All sorts of stuff got liberated. And the bikes were only going to be destroyed otherwise,' Will said. 'You could argue they were protecting something valuable.'

Karen shook her head. 'Right now, I'm not interested in debating the rights and wrongs of what your granddad did. What happened after they buried the bikes?'

'They drew a map. They each kept a copy of it. There weren't any place names to show where it was, because of course Granto and Kenny knew roughly where they'd put the crates with the bikes. The map was just to remind them of the

110

exact details. And then they went their separate ways. They agreed to wait five years and then they were going to go back and dig them up.'

'But that didn't happen.' Sometimes stating the obvious was the best way to push a story on.

Alice sighed. 'No. Kenny died. I'm not sure how exactly, all Granto said was that he'd passed away within a year or two of them being demobbed.'

'So, apart from your grandfather, Kenny was the only one who knew about the bikes?'

She nodded. 'That's right.'

'But he might have told his family the story?'

Alice shook her head. 'He wasn't married. My granddad went to the funeral, he said the only family Kenny had was his sister, who kept house for him.'

'Do you know Kenny's surname? Or his sister's name?'

Will spoke up. 'He was called Pascoe. There's an old photo of them taken at the big house where they were billeted and it says on the back 'Austin Hinde and Kenny Pascoe'. Austin was Alice's grandfather.'

'He came from the North East,' Alice added helpfully. 'Somewhere called Warkworth. I only remember it because Granto used to make a joke out of it. He said going to the funeral in Warkworth was worth the walk.'

Karen flicked a glance at Jason, checking he was getting all this down. 'Did he mention the sister's name?'

Alice shook her head. 'If he did, I don't remember it. He did tell me how upset he was

111

when Kenny died. It was like the two of them shared so much during the war, Kenny was the only one that knew big chunks of his life and now he had nobody who had any idea what they'd got up to. All those spies they'd trained, all those lives they'd changed. People they'd sent off to their deaths, that sort of thing.'

'It's pretty amazing when you think about it,' Will contributed.

Everyone ignored him. Alice went on, 'Granto didn't know what to do then. He knew he couldn't get them out by himself.'

'And he didn't trust anybody to help him,' Will grumbled. 'He was scared it would all come out and he'd get arrested.'

'Anyway,' Alice spoke firmly, 'it was always a sort of family legend, the bikes in the bog. I'm not sure we ever totally believed it. He was a great storyteller, my Granto. But when he died a couple of years ago, my mum and I were going through all his stuff, and I found the map tucked away in an envelope. Which was, like, wow. And Will and I, we decided it would be like a sort of tribute to Granto if we went off and found the bikes.'

'Only it wasn't as straightforward as that.' Will sighed. 'We knew he'd been based at the hunting lodge at Clachtorr but that was all we knew. Stupidly, we thought all we had to do was drive around till we found the layout that corresponded to the map and we'd be sorted. We spent our whole summer holiday last year driving round the area getting more and more frustrated because nothing matched. We'd find

112

somewhere that looked a bit like it, only there would be a hill in the wrong place or one of them sea lochs or whatever. What a waste of time.'

Alice looked at the floor between her pink socks. Clearly this was not the first time she'd heard this rant. 'I didn't want to give up. So I went online. I started checking out forums and groups of people who live up here. I posted a pic of the map and asked if anybody knew where it was. Obviously without the 'X marks the spot' bit.' She giggled.

'And what happened then?'

She looked up and grinned. 'Hamish happened then. He said he thought the map was his grandparents' croft the way it had been back at the end of the war. We started talking and he explained the changes to the buildings and the sheepfold and stuff, and yeah, it made sense.'

'Turned out we'd even checked it out last year but we dismissed it because it was too different.' Will shook his head in disgust. 'We could have saved ourselves a year.'

'No, we couldn't, Will. We could never have done it without Hamish's help. He's been amazing.'

'So when he got in touch, you asked Hamish Mackenzie for help?'

'He *offered*,' Will said. 'He was as keen as Alice was to see what was down there.'

'No reluctance on his part, then?' It was a question Karen couldn't ignore.

'Totally the opposite. He said people were always finding bits and pieces of stuff when they were working their land, but nobody had ever found anything that exciting. I got the impression there's not much excitement around here,' Alice said.

It was, Karen knew, a mistake outsiders often made about the apparently bucolic Highlands. They might not have many murders in these parts, but there was no shortage of illicit and illegal activity. Not to mention the perfectly legitimate social activities. She'd have bet there were more routine events in this corner of the world than in the Somervilles' Home Counties redoubt. 'So you made a plan?'

'We agreed a date that we would come up and excavate the site. Hamish reckoned a metal detector would help us to narrow it down. We arrived the day before yesterday, and we were so excited, weren't we, Will?'

'We were. We couldn't wait to get started. I tell you, if we'd known then what we know now, we'd have got in the car and headed back south fast as you like.'

Alice's bottom lip trembled. 'I thought it was going to be a dream come true but it's turned into the worst nightmare. I wish we'd never set eyes on the place.'

19

2018 — Dundee

River was on the outskirts of Dundee when her phone rang. The dashboard computer told her it was John Iverson, so she hastily accepted the call. 'Hi, John. Thanks for getting back to me so soon,' she said cheerily, knowing it was a waste of positive energy.

He exhaled noisily. 'Well, it wasn't exactly a challenge you set me,' he grumbled. 'You could have googled it yourself and saved me the bother.'

'Sorry, John. But I wouldn't trust myself to get it right. There's so much detail on these shoes, it needs an expert like you to pinpoint exactly what we're looking at.' River took one hand off the wheel and mimed sticking two fingers down her throat.

'Anybody who knows anything about sneakers would know exactly what you've got here.'

'Even with the staining and the discolouration?'

'That does make it a bit more challenging, I suppose,' Iverson said grudgingly. 'But there's no mistaking the shape and the contours, the wave pattern and the keynote minimal swoosh.'

River rolled her eyes. 'And what does that say to you, John?'

'Well, Dr Wilde, you're looking at an iconic sneaker here. This is the Nike Air Max 95, designed by Sergio Lozano. It was a running shoe like no other. He based the look on the striations of the Grand Canyon, except he also incorporated the contours of muscles, and eyelets that were like stylised ribs.' He was off now and there was no stopping him. 'This was the first shoe with visible air in the forefoot and the rear sole. It was a revolution. It inspired whole generations of sneakers since. Nike even produced a twentieth-anniversary reworking of the original.'

'And this couldn't be one of those?'

He breathed heavily. 'No, they did it in a different colour-way. Platinum, silver and black. But the styling was the same, especially the gradient pattern on the women's edition.'

'Amazing,' River said. 'So when was this particular shoe introduced?'

A weary sigh. 'The clue's in the name. Air Max 95. It first went on sale in 1995 and it very quickly became a collector's item.'

River thought for a moment. 'So, what? It was a fashion statement rather than a serious athlete's shoe?'

'It was both. It was designed as a running shoe, at a time when most of Nike's attention was focused on basketball shoes. This was their attempt to make an impact on the growing running market. Runners and field athletes liked it but so did kids who wanted to look cool.' The note of disdain in his voice was unmistakable. 'Here's an interesting fact about the Air Max 95. It was the second most common shoe print that UK police found at crime scenes in the late 90s and early 2000s.'

River knew Karen would love that nugget of information. If their victim moved in criminal circles, it might help to make sense of his bewildering presence in the peat bog. 'Was it an expensive shoe?'

'Oh yes. It cost ninety-nine pounds in 1995. That was the equivalent of a month's rent in a council flat in the North of England.' It was a curiously precise measure, but River didn't doubt it for a nanosecond. Not from grumpy John Iverson.

'Did it stay on sale for a while?'

The sound that came from her speakers was a cross between a rumble and a groan. 'That's not an easy question to answer. It sold out in a matter of months in its first iteration but there was a massive second-hand market fuelled by the Japanese. People would pay as much as a thousand dollars for a mint pair. But by the looks of the photographs you sent me, your owner treated them as shoes, not trophies.'

'Is there any way of tracing the individual pair to a retailer?'

A short bark of laughter. 'I know I said these were iconic shoes, but really, Dr Wilde? Back then, records were skeletal. I would say there's no chance, not even if you had the original box and receipt.' He laughed again. 'Now, that's all I have for you, Dr Wilde. I'll invoice your department as usual for my time.' And the connection dropped out.

River allowed herself a moment of gratification. Inch by precious inch, they were getting closer to their man.

20

2018 — Wester Ross

Karen gave Alice space to compose herself, then said, 'I know this is upsetting for you, but we're going to have to go through exactly what happened yesterday.'

Alice shivered. 'It was horrible. I mean, when I saw that arm sticking out of the peat, all sorts of things went through my head. I even wondered whether it was Kenny in that hole. And if it was, what did that say about my Granto?'

'Thankfully, Dr Wilde has been able to put your minds at rest on that score,' Karen said. 'We think the man whose body you discovered was put in the ground a lot more recently than 1944. Sometime in the last twenty-five years, to be a wee bit more precise.' She gave a wry smile. 'Which counts as 'relatively recently' in our terms of reference.'

'How far back do you go?' Will asked.

Karen didn't think he was trying to distract her, so she said, 'We generally draw the line at seventy years, from a police point of view. There's no realistic possibility of finding a living suspect beyond that. The historians and the forensic anthropologists like Dr Wilde take a much longer view. Nothing's too old for them. But this man whose body you unearthed — he had friends, parents. Maybe even a wife and kids.

People who don't know what happened to him. And I need your help to bring him home to them. Alice, did anybody else know about your granddad's map?'

She thought for a moment. 'Well, he talked about it sometimes with family. But like I said, we all kind of half-believed it was one of his tall stories. Exaggerating what a big deal his war work had been. But I don't remember anybody ever talking about seeing the map. And like I said, it was tucked away in an envelope in a drawer.'

'Did he have pals from his wartime days? Maybe at the local British Legion, or men he met up with socially?'

Alice shook her head. 'Not that I know of. I spent a lot of time with him and my granny when I was little, and I don't remember that. He wasn't much of a drinker, he didn't really go out to the pub much. He played bowls a lot, but I don't think any of his pals from the bowling club went that far back.'

'So as far as you're aware, nobody ever came asking about the bikes?'

Will butted in. 'He'd have said something, wouldn't he? When he was talking about it to Alice. He knew he couldn't do it alone, so if somebody had turned up with an interest, he'd have made some sort of a deal with them, wouldn't he?'

Karen nodded. 'You'd think so. But I need to be as clear as possible about the circumstances surrounding these bikes and the map leading to their discovery. I take it you've still got the map?'

Startled, Alice sat up straight, hand to her mouth. 'God, no! It's still at Hamish's house. We took it over to compare with the maps he'd researched. And we were in such a state, we never picked it up.'

'That's fine, I'll take a look at it over there. We might need to hold on to it for now, but if we do, I'll make sure you get a receipt and a copy of it.'

'Why do you need the map?' Will demanded.

'Because it turns out it's actually a set of directions to a body disposal and I need to be certain nobody else made use of it before you did.' Karen held on to her patience with grim determination.

'How will you know that just by looking at it?'

'We have people called forensic document examiners who uncover all kinds of trace elements from bits of paper that you and me can't even imagine. And while I'm on the subject, I'll be getting a uniformed officer to come over and take your fingerprints and DNA samples. I presume you've no objection.'

Will looked as if he was about to object but Alice took control. 'Of course we've no objection. Like I said. We want to help.'

'Thank you. So, let's go back into the more recent past. Tell me what happened yesterday.'

Alice took a visibly deep breath and told Karen everything up to the point where Hamish had said there was a body in the pit and Alice had screamed herself hoarse. 'Then Hamish called the police,' she said, her voice dull and sad.

'Obviously, whoever he is, he's nothing to do

with us.' Will said. 'So, will we be able to take the other bike back with us? The one from the other crate?'

Even Jason turned and stared incredulously at him. 'I don't think it belongs to you,' he said. 'Just for starters.'

'What about treasure trove? Finders keepers?' Will wasn't giving up without a fight.

'DC Murray's right,' Karen said. 'You've got no legal claim to either of those motorbikes. And treasure trove only applies if nobody knows who the rightful owner is. Which in this case, isn't so. Either the US Army or the MOD has first dibs on those bikes. But right now, that's the least of my concerns. I've got a murder victim to identify and a killer to track down. You'll find that's everybody's priority round here now.'

Will glared mutinously at her. 'If it hadn't been for us taking the initiative here, nobody would have been any the wiser about your dead man. We should get some kind of recognition for that.'

Karen struggled to keep her contempt under control. 'Don't pretend there was anything high-minded going on here. If Alice's grandfather had buried a box of rocks, no way would you be mounting an expedition to find them. You were on the make, Mr Somerville. If all you'd found had been a pair of motorbikes, you'd have had it away on your toes with them, cleaned them up and flogged them to the highest bidder and told yourself you weren't breaking any of the several laws you'd be in flagrant breach of. You don't get a pat on the back for any of that.'

Alice looked as if she'd been slapped. Will sat scowling at a point somewhere to the side of Karen's head. Karen hoped she'd got everything she could from Alice Somerville. She didn't think she'd be getting anything more now. She got to her feet. 'Thanks for your time. An officer will — '

Will jumped up. 'Can we go home now? Since you won't let us take our bike back, there's no reason for us to hang about in this godforsaken dump.'

The thought of never having to see Will Somerville again warmed Karen's spirits. 'You'll have to wait till we've got your prints and DNA. But after that, you're free to go. If this body's the age we think it is, you're certainly not suspects. You'd still have been at school when he was murdered.'

Karen turned and made for the door, Jason at her heels. As they left the room, Alice called after them, 'Good luck. I hope you find out who he is.'

Karen stomped back to the car, head down into the gusting wind that had sprung up from the north-west. 'Where do these people get it from, that sense of entitlement?' she muttered as she slammed the passenger door. 'How can that self-absorbed wee *hipster*' — she made it sound like a swear word — 'sit there with a dead man on the doorstep and bother his arse about a motorbike that doesn't even belong to him?'

'Beats me, boss. Plus, how does he think he's going to sell it with no paperwork except a scruffy wee map?' This wisdom from Jason, a man who'd encountered more undocumented

122

vehicles than he cared to admit to Karen. Having a polis for a brother was a perpetual red face for his big brother Ronan. The late DS Phil Parhatka had once met Ronan at a Raith Rovers match and had sussed him out on the spot. 'You'd do well to make sure Karen never meets your brother,' he'd said as they'd walked down the hill from Starks Park after the final whistle. Jason had understood and obeyed. Some things, the boss didn't have to know.

He had no idea that she'd always known. Of course she had.

'They've not even got their scruffy wee bit of paper any more,' Karen said grimly. 'That is going to be in an evidence locker till we get this killer banged up for life. Now, let's see whether Hamish Mackenzie lives up to his coffee.'

21

2018 — Wester Ross

There was a note on Hamish Mackenzie's front door: 'Back by 5'. Karen checked her watch. Another forty minutes. Maybe more, given the relaxed attitude country people often had towards time. 'Let's go and take a look at this eco-yurt we're supposed to be staying in,' she said.

They drove down the track past the excavation site. Karen had moved her car earlier to sit alongside Hamish's Toyota, and now only three vehicles remained — a police Land Rover, a white van and a Nissan 4x4. 'That'll be the forensic techs still at it,' she said. 'I can't believe the local tackety boots boys shovelled all the peat off the body. I bet the techs are cursing them. They'll have to go through that whole pile of muck on the off-chance that there's some crucial piece of evidence in there.'

'They'll pay for it,' Jason said as they passed. 'They'll have to guard the crime scene till the techs are done with it. I wouldn't fancy a long night shift out here in the middle of nowhere.'

The track fell away after another small rise to reveal a narrow glen leading to the sea. A squat circular building was perfectly placed to benefit from the sheltering shoulders of the hills on either side as well as a stunning view out to sea, complete with the distant smudge of the Isle of Lewis skyline. 'That'll be it, then,' Karen said.

Jason turned off the track on to a gravelled parking area. Curious, they stared at the eco-yurt. It had a foundation and a chimney stack of local stone. Above that, the straw bale walls had been harled and whitewashed. An array of picture windows took advantage of the view and a narrow wooden porch jutted out on the landward side. The gently sloping roof was covered in vegetation; it resembled a heather moor. Karen half-expected a brood of red grouse to come tumbling out and fix her with their beady eyes.

'Shall we chance it, then?' She headed for the door, not sure whether it would be locked. The handle turned easily and the door swung open. They walked into a bright half-moon-shaped room, with big triple-glazed windows round the outside walls. The uninterrupted view was even more spectacular than from the road. Being so close to the sea made Karen feel instantly at home, although this prospect of water and mountains was on a far grander scale than the view of the Firth of Forth and Fife from her flat.

'Cool,' Jason said, prowling round the perimeter. Handmade wooden cupboards lined the walls and a kitchen area provided a fridge, a coffee machine and a microwave. Through the window, Karen could see an outdoor cooking area with a brick oven, a barbecue grill and a picnic table all huddled under their own turf roof. The room was furnished with the kind of chairs that invited sprawling, each with its own convenient little table.

Karen investigated the three doors in the long wall that divided the yurt. The first was a wet room complete with a contraption that identified itself as a body dryer. She eyed it with some suspicion but decided she'd give it a go. Next was a narrow single room — bed, chair, hanging rail and a low chest. A monastic cell for Jason, obviously.

The final room was also filled with light. A king-sized bed looked out across the constantly shifting sea. To one side, a desk with two pillars of drawers. Another hanging rail and a couple of chairs completed the furnishings. Simple but sufficient, a marriage of form and function. *I could live here.* Then reason kicked in and she realised she'd never survive without her friends, her family, her job. The streets she walked at night. Losing Phil had taught her that you couldn't outrun what lived inside you; you could only make accommodation with it. And for her, running away would never be the answer.

'This'll do fine,' Karen said, returning to the living room.

'There's Wi-Fi as well,' Jason said. 'So it doesn't matter that there's no telly. One of the locals told me there's a pub about five miles down the road where we can get some grub, so we'll be OK.'

By the time they returned to the croft house, the note had disappeared. Before they could knock, Hamish opened the door. 'I heard the car,' he said. He'd swapped his overalls for an Aran sweater, a kilt and thick socks concertinaed round the bottom of sturdy calves and his hair hung fashionably tousled to his shoulders. Definitely working the look, Karen thought.

'I suppose you notice anything that disturbs the peace hereabouts,' she said.

He chuckled as he led them indoors. 'It's not that peaceful. The sheep, the birds, the wind . . . But yes, you do notice other people's engines. Come away through.'

After the clever design of the yurt, Hamish's kitchen wasn't as much of a surprise as it might otherwise have been. Even so, Karen recognised that it must have cost a lot to look this simple. She followed her country's politics enough to understand that subsistence farming in the Highlands was just that — subsistence. There was money on display here that didn't come from running a flock of sheep on a Wester Ross hillside. There was something lurking behind his charm, and she needed to be very careful not to be seduced into missing what it was.

'Coffee? I make a very fine cup of coffee, Chief Inspector.'

Karen shook her head. She was already in this man's debt for the roof over her head and she needed to maintain a little professional distance. 'We're fine, thanks. By the way, we checked out the yurt, which will suit us perfectly for tonight. With a bit of luck, we'll be able to finish up tomorrow and be out of your hair.'

He waved off the suggestion. 'Stay as long as you need to. You'll be doing me a favour — there's always little niggles when you bring a new property on stream.' He grinned. 'Like I said, you can be my snagging crew. I'm slightly anxious when things come in ahead of schedule. I can't help wondering what corners have been cut.'

'We'll be sure to bring any complaints straight back to you. Mind if we sit down? I know you'll have talked to the local officers, but we've taken over the investigation now and I need to run through it all again. Sorry about that.' The apology was deliberately cursory.

'No problem, make yourselves comfortable.'

They sat round the breakfast bar, Jason with his notebook open and chewed biro at the ready. Hamish had no sooner settled than he was up again. 'I need a coffee, sorry,' he said, busying himself with buttons and knobs, disrupting any attempt at conversation with grinding and hissing.

Karen let it wash over her. She wasn't thrown off her stride so easily. She waited till he sat down again with a tiny cup of espresso that looked like black oil with a halo of crema round the edge. 'So, let's go back to the beginning. How did you first encounter the Somervilles?'

'We've got a Facebook forum for Clashstronach. It helps people stay in touch. Not everybody who owns property hereabouts lives locally all year round, and this way they can keep their finger on the pulse. Or get tipped off if there's an issue they need to be aware of. Young people move away but they still want to know what's going on back home. And for everybody else, it's an easy way of spreading the word about a party or a ceilidh. Or a funeral, even. So Alice tracked us down and posted a copy of her granddad's map.' He reached for a small pile of paper at the end of the breakfast bar and selected one. He placed a printout of a hand-drawn map in front of them.

'That's what she put up online?' To Karen, it looked pretty vague. A glen, a couple of hills, a sea loch and a few structures.

'Yeah. And she mentioned that the old man had been stationed at Clachtorr. That's yon run-down old pile you'll have passed set back from the road a few miles south. It used to be a grand hunting lodge, but the government commandeered it during the war and it never really got restored to the glory days afterwards.'

'And you recognised this sketch?' It was hard not to sound incredulous.

'I did. Because I spent a big chunk of my childhood running about these hills. This was my grandparents' croft and I had a hand in a lot of the things that have changed since this map was drawn. Even when I was wee, I was always given bits of jobs to do. So yes, I recognised the layout in relation to that arm of the sea loch and the relative position of the hills.'

'That's pretty amazing,' Jason said. 'Mind you, I failed geography.'

Karen ignored him. 'So you replied to Alice?'

Hamish sipped his dark brew. 'I did. I asked her why she was so interested in that particular piece of land. And she asked to email me privately. Next morning, I got an email with the story I'm sure you've heard already. Buried motorbikes, granddad's treasure hunt.' He laughed. 'Who could resist that?'

'Not you, apparently.'

'Och, I thought it would be a bit of fun. And no skin off my nose if it came to nothing. Anyway, we emailed back and forth a wee bit till eventually she realised she was going to have to trust me with some more information if we were going to get anywhere. I'll still have all the emails on my laptop, I can forward them to you if you like?'

'Thanks. I'd appreciate that. If you ping them across to Constable Murray here, he can take a look at them.' Jason nodded glumly. 'So Alice gave you more details?'

He produced a second map, almost identical to the first except that on this one, a faint red X appeared. Even Karen could see that it was a pretty good approximation of where the body had been unearthed. 'X marks the spot.' Hamish tapped the cross. 'So we made arrangements for them to come up and we'd have ourselves a wee treasure hunt.'

'You struck lucky remarkable easily,' Karen said. 'Anybody would think you knew where to look.'

Hamish looked startled. Then he laughed again. It was a big, rich laugh, the sort she imagined people found hard to resist. 'Nothing sinister, I promise you. I'm not daft, Chief Inspector. No way was I planning on spending a week poking about the peat at random. No, I borrowed Archie Macleod's metal detector and made some preliminary investigations in the general area indicated on the map. It took me about an hour of dottering about before I found what I thought I was looking for.'

'Were you not tempted to have a look?'

He stroked his beard, eyeing Karen warily. 'Of course I was. I'm only human. But I restrained myself. It wasn't my treasure to dig up. All I did was stick a couple of iron stakes in the ground and mark out the area with some baler twine.'

'And you didn't tell anybody else about it?'

'Not even Archie. I told him I'd heard about somebody down in Arisaig finding some guns that had been buried at the end of the war and I wanted to have a wee trip over to Clachtorr to see if I could find anything.' His smile was rueful. 'Archie's going to be majorly pissed off with me. That's going to cost me a bottle of decent malt.'

Karen took him through the excavation. His story tallied in every detail with Alice and Will's. 'You've spent time in these parts since you were a boy, you said?'

Hamish nodded. Again the wary eyes, the smoothing of the beard. 'It was my second home growing up.'

'Do you recognise the man whose body you found on your land?'

It was a loaded question. But Hamish didn't dodge the bullet. 'No,' he said firmly. 'I have never seen that man before. He's not from round here.'

22

2018 — Bridge of Allan

It takes a brisk walker a fraction under half an hour to make a circuit of Airthrey Loch, the body of water at the heart of Stirling University's campus. The woman with the fox terrier made the circuit twice most days — once before she left for work and a second time before she went to bed. The mile and a half gave her space to focus on the day from either end. The dog ran three or four times as far as she walked, which meant that later he'd tolerate the short walk round the block which was all he ever got from the woman's elderly mother at lunchtime.

Airthrey Loch suited her. The path was mostly well-lit. Because of the surrounding campus, it never felt isolated. She hardly ever completed her walk without passing someone — a runner striding out; a couple intertwined in first love; a lecturer, head down, brow corrugated in thought; a gaggle of students coming back from the bar to their residences. Nobody gave her a second look, which was how she liked it.

It had been after ten when she'd parked the car and set off. A lazy wind swept down from the hills, but she was dressed for the weather and it didn't penetrate her soft cashmere scarf. She strode out, deep in thought, searching for a solution to a clash between two junior colleagues.

So when the man stepped out from the cover of a thicket of rhododendrons, her chest clenched tight, startling her out of her stride. Pulse racing, she stumbled slightly before steadying herself, arms angled in front of her body in a defensive pose.

'Sorry, ma'am, I didnae mean to frighten you,' DS Gerry McCartney said.

'What? You think creeping up on women in the dark is calculated to put them at ease?' ACC Ann Markie seldom let her guard slip, but this time she sounded as furious as she felt. She dropped her hands to her side and carried on walking. McCartney had to hustle to keep up. 'Why the cloak and dagger, Gerry?' she demanded.

'I thought you wanted me to be discreet?' He sounded wounded.

'Discreet means you don't behave in a way that would set tongues wagging from Jedburgh to John O'Groats if anyone were to see you. Discreet means casual encounters in the course of everyday business. Not acting like you're in an episode of some bloody Channel 4 conspiracy thriller.'

'Sorry.'

'How did you know I'd be here anyway? Are you stalking me?' She stopped dead, turned on her heel and glowered at him.

McCartney thrust his hands into the pockets of his inadequate jacket. 'Garvey, the head of security at the university? He was a sergeant in Falkirk.' He scoffed. 'Everybody knows you walk the dog out here, morning and night.'

'Christ. So much for security.' Markie

marched off again. 'So, why are you interrupting the only bit of peace I get in my day?'

'You wanted to know about DCI Pirie.'

'Fast work, Gerry. You've only been there two days. That's no time at all to come up with the goods.'

The next street light picked up the worried look on McCartney's face. 'I wouldn't say I've exactly got the goods. But I thought you might appreciate an update.'

Markie rolled her eyes. 'Why? What's going on?'

'She's off the reservation. She's away up to the Highlands on River Wilde's say-so.'

Markie stopped in her tracks and turned to face him. 'What? You'd better explain yourself.'

'According to that ginger ninja she has working for her, Pirie got a call from Wilde saying N Division had come up with a body that was probably a cold case,' he gabbled. 'So Pirie dropped what she was doing and legged it across to Wester Ross. She was practically at the crime scene before she finally deigned to talk to the SIO and tell him she was swiping his case out from under him.'

Markie wondered how Pirie had survived in the job as long as she had. The woman seemed to have no understanding of how relationships with colleagues were built. How had she been allowed to spiral so far out of control? Closing cases was all well and good, but in the modern police service, being a team player involved more than a team of two. Clearly Pirie couldn't be brought to heel. She had to be replaced. And once Markie had the HCU sorted, it would be a very different sort of operation. One that understood the importance of a chain of command. And didn't see insubordination as a badge of pride. 'And was it?' she asked, cutting straight to the point and setting off along the path again.

'Was it what?'

'A cold case.' The unspoken 'you idiot' hung in the air.

'I don't know. I've not heard back from the ginger ninja. The thing is, if it is a proper case, she should have taken me, not him. I'm the senior officer. And she's left me on this complete balls-ache of an inquiry that's going nowhere. I'm driving all round the country talking to people who owned a Rover 214 in 1986 on the off-chance that one of them is going to put their hands up to an old series of rapes that might just squeeze out a single rape-murder. As if. Murray should be doing that, not me. It's about all he's up to.'

Markie slowed and stopped, staring out over the rippled darkness of the loch. 'Do you think she suspects I've put you in there to report back on how she's running her wee empire?'

'I don't know.'

'There's a lot you don't seem to know, Gerry. You used to have your finger on the pulse back when you were my bagman. Don't tell me you've lost your touch. I wouldn't want to think I'd misplaced my belief in you.'

He sighed. 'I think she doesn't trust anybody except Murray, and that's only because he's too stupid to betray her.'

'Well, your job is to make her trust you.'

'I'll do what I can. I just . . . '

'What? You just what, Gerry?' Markie sounded friendly now. Anyone who knew her well would have run for the hills.

'I'm not sure what this is all in aid of. That's all.'

'Don't worry about things that are permanently going to be above your pay grade. Do what I ask of you and you'll be fine. You don't want to disappoint me, Gerry.'

He swallowed the lump that seemed to have formed in his throat. 'I get that. But if I knew — '

'You want to go back to the MIT, don't you?'

Right then, he wanted to go anywhere Ann Markie wasn't. 'I'll sort it,' he said.

'Good. And don't pull a stunt like this again, Gerry.' Contempt dripped from her voice. She put two fingers to her lips and let out a piercing whistle. The dog came crashing out of the shrubbery and jumped up on Gerry McCartney, smearing his trousers with mud.

He skittered away, wondering whether she'd trained the yappy little bastard to do that. It wouldn't have surprised him in the least. For a fleeting moment, he wondered whether he'd backed the wrong horse in a race he hadn't even known was being run.

23

2018 — Wester Ross

For a woman accustomed to attacking insomnia by quartering the labyrinthine streets of Edinburgh with its wynds and closes, its pends and yards, its vennels and courts, where buildings crowded close in unexpected configurations, the empty acres of the Highlands offered limited possibilities. Once Jason had gone to bed, Karen had soon realised sleep was going to be elusive. The only option was her usual remedy.

So she put her walking boots back on, shrugged into her jacket and set off into the night. The sky was clear and the light from the half-moon had no competition from street lights so the pale glow it shed was more than enough to see by. She turned right out of the yurt and followed the track for ten minutes till it ended in a churned-up turning circle by what looked like the remnants of a small stone bothy. Probably a shepherd's hut, Karen told herself, based on what she knew was the most rudimentary guesswork. The wind had stilled and the sea shimmered in the moonlight, tiny rufflets of waves making the surface shiver. She stood for a while, absorbing the calm of the night, letting it soothe her restlessness.

But it was too cold to stand still for long, and, sooner than she'd have liked, she retraced her steps up the track, past the yurt and beyond the crime scene, letting her thoughts spool back. She'd had dinner with Jason in the nearest pub — five miles up the road, over the county border into Sutherland. Cleverly, they kept the food menu simple — a range of pies from the famous shop in Lochinver, accompanied by hand-cut crispy chips and home-made baked beans. Until the food had been put in front of them, Karen hadn't realised how hungry she was. Afterwards, she mentally scolded herself for being remiss; she should know by now that when she didn't eat, her brain was the first organ to slow down.

As they drove back, she reflected on the tail end of their interview with Hamish Mackenzie. The thing that had puzzled Karen was how the body had come to rest in the bog without anyone noticing. This was clearly a working croft, and from what Hamish had said, that had been the case when he had been growing up too. How then could someone dig a coffin-sized hole in the peat then fill it in without anybody noticing?

Hamish had been adamant that his grandparents had known nothing about the bikes or the body. When Karen asked how that was possible, he'd been puzzled too. 'When do you think this happened?' he'd asked.

'We're not sure. But probably between twenty and twenty-five years ago.'

Hamish nodded, light dawning in his face. 'We moved to America in 1994 when I was twelve,' he said. 'My dad got a job at Stanford. Apart from a couple of short visits, I didn't come back to the UK properly till I went to university in

Edinburgh in 2000. And by the time I came back, to be brutally honest, the croft was in pretty sorry shape. My gran was in the early stages of dementia and my granddad was getting more and more frail. I started spending my holidays up here, trying to get things straightened out. Doing the hard physical labour that my granddad couldn't manage on his own any longer. So I'm guessing that all sorts of things could have been happening on the land during those few years, and nobody would have noticed. You can't really see that bit of the bog from the house, the way the land falls away. And nature's quick to reclaim her own in these parts.'

As was so often the way with cold cases, what looked at first like an unhelpful response could be open to another interpretation. A twist of the kaleidoscope and Hamish's answer actually provided a window of opportunity. Those six years when he was California dreaming and the wheels were coming off his grandparents' lives had provided a serendipitous opening for someone who knew what was hidden beneath the bog.

'How long would it take to dig down to the crate without a digger?' Karen had asked. 'My experience of agriculture is limited to growing tomatoes on my balcony. And not very successfully at that.'

He shook his head. 'Unless you've got a cold frame or a wee greenhouse, you'll struggle with tomatoes in Edinburgh. The wind's too cold.'

'I like a challenge. How long, though?'

He drained his cup while he considered.

'There must have been two of them at least, right? The victim and the shooter?'

Karen raised her eyebrows. She hadn't mentioned the involvement of a gun.

Hamish shrugged one shoulder. 'The local cops were talking about it when I took the coffee up, they didn't seem bothered about me being there.'

'They don't get out much,' Jason muttered, shaking his head in morose disapproval.

'OK,' Karen said. 'At least two, yes.'

'Probably two or three hours, then. If they were going flat out and they were in decent shape.'

At least he didn't know everything, she thought. Their victim had definitely been in more than decent shape. 'So you could do it overnight?'

'In the right conditions? Yeah, no bother. Especially if you'd had a spell of dry weather.'

And that had been that. Turning it over in her mind took her past the croft house — in darkness at this late hour — and up to the tarmacked road. She turned right and walked as far as the track that led down past the low stone cottage where the Somervilles had stayed. They'd cleared out as soon as their biometrics had been sampled, Will Somerville still huffy at being deprived of what he saw as his wife's rightful inheritance.

Now Karen's thoughts turned to the crime scene photographs she and Jason had pored over when they got back from the pub. The degree of preservation of the soft tissue still surprised her.

140

He looked like he'd been dead a matter of hours, not years. But studying the photographs in detail allowed Karen to see past the victim himself to the wider picture.

The position of his body looked odd, somehow. He was twisted at the waist, as if the bottom half of his body had been immobilised when the gunshots spun his torso to one side. Karen had thumbed through the relevant shots, spreading them out on the top of the cabinets in the yurt. 'Tell me if you think I'm full of nonsense,' she said. 'And it's hard to be sure when I've only got the pix to go on, because by the time I arrived at the crime scene, the bike had been moved. But to me, it looks kind of like the bike was partly on top of him. Now, it might have fallen over that way. But I'm thinking maybe he was lifting the bike out of the hole when he was shot?'

Jason had studied the photographs one by one, breathing heavily through his nose as he weighed up what Karen had suggested. 'You could be right, boss. But why would you go to all that trouble to dig the bike up then shoot the big guy before you've got it out the hole?'

That had been the killer question. Earlier, Karen had struggled to make sense of it. She'd wondered whether murder had been the point and the uncovering of the bike merely an excuse to persuade the victim to dig his own grave. It seemed far-fetched.

In her experience, far-fetched happened more often than was plausible.

But walking often cleared up the intractable,

the intransigent and the implausible. Following the track under the moonlight, she realised what had eluded her earlier. Sometimes, Karen thought, Jason was not the only numpty in the HCU.

She stopped walking and took out her phone. She pulled up the crime scene photos, sliding her fingers over the screen to enlarge one section. The first Indian, in all its glory. The detail that had slipped away from her previously was clear, even though at that magnification the focus was slightly blurred. She summoned up the images of the second bike, the one that had been exposed to the elements.

Karen peered at the screen, aware that the peaty detritus on the bike might make her task impossible. If so, she'd have to wait for morning and check it out in person. But she needn't have worried. The evidence of what she thought she'd remembered was in front of her eyes.

The leather panniers on the bikes were each secured with a pair of buckled leather straps. On the first bike, the one that had apparently been untouched since its burial, the straps were fastened.

On the second bike, they hung loose.

24

1944 — Antwerp; Wester Ross

As he'd expected, it had been the Canadians who liberated Antwerp in the end. Arnie Burke handed himself over to them; he was debriefed by a major in Army Intelligence and told he'd be passed back down the line to the Americans in a day or two. He wasn't sure how easy it would be to get back to Antwerp once he'd been exfiltrated; it left him with a dilemma. Leave his loot in its hiding place and hope nobody would stumble over it, or take it while he had the chance and risk being rumbled when he returned to the fold?

He decided a bird in the hand was better than two in a hole in the wall. Early one morning, as dawn was gradually revealing the river and the city behind it, he walked out of his billet and made his way back to the obscure backyard where he'd stashed the black velvet bags. Working quickly, he freed the brick facing and found what he'd come for. He had a money belt fastened round his waist and he slipped the bags inside.

Back at the school gymnasium the Canadians had taken over, he took his kitbag into the toilet cubicle and made a slit in the lining. He fed the bags through the gap and flattened their contents against the bottom of the holdall. If you were really looking for contraband, you might find them. But a casual search would come up clean.

As it turned out, by the time he got back to an American unit a week later, nobody had a spare moment to give a shit. He could probably have driven in on a Wehrmacht motorbike and sidecar and not raised an eyebrow. Well, maybe that was an exaggeration, but not much of one. He had to tell his story all over again to a US Army Intelligence lieutenant; it resulted in him being bought bottle after bottle of strong Trappist beer that evening.

The morning after, his head splitting and his stomach roiling, he was told he was being sent back to Scotland, where he'd trained for his fieldwork ahead of Antwerp. 'We've got some guys up there who could use your experience in the field. We might have the Krauts on the run, but there's still the Japs to finish off in the Pacific. You know yourself, the Brits've got a great training operation up there. A few weeks in the Highlands and then we'll ship you home,' a pugnacious captain told him.

A choppy crossing of the Channel then an interminable train journey crammed into a cattle truck full of paras who hadn't seen hot water in a while. Finally, at some godforsaken windswept station in the dead centre of nowhere, a Jeep turned up driven by a hard-bitten GI who didn't want to chew the fat. An hour later, Arnie was dropped off at every American's idea of a fairytale castle. Grey granite, turrets on every corner, a massive door you could have marched a battalion through. It was on an even grander scale than the hunting lodge where he'd been based while he was learning the tricks of the tradecraft.

A wiry little terrier of a corporal in a uniform that looked like it had been scavenged from the cast-offs of at least three different regiments led him to a tiny bedroom in the attic. A single bed, a chair and a chest of drawers, but it felt like paradise to Arnie. He couldn't remember the last time he'd been able to sleep without the low thrum of fear in his chest. Nobody was going to burst into this room to denounce him; no stray bullet was going to cut him down as he went about his business; no bombs were going to blow up his world.

For the next ten weeks, he worked with the Brits, giving potential field agents the benefit of his experiences. It was easy on the nerves and Arnie began to feel more like the man he used to be before he'd found himself living on a knife-edge. His old self-confidence grew by the day and he couldn't wait to get back to America and start the new life that the contents of his velvet bags would give him.

And then things got complicated. He was given a date for shipping out. A berth on a US Navy supply ship that was returning material that was no longer needed in Europe. Which was great news, except that he heard from one of his new friends in the military police that there were stringent searches in place for anyone travelling on the ship. 'There's been too many stories about looting,' he'd said. 'Nobody cared when it was just the odd German pistol or Iron Cross, but some guys have been pushing their luck. Some dumb fuck in Signals was caught with a Rembrandt in the bottom of his kitbag — he'd sliced it out of its frame in some rich bastard's house in Brussels, thought he could ship it home and make a killing.'

That evening, he retrieved the velvet bags and amalgamated their contents into a single package. He borrowed a bike and rode down to the quayside on Loch Ewe where preparations for loading were under way. Arnie hadn't come this far to be frustrated by a bunch of self-righteous bureaucrats. He needed to find a way to get his package on board. Once they were out in the Atlantic, he'd figure out how to retrieve it.

He walked briskly among the newly redundant paraphernalia of a fighting force, looking as if he had business there. All the while, he was studying the ship, scanning the cargo, calculating possibilities. It was soon clear he wasn't going to be able to sneak aboard and stash the bag. He'd almost given up hope of a solution when he reached the last row of items. Right at the back were a pair of brand-new Indian Scout motorcyles. They looked as if they'd never been driven. The paintwork was pristine, the tyres without a trace of dirt. Each bike had a pair of panniers fastened over the rear wheel.

Arnie looked around, checking nobody was interested in him. Then he crouched by one of the bikes, opened a stiff leather strap and dropped the bulging black velvet bag inside. In thirty-six hours, he'd be setting sail for America, his future secure in the hold of the ship.

He cycled back to the castle, not caring about the hills. What were a few hills to a man who was going to scale mountains?

25

2018 — Wester Ross

Karen expanded the image on her laptop screen then clicked between the two. 'Do you see what I see?' she demanded.

Jason, who had never been what might be described as a morning person, burned his mouth on the hot coffee and winced. 'Ow!'

Karen flicked between the two screens again. 'Come on, Jason.'

'One set of panniers is buckled up and the other one isnae,' he sighed. 'So it looks like you were right, it was never the bike they were after. But it doesn't take us any further forward, does it? I mean, there's no way of knowing what they were looking for. Or who put it there. Or even if it was there at all.'

Karen leaned back in her chair and stared out at the sea. 'I think there was definitely something there. Otherwise both bikes would have been excavated.'

'Unless it was all a plot to get the victim to dig his own grave.' Jason looked eager.

'That's a bit convoluted. I mean, if that was what was going on, any hole in the Highlands would have done, as long as the killer had a plausible cover story. This hole was very specific, so if it wasn't about the bikes, it had to be about something else. And we do know that whatever it

148

was, it was small enough to fit unobtrusively in a bike pannier. Because if it had been bulky, Alice Somerville's granddad would have either spotted it or known all along it was there. And if he knew there was something there, why not tell her?'

'Aye.' Jason sighed. 'By the way, boss, why did you leave that note on the sink?'

Karen flushed. The note in question was a sheet of lined A4 from the notepad she used to draw connective maps between witnesses and suspects and events. She'd written it at half past two in the morning after her return from her late-night walk. She'd gone into the bathroom to pee and clean her teeth before she went to sleep but she hadn't turned the light on because it was connected to the extractor fan and she didn't want to waken Jason. It was hard enough having a sensible conversation with him when he was wide awake, never mind startled out of sleep.

Somehow, she'd caught her earring on her watchstrap and pinged it out of her ear. Desperately she'd tried to catch it. Then the plink of silver on porcelain, the clink as earring met plughole and the clatter as it bounced down the drainpipe. 'Fuck,' Karen hissed, lips pulled tight against her teeth. The only jewellery she'd ever had that she gave a damn about had just disappeared down the bathroom sink.

A quiet moan escaped from her as she laid her forehead on the cool edge of the sink. On the anniversary of their first night together, Phil had presented her with a pair of Tiffany High Tide silver earrings. She'd been speechless. Nobody had ever given her anything so beautiful. Their smooth wavy lines recalled the ever-changing Forth Estuary they loved to sit and watch while they slowly worked their way through the Sunday treat of a nougat wafer. She'd worn them every day since.

And now one of them had been ripped from its moorings. Thinking about it, she decided it hadn't tumbled very far. It was, she reckoned, trapped in the U-bend. Maybe in the morning Hamish could recover it?

If he was to have any chance, no more water could be allowed to descend into the pipe. So Karen had written the note. In very big capital letters with a Sharpie. JASON: DO NOT USE THIS SINK UNDER ANY CIRCUMSTANCES. I MEAN IT. She'd got up to find him shaving in the kitchen sink. He'd waited till now to ask so she explained. 'I see why you were so bothered,' Jason conceded. 'That's the ones that Phil gave you, right?'

'Right. Thanks for doing what I asked.'

His look said, 'As if I'd dare to do anything else.' Before he could say anything, Karen's phone rang. A glance at the screen and she pulled a face. 'Bloody hell, it's the Dog Biscuit.' She ignored Jason's baffled look, pasted a smile on and answered. 'Good morning, ma'am.'

Ann Markie sounded as bright as freshly squeezed orange juice. 'And is it a good morning where you are, Karen? I ask because I believe you're well outside the Central Belt.'

'You're well informed, ma'am. I'm in Wester Ross, where the sun is doing its best to find a space in the clouds.' Karen rolled her eyes at

Jason and mimed being hanged.

'Would you care to explain what you're doing in Wester Ross?' The voice was honey and silk. Karen was amazed to realise she'd have preferred the snide sniping of her old boss. At least you knew where you were with the Macaroon, even if it was usually in the shit.

'I'm investigating a suspicious death. Well, to be honest, I'd stick my neck out and say, a murder. Two bullet wounds and no weapon does tend to militate against suicide.'

'Is that not a job for N Division's CID?'

'Normally it would be, but it's evident from the circumstances that this is a historic case. The body's been in a bog for somewhere around twenty years, Dr Wilde estimates.' As soon as River's name left her lips, Karen knew she'd tripped up.

'Ah yes, Dr Wilde. Apparently she's now assigning my detectives to cases.'

'She made a phone call that saved me anything up to six or seven hours driving, ma'am. I'd have thought getting stuck into this case was a better use of my time than driving down the A9 and back up again.'

'Did you really need to visit the scene of the crime? Generally speaking, you never have that luxury.'

Now Karen was starting to feel riled. 'All the more reason to take advantage of the opportunity,' she said, forcing herself to smile. You couldn't snarl when you were smiling. 'It doesn't hurt to have a wee refresher on crime scene practice.'

'And you don't think that, given your lack of recent game time at crime scenes, it might have made more sense to take DS McCartney with you rather than DC Murray?'

Nice to have those suspicions confirmed. 'DC Murray needs more experience at the sharp end,' Karen said firmly. 'I left DS McCartney to carry out a series of inquiries that, frankly, require experience and sensitivity. Are those not among DS McCartney's strong points? Have I misunderstood?' Damned if she was going to let Markie push her around.

Jason was openly listening now, the mention of his name permission enough in his world. He gave Karen a quick thumbs-up.

Markie paused for a moment. 'I rather think DS McCartney is a tad overqualified for a last-ditch investigation that's likely to go absolutely nowhere. I take it you'll be heading back to base soon?' It was a retreat of sorts.

'I hope so. It depends what progress we make in terms of ID.'

A sigh from the Central Belt. 'I hope this isn't going to turn into a budget buster, Karen. You know how much pressure we're under in terms of using our resources wisely. And nothing eats up resources faster than the endless battery of tests you cold case detectives love to order.'

The sheer unfairness of Markie's accusation nearly provoked an ill-judged response from Karen. The bureaucratic besom had been away from the front line for too long. Instead, she thought on her feet. 'It's a peat bog, ma'am. The body's very well preserved. I'm confident we'll

152

be able to get an ID from a photo. The media will be all over it, they love this kind of story. So with a bit of luck we'll not need all those expensive tests that we usually have to rely on for a result.'

'Make it so, Karen. I don't want this one to drag out.'

And the call was over. ' 'Make it so, Karen.' Who the fuck does she think she is? Captain bloody Picard?'

Jason tried a tentative grin. 'You don't look very like Mr Data, boss. I take it we're not flavour of the month with the ACC?'

Karen shrugged. 'All she wants is the kind of cases that let her hold press conferences on *Reporting Scotland*. We're only here for the greater glory of Ann Markie.' She stood up and headed for the coffee maker. 'I need to phone River. But first I need more coffee.'

As if on cue, there was a knock at the door. Karen nodded at Jason, who opened the door to reveal Hamish Mackenzie in kilt and a much-darned jumper, his hair rippling in the breeze. He held up a bright turquoise insulated bag. 'Bacon and avocado rolls,' he announced, thrusting the bag at Jason.

'Are you trying to bribe us?' Karen said.

'Is that all it takes?'

Jason grabbed the bag. 'Sometimes not even that much, if she's not had her coffee.'

Hamish grinned. 'I woke up this morning and realised I hadn't stocked the fridge. This is my attempt to make up for being a lousy host.'

Jason opened the bag and took out two

foil-wrapped packages. 'Thanks.'

'Did you sleep well?' Hamish asked, his eyes on Karen.

'The bed's really comfortable.' She paused, trying to find the right way to say what she needed. 'There's one slight problem.'

Immediately he was on the alert. 'A problem?'

'Nothing to do with the yurt, everything's really lovely. Comfortable, perfect. Really. This is my fault, entirely. I dropped an earring down the sink last night. I think it's probably in the U-bend. I wondered whether . . . ' Karen hated to be dependent on anyone else. Especially someone who was at best a witness, at worst a suspect and also the person already doing her a favour.

'Sure, I'll take a look later.'

'I appreciate it.' She took the remaining earring out of her pocket and unwrapped the toilet paper she'd protected it with. 'It's the partner of this one.' She held it out on the palm of her hand.

'May I?' Hamish asked. She nodded and he picked it up, examining it. 'I think I'll know it when I see it.'

'It's Tiffany,' Jason said.

'More to the point, it's got sentimental value.' Shocked at having revealed something personal to a virtual stranger, Karen hurried on. 'We haven't run any water down the plug since I dropped it. I'm really sorry to be a nuisance.'

He shrugged. 'Not a problem. Oh, but just to let you know . . . ' Hamish said, his nonchalance slightly overcooked, 'the media have arrived.

154

Well, I say the media, but it's actually only a guy from the *West Highland Free Press* and a freelance who does stuff for the BBC and the nationals. The uniformed constable up by the tent told them there was nothing to see and nobody to talk to, but they're still hanging about.'

Karen unwrapped her fragrant roll and sighed. 'I'll come up in a wee while and give them a quote.'

Hamish nodded. 'I'll tell them. See you later.' He sketched a wave and left.

'There's a man who knows not to outstay his welcome,' Karen said absently, surveying her unexpected breakfast with delight.

'Nice guy,' Jason said.

'Maybe too nice,' Karen muttered. 'Take a careful look at those emails from Alice Somerville, Jason. Maybe you can take a run down to the pub later, ask around, see whether Hamish Mackenzie is as advertised. They'll maybe be more forthcoming if I'm not around.' Then she bit into the sandwich and moaned through a glorious mouthful. 'How do you get perfectly ripe avocado in the Highlands, Jason? When we used to come up here for our holidays when I was wee, you'd be lucky to see a green vegetable that wasn't cabbage. We're definitely not in Kansas any more, Toto.' *

When she'd finished, she stepped outside to savour the fresh air and secure some privacy for her call to River. Karen got straight down to business. 'I've had the Dog Biscuit on my case already,' she said.

155

* Tonto

'Don't tell me. We've not to spend any money on some guy who's been dead for twenty years without anybody noticing.' River was resigned rather than bitter.

'Got it in one.'

'That's OK.'

'Really?'

'Karen, I've never seen a better-preserved body. This guy's got NHS dental work. Somebody in the UK's going to recognise him from a photo. I've got Callum working on it right now.'

Callum Phelan was the facial reconstruction specialist who worked in River's department. He made convincing faces from bare skulls; the HCU had put one killer behind bars as a direct result of his work. Karen had seen enough to know he'd do a good job. 'How long?'

'Any time now. He said it was straightforward. Lighten the skin tones and give him some blue eyes and he'd be presentable.'

'Brilliant, thanks. I swear, that woman is only interested in how much I can boost her image.'

'I'll do the tests regardless. On my department budget. It's great hands-on training for the students. So you'll get the benefit anyway, if you need it.' Karen heard the ping of a message arriving on River's computer. 'Even as we speak,' she said. 'Callum has delivered. I'll send it straight across to you.'

Ten minutes later, Karen was knocking on Hamish's door. She'd sent Jason down to the crime scene on the off-chance that the cop on sentry duty might recognise the man Callum had recreated for them and now she wanted to try the same experiment on Hamish.

She followed him into the kitchen. 'I'd like you to have a look at something,' she said. 'I know you said you didn't know the man in the bog, but this is closer to what he'd have looked like when he was still alive.' Karen held her phone out to Hamish.

He frowned at the image, studying it carefully. Callum had done a good job. The victim didn't look freakish or frightening. More CGI than dead. Hamish stroked his beard, eyes thoughtful. 'I wish I could help you. But I'm positive I've never seen this dude before. I'm pretty sure I'd remember if I had. He's the kind of guy you'd notice.' He handed the phone back. 'Cup of coffee before you go?'

It was hard to resist. All she had waiting for her was an impromptu press conference. 'Why not? Smells great in here.'

He fussed with his fancy machine and Karen enjoyed the moment of emptiness. It was good to have nothing more to do than watch someone do something competently. He placed the mug in front of her with a flourish. 'You clearly like your coffee. Where do you go in Edinburgh?'

Karen gave a little reminiscent smile. 'You'll not know it. A wee place down on Duke Street. Aleppo.'

He actually took a step back. 'You are kidding.'

'No, it's my regular spot. How? Have you been there?'

He tipped his head back and roared with

laughter. 'Unbelievable. Unbelievable.'

'What? What is it?' Karen was laughing too, though she couldn't have said why.

Hamish managed to recover himself. 'Do you never go to Perk? Three doors down from Aleppo?'

'Not since Aleppo opened. I used to grab a cortado from there sometimes. And I stop in at their hole in the wall on George IV Bridge when I'm up that way. Why?'

He shook his head, grinning. 'They're mine.'

Karen couldn't quite make sense of what he'd said. 'What do you mean, they're yours? You go there?'

'I own them. And the one down on the front at Portobello.'

'You own a chain of coffee shops in Edinburgh?' She was struggling to understand. 'But you're a crofter. In Wester Ross.'

'Only part-time. I usually drive up here late Sunday night and back down on Wednesday night. Teegan and Donny do most of the work on the croft. These days I'm just a hobby farmer really.' Embarrassment turned him into a small boy, grinding one toe into the floor tiles.

'You never said.'

He shrugged. 'Nobody asked. You all assumed. From the Somervilles on down.'

Karen wasn't quite sure what to make of his revelation. Had he been dishonest with her? Or was he right, and she'd leaped to the conclusion there was no more to him than met the eye? Not a simple hospitable Highlander but a hipster barista? She was going to have to rethink all that now. Jason was definitely returning to the pub. To her surprise, she felt an indefinable twinge of regret. 'And are you planning on going back to Edinburgh tonight?' she asked flatly.

'I suppose that depends if there's still a crime scene tent on my land,' he said.

'I think that'll be gone by the close of play today,' she said, sensing a coolness between them.

'Then so will I. And you?'

'That depends on whether we get a result from the media on our bog body.'

Hamish nodded. Like her, he realised his admission had somehow changed the ground between them. 'You're welcome to stay on at the yurt as long as you need to.'

'Thanks, but since you're convinced our victim's not a local, one way or another we'll be heading out.'

She thought she saw disappointment in his eyes. 'Maybe I'll bump into you in Edinburgh one of these days. Up on George IV Bridge.'

'Maybe.' She drained her cup and put it down on the counter. 'You never know. It's a wee city, after all.'

And she stepped out into the bright morning, completely unable to work out what had just happened.

26

2018 — Portpatrick

Detective Sergeant Gerry McCartney was not a happy man. He'd been on his way home from his bruising encounter with Ann Markie the night before when his phone had rung, an unfamiliar number on the screen. He'd considered ignoring it but realised Markie was perfectly capable of calling him from a burner to keep him on his toes.

So he'd answered it. Then wished he hadn't. When he'd dragged his weary arse all the way down to the bottom left-hand corner of Scotland on Karen Pirie's wild goose chase, in an uncharacteristically dutiful moment he'd given his card to the nosy next-door neighbour of Gordon and Sheila Chalmers. According to DVLA, they had once owned a red Rover 214. According to the neighbour, they were currently inhabiting their apartment somewhere on the Costa del Sol.

At first, he'd struggled to place the female voice on the end of the phone. Then he understood the heavy breathing was not sexual but rather the result of a lifetime of Lambert & Butler. 'It's me, detective. Sandra Shaw from Portpatrick. They cry me Sandie, mind? Sandie Shaw? *Like a Puppet on a String*?'

The nosy neighbour with the stupid name.

160

'Hello, Sandie. How can I help you?'

'It's me that can help you,' she said, her tone arch.

'How's that?'

'Mind I told you Sheila and Gordy weren't due back till the weekend? Well, guess who turned up in a taxi five minutes ago?'

'Sheila and Gordy?' *So fucking what.*

'No.' Two letters morphed into three syllables dripping with self-satisfaction. 'Just Sheila. No Gordy. You'd have to wonder what's going on there.'

If you lived next door with nothing else to do, you would. Gerry McCartney wasn't that desperate. However, if one of the couple was in residence, he could take a run down to Portpatrick in the morning and cross another name off Karen Pirie's stupid wee list. 'That's very helpful, Sandie. I appreciate the call.'

'So you'll be coming down to take a statement from Sheila?'

They all watched too many bloody awful cop shows on the telly, that was half the trouble with the public. They all wanted high drama when most of a polis's life was an exercise in tedium. Still, there were some advantages to be screwed out of their expectations. 'Now, Sandie, you know I can't be discussing confidential police matters with you.'

She cackled. 'Right enough. I'll be keeping an eye out for you, mind.'

So he'd left the house that morning at the same time as his bloody annoying teenage daughters, whining and demanding a lift to school even though he was going in the opposite direction. McCartney's life was plagued with women, he thought. Always nagging, always pushing, always bitching about something or other that he was supposed magically to do something to fix. What had happened to the man's world his da had grown up in? Somebody had pulled the rug out from under men's feet, leaving them staggering about trying to stand up for themselves. And yet, he still cared what they thought of him, still needed to feel like they looked up to him, like he really could fix the world.

The long drive down the Ayrshire coast had only served to annoy him further. Pensioners, ditherers and tractors had all conspired to turn what should have been a two and a half hour drive into more like four hours. He had no eyes for the beauty of the countryside or the drama of the coast. He had the radio tuned to Radio Scotland for the pure pleasure of release that shouting at the presenter and her guests gave him.

Bloody Portpatrick. Why would anybody choose to live there? It was the end of the world. Stuck on the outside edge of a hammerhead peninsula that looked like it had been tacked on to the coastline as an afterthought. Sure, it was pretty enough if you liked picture postcard Scottish harbours with painted houses and gift shops and the inevitable golf course. Pleasant enough on a summer day, but mostly it was exposed to whatever the westerlies blew in from the North Channel. McCartney reckoned it would have the kind of winter weather that made the Costa del Sol a dream destination.

He parked a couple of doors down from the Chalmers' house, hoping he'd escape Sandie Shaw's curtain-twitching.. The woman who opened the door to him didn't look well. In spite of the tanned wrinkles that made her skin look like a distressed leather jacket, she seemed somehow pale, the bags under her listless eyes a dark grey. Her hair was lifeless and looked as if she hadn't touched it with a brush since she'd crawled out of bed. McCartney seldom paid much attention to what women were wearing once they'd left their twenties, but even he registered the clash between purple tartan trews and a black-and-white striped blouse.

'Mrs Chalmers?'

She nodded, her mouth fidgeting as if she'd forgotten what to do with her lips.

'I'm Detective Sergeant Gerry McCartney. I wondered if I might have a word?'

She didn't look surprised. He assumed Sandie Shaw had wasted no time in passing on the information that she was wanted by the police.

But he was well wide of the mark. 'Is this about the . . . the arrangements?' Sheila Chalmers stumbled over the words.

'The arrangements? I'm not sure I — '

'To bring Gordy home. They said I'd have to contact a local undertaker but they never said anything about the police.' Her eyes filled up and she blinked repeatedly to stop them spilling over.

Fuck. 'I'm sorry, Mrs Chalmers. Has something happened to your husband?' It took all his willpower not to back away down the drive.

163

She cocked her head, as if she was convinced she'd misheard. 'Are you not here about Gordy?'

'Mrs Chalmers, I'm really sorry. I've no idea what you're referring to. I'm with the Historic Cases Unit.' Words that almost choked him after years of proudly claiming membership of the Major Incident Team. 'I wanted to talk to you and your husband about the car you drove in the 1980s.'

She was mystified. 'That makes no sense. I understand the words but they don't make any sense. My man's dead and you're talking about cars?'

'I'm very sorry. I had no idea about your husband's death. I don't have to do this right now, I can come back another time.'

She gripped her head with both hands, rubbing at her scalp, revealing traces of white at the roots of her hair. 'I feel like I'm going mad. Look, come away in. I can't settle to anything. It's too soon. I might as well talk to you about whatever nonsense it is you're here about.'

It was the last thing he wanted. But he couldn't think of an evasive tactic quickly enough. So he followed her down the hall and into a conservatory at the back of the house that had a view over one end of the harbour and the cliffs that protected it. 'I'll make tea,' she said. 'I can still manage that.'

As he waited, McCartney comforted himself with the thought that this would make a great anecdote for the pub. He'd edit out the awkwardness and leave in the weirdness. It'd be worth a couple of free drinks, at least.

Sheila Chalmers returned with two small porcelain mugs on a tray with a teapot, milk and sugar. 'I've no biscuits, I'm sorry. I only got back late last night. And the milk's UHT, I hope you don't mind?'

'I don't take milk, so that's no bother to me.' He heaped in two spoons of sugar. 'As I said, I'm very sorry to hear about your husband. Do you mind me asking what happened?'

She tipped milk into her tea and sipped it with ladylike delicacy. 'It was his heart. We've got a lovely pool in the apartment complex where we stay in Spain. Gordy loved swimming in it. Anyway, he dived in last Friday morning. Like every other morning. When he hit the water, it was like he jack-knifed under the surface. His arms were wrapped around himself. I had no idea what was going on. There's no lifeguard so early in the morning, but a couple of other residents jumped in and dragged him out. But he was already gone. I could see right away. The water was streaming off him and his eyes were wide open and his chest wasn't moving at all.' She shivered and the surface of her tea rippled as if someone had thrown a pebble in it.

'That must have been an awful shock.'

'I couldn't believe it. Even though I knew it in my heart.' She bit her bottom lip so hard it left teeth marks when she stopped. 'They had to do a post-mortem. I hate the idea of that. Cutting him open like that. I know my Gordy isn't there any more, but still. It feels like a terrible insult.'

He dredged his mind for something sympathetic to say. 'An awful thing to have to go through on your own. At least you're back among your own now.'

'Aye. I suppose.' She put her cup down and physically straightened her posture, squaring her shoulders and breathing in deeply through her nose. 'But this isn't what you came here for. I need to get used to carrying on. You said something about a car? And historic cases? Is that right?'

McCartney set his own cup down and mirrored her posture. He'd done all the training courses and even though he thought most of the body language stuff was bollocks, there was no harm in giving it a whirl. 'It's something and nothing, Mrs Chalmers. We're looking at a series of crimes that were committed in the mid-1980s. For obvious reasons, I can't go into the details. But we've recently had a witness come forward and describe a car she saw at the scene of one of the crimes.'

The woman shook her head, taken aback. 'What? After thirty years she remembers something? That's hard to believe.'

'There are reasons, believe me,' McCartney said. 'Anyway, we're looking for the driver of a red Rover 214 with the initial letter B on the number plate. We need to exclude everybody who drove one of those so we can narrow our search parameters.' Meaningless tosh but it was amazing how often people fell for it. 'Now am I right in thinking you and Mr Chalmers had a red Rover 214 back then?'

'Well, it was Gordy's car,' she said. 'I never learned to drive. I never had any call for it.'

'I have to ask this. And I'm sorry if it sounds really heartless, but it would let me cross another name off my list if I could eliminate Gordy.' *Eliminate. Bloody hell.*

'Of course. How can I help? I mean, he's not here to tell you himself.'

'The gold standard of forensic evidence is still DNA,' McCartney said, an apologetic smile failing to soften the blow. 'Would you have Gordy's toothbrush or electric razor, by any chance?'

Grief had rendered her docile. 'We've got electric tooth-brushes in the bathroom. I can give you the head off his?'

McCartney stood up. 'That would be perfect. If you could maybe show me?'

He followed her through a bedroom strewn with the contents of a pair of suitcases, Gordon Chalmers' clothes scattered among hers. The bathroom smelled stale, presumably because it had been unused for weeks. Sheila pointed to the electric toothbrush. 'It's the one on the left.'

McCartney tore off a sheet of toilet paper and picked up the well-used head, dropping it in a paper evidence bag. 'That's a great help.' As she led him back through the bedroom, he asked whether her husband had ever driven to Edinburgh.

'I don't think so,' she said. 'We led a very quiet life. We'd only ever go to Glasgow when we were flying to Spain. What would Gordy be doing in Edinburgh?'

'Maybe something to do with his work?'

'How? He worked on the ferry from Stranraer

to Larne. He was the chief steward, you know. Forty-five years, man and boy, across the North Channel to Northern Ireland and back again. And you know what he loved most of all? You'll maybe laugh, it's such a daft thing.'

McCartney had what he needed; he wanted to be gone. But still. The woman had just lost her man. 'Tell me.'

'He loved the sight of the gannets plunging into the sea. They come down like dive bombers, he'd say. Like a streak of white lightning with a yellow tip exploding into the sea.' Now the tears were more than her eyes could contain. They spilled down her cheeks and dripped from her jaw on to her blouse. She didn't bother trying to wipe them away. 'He'll never see the gannets again.'

'But when you see them, you'll think of him,' McCartney said, surprising himself with a twitch of empathy. Then he remembered there was one last question he needed to ask. With the stress of dealing with Sheila Chalmers' grief, he'd almost forgotten, and how Karen Pirie would have enjoyed that. 'Before I go, there's one more thing. Did anybody else ever have the use of the car?'

Sheila wiped her nose with the back of her hand. He had the feeling it was a gesture she'd normally have despised. 'Katie and Roddy were too wee to be driving back then.'

He was halfway to the front door when she spoke. 'He gave Barry driving lessons, though.'

'Barry?' McCartney swung back to face her.

'My nephew, Barry. Barry Plummer. His

parents were divorced. He hardly ever saw his useless workshy dad. So when he turned seventeen, he had nobody to teach him how to drive. Gordy offered, he was like that with family. Nothing was too much trouble — you should have seen him with my mother.'

'And Barry used the car after he passed his test?'

Sheila frowned. 'I don't remember. But you could ask him yourself. He lives up in Motherwell. You could give him a phone.'

He walked back to his car feeling like the day had maybe turned a corner. He seriously doubted whether Gordy Chalmers had had a double life. By McCartney's reckoning, he'd barely had a single one. But at least now he had a lead of his own to chase up, which was infinitely preferable to the ginger ninja's leftovers. With a bit of luck, he could make tracking down Barry Plummer last a couple of days. A couple of days without Pirie or Markie breathing down his neck looked pretty close to paradise.

He had a vague recollection of a quiet wee pub in Stranraer that did a braw steak pie and a range of decent beers. At least one of them had his name on it. Now that was a real result.

27

2018 — Wester Ross

Karen's habitual disregard for protocol had already put Walter Wilson's nose out of joint in this investigation. She didn't want to have to trail down to Ullapool for a press conference when the press were already here, all two of them camped in their cars on the track staring glumly at the white crime scene tent. Maybe Muhammad would come to the mountain if she asked him nicely enough.

She walked away from Hamish's croft house, determined not to pick apart their encounter and make something of it. He was the kind of guy who had natural charm and couldn't help exercising it. That was all. She'd been watching too many late-night episodes of *Outlander*. Tutting at herself, she took out her phone and sent Callum Phelan's reconstruction to Wilson. She counted to seventy-three before her phone rang.

'That's quite the picture.' No happy greetings from Wilson today.

'He's quite distinctive,' she agreed. 'I've got a feeling we're going to get lucky with this one. How do you want to play this? There's a couple of journalists up here already so it would make sense to talk to them at the same time as we release it via the press office. Do you want to come up here and join me?'

'I've got a meeting in Poolewe in an hour.' He spoke slowly, considering. 'I tell you what, it's your case now. You might as well do the press release and talk to these boys since they're on the doorstep.'

It was quite a change of heart from the previous day's huffiness, but Karen would settle for it. She reckoned Wilson had realised overnight the advantages in handing off an awkward case that might never be resolved. 'I'll keep you posted.' She walked down the track to the reporters' cars. She stopped at the first one and tapped on the window. It slid down, wafting stale smoke and fried onions in her direction. A craggy middle-aged face peered out at her. 'I'm DCI Karen Pirie, Historic Cases Unit. There's a yurt over the hill. If you come down in an hour, I'll have something for you. Tell your pal.' She walked off briskly, waving to Jason to join her.

'We're doing a wee press conference in an hour,' she told him when he arrived, out of breath and a shade of pink that clashed badly with his freckles. 'So you can occupy the time by checking back on mispers from the mid-1990s while I write the release for the press office.'

Karen imported the photograph to a Word document and started writing the text: *The body of a man has been found in a peat bog on a croft at Clashstronach, Wester Ross.* She referred to the details River had sent her after the photograph:

He was between six feet and six feet two inches tall and in extremely good physical condition, being heavily muscled. His age is estimated between twenty-five and thirty-five. He had a tattoo on his right forearm. He had dark hair and probably blue eyes. He was wearing Levi 501 jeans, Calvin Klein boxer briefs, a brown leather belt with a buckle in the shape of a Celtic knot and Air Nike 95 trainers. We believe he was buried no earlier than 1995. If you recognise this man [insert direct contact details. HCU dealing.]

She saved it then turned it round so Jason could read it. He took his time, then said, 'Should it not be metric? His height?'

'Probably,' Karen said, annoyed with herself for not picking that up. 'I'm going to leave the feet and inches in as well, though, because twenty years ago, most people still thought in imperial.' She made the change, then sent the release off to the central press office, marked for release to coincide with when she was seeing the reporters. She yawned and stretched.

Jason caught the move. 'Are we going back tonight?' He sounded eager.

'Maybe. Have you got plans?' Her inquiry had been casual. Sometimes he played five-a-side football, sometimes he went through to Kirkcaldy for a night out with his mates from schooldays. But he blushed the deepest plum she'd ever seen him go.

'I'm maybe going to see a film,' he said.

'Any film in particular?' She knew he couldn't stand up to her teasing him, but she wasn't going to be mean.

'I don't know,' he mumbled. 'I didn't get the tickets.'

'Bloody hell, Jason, that's a result. Not only did you get a date, you got her to spring for the tickets.'

'I'm getting the dinner,' he said.

'Lucky lassie.' Karen meant it. He was, she thought, a decent if limited man. His mother had done a good job, Phil had mentored him towards manhood and Karen was sanding off the last of the rough edges. 'Anybody we know?'

His ears actually turned purple, as if he'd been munching hot chillis. 'I don't want to tell you. In case it all goes to shit and you decide it's her fault.'

Karen burst out laughing. 'Oh, Jason, you crack me up sometimes.'

'Phil used to say you were like a tiger when it came to defending your team. And I remember how you sorted out that dickhead I used to share the flat with.'

It was true. She had sorted out the dickhead to such a comprehensive extent that she suspected he'd stay sorted well into the next decade. 'You may be right. Well, don't hold your breath for getting back tonight. Better warn her now rather than drop it on her toes at the last minute.'

Crestfallen, he nodded and went back to his screen. While he searched the records, Karen stared at the image of the dead man, trying to think of a scenario that made sense of what they knew so far. But by the time the journalists pitched up at the door of the yurt, she was no further forward.

Jason ushered them in. The man Karen had

briefly spoken to was short and stocky, wearing creased grey trousers and a black anorak over a pale blue shirt whose buttons were battling the bulge of his stomach. A band of stubble circled his head below the bald crown. The acrid stink of cheap cigarettes hovered around him. 'Duncan McNab, *West Highland Free Press*,' he announced, plonking himself down on a chair.

The woman who came in behind him was dressed for the landscape in walking shoes, windproof trousers and a padded jacket over a lightweight knitted undershirt. A red fleece band circled her short blonde hair. 'And I'm Cathy Locke. Freelance, but I do a lot of work for the BBC and the nationals.' She put her backpack on one of the worktops and took out her recording equipment. In a miracle of miniaturisation, the mic was bigger than the recorder.

Karen introduced herself and Jason but before she could say more, McNab chipped in. 'Is it not unusual for Historic Cases to be on the ground as soon as a body's discovered?' He had the softs' sounds of the islands, but that didn't camouflage the hard edge to the question.

'When it's obviously a historic case, there's no point in hanging around,' Karen said. 'It is unusual for us to be present at a fresh crime scene, though. Normally we're working from old case files.'

'A wee bit of a change, then.' McNab laughed, a terrible phlegmy wheeze. 'Does that mean it's a murder?'

'We're treating the death as suspicious.'

'What can you tell us about the circumstances

of the discovery?' Locke said.

'You'd need to speak to the landowner about that,' Karen said. 'I'm sure Mr Mackenzie can tell you the full story. What I'm concerned with at this point is identifying the man whose body was excavated from the peat bog here.' She turned her screen to face them. 'I'm sorry I don't have a printout, but if you give DC Murray your details, he'll email a digital copy across to you.' While they peered at the screen, she ran through the details on the press release.

'Twenty years ago, you say?' McNab sounded thoughtful.

'Between twenty and twenty-five, we think.'

'Based on what?'

'His shoes. He's wearing a pair of trainers that were first manufactured in 1995.'

McNab scratched his chin and reached automatically for his cigarettes. He held the packet close to his stomach like a talisman. 'I think I know who that is,' he said slowly.

'Honestly?' Karen wasn't sure what to think.

'A big lad, you say?'

'Aye. Really muscular.'

McNab nodded. 'I've been covering Highland games all over this patch for the last thirty years. You get to know the faces. If it's who I'm thinking of, he was a heavy athlete.'

'What's that?' Jason asked.

'The big musclemen that do the strength events. Tossing the caber, throwing the hammer, throwing the weight-for-height.' McNab drew the screen closer. 'What was his name, now? Weight-for-height, that was his big event. Near

175

the world record, he was.' He sighed and stared out of the window at the restless sea. 'Johnny . . . Joe . . . Something like that.' He frowned. 'Joey! That's it. Joey Sutherland. If that's not him, he's got a twin.'

'Are you sure?' Karen couldn't believe it. This wasn't how things panned out in her world. Sometimes it took months or even years to identify a body.

'Like I said, unless he's got a double, that's Joey Sutherland.' McNab leaned back in his chair, delighted with himself. 'That's a wee scoop for us today, Cathy. It's not often we beat the police to an ID.'

'It's not actually an ID at this point.' Karen wasn't about to let this spiral away from her. 'We need to confirm this with somebody who knew Joey Sutherland. A family member or a close friend. Do either of you know where he came from originally?'

The two reporters swapped baffled looks. 'No idea,' McNab said. 'Over to the east, I think. He wasn't from these parts. Or from An t-Eilean Fada.'

'Where?' Karen asked.

Cathy gave a weary sigh. 'He means the Outer Hebrides. Duncan likes to confound those of us who don't have the Gaelic.'

'So not from round here. But before we go any further, what happened to this Joey Sutherland? Did he actually disappear?'

McNab took a cigarette from his packet and rolled it between his fingers. Karen could sense the nicotine craving coming off him in waves. 'I

176

don't recall anybody saying anything specific. You have to understand, these guys perform all over the world. There are more Highland games abroad than there have ever been in Scotland. America and Canada, Australia, New Zealand, South Africa. And other places, they have these Strongest Man competitions. Big money, some of them. I hear tell that you can spend the whole summer moving from one to the other and living off the prize money. If you're any good, that is. So not seeing one of them around didn't mean anything sinister. It'd likely be a while before it dawned on anybody that he wasnae about the place. And there could be plenty reasons for that. Retiring through injury. Meeting some lassie and settling down.' He shrugged.

The missing missing, Karen thought. People who had fallen off the radar without anyone paying any heed to their absence. The reasons weren't always sinister. But more often than not, there was pain at their root. She wondered momentarily whether that was what had happened to this victim. 'Any idea where we might find somebody who could maybe tell us something about Joey Sutherland? Always supposing this actually is Joey Sutherland.' The note of caution added in the hope it would give the journalists pause.

Locke looked at McNab. 'What about Ruari Macaulay?' She sounded hesitant.

McNab. 'Big Ruari? Aye, he was on the circuit then. He retired in 2000. I mind, he said one millennium was enough for him.'

'Ruari Macaulay was one of the stars of the

nineties,' Cathy said. 'Face like a train wreck but a body like a god. When he retired, he set up a fitness camp in the middle of nowhere in the hills above Beauly. It's a bit like a boot camp. You pay an arm and a leg and you get an individually tailored regime based on your fitness level, age and weight. Diet, exercise, well-being. No more than six people at a time.'

'Rich fat bastards,' McNab muttered.

'Rich fat bastards who get hooked and come back time after time,' Locke scoffed. 'I get a feature a year out of Ruari. I cycle him through the glossies, the health magazines, the Saturday supplements. People will pay an insane amount of money rather than actually make a few crucial changes that would transform their lives.' *Like me* hung unspoken in the air.

Karen had never had much time for the self-righteous, though she acknowledged Locke had a point. But she wouldn't wish on anyone the crucial change that had improved her own fitness. 'And he would have known Joey Sutherland?'

'Bound to,' Locke said.

'Well, that sorts out my afternoon. But until we get a formal ID, you're going to have to keep the lid on this.'

'But it's a great story,' McNab protested. 'And we gave you the information. That's not how a press conference generally works.'

'I appreciate that. But go and talk to Hamish Mackenzie. There's a great story that you *can* tell sitting waiting for you.'

'We tried to talk to him earlier and he 'no

178

comment'-ed us,' McNab grumbled.

'Give me quarter of an hour to wrap up here and I will personally introduce you to Mr Mackenzie and ask him to tell you why he was digging a hole in the middle of his bog.'

The journalists exchanged another look, calculating the relative value of what they had against what they might get.

'OK,' Locke said. 'But it better be good.'

'Trust me, it's front-page good.' Karen stood up. 'I'll need directions.'

28

2018 — Teavarran

There were places in Scotland where satnav was as much use as a chocolate compass. Wester Fearn House was one of them. It was nominally part of a hamlet called Teavarran, which the officious woman who lived in the car's computer believed she'd brought them to. But it wasn't really a place, just a road through a wood that opened out on to high moorland. They passed a beautifully renovated stone house and a writers' centre before Karen was able to make sense of the map Cathy Locke had drawn for them.

'There's a track coming up on the right. Looks like a forestry road. We need to take that,' she instructed Jason.

As they turned, she saw a small metal sign fixed to a tree. 'Wester Fearn. Private Road.' Karen snorted. 'Aye, right. Amazing how many landowners think the right to roam doesn't apply to them.'

They drove through the conifer plantation for a couple of minutes, then the track swung round to the left and a wide clearing opened before them with a stunning panorama north across the River Beauly valley to the mountains beyond. The view was so breathtaking that at first Karen hardly noticed the building that sat over to one side. At the heart of it was a traditional square stone house, substantial enough to withstand the winters at this elevation. Thrust out from either side were long low wings, timber clad with arrays of solar panels along the roofs. There were no windows to break up the wood, which gave the building a forbidding appearance. Set into the woodland itself was a stone shed that housed half a dozen cars and SUVs. Karen noticed security cameras mounted on the trees, covering the clearing and the house itself.

'This must have cost a bob or two,' Jason said. 'I suppose there's big bucks getting rich folks fit. Ever think we're in the wrong game, boss?'

Karen shook her head. 'Never, Jason. Park up, and let's go and see what's what.'

They walked up to the back door of the stone heart of the building. Before they could press the bell, the door opened and a barefoot young woman in yoga pants and a sloppy sweater greeted them with a broad smile. 'Hi, how can I help you?' Her accent placed her from the other side of the Atlantic.

Karen introduced them. 'We're here to see Ruari Macaulay.'

'Sure. He's working with a resident right now, but you're more than welcome to come in and wait till he's done, Officer.'

'How long will that be, do you think?'

The woman glanced over her shoulder. 'Let's see. It's twenty before the hour now. He should be through in about fifteen minutes.'

'Thanks. In that case, we'll take you up on your offer.'

The house had been stripped back to its bare bones then replastered and painted a shade of off-white that probably laboured under a name like Rabbit's Oxter. They followed their guide down a narrow hallway decorated with a couple of abstract paintings that Karen assumed were meant to induce a spirit of tranquillity. That would be a waste of money, then.

Halfway along, they turned into a room that was half office, half sitting room. Expensively functional yet comfortable. 'Why don't you take a seat and I'll fetch you something to drink.' Another cheerful grin. 'I'm Madison, by the way. Now, we have a range of fruit and herb teas, or there's a variety of juices. What kind of thing do you like?'

'I suppose a coffee's out of the question?' Karen tried not to sound grumpy.

The corners of Madison's mouth turned down in exaggerated disapproval. 'We don't do caffeine. Ruari likes our residents to have a real detox when they're here.'

'I'll take a juice,' Jason said.

'Nothing for me,' Karen said. Madison slipped out, leaving the door open. 'My body's a temple to a different god from hers.' The room felt odd, and it took her a moment to realise that was because it had no window. Where a window ought to have been there was a huge flat-screen TV that appeared to be showing a live webcam feed from a rocky beach with a view over the sea to mountains. Unlike the paintings, this did feel tranquil.

Madison returned with a tall tumbler of something green. Jason looked at it suspiciously. 'What's this?'

'Melon, kiwi, apple, cucumber and kale,' she said brightly. Karen congratulated herself on dodging a Nutribullet. 'I'll make sure Ruari comes along as soon as he's clear.' And she was off again.

Jason sniffed suspiciously at his glass then tentatively tasted it. 'I've had worse,' he said. 'But mostly when my mum thought I was coming down with something.'

Karen flipped open her laptop and jumped on board Wester Fearn House's guest Wi-Fi. She'd hoped that the press release might have shaken some more information out of the trees, but so far Duncan McNab was still the only show in town. She was about to start checking the news sites to see who had picked up on the story when Ruari Macaulay strode in, directing a cautious smile at them.

'Don't get up,' he said as Karen struggled to close her laptop and rise from the chair. He was wearing a muscle vest with a light cotton shirt thrown over it and lycra leggings that came halfway down massive calves. Although he was in his fifties, he still had the physical condition of a much younger man. There was no sign that Ruari Macaulay had come within a hundred-yard dash of running to seed. His shaved head was polished, a contrast to a face that looked as if it had been shaped more by fists than genetics. Karen imagined nobody messed with him.

Macaulay sat down opposite her. 'What brings you up here?' he said. 'What can I do for a detective chief inspector of polis?' There was a teasing note in his voice. He sounded as if he had nothing on his conscience; he could afford lightness of tone with her.

Karen opened the laptop again and clicked on the picture of their victim. 'I'm hoping you can help me. I wonder whether you know this man?' She turned the screen to face him.

Macaulay's face registered genuine surprise. 'Joey Sutherland? Damn right, I know him. Used to be king of the weight-for-height in these parts. Let me see.' He held out a hand for the laptop. 'Aye, that's definitely him. What's he done now?' he said as she passed it over. Then as he studied it more closely, he let out a low whistle. 'I see it's no' what he's done. It's somebody that's done him, right? That picture's no' been taken from the life, has it?'

'I'm afraid not.'

Macaulay passed the laptop back to her. 'So why are you here? It's more than twenty years since I saw Joey. And to be honest, I wasn't expecting to see him again.'

'We had a tentative ID from someone this morning. They suggested you might be able to give us some more information. Why were you not expecting to see him again?'

Macaulay looked startled. 'I didn't mean that the way you've taken it. I wasn't expecting to see him again because when he took off he owed me a wedge of cash he didnae seem keen to pay back.'

Karen felt a glow of satisfaction. It was a real bonus this early in the investigation to find a witness who really knew the victim. 'Take us back, if you would, to when you knew Joey

184

Sutherland. When did you first meet?'

He ran a hand over his head, smoothing down his phantom hair. He drew in a whistling breath while he considered. 'Must have been the late eighties. He showed up on the Highland circuit. He was only a boy, but he'd worked hard to get himself in shape. He was big, but it was all working muscle, you know what I mean? It wasnae for show. You get to know the other guys on the circuit when you're doing the heavy events. You run into each other every other weekend right through the season. You watch them mature and develop, you watch them hit their peak and then decline. You go out drinking together, you eat together. Some you get to be pals with. Some you just know in passing, you know what I mean? Be a bit like that in the polis, I expect.'

'A bit,' Karen said. 'So what kind of lad was Joey?'

'The crowds loved him. He had something about him. Charisma, I suppose. Women wanted to take him home and the bairns hero-worshipped him. He was better looking than most of us — I mean, you see it all.' He pointed to his face. 'Most of the heavy guys look like me. Like we had a run-in with Chewbacca and came off worst. Joey never did any boxing or bare-knuckle. He was a braw fella. He had this wee cowlick that fell on his forehead, like Christopher Reeve in the *Superman* films.'

Macaulay looked at the floor. 'Some guys on the circuit like to take a shortcut to the muscles. They get into the steroids. That messes with pretty much everything in your body. Including your moods. So some of the guys can be quick off the mark when it comes to losing the plot. Quick to take offence, quick with their fists.' He met Karen's eyes. 'Joey was never like that. He was an easygoing boy.' His mouth twisted in a grimace. 'Didnae stop him taking the piss, given half a chance, though.' He sat back, lips pursed, waiting for the prompt, not wanting to be thought treacherous to a pal.

Karen obliged. 'How do you mean?'

'The reason I thought I wouldnae see him again? The money? Joey liked to look the part. Always dressed nice, always clean and well-groomed. He was doing well on the circuit, but not well enough to live the way he wanted. A lot of the guys, they live in their camper vans. That's the only way they can afford the life. Joey's van was pretty poor, you'd have to say. Not a place to take a lassie you were trying to impress. He wanted to trade up. And he didn't have enough ready cash. So he came to me for the top-up. I was doing well by then, and I had a wee gym in Inverness that washed its face and then some.' Macaulay shrugged. That simple gesture probably used up all the calories in a Mars bar, Karen thought.

'How much did you lend him?'

'Five grand. It doesnae sound too much now, I suppose. Especially when you look at this place. But it wasnae a flea bite. He was due to pay me back in the September. This would be 1995. We were both at the Invercharron Games in the middle of the month and I reminded him the

186

money was due. He was a wee bit shifty, wouldnae be pinned down. Anyway, later that afternoon, when we were all packing up to go, he comes up to me cheery as a Christmas card and goes, 'Hey, Ruari, I'll have that money for you at the end of the week.' Which I was very glad to hear, obviously. And that was the last I saw of Joey Sutherland and his top-of-the-range camper van.' He shook his head, a rueful expression on his face.

'What happened to change his attitude to the debt, do you think?'

Macaulay shifted restlessly in his chair. 'I don't know for sure. What I do know is that he was hanging about with an American lassie that afternoon. I say American, but I suppose she could have been Canadian. And I wondered if that put the idea in his head to relocate, so to speak, rather than pay me back. There's plenty of places for a lad with Joey's talent and strength to make a living. Folk are fascinated by the like of us. It's the nearest they get to superheroes.'

He sighed. 'And if he had've done a runner, owing me money like that, he'd know he couldnae come back and pick up where he left off. I couldnae afford to lose face like that. Friend or no, I'd have had to draw a line.' He drew a hand over his face, suddenly struck by the enormity of what Karen had shown him. His eyes softened, gazing over her shoulder into the middle distance. 'Listen to me, talking like he's just stepped out the room. But you're telling me he's gone for good. Away the Crow Road. I cannae take it in. When he's crossed my mind,

I've always pictured him out in the world, being Joey. Not dead. What happened? Where did he die? Was it in America right enough?'

Karen shook her head. 'A crofter found his body in a peat bog in a wee place called Clashstronach. About an hour out of Ullapool, round about where Wester Ross turns into Sutherland.'

'Clashstronach? Never heard of it. What the hell happened to him?'

'We think he was helping somebody dig up a couple of motorbikes that were buried there at the end of the Second World War — '

'Motorbikes? Joey never had a bike. He never had any interest in bikes that I knew.' Macaulay looked confused. 'So what happened? Did he get sucked into the bog? That can happen, I've heard tell.'

'There's no easy way to say this, Mr Macaulay. Joey appears to have been shot.'

A long silence. 'Shot?' It was barely above a breath.

'That's what it's looking like right now.'

His lips quivered. 'That's . . . that's brutal. Joey never deserved that. What the hell could he have done to bring that on himself? I'd maybe have credited it if he'd been caught out with somebody's wife, but digging up motorbikes? That's mental.'

Karen let Macaulay sit with this new knowledge for a moment. When he seemed more composed she said, 'Did he have any enemies? Rivals who might have wanted him out of the way?'

Macaulay winced. 'He had rivals, right enough. But the games and the strongman circuit isn't the kind of world where you bump off somebody that can throw the hammer a wee bit further than you. End of the day, we're pals. Sure, you get a couple of guys getting into a wee ruck sometimes, but never anything serious. And like I said, everybody liked Joey. I'm not just saying that because he's dead. Ask anybody that knew him, they'll say the same.'

'With all that charm, did he have a girlfriend? Anybody he saw regularly?'

A wistful smile. 'He liked his fun, did Joey. But he never made any promises or stuck to any one lassie. He said he wasnae ready to settle down.'

'Did he introduce you to the American lassie in Invercharron?'

Macaulay snorted with laughter. 'No chance of that. He was keeping her to himself.'

'What about friends? Was there anybody he was particularly close to?'

Macaulay pointed to his chest. 'Who's the one he came to for the money? I was his pal. I took him under my wing right from the get-go. I could see he was going to be a star and it never hurts to be pals with the stars. That's how it started, but it turned out we actually enjoyed hanging about with each other.'

'We need someone to formally identify Joey's body — '

'I'm not doing that!' It was almost a shout. 'I can't, I can't look at a dead body.'

It was an extreme reaction. Almost a suspicious one, Karen thought. Macaulay had

189

given a splendid performance of candour, but it might be just that — a performance. If he'd killed Joey Sutherland, the last thing he'd want would be a confrontation with the body. Especially all these years later. Karen parked the idea for further consideration and said, 'So can you put us in touch with any family members? Parents, perhaps, or siblings? Where did he come from?'

'His family came from Rosemarkie on the Black Isle. Joey couldn't escape fast enough. He hated life on the land. Didnae much like his family either. He had a sister. She got the brains, he got the brawn. She went to the university at Edinburgh. She's a lawyer now. Well, she was the last I heard. Donalda, that's her name, though everybody called her Dolly.'

Jason added the name to his notebook.

'Are his parents still on the Black Isle?' Karen asked.

Macaulay shook his head. 'I saw their place up for sale five or six years back. I heard they'd moved down to Edinburgh. Dolly bought them some wee retirement flat without so much as a window box. The chat in the pub said old man Sutherland had had enough of breaking his back for next to no reward. Never wanted to turn a spit of soil again.' He gave a short bark of laughter. 'Ironic, given where Joey ended up.' He frowned and fixed Karen with a shrewd look. 'Do you think he was killed right after Invercharron? That he never ran away at all? That all this time I've been thinking ill of him when he was lying dead?'

There was no way to sweeten the pill. 'It looks that way,' she said. 'You weren't to know.'

Macaulay clenched his fists and banged them on his knees. 'Aye, but all the same . . . What kind of friend jumps straight to thinking the worst? What kind of friend doesn't even bother telling the polis when somebody disappears?'

'He was a grown man, Mr Macaulay. Whatever happened to Joey, it wasn't your fault.' It was inadequate, she knew. But it was better than telling that other truth: that Joey Sutherland had been responsible for the choices that had led him to a shallow grave in a Wester Ross peat bog. He probably hadn't deserved what had happened to him. But he'd chosen the road that had taken him there.

29

2018 — Edinburgh

It had been too late for Jason's visit to the cinema by the time they'd made it back to Edinburgh, but Karen had persuaded him to invite the lassie for a late drink to make up for it. Her good deed for the day, she thought, dropping him outside a chain pub on George Street before heading home.

There was an email waiting for her from McCartney, outlining his interview with Sheila Chalmers and his intention to speak to Barry Plummer in the morning. The subtext was that this was all a waste of his precious time but she was the boss. Karen fired off a quick, 'Well done, good luck tomorrow,' and left it at that.

She stared into the fridge. She'd hit the supermarket the week before but nothing suited her mood. She should have been buzzing with delight at their progress, but there was something about Joey Sutherland's murder that had got under her skin. Although on the face of it, nobody had missed Joey Sutherland when he disappeared it was clear that he would be mourned. On the long drive south, she'd kept running over how Ruari Macaulay had spoken about the dead man. Warmth, affection, regret. All markers for loss. And nobody understood loss better than Karen.

It was, she decided, a night for comfort food. Potatoes and onions from the fridge, coriander leaves from the freezer, red lentils from the store cupboard. She chopped the onions and threw them in a pan with a slug of olive oil, then diced the potatoes and added them. A couple of handfuls of lentils, then boiling water to cover the contents of the pan. She remembered to add a chicken stock gel, then chopped the coriander. Half now, half when she was about to dish up. Lentil stovies had been her own invention when she'd lived alone and in spite of Phil's reservations as a red-blooded carnivorous Scotsman, it had become his favourite scratch supper. The sensible Karen knew it was daft to find significance in lentils and tatties, but the emotional Karen couldn't deny that she felt Phil's presence when she ate the food they'd enjoyed together. She didn't care if it was sentimental nonsense. There was nothing maudlin about it. It simply revived the good memories of the brief time they'd shared.

After she'd eaten, Karen opened her laptop and went to the website of the Law Society of Scotland. She typed Donalda Sutherland's name into their search engine, and struck gold. Donalda Mary Sutherland was a solicitor in a family law firm with offices in George Street. She specialised in conflict resolution and mediation. Messy divorces, in other words. Karen's pal Giorsal, a senior social worker over in Fife, had once commented wryly that the unintended consequence of equal marriage had been equal divorce and the concomitant bonanza for family lawyers. Karen didn't imagine Dolly Sutherland was anywhere near the breadline.

Not that money was any kind of salve for grief. Losing her brother would be the same blow regardless. But at least the family would be spared the desperate problems that came with losing a breadwinner. Even coming as late to the party as Karen usually did, she'd seen too often the shattering effects on a family of losing someone they depended on as well as loved.

For once, although it was barely after eleven, Karen felt sleepy. 'Like a normal person,' she muttered as she got ready for bed. She was about to drift into sleep when what she'd missed hit her. 'Ah, shite,' she groaned. The obvious question. If Joey was in the ground, where was his swanky camper van? She grabbed her phone and composed an email to Ruari Macaulay.

Sorry to bother you again, Mr Macaulay. But I was wondering whether by any chance you might have a photo of Joey with his camper van? We'd like to track down the van and any details would help — make, model, colour, number plate. I know it's a long shot but in my experience, sometimes those long shots pay off. All the best, DCI Karen Pirie.

The chances were slim, she knew. But it was worth chasing.

And now she was awake.

★ ★ ★

Morning brought lashing rain and the sort of east wind that exfoliated anyone caught in its grip. Even Karen had her limits. She took the bus up from Ocean Terminal to George Street, squeezed between the cold window and an elderly man who smelled of wet dog. It was almost a relief to step out into the bitter weather.

Family lawyers didn't spend a lot of time in court. Karen reckoned she'd find Donalda Sutherland in her office. And if not, she was only a few minutes' walk from her own desk.

A discreet brass plaque marked the entrance to RJS, the firm that listed Donalda among its partners. Glass doors opened into an anonymous foyer that could have belonged to any kind of business. A receptionist sat behind a curved white desk; four white leather two-seater sofas sat around the room; the low tables held a selection of that morning's newspapers and a few apparently random magazines.

Feeling too bedraggled for the room, Karen waited while the receptionist finished a phone call then said, 'I'd like to see Donalda Sutherland.' She held up her warrant card.

'Do you have an appointment?' It was an automatic response, without thought.

'No.'

She lifted her phone handset. 'Can I ask you what it's in connection with?'

'You can ask, but I won't tell you. It's official police business.'

The woman's professional smile tightened. 'Take a seat and I'll see what I can do.'

'I'll just wait here,' Karen said, matching the

smile. She wasn't going to be kept dangling by some snotty receptionist who thought lawyer trumped cop in the valuable time stakes.

The woman tapped a couple of keys, waited, then said, 'Angie, I've got a police officer here who wants to speak to Ms Sutherland. Does she have a free slot this morning?' She waited, avoiding Karen's eye. 'She can? OK, leave it with me.' She replaced the phone and said, 'She's in a conference right now. She can see you in half an hour.' She looked pleased with her small victory.

'Great.' Karen checked her watch. 'I'll away across to Burr and get a cup of coffee and come back in half an hour,' she said cheerily, refusing to give the receptionist the satisfaction of pissing her off.

Settled with a flat white on a comfy banquette at the back of the café, Karen opened her laptop and checked the news sites. As she'd expected, the story of the mysterious bog body had been picked up across the board. Even the London-based nationals, notorious for the paucity of their coverage of anything north of Hadrian's Wall, had found it intriguing enough to give it a good show. Karen chose one of the Scottish dailies, figuring it was most likely to cram in as much information as they could get their hands on. The piece was topped by the reconstruction of Joey Sutherland's face. The reproduction made him look like a character from a Pixar animation. But Karen thought anyone who knew him would recognise Joey. She hoped Donalda Sutherland wasn't a news junkie.

When crofter Hamish Mackenzie went digging for treasure, he got more than he bargained for. As well as the vintage motorbikes he was looking for, he uncovered the perfectly preserved body of a man buried in a peat bog.

Mr Mackenzie, 37, who farms at Clashstronach in Wester Ross, said, 'It was a terrible shock. I'd heard about peat bogs preserving bodies but you never think one will turn up on your land. It was the last thing I expected.'

The excavation took place after Mr Mackenzie was contacted by a couple from the South of England. 'The woman said her grandfather had been stationed near here during the Second World War. He was one of the trainers for Churchill's Special Operations Executive — the people who were trained as spies and saboteurs and sent behind enemy lines.

'At the end of the war, they were told to destroy all the equipment. But there were two brand-new Indian Scout motorbikes that had only just arrived from the US, and the woman's grandfather and his best mate couldn't bear to break them up. So, under cover of darkness, they wrapped them in tarpaulins, crated them up and buried them on the croft. My grandparents knew nothing about it, obviously.'

The couple who got in touch with Mr

Mackenzie had a rudimentary map and with the help of a borrowed metal detector, the treasure hunt began. 'I used my wee digger and about four feet down, we hit the top of the first crate. When we opened it up, we found a motorbike in pristine condition.'

But the second crate was a very different proposition. 'Right away, I knew something was wrong. The top of the crate had been disturbed. And when we started to clear away the peat and the planks, we realised that what we were looking at was a human arm. There was no mistaking it. We could see the fingernails and everything.

'It was a hell of a shock. We climbed out as fast as we could and called the police. When they arrived, they soon established there was a man's body down there. They told us afterwards that the rest of the body was as well preserved as the arm.'

Detective Chief Inspector Karen Pirie of Police Scotland's Historic Cases Unit later confirmed that a man's body had been recovered from the peat bog at Clash-stronach. She revealed that the body is not thought to date from the end of the war. 'We have reason to believe that the dead man was only placed in the makeshift grave at some point in the last twenty-five years,' she said. 'We are treating this as a suspicious death.'

The piece ended with the details from Karen's press release. She was grateful to the journalists

198

for respecting her request not to reveal Joey's identity. Bad enough if his family saw the picture. Much worse if their worst fears were confirmed in so brutal a fashion.

Tomorrow, Joey Sutherland would be all over the news media. If they got lucky, somebody's memory might be kick-started. Historic cases weren't like live ones. You couldn't shake the witness tree by going door to door or interviewing everyone who'd been present at the events leading up to the crime. Ruari Macaulay seemed to think the Invercharron Highland Games was Joey's last public appearance. Maybe somebody heard or saw something that afternoon that would push their investigation forward. These were the fragile links Karen relied on to build a chain of evidence. And maybe Donalda Sutherland could provide her with a few of her own.

30

2018 — Edinburgh

When Karen returned to RJS twenty-five minutes later, a different woman was behind the desk. Younger and apparently happier with her lot. As soon as Karen explained that she was expected, Receptionist 2.0 directed her down the hall to the second room on the left.

Karen knocked and entered a small interview room. It was about 300 per cent more inviting than its equivalent in the police station. Three comfortable armchairs, a low table with a box of tissues, soft lighting that had been designed rather than merely installed. A long high window revealed a sliver of sky above rooftops. Nobody else was there, but she took off her coat anyway and slung it over the arm of a chair.

'Chief Inspector, I'm so sorry to keep you waiting.' The only resemblance between the woman who walked in and Joey Sutherland was that she was taller than average. She looked to be in her late thirties; scant make-up, thick black hair streaked with silver, cut in a long bob. She wore a black jersey dress that clung to her slim frame, low-heeled pumps and a pair of chunky earrings that sparkled like the real thing. She wore oversized black-rimmed glasses that gave her an intellectual air, but her smile and her voice radiated warmth. She stretched out a hand to shake Karen's then waved her to chair.

As she sat, she said, 'I'm sorry, I don't know your name. Rachel, who was on the desk when you arrived, didn't make a note. Call me Donna, by the way.' She crossed her feet at the ankles, setting her legs at an angle.

Donna now. Obviously she'd decided nobody would take seriously a lawyer called Dolly. 'I'm Karen Pirie. I'm with the Historic Cases Unit.'

'Interesting. And how can I help you, Karen?' Her expression was one of intelligent interest. She was clearly accustomed to quickly putting people at their ease.

'I'm afraid I have some bad news.' There was never a way to sugarcoat it.

A quick wrinkling of the eyebrows. 'A client?'

'No. Donna, when did you last hear from your brother?'

She drew in her breath sharply. Her right hand clutched her left. 'Something's happened to Joey.' Not a question. 'I knew it. I've always known it. He might go off without a word but he'd never have kept that up for twenty-three years. He had his differences with my parents but he didn't hate them. And you'd have to hate someone to do that to them.' She closed her eyes momentarily then visibly drew herself together. 'Tell me,' she said.

'A body was found in a peat bog in Wester Ross earlier this week. It was very well preserved because of the soil conditions. We had a forensic expert prepare a picture of what the dead man would have looked like and a local journalist at the press conference thought he recognised your brother.'

'Let me see. You have it with you?'

Karen took out the copy she'd printed that morning and handed it over.

Donna's face crumpled. She took off her glasses and rubbed her eyes. 'How much work did your forensic artist have to do?' Everybody clung to hope, even when they knew it was futile.

'Very little. The eye colour was an educated guess. He lightened the skin tone because of the peat staining. But what you see is more or less how the man looks. Would you say that's your brother?'

'I would say that's what my brother looked like when I last saw him twenty-three years ago. Does that fit? Has this body been there that long?'

'We think so.' Karen produced another photograph, this time showing the dead man's belt buckle. 'Do you recognise this?'

Donna's shoulders slumped. 'That's Joey's. He won it the first year he took part in the Isle of Skye games. He always wore it with his kilt when he was competing. And on his jeans when he wasn't.' She wrapped her arms around herself as if she'd suddenly grown cold. 'There's no doubt about it, is there?'

Karen shook her head. 'We will do DNA testing to confirm it, but yes, I think there's no room for doubt.'

'What happened? Was it some sort of accident?' Her eyes were anguished. Donna had had more than twenty years to get used to the idea of her brother not being around; that didn't

202

mean her distress was any less intense.

'I'm afraid not. We're treating your brother's death as suspicious.'

'You mean he was killed? I'm not a child, Karen. You don't have to resort to euphemisms with me.'

'I've not had the post-mortem results yet. But preliminary examination suggests he was shot with a small-calibre gun. In the chest and in the neck. I'd say it was probably a quick death.' Really, she had no idea whether that was true. But nobody was going to contradict her and it was, she supposed, a kind of comfort.

'Shot?' Donna was incredulous. 'How? Why? Joey wasn't a criminal. He didn't mix with people who have handguns. I mean, of course he knew plenty of people who have shotguns or even rifles for hunting. But that's normal in the Highlands. Guns for game. Not for shooting people. That's what happens in the city. Gangsters. Drug dealers. People smugglers.'

'We think this probably happened before Dunblane. Before the gun laws changed. There were a lot more handguns around back then.'

Donna's mouth twisted in a grimace. 'Of course. I'd forgotten how things used to be. But even so, Joey didn't mix with the kind of people who resolved things by shooting each other.' Her expression changed as something else occurred to her. 'And what was he doing in Wester Ross?'

'We don't know. We think it was connected to a pair of motorbikes that were buried there at the end of the war.'

Donna shook her head, as if trying to clear a

fog. 'Motorbikes? Buried motorbikes? The war? This is surreal.'

Karen explained how the bikes had come to be interred in the peat. 'I'm thinking maybe Joey was hired to help excavate them. And then something went very wrong.'

'Hard to think how much more wrong it could have gone.' She licked her lips and took a deep breath. 'Somebody did this to my brother. Shot him like a dog and presumably buried him to cover their tracks. What are you doing to find this person?' There was a new edge in her voice now the shock had subsided enough to let anger creep in.

'Everything I can. I work in Historic Cases because I believe people deserve answers. There are few things harder to live with than not knowing the fate of people we love. I understand that.'

Donna acknowledged Karen's sincerity with a dip of the head. 'Fair enough. So what do you need from me that will help you?'

'I need to know a lot more about your brother.'

She glanced at her watch. 'I'm sorry, I have a meeting in five minutes. I need to cancel it.' Abruptly she stood up and walked out, stiff as a drunk trying to fool the room.

Donna returned almost immediately. 'I've ordered coffee. Probably too early for a proper drink.' She sat down on the edge of the chair, elbows on her knees, arms folded across her body. 'Ask away.'

'Were you close?'

'There were four years between us, which is quite a lot when you're wee. He was a very protective big brother, though. He made sure I was never picked on or bullied. By the time he was eighteen, he was off on the road, competing in the heavy events. He did well. He got invited to games all over the place. By the time he was twenty, he was travelling around Europe and North America. We hardly saw him. Whenever he did come home, there were always rows. My dad thought he should still be helping out on the land, or putting his hand in his pocket to support the farm.' She gave a short sharp sigh. 'Joey argued that he'd earned it by his own hard work. That nobody else had any right to his time or his money. It did not make for harmonious visits.'

'I can imagine. You said he went off without a word. Can you tell me about that?'

Donna raised her head and studied the ceiling for a moment, blinking hard. 'It was round about when I started at university. He'd dropped by one Sunday at the end of August. He'd been doing a Highland games near at hand and he came over to show off his swanky new camper van. It was a beauty. Complete with a shower and a microwave. I have to admit I envied him a wee bit. He had the usual argument with Dad then drove off before it got dark. That was the last time I saw him. By the time I went to Edinburgh, we'd heard nothing from him for at least a month. I remember because Dad was really bitter about me going. 'You'll be like that brother of yours: as soon as you get a sniff of the big city lights, we'll no' be good enough for you any more.'' A wry little laugh. 'Which was funny, because there's generally not many big city lights on the games circuit.' Her voice cracked and she cleared her throat.

'Did you try to get in touch with him?' It was a gentle probe.

'I didn't know how, to begin with. There wasn't social media back in the late 1990s, remember. And I was too busy with student life to waste my weekends chasing round the Highland Games circuit. Why would I be bothered about a big brother who couldn't be bothered with me?' Donna's face crumpled, the pain showing through the bravado. 'And then it was too late. By the time I'd finished my degree and my training, I was moving in a different world. People like me didn't hang about watching grown men chucking lumps of metal around a field.'

'Once you lose touch, it's easy for it to stay lost.'

Donna gave Karen a sharp look. 'When my parents gave up the croft and moved to the city, I did make a bit of an effort. I didn't like to think of him maybe coming home and there being no home to come back to. I'd taken to googling him every few months. I thought if he'd settled abroad, he might show up in some local paper article. But he never did. There were Joseph Sutherlands and Joe Sutherlands but, as far as I could make out, none of them was our Joey.'

A knock at the door and a nervous-looking skinny young man in shirtsleeves came in with a tray. A coffee pot, two mugs, a milk jug, a bowl with paper sticks of sugar. 'Your coffee, Donna,' he said, crossing between them and putting it on the low table. He backed out of the room, an anxious approximation of a smile on his mouth. The women treated the intrusion as if it had never been.

'I don't suppose you took a photo of Joey with his camper van, that day?'

No such thing as a casual question where a lawyer was concerned. Donna was seeking significance everywhere. 'No. Why? Is there some issue with the van? Has it been involved in something else?'

'Not at all. Quite the opposite. We're simply trying to find out what happened to it.'

'In case it leads you to his killer?' She shook her head. 'You'd either have to be very stupid or very sure of yourself to hang on to such a conspicuous connection to somebody you'd murdered.'

'He hadn't had it for long at that point. I don't think there were necessarily that many people who'd automatically connect it to him. And you'd be amazed at the things some people think they can get away with, Donna.'

Donna winced. 'You're forgetting what I do for a living. Trust me, I've had my breath taken away by some of the nonsense my clients and their partners try to pull.'

A wry smile. 'At least it makes our job a wee bit easier sometimes. Now, we think the last time Joey competed in this country was at the Invercharron Games in September 1995. One of my officers has been checking with the Highland

Games Association and that's the last entry record they have for him. We know he won the weight-for-height there. But I've got a witness who says Joey was talking to an American woman that afternoon. Or possibly Canadian. Does that mean anything to you?'

Donna shook her head with a sigh of frustration. 'Nothing. If she was anything more than a casual fling, we certainly didn't know. The last girlfriend I knew about was when he was still at school. A local lass from Rosemarkie. But they split up not long after he started on the circuit and I don't think either of them lost any sleep over it. He never said anything about a woman from America.'

She hunched her shoulders protectively, wrapping her arms around herself. 'All these years, I wanted to believe he'd found someone to love, somewhere far away. I imagined him remaking himself with a wife and a family of his own. Teaching kids to play American football or running a gym or something. I couldn't let myself think he was dead.' She gave Karen a frank look. 'You must think I'm an idiot. Not to work out he was long gone.'

Karen thought nothing of the sort. If there had been any way for her to convince herself that there had been a terrible mistake and that Phil was still alive, she'd have clasped it to her heart and never let it go. 'Hope is our default when it comes to people we love who've disappeared. Until you have evidence to the contrary, it's the natural state to be in.'

'No hope now, though.' She shuddered and sat

up straight. 'You'll be needing a formal ID,' she said wearily. 'Give me ten minutes to sort out my diary for the rest of the day and I'll be with you. I take it he's still up in the Highlands?'

'No, he's in Dundee. That's where the lab is.'

'I suppose that's a blessing.' Donna made an ironic shape with her mouth, 'Not a phrase one hears very often in relation to Dundee.'

'I'm sorry.'

Donna shook her head. 'Somewhere in my head, I've known this was coming. I've been expecting you, DCI Pirie. You or someone very like you.'

31

1944 — Wester Ross

Arnie leaned on the taffrail of the ship, watching the naval ratings loading the last of the cargo. He was flanked by a couple of other GIs on their way back home like him. He'd stowed his kitbag in a cabin shared with three others and now he was making sure everything went to plan. It was as well he'd removed his loot; the MP who had searched his kitbag had noticed the broken stitches and had thoroughly probed the lining of the bag's bottom.

The other two soldiers at the rail were joshing each other about what they'd do first when they got back on American soil. Arnie thought their talk of girls and bars revealed a depressing lack of ambition. He had higher goals. He was going to set the town on fire in a different way altogether. He was short on the details, it was true, but he'd put himself in a position where he was poised to answer when opportunity knocked.

The ratings were working fast. Now only a couple of dozen items remained on the quayside. And then, without warning, they stopped. A sailor in a heavy jersey walked out from the hold and seemed to be telling them something. And then he went back on board and before Arnie could process what he was seeing, the gang-planks were being drawn on board and the cargo hold closed up. 'What's happening?' he demanded loudly. 'Why are they leaving the rest of the kit behind?'

One of his companions gave him a curious look. 'I guess they reached their limit,' he said. 'What's it to you, bud?'

'Nothing,' Arnie gasped. He genuinely felt his heart contract. His head swam and he wondered whether this was a heart attack. The impulse to weep swept through him and he had to turn away as the ship's engines grew louder and matelots cast off the mighty mooring ropes.

Two days passed before he managed to get a grip on himself. When asked what was up, he'd claimed he was upset at having to leave his girl. They laughed at him for being so soft-hearted, but better that than having them guess the true reason for his grief. He spent the next couple of days working out who would be able to answer his questions about the fate of the bikes and his future.

The cargo master, he discovered, liked to play poker. There was a perpetual low-stakes game in a storage locker near the engine room. Arnie snagged himself a seat and joined the game. He'd played in poker nights where the fierce competition and concentration imposed virtual silence round the table. But thankfully, this wasn't one of those. The men talked and laughed, cracking lewd jokes and telling filthy stories. On his third session in the game, he'd casually asked why they hadn't loaded all the cargo.

'No space,' the cargo master said. 'I fucken told them half a dozen fucken times they were

211

being way too optimistic.'

'So what happens to that stuff now? Will it come on another boat?'

'I don't think so. It's too much fucken trouble to go all the way up there for a few bits and pieces. They'll tell the Brits to get rid of it.'

'Get rid of it?'

'Yeah. Burn it or bury it, that's what they'll be told to do.'

Arnie played one more hand then excused himself. He felt physically sick. All his plans, literally going up in flames. He couldn't bear it. What he'd done to get his hands on a bag of diamonds . . . And now it was all for nothing.

32

2018 — Dundee

In spite of Karen's insistence on driving her back to Edinburgh, Donna had caught a train. 'I need to be by myself,' she'd said, as assertive as the detective herself. 'I'm going to have to break the news to my parents and I need time to prep myself.'

As she opened the door of the taxi River had called to take her to the station, Donna paused. 'Thank you, DCI Pirie. You've been very considerate. This wasn't the outcome I wanted for my brother, but it's better to know the truth.' Then she was gone, off to perform a duty nobody would choose.

Donna had spoken freely about her brother on the drive up to Dundee but none of it had felt useful to Karen. It hadn't been current enough. She'd learned more about life on the Highland games circuit, but nothing that gave her a clue to who might have wanted Joey Sutherland dead. As Ruari Macaulay had indicated, he seemed to have been a man without enemies. She went back inside and found River in her office off the main dissecting lab.

'I'm beginning to think Joey Sutherland's a red herring,' Karen said, slumping into the visitor's chair.

When Karen wanted to work things out aloud,

there was no point in trying to ignore her. River saved what she was working on and gave her full attention to her friend. 'What do you mean?'

'It's early days yet, but if this is all about what was in the bike pannier, Joey's an irrelevance. It could have been anybody. Well, anybody big and strong enough to dig a hole and shift a bike. Because they'd have to believe in their ability to lift that bike, otherwise they wouldn't have taken on the job.'

Half of River's mind was still occupied with what she'd been working on. 'Sorry if I sound like Jason, but you've kind of lost me.'

Karen grinned. 'My fault, thinking out loud. Say you know there's something valuable buried in the pannier of one of those Indians. But you also know you're not strong enough to dig down through the peat or to shift the bikes if they're lying in a way that you can't get at the panniers. What do you do?'

River smiled as light dawned. 'You hire somebody who can.'

'Exactly. And you hire somebody who's strong enough to lift five hundred and fifty pounds. Not that many of them kicking around. The good thing is, guys that strong are accustomed to being paid for what their bodies are capable of. Tailor-made for Joey.'

'But why kill him? Why not just collect what you came for and pay him off?'

'I don't know. But I'd guess that whatever you came for wasn't yours in the first place. And you didn't want some Highland strongman telling all his pals about the weird wee job he'd done for you. Some American lassie, maybe . . . ' Her voice tailed off as she remembered what Ruari Macaulay had told her.

'Now you've definitely lost me.'

'The last competition Joey was seen at was the Invercharron Games. And according to his best pal, he was hanging about with an American woman. Or possibly Canadian. Back in '95, either one would have been pretty exotic in a wee place like Invercharron. It's not likely they'd be able to tell the difference.'

'And you think this mysterious stranger hired Joey to recover whatever was in the bike pannier?'

'Makes more sense than luring Joey into digging his own grave so you could shoot him. If that's what the killer wanted, there's plenty of places in the Highlands to dump a body without going to those lengths. If it was me — ' Her phone interrupted Karen. 'Jason? What is it?' she demanded.

'I thought I'd better tell you,' he said.

'Tell me what?'

'There's an interview with the Somervilles in the *Mail Online*. And they're not very nice about you,' he gabbled.

'Oh, bloody hell,' Karen muttered. 'OK, I'll take a look.'

'Sorry, boss.'

'No, not your fault, thanks for letting me know.' Karen ended the call and grumbled.

'Problems?'

'Can you bring up the *Mail Online*? Jason says the Somervilles have been shooting their mouths off.' She moved behind the desk so she could see River's screen. Moments later she was confronted by an unflattering photograph of herself several kilos heavier and still raging with grief soon after Phil's death. 'For fuck's sake. I look like a madwoman.'

'Of course you do. That's what they're aiming for.' River scrolled down. HIGH-HANDED COP TREATS HERO WITNESSES LIKE CRIMINALS the headline screamed.

A couple who discovered a long-buried murder victim in a Highland bog have been denied the legacy they were searching for.

Alice and Will Somerville were on a quest to unearth two WWII vintage Indian Scout motorbikes cached by Alice's grandfather when they came across the body of a man who's thought to have died of gunshot wounds.

Now the bossy chief of Police Scotland's Historic Case Unit, DCI Karen Pirie, has told the couple they have no right to the bikes which were uncovered at the same time.

Alice said, 'My granddad was stationed at Clachtorr Lodge in the Highlands. He was training British agents to go behind enemy lines as spies and saboteurs. When the war ended, he was ordered to destroy the bikes.

'He thought that was a waste and he asked if he could keep them. His commanding officer said he could, as long as nobody found out where they'd come from.'

'That's bollocks,' Karen exploded. 'They're making it up as they go along. She said nothing about permission from a senior officer.'

Close to tears, Alice, 32, said, 'His dying wish was for us to recover the bikes. He'd never managed to organise getting them back while he was still alive and he wanted us to have them.'

Husband Will, 34, said, 'But DCI Pirie as good as told us we were thieves. She said we had no right to the bikes, which is obviously nonsense, since Alice's granddad was told he could have them.

'It's outrageous. If it hadn't been for us, that poor man's body would still be lying in the bog. But she never so much as said thank you. And our only reward for all our hard work is to be told we can't have what's rightfully ours.'

DCI Pirie was not available for comment. A spokesman for Police Scotland said, 'We cannot comment on an ongoing investigation.'

'Bastards.' Karen stomped back to the chair and threw herself into it. 'How dare they? They've got no claim to those bloody bikes. And it was Hamish Mackenzie who did all the hard work. 'Hero witnesses' my arse.' Just then her phone buzzed with a text. It was from Jason. Dog Biscuit in the building, it read.

Karen groaned. 'Any minute now . . . '

'What?'

Karen held her phone up, waggling it in the air. 'Any minute now . . . '

They both stared at it. Seconds ticked by. Then the phone lit up and vibrated in Karen's hand. 'ACC Markie' flashed across the screen. 'Told you,' Karen said, swiping to take the call. 'Yes, ma'am?'

'Have you seen the *Mail Online*?' The ACC's voice was crisp.

'If you're referring to Alice and Will Somerville's excursion into fiction, ma'am, yes. I have.'

'Fiction?'

'The version of events they're peddling now is not the one they gave in their formal statement. They've had time to think about it and they've come up with this steaming pile of nonsense in a bid to embarrass us into handing over the bikes. That's the top and bottom of it.' Karen kept it light. God forbid the Dog Biscuit would realise how much the Somervilles had enraged her.

'Be that as it may, it's out there now. This is not the kind of publicity we want for the HCU.'

'I can't help it if people tell lies to the press, ma'am.'

'They wouldn't be telling lies if you hadn't upset and annoyed them,' Markie snapped. 'How hard is it to keep things running smoothly with your witnesses?'

'They have no legal right to those motorbikes,' Karen said, lips tight against her teeth in a snarl she'd have had to forego

218

if Markie had been in the room. 'They belong either to the MOD or the US Army.'

'Maybe so. But you could have saved that blow for later. Till the case was out of the headlines and nobody cared about the Somervilles and their claims. But no, you had to wind them up at a point in time when you must have realised journalists would be all over them.' Now venom was seeping through Markie's urbanity.

Karen squeezed her eyes tightly shut. 'They wanted to take the bike with them. The one that isn't technically evidence. What was I supposed to say?'

'Whatever it took. You need to get a grip on things, DCI Pirie. So far, I'm not impressed with the workings of your unit.' The line died.

River grimaced. 'She's not happy.' It wasn't a question.

'Understatement. I don't get it. We do good work in HCU. We get results. Not all the time, obviously, but we've got a pretty good strike rate. And yet the Dog Biscuit's been on my case since the minute she walked through the door.' Karen exhaled noisily.

'You know why, don't you?'

'She's one of those women who see other women as a threat?' Karen hazarded.

'Maybe. But that's not what this is about. This is dogs and lampposts. She wants control of HCU. And that means ownership. She can't have that while you're running it, because you were in with the bricks, and doing good work there long before she took over. Your successes are the source of her frustration. She wants you out, Karen.'

33

2018 — Motherwell

Steel grey clouds lowered over Motherwell's matching grey town centre. Unlike the clouds, the monochrome streets were broken up by garish shop signs in primary colours or occasional splashes of colour in the clothes of those inhabitants who remained defiant against the weather and the retail experience.

There were a handful of Lanarkshire towns that always depressed and angered Detective Sergeant Gerry McCartney, and Motherwell was right up there. There had been a sense of community back in the days when the town had been known as Steelopolis, the monumental cooling towers of the steelworks lowering over the cramped streets. But the closing of Ravenscraig twenty-five years before had shattered that. Westminster politicians had ripped the heart out of Motherwell, in McCartney's opinion, just as they had in so many other Scottish towns. That was what fuelled his rage.

Now the politicians trumpeted the call centres and business parks that had brought new jobs in recent years but McCartney knew the scars were too deep to be papered over by jobs that lacked much sense of fulfilment and commanded little respect. He was lucky to be a polis. He made a difference.

Well, he had until he'd let Ann Markie persuade him off the front line into this bloody backwater at HCU. He wasn't sure what she was after, but he knew he'd do his damnedest to come up with it. That was his ticket back to chasing proper villains, not dicking about with cases so old they should be in a museum.

He found a space at the far end of the Aldi car park. Parking was cheap in these parts, but free was even better than cheap. He might pick up some of their excellent New Zealand pinot noir after he'd done with Barry Plummer. No point in the journey being completely wasted. He walked out of the car park, head down against the drizzle, towards the bed store Barry Plummer managed.

At ten in the morning in the rain, the main shopping street was eerily empty. A homeless man whose grubby layers failed to hide how skinny he was failed to sell McCartney a *Big Issue*. The sergeant marched on, determinedly ignoring his pleas. The guy wasn't even from round here, the sergeant thought bitterly. What had happened to all the local homeless guys? He was convinced the beggars in Glasgow were all in some racket. They looked like they were all from the same family and it wasn't a Scottish one. He'd brought it up with the uniforms that patrolled the city centre, but they'd only laughed at him.

He slowed as he came alongside Barry Plummer's empire. There was no doubting what BEDzzz sold. The whole of the double-fronted plate-glass window was packed with beds. Bunk beds, brass beds, single, double and king-sized

222

beds. There was even a circular one. How the hell did you figure out where to put the pillows? Further back in the shop, wardrobes peeped out behind the frames and mattresses. In spite of the plethora of stock there was something profoundly dispiriting about the shop. McCartney was glad he'd given in to his wife's demands to go to John Lewis for their bedroom furniture.

He pushed open the glass door and stepped inside. There was a chemical smell of plastic and air freshener and no sign of a sales assistant. He supposed there wasn't much likelihood of shoplifters. He ventured further into the store and heard a distant buzzer. Almost immediately, a young man in ridiculously tight black trousers and a shirt that might have fitted him comfortably three kilos ago appeared from the back of the shop. His mousy hair was a mop of incongruous dreads. 'Good morning,' he called cheerily, his face an animated mask of delight. 'And how can we make your nights better?'

'I'm looking for Barry Plummer.' McCartney took out his warrant card. 'DS McCartney. Police Scotland.'

His eyebrows shot up his spotty forehead. 'Jings! What's Barry been up to?'

'Is he here?'

'I'll go and get him. This is the most exciting thing that's happened since I started here.' He bounced off.

McCartney didn't have long to wait. Barry Plummer emerged moments later, also grinning like an idiot. He was a nondescript middle-aged man in a nondescript suit. Mid-brown hair in a nondescript style and a face it would be easy to forget apart from a nose that stuck out like the prow of a ship. 'This is an unexpected visit,' he said. 'I don't think we've ever had the police in here before. I can't imagine what brings you here.'

'Is there somewhere a bit less public where we can have a talk?'

Plummer looked mildly disconcerted. 'I suppose we could go into the office. Sorry, I didn't catch your name?'

'Detective Sergeant Gerald McCartney.' Again he held up his ID.

Plummer flashed a quick tight smile and led the way back to the door he'd appeared through. It led to a narrow hallway. The first door opened into a tiny overstuffed office. Cardboard advertising placards were stacked against the walls, promising discounts and comfort. A scabby desk with peeling veneer and a very old computer dominated the space. There was an office chair behind it and a small chair leaking yellow foam facing it. McCartney shifted it so he could actually see past the chunky grey monitor and sat down without being asked.

Plummer unbuttoned his suit jacket and lowered himself into the boss chair. 'So, to what do we owe this visit, Sergeant?' He was still aiming for affable, but there was a hint of concern in the way he blinked fast and furious.

'I work with the Historic Cases Unit,' he said.

'Oh, that sounds intriguing. Like *Waking the Dead*?'

'Not really. Mostly it's reassessing old evidence

in the light of new information and forensic techniques. And we don't have some old woman off *Brookside* telling us how the bad guys think.' McCartney cracked a smile, aiming to get Plummer to relax.

'So, what brings you to BEDzzz? You need me to identify a bedroom suite for you?'

A chuckle. 'Nothing like that. I need you to cast your mind back about thirty years.'

'Let me see. That would be round about when Motherwell got promoted back into the Premier Division, right?' Plummer smiled widely, showing surprisingly good dental work for his age, nationality and class.

'I'll take your word for that. I'm for the Hoops myself. You were learning to drive back then. In your Uncle Gordy's car. Am I right?'

Plummer shifted in his seat, as if he was trying to get further from the sergeant than the proportions of the room allowed. 'Aye. Poor Gordy, did you hear he just passed? What a shock for us all. Poor Sheila. But I don't see — '

'You remember the car?' McCartney leaned forward, elbows on the desk.

'It was a red Rover 214. Same as hundreds of others.'

It was a misstep and McCartney recognised it. Why bother commenting on how common the car was unless you were trying to hide a needle in a haystack? 'Not so many others, really. Not with a registration number like Gordy's.' A pause. Plummer didn't flinch. 'And once you passed your test, you used to borrow it sometimes?'

225

'Did I? I don't really remember.'

'According to Sheila, you did. No reason why she'd lie to me, is there?'

There was a faint sheen of sweat on Plummer's top lip. 'Of course not. It's a long time ago, I don't really remember the details.' He tried a laugh that came out more like a cough. 'I was a young lad, busy enjoying myself. Out and about, pubs and clubs. You'll have done the same yourself, right?'

McCartney let the words hang. 'I didn't get up to anything like that any time in my life.'

Plummer frowned. 'I don't understand. You still haven't told me what you're investigating. And why you're here.'

'Back in the mid-eighties, there was a series of very nasty rapes, Barry. In Edinburgh and Falkirk. A couple of possibles in Stirling too. One of the victims, Kay McAfee, was so badly beaten she ended up in a wheelchair with all sorts of medical problems. She finally died a few weeks ago. Her family think that even though it took her thirty years to die, she was murdered.' McCartney's tone was even and measured.

'That's terrible, so it is. But I still don't see what — '

'When somebody dies like that, it jogs people's memories. They remember things that maybe didn't seem important at the time. Or maybe they were too scared to tell us what they knew. But times change and people's lives change. And now we're interested in anyone driving a red Rover 214 with a particular registration.' He leaned back in his chair, spreading his arms expansively. No question who was in charge here, his body language said.

Plummer's eyes were wide with shock. 'I never.'

McCartney smiled. 'Nobody's saying you did, Barry. Just for interest's sake, did you ever take Gordy's Rover across to Edinburgh?'

He shook his head vigorously. 'No way. I'd not long passed my test. No way was I going to drive across the motorway. That M8 was as mental then as it is now.'

'Fair enough. I had to ask. Something else I have to ask? We need to take DNA samples of everybody known to have driven a red Rover 214 back in the day. It's for elimination, you understand?'

'But I've already told you, I never went to Edinburgh in the Rover. I don't think I ever went to Edinburgh back in those days except for the football. When we went through to play Hearts or Hibs. And even then I went on the train, I never drove.'

McCartney nodded benevolently. 'I understand, Barry. But I've got a job to do. My boss'll kick my backside into the middle of next week if I come back without the right number of samples. It's not like you're being singled out. I've got more than a dozen of these in my car already.'

'What if I don't want to?'

McCartney shrugged. 'You're within your rights to refuse. But honestly, Barry? I wouldn't if I was you. It looks bad, you know what I'm saying? It looks like you've got something to hide. And I can see you're not that kind of guy. Trust me, as soon as we see you're not the one we're looking for, your sample gets destroyed. There's nothing to be feart about.' He reached into his inside pocket and took out the DNA sampling kit. He tore open the paper sachet and removed the plastic wrapped wand with its absorbent tip. 'It doesn't hurt, Barry. A cheek-swab, that's all. You'll have seen it on the telly. It'll be done with in seconds. And since you didn't go to Edinburgh in the Rover, you'll be free and clear in a matter of days.' He stood up and rounded the end of the desk.

Plummer's eyes flicked from side to side. He was cornered. It didn't mean he was guilty. Well, not guilty of these crimes, at least. Plummer nervously chewed at the skin round the nail of his index finger. 'OK. OK. I've got nothing to hide.' He leaned back and opened his mouth. McCartney moved swiftly, before the salesman could change his mind.

'Brilliant. Chances are you'll never hear from us again,' he said cheerily as he put the swab in its sterile tube and scribbled the details on the label.

'I hope you get him,' Plummer said. 'Guys like that? They're scum.'

'We'll get him, don't you worry. You know what they say,' McCartney added over his shoulder. 'You can run, but you can't hide.' He didn't wait for a response. 'I'll see myself out.'

34

2018 — Edinburgh

Sitting in the crawling queue to get over the Queensferry Crossing, Karen almost regretted staying overnight in Dundee. But she knew herself well enough to understand that a Thai meal and a few beers with her closest friend was exactly what she needed when she felt pressure coming at her from all sides. When the people who were supposed to have her back turned out to be the ones with the knives, spending time with someone she could trust was the best bulwark against self-doubt. No detective could do their best work if they were constantly questioning their own judgement.

When she finally arrived in the office, she wasn't surprised that Jason was the only other occupant of the HCU. 'Bloody traffic on the bridge,' she said. 'I thought I'd left Dundee early enough to miss the rush hour.'

Jason scoffed. 'Only time there's not a queue for the bridge is about three in the morning. On a Sunday.'

'Aye. So much for the new bridge easing congestion. So, what's happening?'

'Nothing much. Your woman from the art gallery was on, about the dodgy painting you went to look at. She's going to send you some slides later.'

229

Karen threw her coat over the chair. 'Be still, my beating heart. No sign of Sergeant McCartney? He's not gone across the street for coffee or anything useful like that?'

Jason looked awkward. 'He said he was going to swing by Gartcosh to drop off the DNA samples at the lab personally. I said he should try and talk to Tamsin and tell her they're for you.'

'Well done.' Karen tried not to show her surprise at Jason's initiative. He was defying all her expectations and getting better at his job. 'What would Phil do?' was clearly working. It didn't occur to her that how she operated was having just as much influence on her wingman's development.

Strictly speaking, DNA analysis was nothing to do with Tamsin Martineau, a digital forensics specialist. But she had a way of persuading her colleagues to go the extra mile for Karen's team. 'Tamsin always looks out for us. I think she gets a kick out of using her box of tricks to catch the bastards who have been living free and clear all those years.'

'She's not the only one.' Jason stood up. 'Will I away and get some coffees?'

But before she could respond, the door opened and a flushed DCI Jimmy Hutton stepped in, closing the door swiftly behind him. 'Karen,' he said, 'I need to talk to you.'

'I was heading out for coffee,' Jason said.

'Take your time,' Jimmy said. 'Mine's a cappuccino.' He stepped aside to give Jason room to leave then leaned against the door. In spite of his high colour, the skin around his eyes was pale and his jaw was tight.

'What's wrong, Jimmy?'

'A clusterfuck, Karen. That's the simplest way of putting it. That conversation you overheard in Aleppo? The one you told me about the other night?'

A cold apprehension made the hairs on Karen's neck quiver. 'You're kidding?'

Jimmy bit his lip and shook his head. 'I wish. But it's even worse than you imagined. It all went off last night. A woman called Dandy Muir is dead. A guy called Logan Henderson is on the critical list at the Royal. And his wife, Willow Henderson — the woman you overheard in Aleppo — was allegedly too traumatised to speak to us last night.'

Karen's chest tightened. Sudden violent death usually only became her concern in retrospect. She'd seldom been directly confronted with it in the present tense. But each of those occasions had left its mark on her. Some of her colleagues, she knew, had perfected the skill of professional detachment. But not even the most experienced cops and forensics experts were completely immune. One of Karen's former colleagues from Fife had been seconded to a UN investigative team in Iraq. Confronted by the mutilated body of a girl the same age as his own daughter, his defences had collapsed, leaving him sobbing on his knees like a child. Back when he'd told her about the experience, Karen had never gone through anything comparable. She'd been convinced she was strong enough to deal with whatever the job threw at her.

She'd been wrong. The first time she'd been faced with the immediate aftermath of murder, all her barricades had crumbled. It had taken all she had not to show how close she'd come to emotional meltdown. Somehow, over the years, she'd grown more adept at concealment. It didn't mean she'd escaped those searing moments of empathy.

But she wasn't about to show that. Not even to Jimmy, who had seen her grief and matched it with his own. 'How did Dandy die?' she said.

'Stabbed with a kitchen knife.'

'In the kitchen?'

'Where else?' Jimmy's mouth twisted in a bitter line.

'Fuck. I even said that to them. Kitchens are bad places for confrontation. I told them. What about Logan?'

'Multiple stab wounds.'

'And Willow's said nothing?'

Jimmy gave a dry little laugh. 'I never said that. She was coherent enough to tell the first responders that Logan had come at her with a knife but Dandy had stepped between them to save her. And then Willow grabbed a knife to defend herself against him.'

Karen was appalled. Somehow, this was all her fault. If she'd said nothing to Dandy . . . A thought occurred to her. 'Was Logan stabbed with the same knife as Dandy?'

Jimmy shook his head. She could feel the suppressed rage coming off him like a wave of heat. 'Oh no. That would have been a schoolboy error, wouldn't it? Ironically, that second knife may have been what's keeping Logan alive. It had a shorter blade. Did less damage.'

'Christ. This is down to me,' Karen said, feeling the prickle of tears.

'Stop that right now.' His voice was cold and angry. 'Whatever happened in that kitchen — and we can surmise all we like but we don't know for sure yet — whatever happened, you are not responsible.'

'If I'd not said anything — '

'It would have happened regardless.'

'Dandy wouldn't have been there. Willow was talking about going alone.'

'Karen, stop. I don't need you having a guilt trip. I need you at your sharpest and toughest. I need your help.'

A question dawned on Karen. 'Wait a minute, Jimmy. How is this yours? Your team's all about murder prevention. You don't do sharp end stuff unless it's all gone wrong. How come you know so much about this?'

He sat down at McCartney's desk. 'I happened to be in St Leonard's last night, going through a case that's due in the High Court with one of the E division MIT crew when the report came in. I recognised the names.' He shrugged. 'Given what you know, I thought it was going to be important that you were in the loop. I knew it would get stupidly complicated if one of the MIT grandstanders took it on.'

Karen nodded. Jimmy was too kind to say so, but he was protecting her. 'There are ways of reading this that don't put me in a good light. Mostly because I'm not in a good light — '

233

'Whatever. I thought it would be better all round if I managed to hijack it. And then I remembered you'd said Willow had already reported Logan to the police for trying to strangle her. So I blagged it. I said we'd been looking at the husband so it was an open case on our books.'

Karen stared at Jimmy. 'You did that? To cover my back?'

'It's about a lot more than covering your back, Karen. This is exactly the kind of case my team understands. We'll do it properly. The MIT guys, they're always after something more glamorous than a domestic that's got out of hand. They want to be out there on the streets detecting. Not interviewing fucked-up Morningside ladies in what looks like a sordid open-and-shut case. There's nothing gung-ho about this, so they were more than happy to let me claim it.' His angry flush had subsided now and he gave her a self-conscious smile. 'So if we're right and this is a nasty, devious piece of dirty work, it'll get put to bed properly.'

Karen blew out a deep breath. 'Right enough, Jimmy. What could possibly go wrong? I'm already on the Dog Biscuit's shit list. I might as well go for the top spot. What's next?'

Before Jimmy could answer, there was a timid knock at the door and Jason inched it open. 'Is it OK to come back in now?' he asked. 'Only Sergeant McCartney just drove in and he'll be along in a minute.'

Karen waved him in. He clutched his cardboard tray of coffees to his chest like a shield. 'Thanks, Jason.'

'Nae bother. Only, I thought you might not like the sergeant bursting in on whatever you and DCI Hutton were talking about.'

'Good thinking, Jason. Phil would be proud of you, son,' Jimmy said, taking the proffered cup and getting to his feet. To Karen, he said, 'I'll call you when our traumatised witness feels able to speak.'

On his way out, he passed McCartney, who looked puzzled to see him there. He stared after Jimmy, then said, 'Was that not DCI Hutton? From the Murder Prevention Squad?'

'Aye,' Karen said, staring at her laptop and typing.

'What was he after?'

'A decent cup of coffee, I think.' Distracted, finding the screen more interesting than McCartney.

Frustrated, he dropped hard into his chair. 'That's all anybody round here ever seems to care about.'

Karen looked up and grinned. 'And your point would be?'

35

2018 — Edinburgh

Waiting for Jimmy's call, Karen struggled to concentrate. She set Jason on the task of tracking down who else had been competing at the 1995 Invercharron Highland Games in the hope that Joey had said something to someone about his plans. Or that they'd met the American woman who'd been talking to Joey. There was, Karen thought, an outside chance that she might have approached another of the heavy athletes if she was looking to hire some muscle to excavate the bikes. One who'd refused, but knew something of who she was. Because outside chances sometimes provided the loose end that unravelled the skein that had obscured the past.

McCartney was doing the paperwork on the interviews he'd conducted on the red Rover, occasionally grumbling that it was all a waste of time. Karen blanked his complaints, determined not to let him undermine the unit. She'd figure out a way to ditch him, but not today. Today was for a different kind of calculation.

It was almost noon when the call came. Karen was shrugging into her coat even as she listened to Jimmy. 'On my way,' she said, grabbing her bag and heading for the door.

'Where are you off to?' McCartney said. But the door was already closing behind her.

She left her car in the office car park and hustled up to the taxi rank outside the Playhouse. It would be quicker than trying to find a parking space near the St Leonard's police station and she didn't want to attract attention by asking the front desk for a slot in the car park. She was surprised that Jimmy had brought Willow Henderson in to E Division's headquarters. Given the state of her husband, Karen would have expected Willow's lawyer — and maybe even the doctors — to insist that the interview took place at the hospital. He'd done well to extricate her from that protective cocoon and get her on their turf.

Jimmy was waiting for her in the foyer, as they'd arranged. He led her down to the characterless corridor that housed the interview rooms. Their destination was the final door, which opened on to a dimly lit observation room. There was a traditional two-way mirror but these days it was augmented by a live video feed from two wall-mounted cameras. The room they were looking into had two inhabitants; Willow Henderson, dressed in hospital scrubs, and an expensively suited man who looked like he'd spent a lot more time in a facial spa than a police station.

'Who's the brief?' Karen asked.

'Gil Jardine. The coming man when it comes to defending the rich and discreet. The good news is that he's not done many murders. I'll leave you here for now. I just need to grab my sergeant then it's curtain up. If I think there's any value in you talking to her alone, I'll get the brief out of the room at the end.'

'Thanks. Let's see how it plays out.'

Once Jimmy had gone, Karen moved closer to the glass. There was no denying the night had taken its toll on Willow. Some of it might be artificial — the tangled hair, the lips bare of colour, the disaster of smudged mascara and eyeliner — but the eyes puffy from weeping were the real thing. So were the lines of tension round her mouth. Ironically, she looked good in blue scrubs, until you remembered she was wearing them because the crime scene techs had placed her bloodstained clothes in bags for forensic testing.

She said something to the lawyer, who patted her hand in reassurance, the way men who thought they held all the cards had always done to women. The sound wasn't turned on yet; conversations with lawyers were privileged. The police were not supposed to eavesdrop. Not for the first time, Karen thought she should have learned how to lip-read.

Then Jimmy walked in, followed by DS Jacqui Laidlaw. Laidlaw was a generously proportioned blonde with a face like a child's doll. It would have been hard to find anyone less doll-like under the surface. She was smart and hard and Karen was never going to be her friend. But then, she'd have struggled to warm to whoever had replaced Phil as Jimmy's bag carrier.

Jimmy and Laidlaw sat down with their backs to the mirror. She pressed the buttons on the recording equipment and the audio feed to the observation room sprang into life. Jimmy made

238

the introductions for the tape then said, 'Mrs Henderson, you've come here voluntarily to make a witness statement, is that correct?'

'I wouldn't say that exactly,' she said, her voice slightly tremulous. 'I wanted to talk to you at my home but you insisted we come here.'

'I'm afraid your family home is still a crime scene.'

'We could have gone to my friend Fiona's granny flat, where I've been staying with the children. At least that way I could have changed out of these.' Her face twisted in disgust as she pinched the blue cotton between finger and thumb.

Jimmy ignored her. 'I'd like you to take us through the events of yesterday evening.'

Willow sighed and blinked several times. 'This isn't easy for me. My best friend's dead.'

'I appreciate that. You've been through a very traumatic experience. But we need to understand what happened. I gather you and your husband had been living separately?'

She wiped one eye with a delicate gesture. 'We'd separated. I wanted a divorce. Logan refused to move out of the family home. Fortunately, my friend was able to offer us her granny flat on a temporary basis so I went there with my children.' Her hand flew to her mouth. 'I need to get back to the children. My mother's not able to look after them properly.'

'Why did your marriage break up?' Laidlaw sounded friendly. The sort of woman you could open your heart to.

Willow sighed again. 'Logan lost his job. And

then I discovered all the lies he'd been telling me about our security. He'd been gambling. High-stakes sports betting. He'd gone through all our savings. Remortgaged the house. He hadn't paid the bloody mortgage for months. We were on the verge of bankruptcy.' A bitter edge cut through her piteousness.

'And you didn't think you could weather that together?' Jimmy again.

'No,' she said. 'Didn't somebody say, 'Trust is like virginity. You can only lose it once'? I couldn't contemplate ever being able to trust him again. About anything. So I left and started divorce proceedings.'

'How did Logan react to that?' Jimmy was soft as a cashmere shawl.

'How do you think? How would you react?'

'I'm not your husband, Mrs Henderson. How did he react? Did he become violent towards you?'

Karen couldn't swear to it, but she thought she saw a momentary shift in Willow's expression. It was gone in a flash, if it had been there at all. Willow's eyes dropped to the table. The shame of the victim to a tee. If she was acting, she was good at it.

'I went round to talk to him.' Her voice was a low monotone. 'I wanted him to see sense and move out so the children could come home with me. He said . . . he said the children could come back any time but that I wasn't welcome in the house any more. I told him there wasn't a court in the land that would support that. That he'd be thrown out on the streets as soon as my lawyer could get in front of a judge.' She covered her face with her hands for a long moment. 'He just lost it. He put his hands round my throat and squeezed.' She looked up and gazed imploringly at Jimmy. 'I thought he was going to kill me. I was choking. Everything started swimming, I felt like I was passing out. Then he let go. I fell on to the floor and the next thing? He was on his knees beside me, telling me how sorry he was.' She made a soft noise in the back of her throat.

'I got out as fast as I could. He kept apologising, said he was devastated, that it would never happen again.' A catch in her voice. Textbook stuff, Karen thought, and Jimmy would know that too. He'd seen the real thing more than enough in his work with the Murder Prevention Squad.

'And you reported that incident to the police?'

She bowed her head. 'I wanted it on the record. I was scared. Not so much for myself. For the children.'

'Has he ever been violent towards the children?' Laidlaw leaned in for the question.

Willow let out a shuddering breath. 'No,' she scoffed, 'but then he'd never been violent to me before.'

'Did you share what had happened with your friends?'

'I told Dandy. She's — she *was* my best friend. And one or two others. But Logan told everybody himself. He barged into a dinner party at a friend's house and made this melodramatic confession that he'd nearly strangled me and he was appalled at himself and he wanted everybody to know it was completely out of character and he'd never do it again.' She closed her eyes momentarily. 'It was excruciating.' A faint smile. 'I'm quite a private person. I was mortified for him as much as for myself.'

'We'll need the names of the dinner party guests.' The lawyer nodded and made a note. 'And yet you decided to confront him about the house again.' Jimmy's voice was light but the question was not.

For the first time, the lawyer broke into the interview. 'I think 'confront' is a pretty loaded term, DCI Hutton. What's wrong with 'speak to him'?'

Jimmy dipped his head in concession. 'Fair point. I apologise. What made you decide to speak to your husband about the house again?'

She'd had a chance to collect herself. 'I thought it was worth one last go. He'd been so contrite, you see. I was going to see if I could make a deal with him. I wouldn't press charges on the domestic violence if he moved out and let me move back in with the children.'

'And you decided to take Mrs Muir with you for moral support? Or as a witness if things went wrong?'

Willow shook her head. 'I didn't think things were going to go wrong. Not like that. If I'd thought for a moment . . . I'd never have let Dandy come with me.' Her voice caught again and a tear leaked out from the corner of one eye. 'But she insisted. She said Logan would never do anything if she was there. He'd be too ashamed.' She gave a raw bark of laughter. 'How wrong can you be?'

The police officers gave her a moment to collect herself. Karen couldn't quite make her mind up about Willow Henderson. Either she had a level of emotional intelligence that made the Mint look like a genius or she was a superb actor. But which was it? Karen had met plenty of self-obsessed women over the years; it wasn't a given that this was a performance, she reminded herself.

But Jimmy was talking again and she had to pay attention. 'So what happened when you and Dandy turned up at the house?'

'I let us in. It's my house as much as his. And he hadn't changed the locks. He probably couldn't afford a locksmith. We could hear the TV in the kitchen so we went straight through. He was sitting at the breakfast bar and he jumped off the stool as soon as he realised we were there. He was obviously shocked to see us. He shouted something like, 'What the fuck are you doing here?' I could tell he was rattled.' She reached out for the bottle of water in front of her and took a long draught. 'I said I wanted to make an appeal to his better side. The side that had confessed to our friends and apologised to me.'

'How did he react?' Laidlaw again.

'He didn't really say anything. I offered the deal I'd come up with and he laughed at me. He said he'd never be convicted and told me to fuck off. I said he would be, and after that happened, he'd never be allowed to see his children alone again.'

If ever a line was calculated to push an angry

man's buttons, that was it. Not that Karen had any brief for arseholes like Logan Henderson. But if Willow had done what Karen suspected, that line had probably never been delivered. That whole conversation had probably never taken place.

'You didn't think that might be a bit reckless?' Jimmy asked, mild as a spring day.

A sudden flash of anger from Willow. 'What is this? Blame the victim time? I was defending the interests of my children. Logan needs to understand who comes first in this family.'

'And how did he react to your words?'

She leaned back in her seat, wrapping her arms around herself. She looked like a woman revisiting the worst memory of her life. 'He went mad.'

36

2018 — Edinburgh

Here we go. Karen squared her shoulders and shoved her hands in her pockets. *Showtime.* 'What does that mean, exactly?' Jimmy asked. ''He went mad'?'

'He started screaming that I wasn't going to come between him and his kids. He kept shouting that. Then he said he'd see me in hell first. And it was like a switch had flicked inside him. It was like looking at a stranger, not the man I've been married to for eleven years. We keep the knife block at the end of the breakfast bar. I don't even remember how it happened, but the next thing was he had the carving knife in his hand and he was coming at me.' Her voice was rising in hysteria.

Again the interviewers waited. Then Laidlaw said, 'About how far away was he from you and Dandy?'

Willow shook her head. 'I'm rubbish at measurements. Maybe half a dozen steps away?'

'What happened next?' Laidlaw could put a toddler to sleep with that voice, Karen thought.

Willow screwed her eyes shut and gave a little sob. 'I can't bear it.'

Jardine raised a hand, palm out towards Jimmy. 'I think my client needs a break.'

Willow's eyes snapped open and she grabbed

his arm. 'No. I need to get this out of the way. I don't want to have to go through all this again.'

Aye, right, Karen thought, reaching for the Scottish double positive that signified a negative. More than anything that had gone before, this convinced her she was watching a performance. *This is a rehearsal.*

'If you're sure?' Jardine said, all expensive concern for the little woman.

'I'm sure.'

'So, tell us, Willow. Logan is coming at you with a knife. What happened next?'

A shuddering sigh. 'Dandy threw herself in front of me. She shouted something like, 'Don't be so stupid, Logan,' but he kept coming. And then Dandy was on the floor and the knife was covered in blood and there was blood everywhere and Dandy was making these whimpering, groaning noises. Like an animal in pain.' She stared at Jimmy, her face stricken. 'I'm terrified to go to sleep again in case that's what I hear in my dreams.'

It was a moment of high drama and everyone gave it space. Then Laidlaw took up the baton again. They'd got a good routine going, Karen grudgingly admitted to herself. 'How did you react to Logan attacking Dandy?'

'I wanted to hold her, to help her. But he was screaming again. Saying he was going to kill me. I wasn't thinking. I was just reacting. I backed away, round the other side of the breakfast bar and grabbed for a knife out of the block. Logan lunged at me but I ducked and then I stabbed him. Again and again. I wasn't trying to kill him.

I wasn't thinking anything. All I wanted was for it all to stop.' Now she was crying properly, big hiccupping gulps. Nose running, eyes streaming. It had taken her a while to get there but having reached her climax she was giving it her all.

Laidlaw took a packet of tissues from her pocket and offered one to Willow. She blew her nose loudly and dabbed at her eyes. 'I'm sorry. There are bits that are really clear, but most of what happened is just a horrible blur of shouting and blood.'

'I think Mrs Henderson has covered the salient points of what happened last night,' Jardine interjected. 'What she needs now is to be reunited with her children. We will of course make ourselves available for interview when you've had a chance to develop the evidence further.'

Jimmy nodded. 'Of course. This is only the beginning of a long process. And we're all hoping Mr Henderson makes enough of a recovery to be interviewed soon.' He pushed his chair back and stood. 'Can I have a private word with you, Mr Jardine?' The lawyer nodded, gathering his papers and rising. 'If you wouldn't mind waiting here, Mrs Henderson? DS Laidlaw will arrange a car to take you home.'

He ushered Jardine out of the room. Laidlaw made a note of where Willow wanted to go then turned off the recording equipment. Karen was on the move as soon as Laidlaw reached the door. They nodded to each other, then Karen walked into the interview room.

Willow half-turned and couldn't quite manage

her reaction. Her eyes narrowed and she glared at Karen. 'What are you doing here? I want my lawyer back.'

Karen sat down in the chair Jimmy had vacated. 'Not going to happen, Willow. This is strictly off the record. This conversation never happened.'

'This is nothing to do with you.'

Karen chuckled. 'You think? I'm a witness here. I can testify to what I overheard and what my response to it was. What I said to you both, and what I said to Dandy after you flounced off. Which I suspect Dandy relayed right back to you. Which made you realise you needed to get rid of her as well as Logan.'

Willow said nothing but her jaw shifted, giving her an air of defiance.

Time for a little white lie in the interests of justice. Karen forced a note of sympathy into her voice. 'I don't think you're a cold-blooded killer, in spite of what it looks like, Willow. I think you were driven to despair. You could probably get away with diminished responsibility if you come clean now.'

'How dare you?' Willow had found her anger. 'I've just watched my best friend being murdered. I had to save my life by stabbing the father of my children. And you're acting like I did all this?'

'If Logan lives, it's going to be your word against his. And even if I'm not called as a witness, I can still tell my story to the media.'

'You can't do that. You're a police officer.' There was a note of triumph in her voice.

248

'I wasn't on duty at the time. I was merely a concerned member of the public. You're not the only one who can twist the truth, Willow.'

'You're out of order. You couldn't be more wrong. I'm the victim here. What sort of monster do you take me for?' She leaned forward, her hands fists on the tabletop. 'Let me tell you, if anybody's going to the media, it'll be me. Harassed by a police officer the morning after my best friend was knifed to death in my own kitchen by my deranged husband? How do you think that will play? I'll be paying tribute to Dandy. The best friend a woman could ever have. The woman who gave her life to save her friend. I mean, really, who will they love? Me and my kids, or you?' Her lip curled. 'I can see the coverage now. I bet they've got some great pictures of you on file.'

Karen shook her head. 'You can bluster all you like, Willow. But I've been doing this long enough to know that, one way or another, the truth has a habit of rising to the surface. If you've done what I believe you've done, there'll be evidence somewhere. You'd be amazed at what forensic science can unpick these days. Or maybe it'll be something as prosaic as Dandy confiding what I said to her to someone else. Her husband. Or her real best friend, who obviously wasn't you. Because murder isn't what you do to your best friend.'

'Get out,' she hissed. 'You know nothing. You're full of shit.'

Karen stood up. 'Sure, I'll go. But this isn't over, Willow. Somebody else knows what you did. You think you've outsmarted us? Think again, lady. You've got a very small window of opportunity here to tell the truth. Otherwise, this is not going to end well for you.'

37

2018 — Edinburgh

Willow hadn't been the only one giving a performance in that interview room, Karen thought as she walked down the Pleasance towards the Cowgate. Her parting shot had been empty bluster. They'd be bloody lucky to find forensic evidence that would definitely contradict the story they'd been fed on the record.

Jimmy had been more sanguine about it. 'It all depends on whether the husband pulls through. If he tells a story that fits the forensics better than hers, we'll be in business. If he doesn't? Well, we'll cross that bridge when we come to it.' Karen had opened her mouth to protest, but he cut across her. 'The one thing I know for certain in this case is that it is not your fault. None of it.'

'So what now?'

'While we're waiting on news from the Royal, I've sent Jacqui out to talk to Edward Muir.'

'The grieving husband?'

'Aye. And he is genuinely grieving. They've got two teenage kids boarding at Gordonstoun. One of the teachers is driving them back. So Jacqui's got a wee window of having him to herself. See whether Dandy said anything about the Hendersons in the last few days. And if not, we want a list of her best buddies. The women she'd tell things to in the strictest confidence.'

251

Karen managed a tired smile. 'You know how that works, right? When you get told something in strictest confidence, you can only legally tell your other two best friends. As opposed to everybody in your Facebook friends.'

'See when you say stuff like that? It makes me realise I am never going to understand women. Anyway, if she told anybody, I'd put my money on Jacqui finding it out. She's very different from Phil, but she still gets results.'

Karen had tried her best to look pleased but felt sure she'd failed. 'That's good. Because I'm going to have to disappear into the undergrowth on this one, Jimmy. The Dog Biscuit is dying to get something solid on me, and taking an active part in this investigation is exactly the kind of thing she'd love to beat me up with.'

'I get that, Karen. But you can still make a valuable contribution from behind the scenes. Gonnae let me keep you up to speed, pick your brains when I need to?'

They'd parted outside St Leonard's with Karen reluctantly agreeing to lurk in the shadows of Jimmy's case. She turned right on the Royal Mile, edging through the hapless knots of tourists who blocked its pavements all year round these days, fascinated by the endless parade of shops selling tartan knick-knacks, shortbread in every conceivable shape and overpriced whisky. There were times when she thought people should have a walking licence. Like a driving licence only with stricter penalties for bad behaviour.

She dodged a pair of Japanese teenagers

oblivious to anything except the music on their earphones and cut down New Street. It was like time-shifting into a different city, one whose streets were available only to the natives. Her route took her round the back side of Waverley Station, under the dramatic Regent Place viaduct and up on to Leith Street, mere minutes from her office.

Karen wasn't surprised that Jason was the only person in the office. It was half past four, the cat was away and the wee sleekit McCartney had taken advantage of her absence for an early cut. She didn't embarrass the Mint by asking where the sergeant was. She subsided into her chair with a heartfelt sigh. 'What a day,' she groaned.

Jason, conversely, looked like a boy who'd found the last green triangle in the box of Quality Street. 'Maybe it would improve if you took a wee look at your email?'

'You think? That'd be a first.' Karen woke up her laptop and brought up her emails. Memos, meetings she'd learn magic to avoid, a retirement do for someone she didn't know and finally, a forwarded email from Jason. The subject line read, 'Your question'. She opened it, noting that there was an attachment that looked like a photograph.

Dear Constable Murray, she read.

Nice to talk to you earlier. It brought back a lot of good memories. It made me think. We always talk about sorting out a proper get-together whenever two or three of us from the old days meet up for a drink but we've never managed to get ourselves organised. Hearing about Joey dying so young got me thinking we shouldn't keep putting it off. You never know the day or the hour, right enough.

Anyway. Like I said, I mind the American lassie though, if I caught her name, I've got no memory of it now. Too many dunts to the head in the wrestling bouts! I didn't think I had any pictures of Joey's van, but when I went back through my box of photos, see what I found!

It's not really a photo of the van as such, but you can see it pretty clearly in the background. It's the one on the far right, black with the chrome trim. That's me in the middle, with Joey on the right and Big Tam Campbell on the left.

She didn't read any further but clicked on the download. The fifteen seconds seemed to click down at a glacial pace and then the photograph filled the left-hand side of the screen. Three men in kilts and muscle vests stood grinning at the camera with their arms round each other like the front row of a rugby scrum. She could even see the distinctive buckle on Joey's belt. Behind them, a line of half a dozen camper vans. The black one stood out from all its nondescript companions. 'Nobody thought to mention it was black,' she muttered. But that didn't matter now.

Karen grinned at Jason. 'That's terrific.'

'Third guy I spoke to,' he said. 'Somebody else thought they might have it in the background, for what it's worth. And look . . . ' He turned his screen to face her. He'd blown up the section that showed the front of the van.

It was blurred, but legible. 'You got the registration number.' For a moment, the frustrations of the day slipped away and Karen felt nothing but the pure delight of seeing a case take a leap forward. Finding out what had happened to the van might go nowhere, but equally it might be the break in the case. 'Have you spoken to your helpful contact at DVLA?'

Disappointment creased his face. 'I thought I better wait till you'd seen it. In case . . . ' Clearly there was no 'in case' that he could think of. Just a lingering lack of self-confidence.

'Fair enough.' She glanced at the clock on her computer. 'Too late to get stuck into it tonight. Chances are your lassie will be away home anyway. First thing Monday morning, though — get straight on to it.'

'You got it, boss. By the way, I checked out those emails between Alice Somerville and Hamish Mackenzie.'

'And?'

He shook his head. 'Nothing suspicious. Same as when I asked around in the pub. He seems like a genuinely nice guy. Lives on his own but he's not some weird loner. One of the old men in the pub said Hamish was always first to offer a helping hand when anybody needed it.'

'Makes a nice change. We don't get many of them in this line of work. Look, why don't you take an early cut? You've already done enough overtime this week.' Karen scoffed. 'Listen to me. As if we even have overtime in this unit. But there's not really anything else urgent right now. Go on, bugger off before I change my mind.'

'OK.' He closed his laptop and leaned back to hoick his jacket on without actually taking it off the chair. 'See you Monday morning.'

'Aye. Nice work, Jason.'

He blushed. It wasn't pretty. 'I think I'm getting better at that talking to folk on the phone thing.' Still abashed, he sidled out of the door leaving her to her thoughts. She was honest enough to find space in her head for the notion that Willow Henderson might just be telling the truth. Her cop instincts said otherwise, however. But how much of that was simply because Willow was the sort of woman she didn't have a lot of time for? Was she letting her own prejudices skew the situation?

'Give it up,' she muttered under her breath. She'd meant it when she'd told Jimmy she was backing off, but she couldn't help herself. Some cases had a way of insinuating themselves into the corners of her mind and dragging her in behind them.

But this time her ruminations were interrupted by a soft knock at the door. She frowned. She wasn't expecting anyone and she wasn't in the mood for any of the likely candidates. 'Come in,' she grumbled.

She was astonished when Hamish Mackenzie stood framed in the doorway. 'How did you get in here?' It was an instinctive response. She really didn't mean to sound quite so indignant. 'How did you get past the front desk?'

Taken aback, he stumbled over his words. 'I just bumped into . . . I ran into DC Murray. In the street. Outside.' He gave an anguished smile.

256

'I told him I had a . . . something for you. And what should I do? And he walked back with me and brought me through.' The last sentence in a rush.

She stood up. 'Sorry, I didn't mean to be brusque. You kind of freaked me out for a moment. Members of the public are not supposed to be back here.' She gave a nervous laugh. 'Unless they're under arrest. You caught me by surprise.'

'I hoped it would be a nice surprise.'

Now she had the chance to take him in, she had to admit to herself it was exactly that. His hair was tied back, glossy under the strip lights. He was dressed for town; slim-fit jeans rather than drainpipes over black trainers, a pale grey base layer under an unbuttoned Black Watch tartan shirt and a dark blue herringbone tweed jacket. And a brown leather satchel over one shoulder. She'd probably have looked twice at him if she'd seen him in the coffee shop, though possibly with a mental eye-roll. Chiding herself for being a teenager, she said, 'I like advance warning of my surprises. In my line of work, they're usually unpleasant.' But she smiled, to soften it.

'I won't keep you,' he said. 'I can see you're busy. I only wanted to bring you this.' He dug in the pocket of his jacket and came out with a small tissue-wrapped package. He handed it over with a tentative smile.

Karen had an inkling of what it contained. She unfolded the paper to reveal her missing earring. This time, her grin was wholehearted. 'Thank

257

you so much. I can't tell you how much this means to me.'

'I could tell. But it was easy enough to get it. I took off the U-bend and there it was.'

'It looks like new. Really shiny!'

He looked embarrassed. 'I buffed it up with a silver cloth.' One hand made a small gesture of inconsequence. 'No biggie.'

'But then you took the trouble to bring it round yourself. That's really kind. I don't know how to thank you.'

There was a short pause, then he looked her in the eye. 'You could buy me dinner tonight.'

38

1946 — Michigan; Mid Atlantic

It had taken him two gruelling years to save up enough money for the trip, but at last Arnie Burke was on his way. The *Queen Mary*, still fitted out as a troop ship, wasn't the most luxurious way to spend the best part of five days on the ocean, but it was still a damn sight more comfortable than his voyage back home, when he'd been ravaged by misery and loss.

He hadn't spent the two years sitting on his hands. When he hadn't been working security shifts at the Dodge plant in Hamtramck, he'd been dedicated to finding out what had happened to his diamonds. As soon as he made it to dry land, he wrote to one of his fellow Americans who was still back in Wester Ross. Halfway down his slew of inconsequentialities, he casually wondered what had happened to the kit left behind on the quayside. 'I envy whoever got their hands on those two brand-new Indians,' he'd written. 'What a pair of beauts.' Then he moved on to what it was like returning to the US, describing the joy of biting into a real hamburger and feeling the meat juices running down his chin.

It took his buddy's reply six weeks to get to him. Arnie almost tore the thin airmail pages as he searched for what he was desperate to read. It was almost at the end. 'The Brits were supposed to do a B&B on all the leftover equipment — that's Burn and Bury to you and me. They put the two fieldcraft guys in charge. But I didn't see no bikes getting burned. You ask me, those guys made the Indians disappear a different way. Come the end of the war, they're going be riding around in style! Can't blame them, I'd a done the same given half a chance. So, you got yourself a girl yet? Or are they scared off by your ugly puss?'

'The two fieldcraft guys,' he said. He could picture them. Both medium height, dark hair cropped close at the sides, both with matinee idol moustaches. One was wiry, ropes of muscle across his shoulders and down his arms. Smoked like it was going out of fashion and coughed like a goddamn dog barking. The other was well-set, broad shoulders and narrow hips, a nose that looked like it'd been broken more than once. Arnie had suffered under their tutelage for a couple of days at the start of his training. He'd had to crawl for hours across a heather moor, sun on his back and wet peat under his body. What the fuck were their names?

He fretted at that problem for days and at last it came to him when he was lying on a lumpy sofa listening to the game on the radio, Hal Newhouser pitching for the Tigers and confounding the batters with his left-handed throw. 'Kenny,' he shouted, bouncing upright and sending his ashtray flying. 'The skinny fuck. Kenny.'

It wasn't hard to get Kenny's name. He'd been

trained in deception, after all. He knew the phone number for the castle where he'd been billeted and one Sunday morning he walked into the plant, bold as brass, and let himself into the office of the secretary to the general manager. It took a while to place a transatlantic call, but he waited patiently. The phone was eventually answered by a man with a deep, clipped English voice. Arnie forced himself to sound bright and breezy. 'Good morning, sir,' he said.

'It's afternoon here,' the voice barked. 'Where are you calling from?'

'Sir, I'm calling from the Pentagon. We've just had a medal ceremony here, been giving one of our guys a silver star. He wanted to send a copy of the photograph to one of your boys who trained him up to go behind enemy lines.'

'Splendid. But what has that to do with me?'

'Well, sir, it's a little awkward. Our man can't recall your fella's surname. His Christian name is Kenny and he's one of the fieldwork trainers. Expert in camouflage, apparently.'

'You mean Kenny Pascoe? Sergeant Pascoe? That the man?'

'I guess so, if he's your fieldwork guy.'

Easy as that. It had taken him a little longer and a little bit of cash to a private eye in London to track down Kenny Pascoe. But now he knew where the man was, he could put his hand on him just as soon as he was ready.

And now he was ready.

39

2018 — Edinburgh

She hadn't meant to say yes. Yet here she was, sitting on a hard wooden chair in a quiet corner of her favourite restaurant in Leith with an untouched Arbikie Kirsty's gin and tonic in front of her, waiting for a man she barely knew. She'd walked round the block twice, lingering on the footbridge where the Water of Leith debouched into the Albert Dock, staring at nothing. But still she was early.

Was this a date? She didn't even know. She didn't get together with Phil by going on dates with him. They'd got to know each other from working together in the close camaraderie of a small team with a defined set of goals. The cold case unit in the old Fife force had been distinct from the rest of CID and they'd developed a way of working that suited the three of them. She'd been in love with Phil for a long time before anything happened between them. Turned out he'd felt the same about her, but they'd both been trapped by the conviction that the other couldn't possibly be interested in someone as uninteresting as them.

What had finally overcome that was a case whose resolution had shaken them both to the core. The mummified body of a ten-year-old girl, missing for a dozen years, had turned up stuffed into a suitcase rammed into a defunct chimney. It had come to light when a lorry had lost control on a hill and crashed into the house. The child had clearly been tortured and mutilated before she had died. The forensic evidence had nailed her stepfather, an Episcopalian minister. His wife — the girl's mother — refused to believe in his guilt. Arresting him had been a harrowing experience.

They'd gone back to Karen's house with a bottle of gin but neither of them had any appetite for the drink. It turned out their appetite was for each other. And that had been that. Apart from a certain rueful annoyance at the time they'd wasted, there were no regrets. She'd never imagined she'd find a love like this. And after he died, that was it, as far as Karen was concerned. She didn't expect another man to show any interest in her.

That Hamish Mackenzie appeared to be doing just that made her uneasy. He was a key witness in a murder case that she was investigating. She'd be a fool if she didn't consider the possibility that he might be trying to throw sand in her eyes. Even though Jason's inquiries had given him a clean bill of health, she had no way of knowing what Hamish might have to hide. Maybe he'd known Joey Sutherland. He'd have been in his teens twenty-three years ago. The perfect age to hero-worship a handsome successful athlete. He'd mentioned his grandparents had been struggling with the croft around that time. Maybe they'd taken a backhander to look the other way when someone wanted to dig a hole on their land. Then there was America. He'd lived there in his teens; there was a mystery American woman at the heart of the case. What if there was a connection in there somewhere?

And that was for starters. Hamish had gone out of his way to help the Somervilles in their greedy little treasure hunt. He'd done the same for Karen and Jason. Was anybody that straightforwardly good-hearted? Or had she become jaundiced by the job? Had she grown so underexposed to the milk of human kindness that she didn't trust it when somebody poured her a glass of it?

Maybe this was a terrible mistake, personally as well as professionally. If the Dog Biscuit knew what she was doing tonight . . . But that was the thought that brought Karen up short. She needed to remember she was her own woman. Ann Markie wasn't the arbiter of her actions. Her instincts told her Hamish Mackenzie was a decent man. Just as it told her the ACC was a self-serving careerist.

Besides, if she wasn't doing this, she'd only be fretting endlessly like a hamster on a wheel about Willow bloody Henderson. And that would be an exercise in futility if ever there was one.

Saving her from more febrile speculation, Hamish walked in, looking around with an appraising eye. He caught sight of her and waggled his fingers in a little wave. He'd swapped his shirt for a white collarless one and let his hair down. It brushed his shoulders in gentle waves. Karen wondered what it would feel like between her fingers then scolded herself for her ridiculousness.

He pulled out the chair opposite her and sat down. 'I'm not late, am I?'

'No, I'm not long here myself.' White lie, but a face-saving one.

He looked around the room, taking in the dark wood panelling and soft lighting, the well-stocked mahogany bar and the quiet mutter of conversation at the other occupied tables. 'I didn't even know this place existed. A Room in Leith.' He grinned. 'You have to admit, it doesn't sound promising.'

'I found it by accident. I like walking the city, and I came down the dockside one night and there it was. I read the menu and thought it sounded interesting, so I came back when it was open. It's become my regular Sunday brunch treat. Eggs Benedict with Stornoway black pudding.' *Shut up, for fuck's sake.*

'Sounds good to me.' The waiter hovered and Hamish asked Karen what she was drinking. 'I've heard about that. Single estate, isn't it? Farm to bottle? I'll have the same.'

'You know your gin.'

He made a face. 'Too hipster by half, that's me. What's your excuse?'

She wasn't about to tell him about her Gin Nights with Jimmy Hutton. 'I like a bit of variety.' She picked up the menu. 'Shall we?'

It turned out their taste in food was as similar as their taste in gin. Mussels to start then steak with, at Karen's insistence, a side of mac and cheese. 'Trust me, it's the best,' she insisted.

265

Hamish gave in without a fight. And he handed her the wine list.

'Your treat, your place, you choose.'

So she went with a South African Shiraz she loved. Pointed it out to the waiter and hoped he wouldn't read anything into the name — Cloof Very Sexy Shiraz. Maybe she could keep the label turned away from him.

'You've got the edge over me tonight,' he said.

'How so?'

'You know quite a lot of bits and pieces about me, but I know nothing about you except that you're a hotshot detective.'

Karen laughed. 'I don't think my boss would recognise that description. Where did you get that idea from?'

'I googled you, of course. That's what we all do, right? And there's all those stories about stone-cold cases you've cracked.' He fiddled with his fork. 'That's not nothing. Giving closure to grieving people.'

'All I do is follow where the trail leads.'

'What made you want to do this?'

And so she told him. The conviction that university wasn't for her. Nor were most of the other careers on offer. The police, she thought, would be interesting. And nobody much cared what you looked like.

'Nobody much cares what you look like in a coffee shop either,' Hamish said. 'Though I'm not quite sure why you were so worried about that.'

She was spared further discussion by the arrival of the mussels. Maybe not the best choice, she thought, staring down into the lavish bowlful. Nobody ever ate a mussel elegantly.

As if reading her mind, Hamish took his napkin from his lap and tucked it into his undershirt. 'Fatal error, a white shirt.'

Karen couldn't quite work out what it was about Hamish that made her open up so readily. She'd spent most of her adult life in a state of mild wariness, always cautious about letting people too close. Three or four close friends and Phil; that had been about the limit in recent years. But this stranger had somehow found the knack of putting her at her ease.

When the wine arrived, he caught sight of the label and laughed out loud. 'First time I've had a bottle of wine try to come on to me,' he said.

'Sorry about that. I'm a sucker for Shiraz and it's the only one on the list.'

He took a mouthful. 'Luckily the mussels are rich enough to stand up to it.'

They concentrated on their food for a couple of minutes, then Karen said, 'Now you know about me. What drew you into running coffee shops?'

'When I opened the first one you couldn't get a decent cup of coffee in Portobello. I did a degree in economics here in Edinburgh and got sucked into financial services. Didn't much like it, but the money was a big incentive to stay put, and nothing else had grabbed me.' He focused on his mussels, expertly using a pair of shells like pincers to extract the meat from the rest. 'And then the global financial crash came along and pulled the rug out from under us. All around me

267

people were being fired. They were literally staggering out of the office like they were drunk. They couldn't believe their personal gravy trains had walloped straight into the buffers.'

'You didn't see it coming?'

He shook his head, pursing his lips. 'I'm not that smart. And I wasn't far enough up the greasy pole to have inside information.'

'You got the bullet though?'

Another shake of the head. 'Somehow I escaped the cull,' he scoffed. 'Which made me very unpopular with a bunch of guys I thought were my friends.'

'So what happened?'

'I realised there was no future in an environment where the bosses cut people off at the knees when it suited them. I'd not long moved to Porty and I really liked it down there but I thought there was a definite gap in the market for a good coffee shop. I sat out the worst of the financial storm then I managed to screw a redundancy payment out of the bank and made my bid for freedom.' His mouth twisted in self-deprecation. 'I haven't worn a suit since.'

The ice was broken. The rest of the evening slipped by in easy conversation. Every now and then, Karen caught herself relaxing and enjoying herself. It wasn't how she had expected the evening to turn out. She'd anticipated awkwardness on both sides, a dawning realisation that this had been a bad idea.

Instead, apparently, it had turned out to be a rather good one.

40

2018 — Edinburgh

Jimmy Hutton had been sitting down to dinner with his wife and kids like a normal human being when he'd got the call. It'd been the first time that week that they'd had their evening meal together, but as soon as his phone rang, his teenage offspring rolled their eyes and his wife sighed. 'I sometimes wonder if you're the only DCI in Scotland,' she said. But he knew there was no rancour behind her words. She was proud of the work he did, all the effort he and his team put into protecting the lives of women and children. And even the occasional man.

When he saw Jacqui Laidlaw's name on the screen, he rose from the table to take the call. Walking into the hall, he said, 'What's happening, Jacqui?'

'Logan Henderson's off the critical list. He's been downgraded to 'serious but stable'. The doc says we can talk to him as long as we keep it brief.'

'That's good news. I'll meet you there in forty minutes.' Jimmy stuck his head back into the kitchen to apologise to the family, then set off for the Royal Infirmary. The new site was much easier for him to get to than the stately old Victorian building in the city centre. The old hospital, a dramatic Gothic pile, was about to

269

become the university's new learning hub, hemmed in by apartment blocks that gleamed with glass and money. Instead of crawling through city traffic, at this time of night he could zip round the bypass stress-free.

Laidlaw was waiting for him by the nurses' station, leaning on the counter, chatting comfortably to the two women on duty there. She was good with people, Jimmy thought. She had Phil's easy way about her. He'd been worried that her looks would put a barrier between her and the damaged and abused people they had to deal with. Sometimes people resented beauty. But her manner overcame any resistance to her allure. The bonus he hadn't expected was that men tended to dismiss her as a bimbo. He loved watching them get their comeuppance.

'Good evening, ladies,' Jimmy said cheerily. 'I believe we're good to go with Mr Henderson?'

The senior nurse gave him a cool look. 'I'll get the doctor.'

While she made the call, Jimmy drew Laidlaw to one side, his voice low. 'What do you know?'

'He picked up late afternoon. They wanted to be sure it wasn't just a flash in the pan before they let us near him. I spoke to the doc. He's a bit reluctant to let us loose on Henderson, so he wants to sit in on the interview.'

Jimmy pulled a face. He'd expected as much, but he was an eternal optimist. 'Let's hope he's not the kind that likes to prove they're in charge.'

Before he could say more, Laidlaw touched his arm and cut her eyes at the man who was coming up behind Jimmy on silent rubber soles. 'This is Doctor Gibb, sir,' she said.

Jimmy turned and extended a hand. The doctor wore green scrubs under a white coat, his stethoscope hanging round his scrawny neck. He was whip-thin, with dark smudges under his eyes and hollow cheeks that models would have died for. 'Johnny Gibb,' he said. 'You want to talk to Logan Henderson, is that right?'

'We do. We need to ask him some questions about what happened in his house last night.'

Gibb nodded. 'I appreciate your need to know, but what I need is to make sure you don't put my patient at risk. He's still very weak. So I'd appreciate it if you'd be guided by me as to when he's had enough.'

Jimmy gave his warmest smile. 'I'm in your hands, Doc. If you could just bear in mind that a woman's lying in the mortuary right now and the only voice she has is mine?'

Caught on the back foot, Gibb looked put out. But he said nothing, merely indicating with a gesture that they should follow him. Logan Henderson was in a side room at the end of the ward, distinguished by the uniformed constable sitting by the door. Inside, the blinds were drawn and the light was dim. Even so, Jimmy could see he had barely more colour than the hospital bed linen. Dark stubble stood out against his skin and an ugly bruise spread across one cheek. He was hooked up to a drip and oxygen tubes disappeared into his nostrils. When they filed in, his eyelids flickered then stayed open in narrow slits.

'Mr Henderson, I'm DCI Hutton and this is DS Laidlaw. We're investigating what happened in your house last night and — '

'That mad bitch tried to kill me,' Henderson said, his voice weak and thready. 'That's what happened. She fucking stabbed me. Over and over.' He gasped for breath.

'For the record, sir, who are we talking about here?' Laidlaw, as ever, with the gentle question.

'My fucking wife.' It wasn't much more than a whisper.

'Can we backtrack a bit? How did the incident start?'

He closed his eyes, his breathing shallow. 'I was in the kitchen. Watching the football. Sitting at the breakfast bar.'

They waited while he gathered himself.

'Then they just walked in. My wife and her sidekick. Dandy bloody Muir.' Another pause. 'Willow went straight for the knives. She grabbed two of them and came at me. Like a mad thing. I could feel the blade, going in, coming out. Again and again. Then I was on the floor and she kept at me. Kicked me in the face. Then it's all a blank.' There was a sheen of sweat on his forehead now.

Dr Gibb moved forward and checked the monitors. 'I think he's had enough.'

'One more question,' Jimmy insisted. 'Logan, what happened to Dandy?'

He frowned. 'I don't understand. Nothing happened to Dandy. The bitch just stood there. Didn't do a fucking thing to stop it.'

'Really, that's it, Officers.' Dr Gibb physically

shooed them out of the room. In the hallway, he said, 'Call us in the morning. He might be stronger then.' He turned to go, then looked back. 'That wasn't what you expected to hear, was it?'

Jimmy stared at him. Bloody everybody thought they were a detective these days. 'No comment.' With a jerk of his head, he indicated Laidlaw should follow him.

He said nothing until they were outside the hospital, heading for the car park. 'So what do you make of that?' he asked.

Laidlaw stuffed her hands in her coat pockets against the cold night air. 'Like the doc said. It wasn't what I expected to hear. What about you, sir?'

'It makes me think Karen's theory might be right. That Willow set this up. Logan Henderson wasn't meant to survive. She thought she'd done enough to see him off, then there would be nobody to contradict her version of events. But it's still going to be her word against his, unless Forensics tell us something different,' he sighed.

'It's a mess. Are we going to keep pushing Mrs Henderson?'

'Oh, I think we have to.'

'It's funny. If DCI Pirie hadn't overheard that conversation — '

Jimmy swung round and glared at her. 'Don't go there, Jacqui.'

'But it's thanks to her that we're not taking Willow Henderson at face value,' she protested. 'Where's the downside?'

'Think it through,' Jimmy urged, a note of

exasperation in his voice. He was surprised at Laidlaw. She was smart and emotionally intelligent. He'd expected her to work it out for herself. Instead, she seemed puzzled. 'If Karen hadn't warned Dandy Muir about the possibility of Willow teeing her up to be a defence witness, she might not have been in that kitchen at all. Chances are she told Willow what Karen said, so Willow decided it was more of a risk to her plan to leave Dandy alive to testify to what Karen had theorised. If Karen was the kind of cop that would have kept her mouth shut, Dandy would probably still be alive. And Willow's smart enough to have realised that. The last thing we need is the rest of the world jumping all over it. There's plenty people waiting for a stick to beat Karen with. Success never comes without enemies.'

Laidlaw looked pained. 'I get all that. But what Willow Henderson did, if she did it — it's cold, boss. Not many people have got the nerve to do something like that and not crack up afterwards.'

'I know. Most of the stuff we get in Murder Prevention is spur-of-the-moment loss of control, driven by drink or drugs. The cold-blooded stuff — that's much less common and it takes a particular kind of detachment to carry it through. A rare kind of detachment. I don't know Willow Henderson well enough yet, but she might just be one of those special ones.'

'What struck me was how little distress she showed for her friend. It's like she wanted us to focus on the husband.'

'Exactly. I'm not saying we dismiss the

possibility that her version is the truth. We need to try to keep an open mind, in spite of what Karen overheard. But right now, I'm leaning towards the notion that the husband's the one who's the victim here.'

41

2018 — Edinburgh

There was nothing quite like a classic bright blue Edinburgh morning, Karen thought as she set out for work. She'd spent Sunday with her parents, helping her dad repapering the hall, stairs and landing and the sparkle of the sea that seemed to suffuse the very air with vitality was just what she needed to recover from all the bending and stretching. Even the sandstone tenements stained grey and black with generations of pollution were burnished by the sun. It was hard not to feel a lift of the spirits on a day like this, even if murder was your bread and butter.

But it wasn't murder that was occupying her thoughts that morning as she marched briskly up Newhaven Road. She liked to vary the route she took to work, but for once she wasn't checking out her environment to see what people were up to and what changes were in the wind. Instead she was still turning over her evening with Hamish Mackenzie.

After they'd parted company outside the restaurant with a slightly awkward hug and a peck on the cheek, she'd conducted the first post-mortem on the walk home. She had to admit she'd had a good time. They'd chatted easily. They'd made each other laugh. Even after

276

a few drinks — a gin each, a shared bottle of wine and then a couple of brandies — there had been no sense of his bonhomie slipping into something less attractive. No indications of guard to be let down.

The elephant in the room was only visible to one of them. Lurking over her shoulder all through dinner was the memory of Phil. It was the first time she'd had anything approaching a date since he'd died and it was impossible to escape an uncomfortable mix of guilt and disloyalty. It didn't matter that honest pragmatism told her Phil would never have expected — or wanted — her to spend the rest of her life as a lonely grieving relict. He'd loved her; he always only wanted the best for her. Knowing it and feeling it were, however, very different states.

Karen was sure she'd buried all that well below the surface. She didn't believe Hamish had seen anything other than the uncomplicated version of herself that she'd intended to present.

The question that kept nagging her was why he was bothering with her. He was attractive, solvent, personable, unattached and apparently straight. She imagined he'd have no difficulty finding a woman to have dinner with — and more besides — who'd outclass Karen in every area. She had no illusions about herself. Men like Hamish Mackenzie didn't chase women like her.

It was hard not to believe there was another agenda in play. What better way to derail close scrutiny of a man and his life than to work his charms on the detective in charge of the investigation. She had no evidence that Hamish had anything to hide. But it was early days yet. She mustn't let herself be distracted from what she needed to do. Now *that* would be something Phil would have had plenty to say about.

She'd barely been home five minutes when her phone pinged with a text message. Karen almost hoped it was work-related. Something uncomplicated like a DNA match to a senior government minister in an unsolved murder. But no. It was from Hamish.

> Thanks for a great evening. Next time it's my
> treat.
> Hamish x

Short and to the point. No lines to read between, except that he seemed to take for granted that there would be a next time. It wasn't an unattractive proposition.

What clarified matters to some extent for Karen was that she'd slept. Maybe it was the drink. She didn't think so, because she regularly had at least that much alcohol on her Gin Nights with Jimmy. For some reason, an evening spent in Hamish's company had soothed her into sleep. And that wasn't something she could discount. Her sleep had been shattered since Phil's death. She couldn't remember the last time she'd slept soundly through the night. She'd scarcely credited it when she woke and rolled over automatically to check the time on the radio.

Now, two mornings later, she was still

re-examining her decision from all sides and still the only downside she could come up with was that there might be a secret he was hiding. After all, so was she. Only her secret didn't impact on an ongoing murder investigation.

She was at Gayfield Square before she realised, so lost was she in her circling thoughts. 'You're overthinking,' she muttered. 'Let the chips fall where they will. And get the Hoover out later.'

The empty office was testament to how fast she'd beasted up the road, driven by her churning mind. She should have been concentrating on Joey Sutherland, not the man who owned his last resting place. She'd no sooner settled in behind her screen than Gerry McCartney arrived, with, miraculously, a tray of coffees from across the road. 'Ya beauty,' Karen said, accepting the cup he offered her. She sipped gratefully. 'Oh, that's what I needed.' She looked thoughtfully at her cup. 'Though given the amount of coffee that gets drunk in here, it's about time I treated us all to those nice wee beakers that you can reuse.'

Jason arrived in time to hear this. 'I suppose the washing up'll be my job, then?'

'It's certainly not going to be mine,' McCartney said, passing a carton to Jason.

'We can all wash our own. Surely that's not beyond you guys?' The discussion was cut short by Karen's phone. It was a number she didn't recognise. An offer for recovering mis-sold PPI, or claiming compensation for a car accident she'd never had? Sighing, she took the call. To her surprise, it was Jimmy Hutton. 'Hi, Karen.'

'Have you changed your phone?'

'This is Jacqui's. One of the kids unplugged mine from the charger. Flat as a pancake. I only noticed just now.'

'Wee toerag. I blame the parents.'

'Me too. Listen, we got in for a wee word with Logan Henderson last night.'

'Really? And what did he have to say for himself?' Karen, engrossed in what Jimmy had to say was, for once, oblivious to McCartney, who was nonchalantly drinking coffee right behind her chair.

'Not very much. He's still in a bad way. On a drip and oxygen, and he's got a helluva bruise on his coupon where he says the wife kicked him when he was down. Literally.'

'OK. So what's his version of events?'

'She went for him. Unprovoked. But here's the thing. I asked him what happened to Dandy.'

'And what does he say happened to Dandy?'

'He says nothing happened to Dandy. At least, not when he was conscious.'

'That's interesting,' Karen said. 'You'd think if he was trying to act the innocent he'd find some way of pinning that on Willow.'

'There's a lot that's interesting. What I'm increasingly anxious about is that each of them is plausibly blaming the other. Unless we get some convincing forensics, we could end up with nobody getting charged here.'

'You've a long way to go before you get to that bridge, never mind across it. I think Willow's going to stick to her story, though. There was no

280

sign of her cracking when I spoke to her on Saturday. I think she's the real deal — a stone-cold killer. She'll argue that he's lying because he thinks if she goes down he'll get the kids and the house.'

'It's a persuasive line.'

'Except that she's already reported him to us for domestic violence. The courts won't hand him his kids on a plate. And he has to know that, surely?'

'Who knows? At this point, we're dancing in the dark. Anyway, I'm hoping I can talk to him again today. Let's see where that takes us. Talk to you later, Karen.'

'Thanks for the update, Jimmy.' Karen ended the call and stared frowning out of the pitiful excuse for a window. The sky was still brilliant blue. But she wasn't feeling uplifted any longer. So much for staying out of it.

42

2018 — Edinburgh

Karen had barely ended her call with Jimmy Hutton when Jason yelped like a puppy.

'Is that a happy noise or did you get your finger stuck in the drawer?' Karen asked.

'The lassie from DVLA got back to me,' he said. 'She said it was in the archived records but it wasn't hard to access. The registered owner of Joey Sutherland's van changed on December seventeenth, 1995.'

'That's three months after the Invercharron Games. Three months after anybody admits to having seen Joey. That's interesting. So who was the new owner?'

'A Shirley O'Shaughnessy. There's an address in Edinburgh. Looks like a flat.' He read out the address.

'That used to be one of the accommodation blocks at Napier. What would a student in residences want with a camper van?'

'Maybe cheaper to live in?'

'It's a big capital outlay, though. What did you say the name was?' Karen's fingers were poised over Google search.

'Shirley O'Shaughnessy. You want me to spell that?'

'I think I've got it . . . ' Karen typed swiftly. The search results were almost instantaneous.

282

She opened the first one and skimmed it. Shirley O'Shaughnessy was not at all what she expected. 'Oh,' she said. 'Now that's really interesting.' She clicked on the 'images' tab. There were plenty to choose from. She captured the oldest one she could find that was a clear likeness and attached it to an email.

'What's interesting?'

'She lives in Edinburgh but she's originally from America.'

'What? You think she might be the American who was with Joey in Invercharron?'

'There's one way to find out.'

'You going to call her?'

'Not yet. I've got a lot of ducks to get in a row before I'll be ready to talk to Ms O'Shaughnessy.' Karen searched Facebook and found half a dozen images of other women who looked a bit like Shirley O'Shaughnessy and added them to the email, deliberately jumbling them up so she wasn't first or last. She typed Ruari Macaulay's email address into the recipient's box. In the message, she asked whether he recognised any of the women in the photographs. Before hitting send, she turned to Jason: 'Ping me the email address of the guy who sent you the pic of the van, would you?'

Jason, as always, did as he was told. Karen added that address to the email and sent it off. 'Now we wait and see,' she said.

'Do you want me to start researching into her?'

Karen shook her head. 'Let's hold fire for now. No point in wasting your time if she's not the right American. I do have a wee research job for you, though. I'm beginning to think we're coming at this case from the wrong end. The roots of Joey Sutherland's murder are not in 1995. They're in 1944. Somebody put something in those bike panniers. Something valuable that they wanted back. Fifty years later, a different somebody comes to collect. We've no way of filling in the blanks at this point. But one thing we do know is that only two people knew where the bikes were buried, right?'

'Right.'

'One of them was Austin Hinde, Alice's granddad. And he still had his map. But we don't know anything about Kenny Pascoe and what happened to his map. We should have followed up on that sooner, I let myself get distracted. What I want you to do is find out what you can about Kenny Pascoe — Kenneth, presumably. We know he died in Warkworth in 1946 or '47. Get hold of a death certificate. That should give you an address, then you can check with the voters roll and get the sister's name. She might still be alive. If she is, find out where she's living.'

Jason's look of panic brought home to Karen how thin a thread this was through the past seventy years. She was about to suggest where he could start looking when the door opened. No knock. But Karen supposed if you were the Assistant Chief Constable, you could dispense with manners. Ann Markie stood framed in the doorway, elegance personified except for the thunderous expression on her face. 'Give us the room,' she said to Jason, who hastened to his feet and scurried past her. She closed the door and leaned against it. 'You don't take a telling, do you, Pirie?' Her voice was hard and cold. No wriggle room there.

Karen couldn't be bothered answering. What could she say, after all? 'No' was capitulation. But so was 'Yes'. Instead, she closed the lid of her laptop and met Markie's hostile stare.

'I hadn't realised that spending your days working cold cases meant you were entirely oblivious to the here and now. It's clearly escaped your notice that Police Scotland is under huge pressure at the moment. From the politicians, from the public, from the media. Some of us are trying to fix that. Some of us seem intent on making it worse.'

Karen gave the faintest of smiles. 'Sadly not everybody can manage the same closure rate as the HCU, ma'am.'

Two smudges of scarlet appeared along Markie's cheekbones. 'Don't get smart with me, Pirie. I'm here because, not for the first time, you are the problem, not the solution.'

It couldn't still be the issue of undermining N Division. It had to be Dandy Muir's murder. Of course it was. When nice middle-class women got stabbed in prosperous Merchiston, the great and the good came out of the woodwork and got on the cases of ranking officers like the Dog Biscuit. Nobody would get into Markie's ribs about collateral damage in a domestic in Pilton. But the rich paid their taxes to avoid unpleasantness like this on their doorstep. 'Not intentionally, I can assure you,' Karen said, a matching edge of steel in her own voice. 'What seems to be the issue?'

'I think you know fine what the issue is. But perhaps you'd like to explain to me what you're doing interfering in a current murder case?'

'I take it you're talking about the murder of Dandy Muir and the attempted murder of Logan Henderson?' Karen kept her eyes steady.

'Why? Are there other instances of inappropriate involvement I don't know about yet?'

If Markie knew how ugly that curled lip looked, she wouldn't have done it, Karen thought. 'I had important information to pass on to the SIO,' she said. 'If I had kept quiet, that would have been about as inappropriate as it gets.'

A quick flash of surprise crossed Markie's face. 'How did you come by your information? Apart from your unrecorded interview with a witness?'

'I happened to overhear a conversation in a café between Dandy Muir and Willow Henderson. Mrs Henderson was planning to confront her husband about the family home in spite of him having previously attacked her. I felt I should warn her that this was high-risk behaviour. Which I did.'

'And that's all?'

Karen was reluctantly impressed. The Dog Biscuit was maybe sharper than she'd given her credit for. Now she was going to have to own up to the difficult part. The part that might have cost a woman her life. 'I also spoke privately to Dandy Muir. I pointed out that there was another way of reading the scenario.' She drew in a deep breath. 'That Mrs Henderson might be setting Mrs Muir up as a defence witness if she killed her husband.'

A long pause while the ACC calculated the various possible ways of playing Karen's admission. 'Why did you do that?' she eventually said.

'Murder prevention isn't just about protecting women. Mostly it is, but occasionally it's about extending that protection to men. There was something calculated about Willow Henderson that made my instincts twitch.'

'But Logan Henderson isn't dead. And Dandy Muir is.'

'It's pure chance that Henderson is alive. She stabbed him nine times.'

'Do you really think Mrs Henderson killed her best friend then attempted to do the same to her husband?' Markie scoffed, shaking her head with an air of disbelief.

Karen shrugged. 'If he'd died, would you even be considering that as an option? I don't think so. There would only be one surviving witness, and one with a credible version of events.'

Markie pursed her lips. Evidently she didn't like the possibility of having to take Karen seriously. 'Even so, confronting her without witnesses, without a record of the conversation, was completely out of order. Oh yes, DCI Pirie, I know what you got up to on Saturday. You're not the only one with sources in St Leonard's. You've undermined any possibility of us investigating this case transparently. Your improper behaviour is a gift to any defence lawyer.'

Karen shook her head. 'She's not going to tell

her lawyer about our conversation. If she does, it begs the question, what grounds did I have for suspecting her? And that opens up my conversation with Dandy, which in turn gives the prosecution the gift, as you call it, of an entry into the question of why Dandy was there in the first place.'

'To support her friend, clearly.' Markie was scornful.

'You'd think. Except that I can swear on oath that Willow refused Dandy's help. She insisted that taking anyone with her would only enrage her husband all the more. That's exactly what she said, ma'am.'

'And you think your testimony would be enough to persuade a jury that a respectable mother of two with no criminal record would murder her best friend and attempt to murder her husband just to get her house back?'

Karen couldn't help but be disgusted at her boss's lack of respect for her. 'I'm a senior police officer with a significant conviction rate. I'm one of the few police officers that gets a consistently good press in the Scottish media. What advantage do I get from giving evidence against Willow Henderson in a case that isn't even part of my remit?'

'Making your gin-drinking crony DCI Hutton look good?' Markie registered Karen's surprise. 'What? You think you can spend that much time with somebody else's husband without tongues wagging?'

Karen reared back in her seat, genuinely shocked at the offensiveness of Markie's comment. 'Jimmy Hutton doesn't need me to make him look good. He manages that all by himself. He'd look just as good putting Logan Henderson away for Dandy Muir's murder. And you'd do well to withdraw that insinuation, ma'am.'

The two women glared at each other, neither prepared to back down. 'Don't presume to threaten me, Pirie,' Markie finally blustered. 'Right now, your coat is on a very shoogly peg. Keep well away from Willow Henderson and her husband. And that's an order.'

43

2018 — Edinburgh

Left alone in her office, Karen scowled at the door. She'd disliked the Dog Biscuit before; now she heartily despised her. But even more, she despised the person who'd played Judas. There was only one person who could have betrayed her to the ACC. Laidlaw and Hutton she discounted because it was in their interests to use whatever help they could to nail a killer. But McCartney was another case altogether. He had been in the office when she'd taken the earlier call from Jimmy. He'd been close enough to have heard enough to figure out some of what was going on. Coupled with what Markie would have already known about the case, she could have stitched together enough to confront Karen with.

'Bloody Weegie,' she muttered. Her resolve to see the back of him stiffened. 'Fuck it,' she said, getting up and reaching for her coat. She couldn't bear another minute in the office. She needed to be somewhere else. Anywhere else, really.

On her way out, she passed Jason skulking by the front counter. 'All right, boss?' he said, concern outweighing wisdom.

'No,' she growled. 'I'm going out. If anybody asks, I've gone to make some other poor soul's life a misery.' Frustratingly, it wasn't possible to slam the door.

She stormed down the hill doing a passable impression of Tam O'Shanter's wife Kate — gathering her brows like gathering storm, nursing her wrath to keep it warm. McCartney was going to pay for this treachery. Every shitty tedious job she could think of would land on his toes. And every plum that should have been his would go to the Mint. He'd get the message soon enough. Maybe demand his reward from the Dog Biscuit. She allowed herself a dark smile. She'd like to see him get any change out of her.

Moments before she reached her car, her phone pinged with a message from Jimmy. Check your inbox, it read. She did, and saw Jimmy had sent her a file. She got into the driver's seat and linked her laptop to her phone's hotspot, all the better to download what turned out to be the preliminary forensics on the incident at the Henderson house.

If it had been Karen's case, she'd have wanted to kick the metaphorical office cat. The fingerprints were unhelpful. The bread knife that had killed Dandy Muir had mostly smudges. But what prints were clear belonged to Logan Henderson. It didn't prove he'd killed her; just that his hand had clasped the knife at some point. If you had a devious mind, you'd maybe think that had happened after he'd passed out. Even if they found traces of Willow's prints or DNA on the knife, it proved nothing. She'd lived in the house for years; it would be surprising if her DNA wasn't all over the bloody place. The other knife — the one that had stabbed

Henderson — was covered in Willow's prints. But there was no dispute about who had stabbed the husband. Only the circumstances were unclear, and fingerprints were silent on that subject.

Chances were the blood spatter and the DNA wouldn't be any more helpful. By her own admission, Willow Henderson had hugged Dandy Muir as she lay dead or dying. And she'd had close contact with her husband. The blood, which sometimes told a story, was an incoherent babble of smears and stains.

They'd known they'd need some forensic support if they were to prove a case against Willow Henderson. It wasn't there in this report.

Karen closed her laptop. The heat of her earlier rage had cooled to an icy shard sharp enough to split the skull of anyone unwary enough to cross her. Best to head somewhere the company would be congenial. She made a quick phone call to check that the person she wanted to see was around, then set off down the M8 for Gartcosh.

The Scottish Crime Campus was set incongruously at the heart of woodland, parkland, farmland and wetland. A modern complex, it had been designed to resemble a stylised DNA barcode. From a distance, the black-and-white stripes fostered the illusion. Karen thought it was the only thing about Police Scotland that was remotely glamorous. On the outside, at least.

Inside was more like the headquarters of a bank than a police force. People in suits walked purposefully past, clutching their laptops and tablets, eyes on the prize only they could see. Karen avoided the grimly corporate heart, heading for the labs where more than a hundred scientists and technicians harnessed the latest technology in the service of law enforcement.

Karen found Tamsin Martineau staring at a computer screen that was bigger than the TV in her flat. The bench around her held a scatter of components whose function was a mystery to Karen. Her hair was even more startling than usual. She'd forsaken her platinum spikes for a tousled rainbow array and there were even more rings and studs in her ears than before. Karen loved the notion of her more traditional colleagues encountering Tamsin for the first time.

The Australian barely glanced up when Karen's shadow fell across her desk. 'Hey,' she said. Her fingers danced across the keyboard and lines of text scrolled down the screen faster than the eye could read. Then she pushed back from the desk and grinned at Karen. 'How's it going, girl?'

'It's been better. Have you got time for a coffee?'

'Sure. This fucker is bending my brain like a pretzel. I need to step away.' She led the way to the tiny breakout area at the end of the lab where the techies made grim instant coffee. There were always good biscuits, although in Karen's view that wasn't an equivalent compensation. Personally, she'd trade a box of Tunnock's Caramel Wafers for a decent cup of coffee any day.

They sat at a table jammed in the corner and

Tamsin tore into a packet of Leibniz chocolate biscuits. 'My favourite mathematician, Leibniz,' she said. 'I mean, what's not to like about a man who invented logarithms and got such a fine biscuit named after him?'

'Never mind biscuits.'

'Heresy,' Tamsin muttered.

'I could use some help,' Karen said.

'And not even a packet of Hobnobs for a bribe.' Tamsin pouted, making the stud in her labret twinkle.

There were three things Karen loved about Tamsin. One was the love she had for cold cases, which inclined her towards helping Karen. The second was that she had weaselled her way into every nook and cranny of the Gartcosh forensic set-up, either by charm or by hacking. A modern version of 'by hook or by crook', Karen liked to think. And the third was that she held all authority in good-natured contempt.

'I'm on a mission to piss off Ann Markie even more than I have already.' It wasn't what Karen had planned to say but as soon as she'd uttered the words, she knew it was the truth.

Tamsin grinned. 'Cool. Where do we start?'

'A couple of things. One is my business. I've been lumbered with a Sergeant McCartney, literally for my sins. He dropped off some DNA samples that probably have been assigned the lowest priority possible. I want them hustled through like they mattered.'

Tamsin nodded. 'Can do. There's at least two of the DNA team who owe me massively right now.' She pulled a mock-disappointed face. 'Is that it? I thought you were going to ask me something hard.'

There was a fourth thing to love. Like River, Tamsin was infected with a curiosity for forensic science that went well beyond her own area of expertise. She talked to colleagues, she read the research literature and she inhaled and retained information like one of her own hard drives. Karen could generally be sure that whatever she needed to know, she'd get a steer in the right direction from one of the pair.

'Well, let's see how good you really are,' Karen said. Having been reluctant, now she was mustard. Taking her time with the details, she filled Tamsin in on the Henderson case.

'So there's nothing in the early forensics to suggest which one of the Hendersons is telling the truth?'

Karen shook her head. 'I expect the phones will be coming your way. Maybe there'll be something there?'

'They came in first thing this morning. I've not had a chance to do anything more than download the data on to our system. But it doesn't sound like Willow's dumb enough to have committed anything to her phone.'

'Dandy might have confided in a third party. Passed on what I suggested to her.'

'I'll look. But don't hold out too much hope. We're all a lot more savvy these days about not leaving digital traces of what we don't want to come back and bite us in the arse.' Tamsin helped herself to another biscuit. She nibbled round the edges of the chocolate, her brows drawn together in thought. 'There is one thing, though. How tall is Logan Henderson?'

It was not the question Karen had expected. 'Not sure. I can find out, though. Why?'

'In a minute. What about his wife?'

'About a hundred and sixty-five centimetres, I'd say.'

'And the murder victim?'

'More or less the same. What are you getting at?'

'Wound angles. If everybody was standing up when it all went off, the single fatal wound angle will be different. Henderson would presumably have been stabbing downwards — '

'And Willow would have been on a level. That's genius, Tamsin.' Already Karen was texting Jimmy, asking for Logan Henderson's height.

Tamsin made a rueful face. 'It's not totally straightforward. There's a lot of variables. The shape of the wound looks different when the corpse goes horizontal. Flesh moves. And it's not always a simple straight in-and-out. Plus you have the issue of how you demonstrate it.'

Crestfallen, Karen sighed. 'So we're probably screwed?'

'Give me a minute.' Tamsin pulled out her phone and was instantly absorbed by her screen. 'I heard this post-doc researcher give a five-minute presentation at a forensics expo last year . . . ' She swiped and tapped and then smiled. She turned the screen to show Karen. 'Vaseem Shah. He's a researcher at the Life Sciences Centre in Newcastle.'

The screen showed an Asian guy who looked a lot less geeky than Karen expected for a post-doctoral researcher. Cool haircut, well-groomed facial hair and stylish glasses. 'Dr Shah is currently engaged in a research project that aims to establish methods of visually realising knife wound trajectories in human bodies,' Karen read. Underneath, his email address.

'You think he can help?'

Tamsin shrugged. 'He talked a good game, albeit briefly. Depends how far along his research has gone. Whatever it is, chances are it won't be courtroom-tested, so you're going to need an open-minded fiscal who doesn't mind going out on a limb.'

'That won't be a problem. I know the very woman. But first, we need to get the evidence. I think I need to get him and River in a room together. Can you ping those details to me?'

Tamsin tapped the phone. 'Done.' She got to her feet. 'Now I've gotta go. Crims to incriminate.'

'Thanks. I owe you.'

'You do. Next time, bring some serious biscuits. Those yummy almond ones from that deli across the street from your office, maybe?'

'It's a deal.'

'You'll have that DNA tomorrow. I'll speak to the night-duty guy when I'm going off.'

Karen walked back to the car, glad she'd made the trip. Her anger was a memory now. She didn't believe in bearing grudges.

She believed in killing them where they lay.

44

2018 — Edinburgh

Karen didn't bother going back to the office. She could do what needed to be done as easily at home. Unusually, for she seldom drank alone, she mixed a gin and tonic — Wild Island Sacred Tree from Colonsay, with Fever Tree tonic — and composed an email to Vaseem Shah. She'd already spoken to Jimmy from the car on her way back, and once he'd established why she needed to know that Logan Henderson was 188 cm tall, he'd agreed this might be their best hope. Neither of them expected Willow to crack, and Jimmy's second interview with Logan Henderson hadn't produced any conclusive evidence. Right now it was his word against hers, a stalemate no prosecutor would relish.

Dear Dr Shah, it read,

> I am a detective chief inspector with Police Scotland. I am assisting a fellow DCI who is SIO on a murder + attempted murder here in Edinburgh. A forensic scientist colleague who heard you give a brief presentation of your wound-angle research has suggested you might be able to provide assistance to us. It would be helpful in the first instance if you could contact myself or DCI James Hutton.

She gave their mobile numbers and signed off. Then she forwarded the email to River with an explanatory note. If anything was to come of this, it would need the weight of her court-recognised expertise and experience behind it. Not to mention her ability to explain complex scientific details in terms that lawyers, judges and jurors could understand.

Now the evening stretched before her with nothing to interrupt her research into Shirley O'Shaughnessy, the American who had taken possession of Joey Sutherland's camper van three months after he had apparently disappeared. She'd told Jason to hold fire until they had more information, but that had mostly been because even the most cursory scan of the Google search results had indicated that investigating Shirley O'Shaughnessy was going to take them places where nobody would welcome their interest.

Karen re-ran her search and assessed the results. She settled on a major profile that had been run by one of the glossy magazines that prided itself on intelligent interviews with women who were movers and shakers in their very different fields. It dated from the previous autumn, so she expected it to be relatively up to date as well as wide-ranging.

HOUSE CAPTAIN

India Chandler meets the woman who may have the answers to the boomerang generation.

I met property tycoon Shirley O'Shaughnessy

in her latest home — a penthouse duplex perched above the bustling heart of picture-postcard Edinburgh. The vast windows of her living space have stunning views of all the Scottish capital's classic landmarks — the castle, the Scott monument, the random cluster on Calton Hill, the grand Balmoral Hotel looming over Waverley station. But in the distance, we also look north across the Georgian grid of the New Town towards some of the city's less attractive residential areas. For underneath the glamorous skirts of the Athens of the North are some very shabby shoes.

That's something Shirley is determined to change. She's spent twenty years in the property development business and to celebrate that anniversary, she's announced a collaboration with the Scottish government that she believes will revolutionise the lives of countless people.

She's about to embark on a remarkable building programme aimed not at the luxury market but at the people towards the bottom of the housing ladder. First-time buyers. Families who want somewhere decent to rent at a price they can afford. Young single people who want to make a home of their own. Homeless people who want to find a way off the streets.

We sat at a Philippe Starck Darkside table with matching chairs and sipped a light and fragrant Speyside malt whisky as Shirley explained her philosophy. 'My grandfather always said it was a gift to know when enough was enough. And I realised a while back that, you know what? I have enough. It was time to change the axis of my business away from purely making profit to spreading the good fortune I've had in life.'

Shirley may have had good fortune, but she's mostly worked for it. There was no available silver spoon for her infant mouth. She was born in Milwaukee, where her father worked on the production line in the Harley Davidson factory. In a terrible irony, he died in an accident on the freeway, riding one of the very bikes he'd helped to build. It was only weeks before Shirley's third birthday.

'My grandfather drove down to Milwaukee the very next day and took us back with him to Hamtramck in Michigan. He was head of security at the Dodge automobile plant there. It sounds grand, but really it wasn't much. He should have been so much more, but escaping a blue-collar background took more luck than ever came his way. But he worked hard and he saved hard, so when he died, his legacy was to give me a great start in life.'

Shirley's grandfather's legacy had an impact in more than material terms. He was the reason she chose to go to university in Scotland. 'My grandfather was stationed in the Highlands during the war — '

Karen drew her breath in sharply. Was this — could this be where the seeds of Joey Sutherland's death had been sown?

' — and he said it was the most beautiful part of the world he'd ever visited. And he'd been all over Europe during the war, so he reckoned he knew what he was talking about. When I was a teenager, he told me he'd put enough aside for me to come to Scotland to study. The tragedy is that he died before he got to see me graduate.'

Shirley took a degree in business studies at Napier University in Edinburgh, spending her days on the Craiglockhart Campus whose buildings had been used in the First World War as a convalescent home for shell-shocked soldiers, including the war poets Siegfried Sassoon and Wilfred Owen. The modern reimagining of the space was something that excited Shirley.

'Growing up in America, we don't have that same sense of architectural heritage. We tend to tear things down and start afresh. And that's good in some ways. But it's also important to find ways of making useful what's already in place. Craiglockhart was the first real practical demonstration I'd had of that principle.'

Inspired by that and by her desire to do something literally constructive with the money her grandfather had left her, during her second year at university Shirley went along to a property auction and bought a dilapidated Victorian villa overlooking the Leith Links park and spent all her spare time for a year restoring and repairing it.

'It was a real challenge,' she said. 'My

grandfather was good with his hands and he brought me up to be the same. But I had to learn your British plumbing and electrical systems from scratch. I did most of the work myself, apart from the roof.' She grinned, revealing an impish twinkle. 'I had to hire a bunch of guys to do that.'

What was the hardest part of the project?' 'Living in a Winnebago through an Edinburgh winter,' she said with a shiver. 'I'd ploughed all my money into the development. I had to move out of the student residences after one term because I couldn't afford the rent. So I parked the van in the tiny backyard and lived there. I have never been so cold, not even in the depths of a Midwest winter!'

But at the end of it, Shirley had something to show for all her work. She'd chosen her location well. She sold the house for more than double what she'd paid for it as a wreck. And she was on her way.

Her next purchase was a pair of 1930s semis in a quiet residential suburb. They'd been badly damaged in a fire and one of the roofers who'd worked for Shirley in Leith tipped her off that the insurance company was looking to offload them cheaply. Again she worked her magic and again she made a serious profit.

Looking at her today at 45, it's hard to imagine her in hard hat and overalls, digging a drain or rewiring a Georgian townhouse. She's elegant in a classic Armani trouser suit and Pantanetti Chelsea boots. Her hair is cut in a blunt bob — 'Only my hairdresser Sandro knows how much of my blonde is still real,' she jokes. She has the kind of natural look that takes a great deal of art to achieve. 'Part of me resents the need to look a particular way so that people will take me seriously,' she admitted. 'But part of me quite enjoys making the most of myself.'

And that's what Shirley has been doing for the last twenty years. By the time she'd completed her business degree — 'I got a 2:1,' she said. 'I kind of felt I'd let my grandfather down by not getting a first, but my mother told me to quit feeling sorry for myself because he'd have been just as proud of my business success' — she'd set up a fully fledged property company, City SOS Construction. The week after she finished her final exams, she rented an office and hired her core staff.

'My PA and my architect are still with me. I'd be lost without them. We've grown up in the business together, from small renovation projects to warehouse redevelopments and major new build sites, like the one you're sitting in now. From the outside, this still looks like a grand Victorian building. But that's only a façade. The whole of the interior has been built from scratch, to modern standards, using the best of contemporary materials.'

Her empire has grown steadily, but the recent housing crisis has convinced her she needs to alter her angle of approach to the business. 'It's genuinely tragic that so many people are condemned to living in places where it's impossible to build any kind of life. So I've come up with a plan that offers a series of new possibilities. And I'm happy to say that here in Scotland, where I've made my home, we've got a government with the imagination to embrace that.'

Shirley opened her Mac Air to reveal some of her plans. First up is a development of shipping containers transformed into compact homes. They're stacked four high around a central courtyard. 'This will occupy a brownfield site that used to be a machine parts factory. Sixteen separate homes, each with a bedroom, living room, shower room and kitchen.'

She clicked on a thumbnail and showed me a gallery of interior shots. They had a surprising air of roominess. 'These are forty-foot containers, so they're actually quite spacious once they're kitted out. Everything's modular, so they'll be let at a very affordable rental. We're planning on rolling them out throughout Scotland, from big cities to smaller towns. Wherever they're needed. Which right now is pretty much everywhere.'

Another window opened on a three-storey square block, the exterior painted in earth tones with highlights in primary colours. 'This is a purpose-built block with twelve two-bedroom flats in it. These will be sold to first-time buyers and they'll have covenants forbidding their owners from letting them out. Again, we're expecting to construct quite a few of these, mostly in our cities and big towns.'

Yet another window showed a former office block, all sixties concrete and metal window frames. 'You can just see a corner of that, peeping out from behind the car park over there.' She pointed over to her left, to the ugly top corner of the building. 'We're going to transform that into studio flats. We're working with charities that support the homeless and ex-service personnel, and this building will be used to house people who need to get a toehold back into normal life. There'll be a gym and a library — the First Minister is very keen on the value of reading — and a couple of other communal spaces. This shows what you can achieve with buildings that nobody else wants any more.'

She grinned and chinked her glass against mine. 'And this is only the beginning.'

Karen pushed the laptop away from her. 'Oh shit,' she said to the night sky. 'I'm taking on Mother fucking Teresa.'

45

2018 — Edinburgh

Karen had arranged to meet Jason at the end of his street. She wanted to brief him on Shirley O'Shaughnessy outside the office where there were no disloyal ears to listen in on their conversation. Together they caught a bus to the top of Leith Walk and cut across St Andrew Square to Dishoom for Kejriwal — spicy cheese on toast with a couple of eggs. 'And two side orders of bacon,' Karen insisted. 'My treat.'

'I've never been here before,' Jason said, checking out the Bombay-style Iranian café that had been reinvented for a very different cultural landscape. Bentwood chairs and wooden screens, a conscious nod to the past, not least in the shape of tributes to the Scottish geographer and town planner Patrick Geddes, who'd spent the early 1920s in Bombay. 'Very historical. It's a bit different from your usual Indian.'

'So's the food,' Karen said. 'But listen. I didn't drag you up here so we could sit and blether about the great days of the Raj. I wanted to tell you what I've found out about Shirley O'Shaughnessy.'

'I thought we were waiting till we — '

'I know. But I was at a loose end last night and I was still raging from the Dog Biscuit, so I needed something to take my mind off that.'

He nodded, resigned. 'OK, boss. You think it was the sergeant that grassed you up to the ACC?'

'Unless it was you?' She gave him a steady look, but when she saw he was flushing with genuine hurt, she shook her head and grinned. 'Don't be daft, Jason, of course I know it wasn't you.'

'I would never . . . Honest.' He was painfully earnest. 'Not after what you've done for me. Plus, you know, I respect you.'

Karen felt guilty; sometimes she forgot how thin his skin was in unexpected areas. 'I know. Anyway. Here's what I found out.' She gave him a resume of the key points in the magazine article she'd found.

'She doesn't sound much like any kind of murderer we've ever had dealings with before,' Jason said dubiously. 'They're not usually pals with the First Minister.'

He had a point. 'And that's why we need to get this nailed down at all four corners. I read everything I could find online, and there's one or two interesting wee nuggets that might be worth pursuing. I tracked down another interview, from about ten years ago when she was doing her first big development along the coast near Dunbar. An estate of little boxes between the A1 and the railway line. I suppose if your job's in Edinburgh, they're handy for the commute. So this journalist was asking about how our Shirley got started and she talked the talk about the winter in the camper van.

'But she said a bit more about how much

she'd loved the van. She bought it, she said, from a small ad in the *Evening News*. She wasn't expecting much but it turned out to be quite the luxury van as these things go. What we need to do is find that small ad, see if her story checks out. If it doesn't — well, we've caught her out in a lie before we even get started.'

Jason looked gloomy. He knew that 'we' meant him. But he was a simple man and the arrival of his breakfast was enough to lift his spirits. 'OK,' he said, cutting into his cheese on toast. 'But I've still got that Kenny Pascoe research to finish.'

'Where are you up to?'

'I've got the address where he was living when he died. Percy Cottage, Warkworth, Northumberland. The death certificate gave TB as the cause of death. And I managed to get somebody at the Northumberland County Archives to check out the census returns for that address and it looks like his sister Evlyn lived at the same address right up to the 2011 census. Never got married. She lived there all by herself. She was on the voters roll at that address till 2015.'

Karen sighed. No family to be the repository of stories about Uncle Kenny and the motorbikes. 'Is she dead, then?'

'I don't know. That's what I've still to find out. I haven't been able to track down a death certificate.'

'So she might still be alive?'

'She might be. But I don't know where.'

'OK. Leave that for now, and concentrate on finding that small ad for the van.'

Evidently not even the spicy cheese was

compensation for that prospect. Glum-faced, Jason asked, 'Where do you think they keep the archive?'

'I don't know if they've got a physical archive. But there's an online archive for British newspapers. You can search date and subject. You'll have to plough through all the ads for a camper van or a motor home or a caravan for the three months from Invercharron games to the date DVLA registered the van to her. I know it's the kind of tedious job I should be dumping on McCartney, but I don't trust him to do it right.'

Even the Mint understood that was a compliment. He smiled as he chewed, which wasn't a pretty sight. He swallowed and said, 'If it's all online, do you want me to go home and do it there? Out of his road?'

'That's not a bad idea. And I'll deal with the weasel when he turns up. And in the meantime — ' She signalled to the waiter. 'I'm going to have another cup of chai.'

★   ★   ★

Karen wasn't someone who spent a lot of time thinking about food, but eating well always left her in a better frame of mind. So she managed to find a tight-lipped smile for McCartney when he arrived at Gayfield Square shortly after her, juggling three cartons of coffee. He looked wary and tired. She hoped it was because his conscience was bothering him but thought it was more likely to be his wife or kids giving him a hard time.

'Where's the Boy Wonder this morning?' He passed Karen a coffee and looked around, as if Jason would emerge from under a desk to claim his drink.

'Out and about on a wee job for me,' she said blandly. 'If there's an extra coffee going, I'll take it off your hands.'

He sighed, gave her the extra brew and went to his desk. He opened his laptop then whistled between his front teeth. 'Bloody hell. Miracles will never cease.' The sound of fingers tapping keys, heavy-handed and staccato. 'Have you got some serious blackmail material on the Gartcosh geeks?'

'How?' Karen didn't turn her eyes from her own screen.

'I've got the full set of DNA results through from all those red Rover interviews we did. Unbe-fucking-lievable. Do you know how long it usually takes to get DNA back from the labs? And that's on live cases, where somebody actually cares what happens.'

'People care about what happens in our cases too. The passage of time doesn't diminish the importance of getting answers.'

'I know, I know. This bastard's victims have been living with what he did to them for the best part of thirty years. And Kay McAfee's parents have only had a few weeks to get used to the idea of it finally killing her. But still, MIT never gets results this fast.'

Karen shrugged. 'I think some of the techies feel the same way I do. When people have waited years for answers, you shouldn't make them wait a single day longer than is absolutely necessary. So they do have a tendency to bump us up the queue when nobody's looking.'

He slurped his coffee. 'I'm not complaining, don't get me wrong. I'm just amazed.'

'Any joy?'

'Hold on a minute . . . ' A silence that felt longer than it ought to be. 'Bloody hell! We've got something.'

Karen was on her feet and round behind McCartney almost before he'd finished speaking. She peered over his shoulder at the screen where he was pointing to a section of the results page he'd downloaded. 'Barry Plummer. He's the Motherwell bed salesman. He wasn't on our initial list because it wasn't his car. His uncle taught him to drive in it. Gordon Chalmers, the guy from Portpatrick that died out in Spain. Shit.'

'And you thought this was a waste of time,' Karen said, with a lot less rancour than she felt. 'Turns out it might not have been such a daft idea after all.'

McCartney swung round and held his hands up, palms towards her. 'I totally concede. You were right on the money.'

'I don't want to sound all 'I told you so', but when you've been doing cold cases as long as I have, you learn that sometimes it's the wee things that didn't get noticed at the time or that seemed meaningless that give us the answers now.' She headed back to her chair.

McCartney gave her a shrewd look. 'You'd know about that.'

'Meaning what?'

He raised his eyebrows. 'Come on, Karen. The first thing everybody hears about you is how you got the cold case job in Fife in the first place.'

'Like I said, meaning what, exactly? And it's DI Pirie to you, Sergeant.' Karen felt a familiar cold weight in her stomach. No matter how many years went by, every so often some arsewipe like McCartney thought bringing up her past would make them a big man.

He looked away to the side, a badly stifled sigh filling the silence. 'You dobbed in your own boss. Who is still behind bars, by the way.'

'I know that. It's where he deserves to be.'

'So much for loyalty and teamwork.'

'In my version of teamwork, murder's a deal-breaker. And none of this is any of your business. Let's stick to the matter in hand.' She was stiff and unyielding, hiding the complex swirl of emotions that piece of her history still raised inside her. 'We've got a DNA match for Barry Plummer. But we've no samples from the other victims to compare it with? Is that right?'

McCartney nodded. 'They're missing. Probably misfiled somewhere, but unless we go through every bloody box in the storage warehouse, we've no way of getting to them.'

For the briefest of moments, Karen wondered if she hated him that much. But she'd never get away with it. He'd run straight to Markie and then Karen's chips would be well and truly pissed on. 'So this is all we've got. Is it enough, do you think?'

McCartney looked dubious. 'It's enough to

313

question him, certainly. But charge him? That's a different matter. Easy enough for him to say he was with the lassie earlier but he never battered her. Going with a hoor doesn't make you a criminal.'

'Maybe not for much longer if the Scottish government gets its act together and makes paying for sex the offence. What we need is someone to positively say, 'It was him that raped me.' Ideally more than one. What I want you to do with the rest of the day is talk to the VIPER team and get it organised for tomorrow morning. I want to set up an ID parade tomorrow. Plummer's photograph will be on record with DVLA, they can use that as their baseline. Then I want you to track down the other women we think this perpetrator raped and get as many of them as you can in here tomorrow to do an ID parade. I want at least two. Ideally more. And when you've got all that lined up, then you can arrange for Barry the bed man to come in to answer some questions.'

'You want me to find a bunch of hoors from twenty years ago and get them to stand as witnesses in an identity parade? We'll be lucky if half of them are still alive. Junkies and jakies, the most of them.'

'That's exactly what I want. And like I told you before — I don't care how dismissive you were in your MIT, but in here, Sergeant, we use the term 'sex workers'. Just like you and me, they're human beings.' She turned back to her screen and finished her first coffee. She looked over her shoulder at him. 'Are you still here?'

'Fuck's sake,' he muttered under his breath. 'Just let me print out the last known addresses.' Sighing, hammering of keys, more sighing and finally the exhalation of the laser printer. McCartney grabbed his coat and the papers and stalked out of the room.

Karen felt her shoulder muscles relax as he left. For the first time that morning, she had time and space to think.

And then the phone rang.

46

2018 — Edinburgh

The first time Karen had gone to the Edinburgh City Mortuary on the Cowgate, she'd had to look it up on her phone. She'd noticed instantly with a sense of unease that it was a mere block away in an almost straight line from the Museum of Childhood. Edinburgh was full of those unexpected and awkward cheek-by-jowl relationships. The house of that sanctimonious and censorious prig John Knox right across the street from the World's End pub where two of the city's most notorious murders had their beginnings. Stately Georgian houses with brothels in the basement. Both sides of the city liked to pretend the other didn't exist. It was a duality she was learning to become blasé about.

River and Vaseem Shah were both arriving by train from opposite directions within ten minutes of each other. Karen had suggested they meet by the kiosk that sold freshly baked cookies to save having to run back and forth between platforms in case of delay. She was beginning to regret that now; the smell of hot sugar and chocolate was torment to her. She knew the cookies would be a crushing disappointment but that didn't stop her wanting one. So it was a relief when River came trotting across the concourse towards her.

They embraced, but had no time for further

conversation because they were accosted by a tall Asian man who looked surprisingly like his official photograph. 'Vaseem?' Karen said.

He smiled and nodded eagerly. 'That's me.'

They all introduced themselves as Karen led the way to the station exit and round the curve of Jeffrey Street down the hill to the Cowgate and the mortuary, a modern block surrounded by some of the oldest buildings in the city.

Every step of the way, Vaseem had a question to ask or an opinion to proffer. His enthusiasm was exhausting, especially since in their earlier phone conversation Karen had already heard what he was repeating for River's benefit.

'Wound analysis isn't a simple matter, you know? It's not simply a case of looking at a wound and shoving the knife back in to see if it fits. People have tried to argue that in the past but it's a really crude method and the results are completely unreliable. There's all sorts of variables, you see. The depth of the wound is affected by the state of the blade. Not to mention the resistance offered by the organs and assorted parts of the body. Whether the victim's dressed and what they're wearing. Not to mention the speed of the blow itself. And that's just one measurement.

'The human body isn't a fixed object like a block of wood. Think of it as a bag of shopping. You stand that bag of shopping up in the kitchen and everything is neatly in its place, the way you packed it. Then you knock it over, and everything shifts into a new configuration. That's what your insides are like when you die and they lay your body down.'

He paused for breath. 'Makes sense,' Karen had said the first time. She said it again, for something to say.

'Does that mean you'll want to elevate the body?' River asked, the cold east wind blowing her red hair into her face.

'I'd like to be able to do that, yes.'

She pulled her hair into a knot at the back of her neck as she walked. 'That's not going to be straightforward.'

'No. I'll insert a soft mould of the knife blade into the wound as a holding mechanism while we do that. Once we're in place, I'll slip in a hard model of the blade then I'll study the angle via an ultrasound. The blade model shows up on the screen at the angle it was driven in.' He grinned like a small boy who's just been given all the train sets for Christmas. 'I've been experimenting with this for three years now, and I'm desperate to try it out on a real case,' he added.

'Untested in the courtroom?' River asked.

'So far, yes. Perhaps this case'll change that?'

'It's not easy, getting the courts to accept a new forensic technique.' River thrust her hands deep into the pockets of her ancient waxed jacket. She never dressed up for the city. Always looked like she'd come straight in from walking a pack of dogs on a grouse moor. Karen loved her for it.

'But people have given evidence about wounds before, surely?' Karen was puzzled.

'Opinions,' Vaseem said, in the same way he'd have said, 'tapeworms'. 'Not backed up with any scientific rigour.'

'At least we have the blade that made the

wound, which makes your job easier,' River said.

'Yes. And you said it's a wound to the heart?'

'That's my understanding, from speaking to the pathologist.'

'That's excellent from my point of view. The serosal planes and the fasciae of the pericardial sac often clearly show the shape of the wound. And that makes it much easier to plot the angle.' As he spoke, they turned the corner on to the Cowgate. 'Wow. I've never been down here before. It's like the Quayside in Newcastle. The city's on two levels. Upstairs and downstairs.'

'And we're very definitely below stairs down here,' River said.

'Except that the Parliament's just down the road. And Holyrood Palace. It's the Jekyll and Hyde city, Vaseem.' Karen gestured with her arm. 'This is us. I'm going to wait in the pub on the corner. I don't need to be in the room, and you'll have the pathology prof in there for corroboration.'

River looked momentarily surprised. 'I thought — '

'And it'll be Jimmy Hutton you'll be delivering the report to,' Karen added meaningfully.

Light dawned. 'Oh, right,' River said. 'We'll come and find you when we're done.'

'It might be a couple of hours,' Vaseem said. 'Or more.'

'I'm a very patient woman,' Karen said.

'And a very good liar,' River threw over her shoulder as they walked away.

★   ★   ★

319

Karen would have been perfectly happy to sit in a booth in the pub's afternoon lull with her book. She was currently on a Phildickian kick and the recent TV series had reminded her that she'd never read *The Handmaid's Tale*. She'd read other Atwood dystopian futures, yet somehow she'd missed the classic.

But she'd barely read a page when her phone buzzed with an email alert. If it was McCartney with some long-drawn-out bollocks about not being able to track down witnesses, she'd really struggle not to lose it with him.

It wasn't McCartney.

It was Ruari Macaulay.

Good afternoon, DCI Pirie. I was intrigued by your digital ID parade. It's been a long time since that afternoon in Invercharron, but we didn't get many attractive North Americans turning up at a relatively wee gathering like that. So I did pay attention to her. And as soon as I saw the picture of her, I recognised her right away. I'd happily swear on oath that the woman I saw with Joey Sutherland that afternoon is Number Five in your six-pack. Do let me know if you need some kind of formal statement.

It was a pleasure to meet you.

All the very best

Ruari Macaulay

Macaulay was on the money. Number five in the pack Karen had put together was everybody's favourite property tycoon, Shirley O'Shaughnessy.

Karen cautioned herself about running before she could walk. After all, they still hadn't heard from the other potential Invercharron witness, the man who had supplied the photograph of Joey's van. But they were inching closer to something. She could feel it.

Still, she couldn't help remembering Donald Rumsfeld's line about known unknowns and unknown unknowns. Satirists had had a field day when the American Secretary of State had said it. But Karen understood the point he was making. Right now, she was well aware of some of the things about Shirley O'Shaughnessy she didn't know. But what she was more concerned about was the things she didn't even know she should be trying to find out. And until she'd dragged the unknown unknowns into the light of day, there would be no satisfactory answer to the mystery of Joey Sutherland's death.

47

2018 — Edinburgh

A few hundred yards away, Jason was suffering. His attempts to find the *Edinburgh Evening News* back issues online had failed. Well, not quite failed. He'd found it at the British Newspaper Archive. But the copies they'd digitised seemed to end in 1942. He didn't want to go back empty-handed to Karen so he took another look at Google. Maybe the National Library of Scotland would have the answer.

He was struggling to make sense of the online searches when he noticed it was possible to chat live online with a librarian. It was a prospect that filled him with anxiety. His school library had been run by a cheery young woman who tried to get everyone reading and grew increasingly exasperated by lads like Jason who were only interested in football and the sort of gaming where success depended on how many corpses you could chalk up. He'd avoided the library as much as possible because he quite fancied the librarian and she made him feel guilty about his inability to get into a book.

But he was a grown man now, and although he still never read a book, he watched a lot of documentaries and movies so he wasn't totally ignorant. Hopefully the online librarian wouldn't demand to know the last book he'd read before they agreed to help him.

It turned out to be a completely painless experience. He'd explained what he was looking for and, yes, the NLS had what he needed. Yes, he could come in and look at the back copies on microfiche. They'd order them up for him right away.

The reading room, the librarian told him, was open till half past eight. He'd have at least five hours' reading time, probably more. The thought that he might need to spend five hours staring into a microfiche reader was Jason's idea of hell. He only had a hazy idea of why the boss thought it was important to verify this tiny detail from Shirley O'Shaughnessy's past. But if he'd learned one thing from working with KP Nuts, as he'd now heard her referred to by Gerry McCartney, it was that there was always a point. Anybody who thought otherwise only had to look at her clear-up record.

A couple of hours later, Jason was hunched over a microfiche machine in the library, spooling slowly through pages of small print offering vehicles for sale, accommodation to let, auction room schedules, duty pharmacists and lonely hearts. Every fifteen minutes or so he flicked a glance around to make sure no official was watching him. Then his hand crept surreptitiously into the pocket that housed a bag of wine gums and back to his mouth.

Gradually he realised there was a pattern to the arrangement of the small ads and that most of the car and caravan ads appeared on Fridays. Presumably because back in 1995, people didn't work at the weekends so they had time to go out and about viewing their potential purchases. That realisation speeded things up a little. But it was slow, painstaking work, not least because there were so few camper vans for sale that it was easy to fall into the trap of letting his eyes run down the page without really paying attention.

He stopped after an hour and a half and wandered down to the café for a cup of tea and a scone. It was almost as much of a treat to spend ten minutes not staring at lines of tiny print.

Then it was back to the endless spooling film. Three hours and forty-seven minutes into his quest, he finally found what he was looking for. He almost missed it on the first pass. But there it was. A van for sale that was the same make, model, colour and year of registration as Joey Sutherland's. There was an Edinburgh phone number but no name.

Jason quickly took out his phone and snapped a couple of photos. One close-up on the ad, one wider shot that showed the masthead at the top of the page: *Edinburgh Evening News*, 8 December 1995.

He'd done it. He wasn't quite sure what he'd done, but he'd done it.

* * *

River found Karen staring out of the window at a patch of grey sky and the corner of a tall sandstone tenement, a frown line between her eyebrows. 'You don't look happy,' she said, sliding into the booth opposite her.

Karen sighed. 'Too much unresolved stuff rattling round my head. It's my job to get evidence lined up so a fiscal can prosecute it successfully. But right now, it feels like everything's way too amorphous for that ever to happen.' She roused herself. 'But what happened back at the mortuary? How did it go?'

'I need a drink,' River said, her grin a deliberate tease. 'And so do you.' She slipped out and headed for the bar, returning with a pair of gin and tonics. 'Nothing fancy,' she reported, plonking a glass in front of Karen. 'I haven't got the energy to discuss the gin gantry with the barman.'

They clinked glasses and took a sip. 'Right,' Karen said. 'Stop teasing and tell me.'

'The prof wasn't overly impressed with the theory, it has to be said. But he's a lot more open-minded than some of his colleagues so he was at least willing to entertain it. I was worried the post-mortem would have destroyed or damaged all the potential evidence but we got lucky. Turns out Dandy Muir was Jewish and her family requested a Minimally Invasive Post-mortem.'

'What's that? You have to remember, all my bodies died back when the pathologists' only option was to slice them open.'

'It's a combination of keyhole cameras and CT scanning. Normally it's only used to investigate natural causes. But because there was no doubt about the cause of death and no other signs of violence, it was decided that they could make an exception in this case. Which was very lucky for us.'

'No kidding.' Karen tapped her fingers soundlessly on the edge of the table. She wasn't even aware of it, but River recognised it as a sign of tension she'd seen before in her friend. 'So what happened?'

'More or less what Vaseem told us. He made a pliable model of the blade then slid it in. That was actually the hardest part, easing it in along the line of the wound. Then we used one of the hoists to return the body to the vertical. I'll be honest, I wasn't convinced it would work and neither was the prof. But it did. Then he slipped the hard model of the blade in. And when he fired up the ultrasound machine, there it was, clear as anything. We could see the angle of the blade and the depth of the wound, everything.' She pulled a small piece of paper from her pocket. 'Look. See for yourself.'

Karen took the printout. She recognised the familiar grey and black static of an ultrasound background. But there in the middle of the cloudy image was the clearly defined shape of a knife blade. 'That's clever. And what does Vaseem think it tells us?'

River leaned across and traced the outline with a finger. 'The line of the blade is more or less horizontal. The blow was probably struck by someone roughly the same height as the victim. Or standing at the same level. For example, if they'd been on a flight of stairs, the height difference would be distorted.'

'But they were standing on a flat kitchen floor. And Logan Henderson's about nine or ten inches taller than Dandy Muir. Whereas Willow

326

Henderson is almost the same height.' Her voice was dull, conclusive in its tone.

'Looks like you've got an answer, then.' River took a generous pull of her drink. 'You were right.'

'I should feel pleased about that. But I really didn't want to be right. I didn't want to have to confront the idea that a woman would treat her best friend as acceptable collateral damage in a war she had nothing to do with. Willow Henderson's fight was with her husband. She wanted him out of the picture so she could move back into the big house with her kids. Because she felt entitled to that. And she was willing to pay for that with Dandy Muir's life.' She shook her head. 'You're my best friend, River. If you wanted Ewan out of your life, would you think my death was a price worth paying?'

'Of course not. And neither would anybody who wasn't a psychopath. Or desperate. And from all you've told me, Willow Henderson wasn't desperate. She's one of the exceptions, Karen. The ones you can't bargain for because they're not like the rest of us.'

Karen ran a hand through her hair. 'If he'd let her have the fucking house, none of this would have happened.'

'You can't go down that road.'

'What? All we can do is mop up afterwards?'

River sighed. 'With people like her? Probably. At least she will pay a price for what she's done. When Jimmy Hutton reads Vaseem's report, he'll have a genuine pressure point to lean on.'

Karen's smile was weary and unconvincing.

'Let's hope it's enough.' She drained her glass. 'And now I'm off to catch a train.'

'Where are you going?'

'A small dot in Northumberland called Warkworth. Nearest station's Alnmouth, an hour down the line. I've got a wild goose to chase and with a bit of luck I'll be back before bedtime.'

48

2018 — Northumberland

The River Coquet wound its way through the charming village of Warkworth on its way to the sea, and the tiny stone cottage where Kenny Pascoe had lived and died had been staring out at the estuary for the best part of three hundred years, overlooked by the arresting ruin of a medieval castle. 'It was already ancient when Shakespeare wrote about it,' Karen's taxi driver had told her as they'd swung round the corner of the main street to come face to face with its tall towers and battlements.

Karen had no idea whether the present inhabitants of Percy Cottage would know anything about Evlyn Pascoe, but she was determined to do what she could to tie up the loose end of Kenny Pascoe's map. The taxi driver was content to wait.

She rang the bell and almost immediately the door was opened by a short middle-aged man in a tweed jacket, Fleet Foxes T-shirt and jeans. He looked startled. 'You're not Eliza,' he said.

'No, I'm DCI Karen Pirie from the Historic Cases Unit.'

His surprise grew visibly, his round gold-rimmed glasses sliding down his nose. 'I don't understand. I was expecting a Northumbrian piper. What's happened to Eliza?'

'I'm nothing to do with Eliza, Mr . . . ?'

'Hall. Tobias Hall. So why are you here?'

'I'm looking for a woman who used to live here. Ms Evlyn Pascoe.'

He chuckled. 'I don't think anybody's ever called Evlyn 'Ms' before. Why are you looking for Evlyn?'

'I'd like to ask her a few questions.'

'Oh, that's very intriguing. I've never thought of Evlyn in a criminal context before. Well, as you said, she doesn't live here any more. The house got too much for her three years ago. She's eighty-eight, you know.'

'So where is she?'

'She's in a care home up the road in Lesbury. Friary View, it's called. She's got a nice room, lovely view of the oxbow on the River Aln. They're really good with the oldies there. We go up often and do a little concert for them. I'm a musician. Oh, and here comes Eliza.'

Karen turned to see a large young woman striding down the lane carrying a small leather valise. 'I'll let you get on,' she said, backing away from the door. 'Thanks for your help.'

The care home was a modern stone building, solidly built on the hillside near the station where Karen had arrived earlier. 'No need for me to wait,' the taxi driver said. 'You can walk to the station from here.' She settled up and walked into Friary View.

It smelled of lilies and furniture polish, which wasn't what she expected. A young man in a white jacket sat behind a gleaming wooden desk tapping at a keyboard. He looked up and smiled.

'Hi. How can I help you?'

Karen showed her ID and asked to see Evlyn Pascoe. He frowned. 'I'll need to ask Mrs Leatham. She's the manager. If you'll give me a minute?' He gestured towards a pair of low armchairs in the corner.

He disappeared down a corridor and returned a few minutes later with a thirty-something woman of two halves. Her shapely legs were encased in black leggings and her top half was swathed in a massive terracotta fisherman's smock. She looked as if she was about to take part in a dancing satsumas routine. Karen repeated what she'd already told the young man. Mrs Leatham seemed uncertain. 'Is this going to be upsetting for her?'

'I don't think so,' Karen said. 'It's about her brother. He died over seventy years ago.'

'Would it be all right if I sit in with you? It's just that she's a bit frail, you know? I mean, mentally she's all there, but she doesn't do well with stress.' Mrs Leatham gave a worried smile.

'I've got no objection to that,' Karen said.

The other woman thought for a moment then said decisively, 'Let's go then.'

Karen followed her down a carpeted hallway. Evlyn's room was the last door and they walked in to find her sitting by the window. Tobias Hall had been right, she did have a lovely view. Evlyn was small and shrunken, like most women of her age that Karen had encountered. Her hair was a halo of white frizz, and her face was a crumple of lines and age spots. Her cardigan was buttoned to the neck in spite of the cloying warmth of the

331

room, and her lap was covered with a tartan rug. But her expression was curious and her deep blue eyes bright.

'Evlyn, you've got a visitor,' Mrs Leatham said brightly. 'But it's somebody a bit out of the ordinary. This lady's a police officer and she wants to talk to you about something that happened a long time ago.'

'A police officer? Come for me?' Her voice was high and thin, her accent unmistakably local.

Time to take over. 'My name's Karen Pirie, and I investigate cold cases.'

'Like Trevor Eve on *Waking the Dead*? I bet you get that all the time.' Evlyn twinkled.

'I'm nicer than him,' Karen said.

'We'll see about that,' she cackled. Karen thought she'd never actually heard a laugh that deserved that name before.

Karen sat down on a stool opposite Evlyn. 'I need to ask you some questions about your brother Kenny.'

'Is this about the war?'

'I'm more interested in the period after the war.'

Evlyn shook her head. 'He never did anything criminal after the war. When he came back from the Highlands, he already had the TB that killed him. He was no good for anything in the time he had left.'

'I'm not suggesting he did anything criminal at any time.' Little white lies, but who was to know? 'Did he ever talk to you about a couple of American motorbikes that he and his friend Austin had to do with?'

'Motorbikes? I know they rode around on motorbikes up in the Highlands but I never thought they were American ones. What is it you think he's done?'

'Austin told his family that he and Kenny hid a couple of American bikes at the end of the war. They were supposed to destroy them, but they couldn't bear the idea. They each had a map of where they'd put the bikes. They were planning to go back after the war and collect them but then Kenny died and Austin didn't have the heart to go back. Did Kenny ever talk about it?'

Evlyn gave a reminiscent smile. 'That's just like him. He could never see good things going to waste.'

'After he died, did you find a map? A hand-drawn one?'

'Nothing like that,' Evlyn said. 'Some photos, a few letters and postcards, that's all.' Her face scrunched up in pain. 'He left very little behind, pet. He didn't leave much of a trace on this earth.'

'I'm sorry.'

She sighed. 'He was a happy lad. Until the TB cut him down.'

'Do you mind if I ask you about when he died? I know it's touching on things that must be painful for you to remember . . .'

'It's too long ago, pet. I can think about Kenny without the sadness now, maybe because I'm coming to the end of my own time.'

'Don't be daft, Evlyn. You've years in you yet,' Mrs Leatham said, bracing tones too loud for the room.

'I bloody hope not. I'm tired, pet. Tired right through to the bone. So what did you want to know?'

'I wondered if there was anything unusual that happened around the time he died? Did he get any unexpected letters? Visitors?'

Evlyn gripped the arm of her chair. 'No letters. There was an American came to see him, though. A couple of days before he died.'

'An American?' Was this the connection to Shirley O'Shaughnessy? Had her long shot paid off?

'Aye. He said he knew Kenny from the war. I knew they had all sorts up there in Scotland where he was doing the training, but Kenny never told tales of who he worked with and what they'd done. So I didn't think anything of it. Only, Kenny wasn't at home. I told him, I said, 'Kenny's got a hospital appointment.' He was up at the cottage hospital in Alnwick. I asked the Yank if he wanted to leave a message, but he said not to bother, he'd try and call again.'

'And did he? Call again?'

'I don't think so. I was at work the next day — I had a part-time job in the baker's shop — but Kenny never said anything about him coming back. And the next day, Kenny died. I came home from work and there he was, lying on the living room floor like he'd been trying to get up out of the chair.' She gave a regretful shake of the head. 'It's a shame he never got a last chance to talk about his time in the war.'

'Was it the TB that killed Kenny?' Karen knew the answer but she was hoping for more detail.

334

Maybe even a suggestion that it hadn't been as straightforward as it seemed?

'That's what the doctor said. They'd seen him at the hospital two days before, like I said. I knew one of the nurses there — she lived in the village, her mum had been the postie during the war. She said nobody was surprised. She said it was maybe sooner than they expected, but they all knew it was only a matter of time.'

An American, a missing map and a death that had come too soon. You didn't have to be much of a detective to have a gut reaction to that combination, Karen thought. Her job was like trying to put a jigsaw together without a picture on the box. She couldn't help feeling she'd completed a big chunk of sky.

49

1946 — Northumberland

All that way, and still he hadn't found what he was looking for. Arnie had taken the train from Southampton to London, from London to Newcastle and from Newcastle to Warkworth. Then he'd walked the mile and a half into the town and asked directions to Percy Cottage. And when he knocked, it wasn't Kenny Pascoe who answered the door but a slip of a girl who barely looked old enough to be out of school.

Arnie smiled and raised his hat. 'Hi, I'm looking for Sergeant Pascoe. We served together in the war.'

'He's not in. He's at the hospital. I'm his sister, Evlyn,' she replied. At least, that's what he thought she'd said. The accent was almost impenetrable to his ears.

'The hospital? Has he had an accident?' Please God, no. Not now.

'No, he's got the TB. He's proper poorly with it. He has to gan there for his treatment twice a week.'

'When will he be back?'

'I divn't kna. Can you come back the morrow? Or maybe the day after would be better, he's always knackered after the hospital.'

Arnie raised his hat again. 'Of course. What time is good?'

'Any time, really. I get back from work about two. I work in the bakery, in the main street. I could maybe bring some scones back. But Kenny'll be home all day.'

He walked to the station and caught a train back to Newcastle. He didn't want to stay locally; he didn't want to be quizzed about the purpose of his visit, or to be remembered. He found a cheap and cheerless boarding house near the station and passed the time lying on his bed reading a Dashiell Hammett novel and sleeping. If he'd learned one thing from his wartime exploits, it was how to wait.

He knocked on Kenny Pascoe's door a couple of minutes before ten on the appointed day. It took Pascoe a moment to place him, but as soon as he did, he broke into a smile and invited him in. Arnie followed. He'd hardly have recognised this shrunken husk as the man who had showed him how to disappear into the Scottish wilderness. Somebody once wrote something about the skull beneath the skin, and Kenny Pascoe was the living embodiment of that. His breath wheezed like a grim concertina and he looked twenty years older than he was.

In the tiny overheated living room, he fell into an armchair and signalled to Arnie to sit opposite. Arnie stayed on his feet. 'I'm not going to waste your time, Kenny. From the look of you, you don't have much left. What did you do with the bikes, Kenny?'

Pascoe's cheeks flushed a hectic red against the paper-pale skin of his face. 'I thought you'd come to see me.'

337

'I don't give a flying fuck about you, Kenny. I'm here for the bikes. And I mean to find out what you and your buddy did with them.' He took a step closer, looming over the sick man.

Pascoe shook his head. 'You're threatening a sick man over a pair of motorbikes?' His voice trembled. 'You should be ashamed of yourself.'

'Just answer me, Kenny.' Arnie's voice dropped to ominous darkness.

'We buried them,' he whispered. Then he was shaken by a bout of coughing. Arnie stepped back quickly, disgust and fear possessing him. When he recovered himself, Kenny spoke feebly. 'We sealed them in tarpaulins and crated them up. We were going to go back after the war and get them.' He coughed again. 'Divn't think I'll be doing that.' He gave a terrible skeletal smile.

'Where did you bury them?'

'In a bog.'

'Where?' Arnie almost howled.

'We drew a map so we could find it again. We've each got a copy. You're welcome to mine. It's no use to me now.' He pointed to a small Victorian writing desk. 'It's in the bureau.' Arnie turned. He took a step towards it. 'You didn't have to shout at me, you know. I'd have given you the map anyway. But you Yanks never had any manners, did you?'

Arnie swung back to face him. 'No, all we did was put our lives on the line to save your asses.'

Pascoe wheezed a laugh. 'The Russians would have done it for us if you hadn't turned up.'

Outraged, Arnie grabbed him by his lapels and hauled him to his feet. 'You ungrateful little fuck.

We saved your skin and how did you repay us? You stole our shit.'

Suddenly Pascoe's whole body shook in an uncontrollable spasm. He jerked and twitched, his face darkening as he fought for breath that wouldn't come. He grunted and wheezed and the thin sharp smell of urine rose between them. Arnie let go then, horrified not at what he'd done but at the thought of carrying the dying man's taint on himself.

For he knew Pascoe was dying. He'd seen enough death to recognise its imminence. This hadn't been what he'd planned. But there was no need to let it derail him from his purpose. Arnie took a step backwards and whirled round to face the bureau. He knew how to search without leaving a trace. And he knew he had plenty of time before Pascoe's sister came back from the bakery so no need to rush.

It took more than an hour of careful exploration and even then, he almost missed it. The map was tucked into an envelope containing a 1942 letter to Pascoe from Evlyn, writing to tell him their father had died from kidney failure following an infection. It was exactly the sort of letter you'd keep. Most people wouldn't look any further. But Arnie Burke wasn't most people.

He unfolded the fragile square of airmail paper. It was a basic outline of a handful of landscape features and a few rough squares with triangles above, which he took to be buildings. And towards the top right-hand corner, an X. No names, no indications of where precisely it might be. He checked the envelope again, then

339

noticed there were faint numbers in pencil on the back of the second page. There were ten rows, each with seven numbers. It meant nothing to him. He wasn't even certain whether it was anything to do with the map.

Still, better safe than sorry. He stuck the map and the letter back into the envelope and put it in his inside pocket. A quick reconnaissance revealed the cottage had a back door leading to a tiny yard which in turn gave on to a narrow lane that led back towards the river. Far less chance of being spotted than if he went out the front door. In less than a minute, he was walking along the bank of the Coquet, a man with nothing more on his mind than a riverside stroll on a pleasant morning. Nobody would have guessed how bitter was his disappointment.

50

2018 — Edinburgh

There was a busy bar in Stockbridge where nobody knew Karen or Jimmy Hutton. Nobody to wonder why they were huddled over a small table in the back room. Nobody to grass them up to Ann Markie. Jimmy had texted Karen on her way back from Warkworth. Now she nursed a Diet Coke, Jimmy an Irn Bru. This was a night for clear heads. And besides, Jimmy was still working.

'Where's Laidlaw?' Karen asked.

'We got a list of Dandy Muir's friends from her phone, cross-checked it with her husband. Jacqui's out trawling, seeing whether Dandy said anything to anybody about you giving her the gypsy warning.'

'Hearsay,' she said gloomily.

'Aye, but hearsay from a dead victim sometimes gets heard,' Jimmy pointed out. 'But I'm not holding my breath for Jacqui catching anything. Dandy said nothing to her husband and he reckons if she didn't tell him, she didn't tell anybody.'

Karen snorted. 'I'll never get used to the way men think they know their wives. Something like this, the husband's the last one she'd tell. Especially since the four of them moved in the same dinner party circles.'

'I hope you're right. We desperately need something more. Dr Shah's report is good stuff but, like River says, it's a new area of expertise. The court's always wary of accepting science that isn't tried and tested, then tested again.'

'It's convincing, though.'

He looked sceptical. 'Do you remember the first time the Crown presented vein pattern analysis to identify a paedophile from a photograph of his forearm? Hours of legal argument. And in spite of the sheriff finally agreeing, the jury still made their decision on witness testimony rather than the science.'

Karen nodded wearily. 'They struggled with it. Because they'd never seen vein pattern analysis on *CSI* or read about it online or in the papers. But now, the novelty's worn off and it's accepted by judges and juries. I think people are maybe a bit more open to scientific evidence these days, especially since the expert witnesses have got better at presenting the science in ways that ordinary punters can understand.'

Jimmy shook his head. 'It's as much of a struggle to get lawyers and judges to understand. This theory of Dr Shah's sounds good on paper. Looks good too. But because it's untested, the defence will do their best to demolish it. And you've got to admit, it all sounds a bit creepy. Like the return of the resurrection men. Messing about with corpses in the supposed interest of furthering our understanding.'

Karen was disappointed with Jimmy's lack of enthusiasm for the wound analysis. She'd genuinely thought he'd see it as a breakthrough, as she had. 'At least it's something to push Willow Henderson with.'

He conceded that with a dip of his head and a tip of his glass. 'I need more, though. I need another piece of evidence before I can put her under real pressure, never mind get enough to arrest her. It's frustrating, Karen. I'm pretty sure you're right about what really went down in that kitchen, but for now we're stuck.'

They sat in silence, sipping their drinks, staring glumly at the table. Karen had hoped the new evidence would move things forward. Ann Markie was coming at her from all directions and the woman wasn't going to leave her alone until Karen could protect herself with success. 'Let me know if there's anything more I can do,' she said. 'Everything I touch at the moment seems to be going nowhere. And the Dog Biscuit is snapping at my heels everywhere I turn.' She sighed. 'I don't know why she's got it in for me. River reckons she's a control freak. Trying to get me out of the HCU so she can put in one of her placemen and take all the credit for the cases the unit clears.' She fiddled with her glass. 'Maybe she's right. But it feels more personal than that.'

Jimmy fidgeted. 'Don't let her get to you. You're better than that.'

'Easy for you to say. She's not breathing down your neck, telling you your coat's on a shoogly peg.' Karen fixed him with her eyes. 'I love my job, Jimmy. I know there's not much to HCU, but I've built what there is. And me and the Mint, we do good work. I don't understand why even a control freak would want to put a spoke in my wheel. She already claims the kudos for what we do, we come under her remit. It's hard not to feel it's personal.'

Jimmy's mouth twitched expressively, as if he was holding something back that he wasn't comfortable with. Karen saw his unease. 'What is it, Jimmy? What are you not telling me? I thought we didn't keep stuff back from each other?'

He screwed his face up in an awkward grimace. 'It feels personal because it is personal.' He stood up abruptly. 'I need a proper drink. You want one?'

She nodded. What was so difficult that Jimmy needed a bracer before he could tell her? She watched him push through to the bar and catch the bartender's attention. His shoulders were tense, higher than usual.

Before long, he was back with a pair of gin and tonics. 'Millers,' he said tersely, pointing at the slice of cucumber floating in the drink.

'Never mind that. What do you know about Markie?'

'I never wanted to tell you this. Hell, Phil never wanted you to know about this.'

A cold hand of apprehension gripped Karen's heart. Phil? What had Ann Markie to do with Phil? The idea of them together filled her with dread and nausea in equal measure. 'Know about what?' she growled.

Jimmy's eyes widened in alarm. 'Nothing happened, Karen. For God's sake, you can't imagine Phil would be interested in an ice queen like Markie?'

Karen took a mouthful of her drink. It tasted

like acid on her tongue. 'Get to the point, Jimmy.'

'It was right before you and Phil got together. You remember he went on an interview techniques course at Tulliallan?' The police staff college ran regular courses on a variety of subjects, Karen had endured a few herself. They were always a mixture of genuinely useful information and annoying human interactions.

'I remember. I thought we needed to get better at accessing people's distant memories.'

'Right. Well, Markie was on the same course. She was only a DCI then. I reckon she was more interested in honing her media interview skills than in getting better at screwing information out of villains. Anyway, she took a fancy to Phil. Which was awkward for him, because she outranked him.'

'I outranked him,' Karen pointed out.

'That was different. He'd known you for years, and you never act the high heid yin the way she does. Once he realised, Phil did his best to avoid her but she did make a pass at him late one night after they'd all been in the bar. And he knocked her back in spite of her trying to pull rank on him. He said she was really pissed off with him.'

'She must have felt humiliated.' Karen couldn't help thinking herself into Ann Markie's shoes. She knew all about the pain of knock-backs, even though she'd barely ever made any kind of move on somebody she fancied. And Markie was an attractive woman. Karen guessed she wasn't accustomed to being turned down, especially in the 'what happens in

Vegas' atmosphere of Tulliallan courses.

'I suppose so. Anyway, he made it clear he wasn't interested. But less than two months later, you moved in with Phil.'

Karen sipped her drink, considering. 'She'd have been livid when she found out. He turned down the beautiful high-flying Ann Markie for a dumpy wee woman with bad hair and terrible dress sense. And zero ambition.' Karen gave a rueful laugh. 'How dare he? How would she not take that personally? That is definitely the kind of grievance that rankles. No wonder she wants to see me crawling over broken glass.'

'You're taking it very well,' Jimmy observed.

Karen shrugged. 'It's a pain in the arse to deal with. No getting away from that. But here's the thing, Jimmy. Every time she has a go at me, all I have to do is remind myself that she might have wanted Phil, but I was the one he chose. I was the one he loved. I might not have had him for as long as I wanted, but we had something she'll never have.'

'Ain't that the truth,' Jimmy said. She could see the relief in his face, in his posture. He'd been afraid she'd go off on one when he revealed the reason for the Dog Biscuit's constant hectoring, and like most men, he'd been apprehensive at the prospect of an irate and emotional woman. But she hadn't been angry. She was actually relieved to know what lay behind her boss's hostility. In truth, Karen felt a degree of sympathy for Markie.

Not enough sympathy to cut her some slack, however.

But one thing was clear. Now the final piece of the puzzle was in place, Karen understood what was really going on. That made her even more determined to get all three cases moving in the right direction. There was no way that she was going to concede any ground to Ann Markie now, no matter how hard her boss tried to make it for her.

51

2018 — Edinburgh

As soon as Karen had walked into the office, Jason had presented her with printouts of the only *Edinburgh Evening News* advertisement for a camper van that matched Joey Sutherland's home. 'Is this what you were after?' he asked eagerly.

Her face had lit up as she took in the date at the top of the page. 'Nice work, Jason.' She tucked it into the case file and leaned back in her chair, deep in thought. Then she straightened up. 'Next thing we need to find out is the actual date when she bought that place in Leith. The first one she did up. I need to talk to somebody at Registers of Scotland and get them to look up the historical data.'

'I could do that,' Jason offered. Not so long ago, he'd never have volunteered. But he was growing in confidence, becoming more assured of his ability to dig out information.

'I know you could,' Karen said. 'But I've got another job for you. Here's what I'm thinking, Jason. Shirley O'Shaughnessy spends time with Joey Sutherland at Invercharron. Three months later she becomes the registered owner of his van. DVLA confirms that. Although we know she's met Joey — hung out with him, even — she doesn't buy the van directly from him, but via a small ad in the paper. Now that is, frankly, weird.

Especially since nobody seems to have seen or spoken to Joey after Invercharron.' She raised her eyebrows interrogatively at him.

'It doesn't make sense,' Jason said, hoping that was the right answer.

'Exactly. What we need to do is find out where that van was between the Invercharron weekend and the date Shirley allegedly bought it from its previous owner.'

'She said in that interview you sent me that she lived in it that first winter she was doing places up. Parked up behind the house she bought in Leith.'

'But even if she owned the house then, she didn't officially own the van. If she did use Joey Sutherland to retrieve something valuable from those bikes and then killed him she was clearly determined to cover her tracks. She's not going to then do something so careless as to put that van anywhere connected to her until she'd made everything legal at DVLA. Do you see what I'm getting at?'

'Kind of. So where do you think the van was?'

Karen shrugged. 'Your guess is as good as mine.'

Jason laughed. 'I doubt it, boss.'

She shook her head, amused. 'Where do you hide a needle?'

'In a haystack?' Now he was confident.

'No, Jason.'

Puzzled again, he scratched his head. 'Eh?'

'You hide a needle in a case of needles.'

Light dawned. 'A caravan site,' he said. 'You'd stick it on a caravan site.'

'Exactly. I know this might be a wild goose

chase, because we're looking at a long time ago, but I want you to check out caravan sites that were around in 1995.'

Dismayed, he protested. 'There must be hundreds.'

'She won't have gone far from Edinburgh. She had to be able to access it easily when it was time to move it officially to Leith. Start with a twenty-mile radius, Jason.'

His heart sank. *Start with?* 'Even if I can get a list, nobody will remember one van twenty-odd years ago.'

'They might if it sat on their site for three months and had an attractive American owner. It's got to be worth a shot.'

'Aye, OK. But what exactly does it prove if we do find out where it was?' He was still struggling to figure out what was going on in his boss's head.

'It's another brick in the wall, Jason. And what do we do here?'

'One brick at a time,' he sighed, resigned to his fate. He turned to frown at his computer. What did people do when they wanted to find somewhere to park their caravan before there was an internet? He'd only been a lad back then; he'd never had to think about things like that. He glanced over his shoulder but Karen was already engrossed in her own research. Quickly he sent a text to his mother:

See when I was wee and we went our holidays in a caravan? How did you and dad find out about caravan sites? Before the internet, I mean.

350

Whatever his mother was doing, she always put it aside for her sons. Within a couple of minutes, a message whizzed back:

Guide Books. Out of the library. The Caravan Club had a magazine as well, but after your dad bought it one year he found out that was mainly for folk with their own caravan, not people like us just wanting to rent something for a week or two. We had some lovely holidays in caravans, remember? There was that time at Stonehaven, you were never off the beach. Are you coming for your tea on Sunday? Love, Mum.

Of course. The library. And now he'd discovered how easy it was to ask a librarian without actually having to feel awkward fronting them up, he could do that no bother. He sent his mother a quick thanks, ignoring the Sunday dinner inquiry. That could wait.

Jason connected to the service and carefully composed his question.

I'm looking for a directory of caravan sites and/or caravan pitches for hire in a twenty-mile radius of Edinburgh in 1995. Do you have any-thing that would help me? Thank you. DC Jason Murray, Historic Cases Unit, Police Scotland.

He sent it off and wondered how to look busy while waiting for an answer. Karen was deep into a phone call with somebody about property transfers, so at least he had some breathing space. He decided that what he needed was sugar, so he headed out for the vending machine outside the CID office in the main building.

By the time he returned, a half-eaten Snickers bar in his hand, Karen was adding a note to the corkboard next to her desk. 'I thought I was going to struggle,' she said. 'The guy I got on the phone sounded like he'd been there since the days of the Town Guard.' Seeing his look of bewilderment, she added, 'What they had in Edinburgh three hundred years ago before they had proper polis. But I misjudged the poor man. He was sharp as one of my dad's chisels. All those historic transactions and transfers have been digitised so the info's only a mouse-click away.' She pointed at the note. 'Ownership of the Leith property was registered in Shirley O'Shaughnessy's name on December fourth, 1995.'

'Four days before the ad went into the paper.'

'Exactly. And thirteen days before the van was registered in her name. At which point, she could legitimately park it in her own backyard.'

Jason nodded. That all made sense. But something was still bothering him. 'Why did she wait so long? Why did she not go ahead and buy the house and pretend she'd bought the van as soon as she'd killed him?'

Karen rewarded his question with a smile. 'I can think of two reasons.' She raised her eyebrows, giving him the opportunity to come up with one or more himself. But there were limits to the progress Jason had made and he was stumped.

He screwed up his face in rueful puzzlement.

'Not a scooby,' he said.

'Put yourself in her shoes. She's murdered a man she might reasonably expect to be missed. He was well known on the Highland games circuit. I imagine she'd have found out where he was due next so she could keep an eye out and see whether he turned up as a missing person in the local paper. If I was her, I'd have waited a few weeks at least to make sure nobody was looking for Joey, or if they were, they weren't looking at her.'

'That makes sense,' Jason acknowledged. 'What was the other reason?'

'She had a plan. She had a use for the van, otherwise she'd have forged Joey's signature earlier and sold it on to some unsuspecting dealer or punter, no?'

'Aye, she wanted somewhere to live on site while she was doing up the house.'

'Right. But she didn't buy a house right away, did she?'

Jason shrugged. 'Maybe there was nothing on the market that fitted the bill for what she had in mind.'

'That's possible. But maybe it's as simple as her not having the money. Maybe she needed whatever was in that bike pannier to raise the capital she needed. So she had to put the van in cold storage till she could turn the loot into cash to get started. And that, Jason, is why it's so crucial that we find out where that van was before it turned up in Leith with her name on the paperwork. So we can connect her to it at a time when she had no business being connected to it. Oh, and we need to get the original paperwork from DVLA. She must have forged Joey's signature. We need to let the document examiners loose on that.'

'You want me to sort that as well? I can do that while I'm waiting for the library to get back to me.'

'Perfect.' Before she could say more, McCartney arrived, a swagger in his walk.

'Morning,' he said. 'I've brought Plummer in. He's in interview room three with his solicitor.'

Karen looked up from her screen. 'Any luck with the ID parade?'

'I've managed to persuade two of the victims to come in. One from 1983, one from 1984.'

'If it's Plummer, how come he stopped?' Jason said.

Karen sighed. 'He probably didn't stop. He just wised up. DNA only hit the headlines as a way of identifying criminals in 1987. It's entirely possible he's been raping and battering sex workers on and off for the last thirty years. The women who work on the streets often don't report what happens to them. They think we don't take them seriously.' She shook her head. 'Mostly, they're probably right.' She stood up. 'Right then, let's see what Plummer has to say for himself. Jason, you know what you've got to do, right?'

'Aye, boss.' He turned back to his computer as Karen and McCartney left the room.

'What's the Boy Wonder up to, then?' McCartney asked casually as they walked into the main part of the station.

'Dotting 'i's and crossing 't's,' Karen said. 'Nothing for you to worry your pretty little head about. There's plenty here for you to be going on with.' She gave him her sweetest smile. 'You can leave the big picture to me.'

52

2018 — Edinburgh

Barry Plummer thrust out his chin and squared his shoulders as they walked into the interview room, as if to say, 'I'm an upstanding regular guy with nothing to hide.' What Karen saw was the kind of middle-aged guy you wouldn't give a second glance wherever you encountered him. But when she did give him a second glance, she saw muscles bunching as he clenched and unclenched his jaw. Raw red patches at the side of his fingernails where he'd chewed the skin. The twitchy bounce of his left leg as he tried to contain his anxiety. And his solicitor was a woman. It was such a sex offender cliché — get a woman to defend you, because surely a woman would never defend a man who'd committed a grievous sexual assault.

Karen drew back the chair opposite Plummer and switched on the recording equipment without saying a word. She introduced herself and McCartney, then said, 'Also present is Barry Plummer and — sorry, I don't know your name?'

'I'm Sujata Chatterjee, Mr Plummer's solicitor. I understood this was simply a further clarification of the interview my client had with Sergeant McCartney last week?' She had a nasal Glasgow twang, the sort of voice that always

356

sounds like a challenge.

'Not quite. This will be an interview under caution,' Karen said. She inclined her head towards McCartney, who solemnly intoned the familiar admonition.

'Wait a minute,' Plummer said. 'Are you arresting me, or what?'

'As I said, we want to interview you under caution so there can be no doubt about what's asked and answered.' Karen spoke firmly.

Plummer turned to his lawyer. 'Do I have to answer them?'

'You can say 'no comment' to any question you don't want to answer,' she said. 'This is Scotland. The court can draw no adverse implication from a 'no comment'. You're not under arrest and you can leave whenever you want to.'

Karen smiled. It was the kind of smile that makes small children whimper and cling to their mother's legs. 'Of course, if you did decide to leave, we probably would arrest you.'

Plummer shifted in his seat and folded his arms across his narrow chest. 'Fine. Ask away. I've got nothing to hide.'

Without taking her eyes off Plummer, Karen held out a hand to McCartney and he gave her a thin manila folder. She opened it and took out two sheets of paper. Each contained the black-and-white barcode of a DNA sample. She tapped one. 'This is the DNA sample taken from a rape victim in 1985. We believe this was one of a series of violent rapes that took place over a period of years.' She tapped the other sheet of paper. 'This is the DNA sample taken by

Sergeant McCartney from your client last week.' A pause. 'As you can see, they're a perfect match.' Plummer blinked furiously. He pursed his lips so tightly the skin around them turned white.

She leaned forwards, linking the fingers of her hands. 'I wonder, Mr Plummer, how you explain that?'

Plummer leaned towards his solicitor and mumbled something in her ear. She nodded and said, 'Was the victim of this alleged crime a sex worker?'

'Rape is rape, regardless of whether a woman is a sex worker or not.'

'I'm well aware of that, DCI Pirie. That was not my point. I ask again, was this victim a sex worker?'

Karen knew exactly where this was going. But she couldn't evade the question. 'We believe so, Ms Chatterjee.'

Plummer muttered in his lawyer's ear again. She nodded. He cleared his throat. 'I use prostitutes,' he said. 'I've got a very powerful sex drive.' A tiny smirk. 'So I might well have been with this woman. Doesn't mean I raped her. I've always paid my way. Know what I mean?' He leaned back, suddenly sure of himself.

'That's quite a coincidence. A viciously beaten rape victim with your DNA inside her, and you just happen to have had a consensual sexual transaction with her on the same night?' Karen kept her voice level, refusing to betray her contempt for Plummer.

'Coincidences happen, DCI Pirie.' Chatterjee was right in there.

'I wonder what a jury would make of it?'

Chatterjee gave a light polite laugh. 'I don't see this ever reaching a jury. Man has sex with prostitute? It's hardly hold-the-front-page material, is it? I think you're going to need a lot more evidence than that.'

'And that's exactly what we intend to acquire. Sergeant McCartney has made arrangements for an ID parade to take place this morning, here in the police station. What we need from you, Mr Plummer — '

'I'm not doing that,' he said indignantly. 'You're talking about crimes that took place thirty years ago. I look nothing like I did then.' His face was tight, either with anger or fear, Karen couldn't decide. What she did know was that beak of a nose couldn't have changed much over the years. She was confident he was still recognisable.

'I must protest.' Chatterjee added her voice to the complaint. 'My client is right. Any identification after so long an interval is seriously questionable. I doubt it would have any probative value and frankly it's a waste of time and money.'

'Well, you're getting paid for your time, and how I spend my budget is my business,' Karen said. 'All we need from Mr Plummer is a few moments in front of a video camera and then we'll take a short time to set up the VIPER system.'

'A few minutes? A short time? You've been planning this,' Chatterjee said.

'We'd be negligent if we — '

'What the hell is the VIPER system?' Plummer

cut in. 'What the hell is going on here?'

'It's very simple,' Karen said, in the tone of someone explaining to a small and rather unintelligent child. 'VIPER stands for Video Identification Parade Electronic Recording. It's a system we've been using for the last fifteen years. We have a huge database of videos of people from all over the UK. We video them looking at the camera then turning to the side to show their profiles. We've got a team of experts who put together a package of men who resemble you. Then we're going to film you doing the identical thing — face on, then turning your head. And then an officer who's never seen you and doesn't know which video is you will show the victims the set of films.'

'I'm not doing that.' Plummer pushed his chair back and half-rose before his lawyer patted his arm, indicating he should sit down. He fell back, scowling. 'I'm not doing that. You can't make me.'

'Here's how this plays out, Mr Plummer,' Karen said, her voice low and pleasant. 'Either you cooperate willingly, or I arrest you. Once I've arrested you, the law allows Police Scotland to photograph you. Once we've done that, we can make up a pack of a dozen photographs of men who look like you and show them to the witnesses. Same end result, only you've used up any possible fragment of goodwill you might have earned by helping us out. Plus you're under arrest and held in custody. Now, I suspect you've failed to mention to your wife and kids and workmates that you were coming here today.

When you don't turn up at home at your usual time, your wife might get concerned. She might call her local police station and report you missing. And then they might tell her that you're in custody, being questioned over the rape of a prostitute you've already admitted having sex with.'

'This is outrageous,' Chatterjee complained. 'How dare you threaten my client.'

'Believe me, Ms Chatterjee, if I was threatening your client, he'd know all about it. I was merely explaining to Mr Plummer the choices that are presently available to him. I believe in making informed choices, don't you, Ms Chatterjee?'

The lawyer glared at her, but Karen had left her nothing to grab hold of.

'So what's it to be, Mr Plummer? The primrose path or the hard road?'

★ ★ ★

In the end, it turned out to make no difference. Neither of the two victims was able to make a positive identification of Barry Plummer. One thought it was him but couldn't swear to it. The other, a woman wasted by years of drugs and drink and poverty, had not a clue. And even if she had, Karen knew she'd have made a terrible witness. No fiscal would have entertained a prosecution based on her testimony.

Karen and McCartney were in the HCU office when the VIPER officer came down to break the bad news. Neither had really believed they'd get a definitive result from the witnesses, but Karen had clung to the hope they might get enough to put pressure on Plummer.

This was the hardest part of working cold cases. You reviewed an unsolved crime, or some new evidence surfaced — the car registration, for example. You got a bit further down the road towards a solution. Sometimes, like today, you had a suspect your years of experience told you was almost certainly the one. But then you hit a brick wall. A different brick wall from the one the original investigators had encountered, but one that was equally solid.

'What do we do now?' McCartney answered.

Karen shook her head. 'I think we're screwed. I don't see another angle. The DNA's not enough. If the victim hadn't been a sex worker, it would maybe have taken us across the line. But Plummer's got a legitimate answer to that. The only other possibility is to go through the evidence warehouse box by box to see if we can find the samples from the other cases. That would take weeks, and even if we do find them, there's no guarantee it'll secure a conviction. I hate walking away from something because it's a budget-buster. But this is a no-brainer. We have to let it go.'

McCartney kicked the bin by his desk. It bounced off the bottom drawer with a sound like a cracked bell. 'Bastard,' he said.

'I was under the impression you thought this was a waste of time,' Karen said.

McCartney had the grace to look ashamed. 'At the beginning, aye, I did. But Plummer set my alarm bells ringing. He didn't smell right, know what I mean? And I went and talked to Kay McAfee's parents. Just to see whether any other details had surfaced over the years.' He scoffed, his mouth a twisted smile.

'Makes it real, doesn't it? When you talk to the people that have somebody to grieve for.'

He nodded. 'They never gave up hope, her mum and dad. Her old man in particular. He's well into his sixties now, but he's still fierce. He feels like they let Kay down when she was in her teens. She ran wild. You know how it goes. They're ordinary working class folk from a wee town in West Lothian, they had no idea how to cope. So they did the 'under our roof, you play by our rules', and Kay was offski. And the next thing they know is the polis are at the door, then the doctor's saying their lassie's going to be in a wheelchair for the rest of her life and, by the way, she's not going to be able to talk to you either.'

'That's hard.'

'Aye. So Billy McAfee has had thirty years of guilt as well as thirty years of rage.' McCartney ran a hand along his clean-shaven jaw. 'Talking to him, seeing that pain? I kind of got it. What you said about not wanting the people left behind to suffer one more day than necessary. And I wanted to nail Plummer for Billy McAfee.'

To her surprise, Karen felt moved by McCartney's admission. Maybe she could make something of him yet, if she could convince him that she was the one on the side of the angels rather than the Dog Biscuit. 'We can't charge

Plummer, obviously. But let's make him sweat a wee bit. Away and tell Ms Chatterjee that we need to rerun VIPER. We'll keep him hanging around for a few hours yet. Maybe long enough to make things a bit uncomfortable for him at home.' She gave a grim smile. 'Seems like the least we can do.'

53

2018 — Edinburgh

Left to her own devices, Karen turned her mind to the Joey Sutherland case. She reread everything the internet had provided but kept coming back to what the magazine profile had said about the dawn of O'Shaughnessy's property empire. According to the journalist, she'd started the business with money she'd inherited from her grandfather. If that had been the case, why did she wait so long to get going? It had taken her till halfway through her second year at Napier before she'd made her first foray into the property market.

Maybe she'd felt she had to get a better grasp of business principles before she dived in at the deep end. That was a reasonable explanation. Even a mind as naturally suspicious as Karen's had to concede that.

But maybe it was because the woman hadn't actually had the capital till much later. If the truly valuable part of her inheritance had been buried under a Highland peat bog, that would explain why she'd had to wait until she could find someone like Joey Sutherland to unearth it for her.

Karen had once watched *All the President's Men* on a wobbly VHS tape her dad had borrowed from the video rental shop years before. Her first case as a detective had turned on a forged will. While they'd been digging around the edges of the case, she'd remembered the coarse rasp of Deep Throat's voice as he'd exhorted Bernstein and Woodward to 'follow the money'. It had been the route to resolving that case, and it had remained one of the tools in her investigative box ever since.

The time had definitely come to follow Shirley O'Shaughnessy's money. But how was she going to check it out? If they ever got a case they could take to the Procurator Fiscal, forensic accountants would dissect every penny that had flowed through O'Shaughnessy's company and private accounts. But Karen didn't have that sort of expertise at her command.

If O'Shaughnessy had been Scottish, Karen would have known where to send the Mint searching for her grandfather's will. But she had no idea how these things were done in America. She was going to have to embark on a steep learning curve.

She'd barely typed 'American probate records' into the search bar when McCartney returned. A quick glance at the clock revealed he'd been gone for the best part of two hours. She'd been so absorbed in researching O'Shaughnessy's background she'd lost all track of time. 'Is Plummer still here?' she asked.

McCartney nodded. 'Chatterjee's getting kind of restive, but I pointed out she should be grateful we're not rushing things. In her client's best interests, and all that shite. Maybe give it another hour or so?'

Karen considered. 'No, I think that'd be pushing it. Away and tell him to stop cluttering up our nice tidy police station.'

The sergeant looked less than happy but knew better than to argue. 'OK. Where's the Mint, by the way?'

Karen chuckled. 'You don't give up, do you?'

He grinned back at her. 'I'm persistent. Isn't that a good quality in cold cases?'

'Touché. But never mind Jason, get rid of Plummer. We'll revisit the case at the end of next week, see if either of us has had a brainwave.'

'OK. I'll go and have a cup of tea and a bacon roll, then I'll give Plummer his marching orders.'

Karen turned back to her screen as he left. Time she did something that might lead them out of frustration to a result they could celebrate.

★   ★   ★

Gayfield Square, late afternoon. One of the few bits of metered parking in that part of town, so a car was cruising hopefully round the perimeter. As always, plenty of foot traffic, with people cutting through between London Street and Elm Row. A nice wee park in the middle with a couple of benches on the grass, at least one of which provided an uninterrupted view of the public entrance to the police station. And if it happened to be raining — which it wasn't on that particular afternoon — South Gayfield Lane tucked down the side of the nick, with one or two handy doorways for shelter.

When Barry Plummer emerged with Sujata

367

Chatterjee, they paused on the pavement outside, presumably to discuss what had happened
earlier. Perhaps to develop a strategy should there
be further developments. Neither of them noticed
that the occupant of one of the benches had
leaped to his feet when they appeared. A compact grey-haired man dressed in jeans, trainers
and a nylon blouson zipped to the neck sprinted
across the park and across the street. He was
upon them before either of them registered his
presence.

'You fucking bastard,' he howled, unzipping
his jacket and pulling out a long-bladed carving
knife. 'You fucker. You fucker.' He plunged the
knife into Barry Plummer's gut.

Plummer tried to grab the handle but he missed
and the blade sheared through his fingers as his
assailant drew it out and struck again. Plummer's
high scream mingled with the yells of the man
and the piercing wail of Sujata Chatterjee, who
was battering the attacker's back with her small
fists. He didn't seem to notice. He just kept
pulling out the knife and stabbing Plummer wherever he could reach.

Plummer sank to his knees but the man didn't
stop. He stabbed at his victim's neck and head,
red-faced, spattered and smeared with blood,
still swearing and shouting.

He was still shouting seconds later when half a
dozen police officers ran out of the public entrance,
some still struggling with their stab vests. They
grabbed him from behind and clattered him to
the ground, one of them stamping on his wrist,
forcing him to drop the knife.

Too late. It had taken less than a minute. It was over so quickly that nobody in the square even managed to capture it on their phone. But Barry Plummer was dead. Not from a stab wound, but a heart attack.

54

2018 — Edinburgh

DC Jason Murray returned to Gayfield Square in cheerful mood to find the station in an uproar. There was a crime scene tent on the pavement outside the main entrance and a scrum of reporters barely held in check by a trio of grim-faced tackety boot boys in their hi-vis jackets. He pushed his way through to the foyer, where a uniformed sergeant behind the desk glared at him. 'What's going on?' Jason asked.

'Your lot have caused bloody mayhem round here this afternoon,' the sergeant snarled at him. 'Away and get your own boss to bring you up to speed. That is if she's got a bloody clue about what's going on round here.'

Startled, Jason walked quickly down the corridor towards the HCU, dodging a harassed-looking detective emerging from a doorway holding an evidence bag containing a blood-stained knife. 'Out the road, Mint,' he barked as Jason flattened himself against the wall.

He made it to the HCU office without any further baffling encounters and found Karen on her feet, face to face with Superintendent Craig Carson, the man in charge of Gayfield Square. Karen was pink-cheeked, leaning into the conversation, her body stiff with anger.

Carson was in mid-flow when Jason walked in.

They both turned, shocked out of their confrontation. 'Out, Constable,' Carson shouted.

Jason didn't hesitate. He also didn't go far. He didn't have to put his ear to the door to hear what was going on, since neither officer was bothering to lower their voice. 'According to what my officers are telling me, William McAfee is unrepentantly rejoicing in the fact that he has murdered a man on the steps of my police station. And you think that's OK?' *Holy moly*, Jason thought.

'Of course I don't,' Karen shouted back. 'The man is clearly out of his mind with grief. He lost his daughter less than three weeks ago. She spent the best part of thirty years in a wheelchair because of what some bastard did to her. And Billy McAfee thought Barry Plummer was that bastard. That doesn't make it right but it makes it understandable.'

'And how did McAfee come to believe Barry Plummer was the man who attacked his daughter? Tell me that, DCI Pirie. Tell me how you've turned my station into a fucking circus.'

'We keep families informed if there's credible progress in a cold case, sir. That's standard practice.'

'What? You go round their house and say, 'by the way, there's this guy Plummer. We don't actually have any concrete evidence but, hey, we think he's our boy'? Is that how it goes? No wonder they call you KP Nuts.'

'Don't talk nonsense. I don't know how McAfee got Plummer's name or how he knew the man was going to be here today. But I sure as hell plan to find out.'

'You and me both. But the only source of that info is this office. Your fucking team. You've got blood on your hands, Pirie.'

The door slammed open, bouncing off the wall inside and again Jason flattened himself against a wall. At least now he had a rough outline of what was going on. He counted to a hundred then, cautiously, he edged round the door jamb. 'OK to come in now, boss?'

Karen was slumped in her chair, all the fight gone. 'You heard that, I suppose? They probably heard it on the Castle Esplanade.'

'Barry Plummer got murdered?'

Karen clenched her fists and spoke in tight sentences. 'We interviewed him. We did a VIPER. We didn't get an ID. So we had to let him walk. Kay McAfee's dad was waiting outside. He filleted him with a kitchen knife on the pavement.'

'I wondered why there was a crime scene tent. But how did he know? I mean, I get why he lost the plot, but how did he . . . ?'

Karen slammed her fists on the desk. 'Three people knew about Barry Plummer. You, me and Sergeant Gerald McCartney. And only one of us went to see the McAfees. You tell me how he found out, Jason. You tell me.'

He had never seen her so angry. They'd faced some bloody awful things in their time working together but he'd never seen this white-hot rage grip her. McCartney couldn't have picked a worse moment to walk into the office.

Karen was out of her seat in a moment. He'd

barely closed the door behind him when she was on him. She grabbed him by the lapels and slammed him against the wall. McCartney stumbled, but he didn't cave. He actually smiled. Not a nervous grin of fear, but a genuine, relaxed smile.

'Chill, guv,' he said. 'Gonnae let me go?'

Karen's response was to slam him against the wall again. This time his head connected with a thud and he yelped. 'Ouch, that fucking hurt.'

'You utter piece of shit,' Karen growled, enunciating each word with cold precision. 'A man's dead tonight because of you.' She shook him, and for an awful second, Jason thought she was going to nut him. Personally, he'd have been happy with that outcome. McCartney deserved to have his wee pointy nose spread over his grinning face.

'So? He was a thug. He was a rapist who preyed on women and destroyed their lives. I'd have thought you'd have been happy to see the back of him. You being a feminist and all that.' McCartney tried to free himself, but Karen had him fast. He'd have had to rip the lapels off his jacket to get free of her.

'You fucking told him, didn't you? After I said we'd let Plummer sweat before we released him, you told Billy McAfee we were letting him go.'

'Aye. Back when I went to see the McAfees, I told him we were pretty sure who'd destroyed his family's lives. And then, when it all fell to bits, I phoned him to say sorry, we couldn't pin it on the bastard. And aye, I might have mentioned he might be able to see the little fucker for himself if he turned up at Gayfield Square. I didn't think he was going to do him, though. I thought McAfee just wanted to let off steam. Give him a piece of his mind.'

'And how did he know which one of the people coming in and out of Gayfield Square was Barry Plummer? Did you send him a fucking photo? Because if you did — '

'I'm not stupid,' McCartney spat through tight lips. Now she'd got to him, Jason thought. 'I told him the cunt would be with his brief. An Asian woman in a suit. You don't get many of them coming in and out of here, right?'

Karen slammed him into the wall one last time. 'You disgust me.' She let him go and stepped away from him.

McCartney straightened his shoulders and brushed down his lapels. 'I don't give a shit,' he said. 'The streets are cleaner tonight. We couldn't nail Plummer so McAfee did it himself. When they hear his story, he'll get off with next to no time. Far as I'm concerned, it's a result. You said it yourself — it's our job to give people closure. That's exactly what happened out there today.'

'Get out of my office,' Karen said. 'I never want to see you in here again. You'll be suspended before the sun goes down tonight, but even if they don't can you, you will never work under my command again.'

He shrugged. 'Suits me. This is a fucking Mickey Mouse operation anyway. Youse haven't got the first idea of what it takes to be a polis out there on the streets. I might get a slap on the wrist. But the people that run the show round here, they know who gets the job done. And it's not you. You're a fucking laughing stock.'

Karen neither flushed nor flinched. Phil would have been so proud of her, Jason thought. Fuck, *he* was proud of her.

'Clear your desk and leave,' she said, stepping to one side so he could pass. He grabbed his laptop and snatched a couple of pens and a notebook out of a drawer. It couldn't have been clearer that he'd never had any intention of committing to the HCU. *Good riddance*, Jason thought.

In silence, they watched him leave. Then Karen let out a deep breath and said, 'Do you fancy a drink? I think we deserve one.'

55

2018 — Edinburgh

Karen had never felt less like turning in for work. She wasn't hungover from alcohol; they'd both lost the taste for it after the third drink. She was hungover from the rage and despair that Barry Plummer's death had provoked in her. She didn't always play strictly by the book, she acknowledged that. But she knew the difference between what she did and what McCartney had done. Bending the rules to make due process possible was light years away from setting someone up to be killed. She didn't think that was what McCartney had planned. But he'd made it possible. And that, in a way, was worse. To be so careless, so heedless of what might happen was completely alien to Karen.

And now she was going to have to carry the consequences. As she'd predicted, McCartney had been suspended pending an internal inquiry. His career would be over unless Ann Markie had his back, which was a big ask. But it was Karen's unit that was tainted by what had happened. When the finger pointed, it would be the HCU in the frame. It was already all over what Karen liked to think of as the anti-social media.

The white tent had gone from outside the police station. The forensic techs would have worked flat out to clear this particular crime scene. It didn't look good for Police Scotland to have such an unequivocal symbol of serious violent crime on their literal doorstep.

The media had dispersed too, their short attention span captured by something else. There would be a press conference later, she was sure of that. But the Dog Biscuit would hold that somewhere far away from the scene of the crime in a bid to distract people from the locus of the murder.

Some poor sod had been set the task of scrubbing the concrete pavement slabs. But the stain had penetrated the surface, and a brown shadow persisted where Barry Plummer's blood had leaked away. That was going to be a salutary reminder for a long time to come, Karen thought as she set a path for the door that avoided walking on the stigma.

She managed to make it all the way back to her office without encountering anyone. She tried to summon up some enthusiasm for the task she'd begun the previous afternoon, while Billy McAfee was wrapping a dish towel round the family carving knife and driving along the motorway to Edinburgh, his head fizzing with the need for vengeance.

She'd barely typed in her search terms when she heard a sound that filled her with dread. The brisk staccato tap of heels on vinyl flooring, heading her way. Karen braced herself as the door swung open, framing ACC Ann Markie. She looked as if she'd stepped straight out of a beauty salon after a makeover. From which Karen deduced that a press conference was imminent.

For a long moment, Markie said nothing. Her eyes scanned what she could see of Karen behind her desk, travelling from her waist to her head, disdain in the line of her mouth. 'This really is your week for dragging Police Scotland through the mire, isn't it?' she said at last.

Karen stood up. She knew her cotton jumper and black jeans were no match for Markie's perfectly tailored uniform and crisp shirt, but she really didn't care any more. She was done with feeling inferior to a woman who didn't outrank her in any of the ways that mattered to her. 'Not me,' she said calmly. 'The only person out of line here is McCartney. The man you imposed on my unit.'

'But it is your unit, DCI Pirie. You have to take responsibility for what happens here. And right now, I'd say you've got one foot in the grave.'

'Not my foot, ma'am. I'd be very happy to defend myself to Professional Standards. Because the only person at fault here is your sleekit wee lapdog.'

Markie's eyes widened. 'How dare you speak to me like that!'

Karen kept her gaze steady and her face immobile, determined not to give Markie the satisfaction of seeing the anger and hurt that burned in her gut. She knew she should say nothing, but the time for that was past. 'Because somebody has to. This unit does an important job and we do it well. We take pride in how we conduct ourselves. But you imposed an officer on my unit without consultation. He's been consistently disruptive and bad for morale. And now a man's dead because Gerry McCartney was indiscreet and reckless. Why would you impose an officer with those qualities on this unit, unless you were deliberately trying to fuck us up? And why, ma'am, would you want to fuck up an officer who actually delivers the sort of positive PR that you love to bask in?'

Markie took a step backwards. 'You are out of order, Pirie. You don't speak to a senior officer like that.'

Karen sat down. 'So report me to Professional Standards. I'll happily take the lid off this can of worms. Because you should know by this time that there are no secrets in a nick. Now, if you don't mind, I have work to do. As I'm sure you do too. Your placeman has left one hell of a mess for you to gloss over.' Beneath the desk, her legs were trembling but she was determined not to let Markie best her. The woman was in the wrong; it was as simple as that. But Karen knew she was out in the middle of the high wire without a safety net.

There was high colour in the ACC's cheeks that even her cosmetic skill failed to camouflage. 'This isn't over,' she seethed. 'You're not untouchable.'

Karen scoffed. 'That makes two of us, I suspect.' She woke her laptop from its slumber. 'If you'll excuse me. I'm sure our public will be waiting for you.' She glanced back up. 'You know, I thought having a woman boss would be a good thing. Sisters under the skin, and all that.' She gave a short bark of laughter. 'I should have been thinking Margaret Thatcher, not Nicola Sturgeon.'

379

'You're lucky I'm not recording this conversation. Next time, I will be.' And Markie turned on her heel and stalked out.

It should have felt like a victory, but instead it left Karen feeling miserable. So few women made it to the top of the tree and for every one of them who understood the importance of solidarity, there was one ready with an axe to chop any other contender off at the knees. It wasn't just lonely at the top. Sometimes it was lonely all the way from the ground up.

She held her arms out at her sides and gave her hands and wrists a good shake. The physical action made her feel as if she'd shucked off the encounter with the Dog Biscuit. She knew it wasn't that simple and that it would return to plague her later, but for now, she'd parked those complicated emotions. She was an investigator; time she did some investigating. Jason was out in the field trying to track down camper van records from 1995. The least she could do was try to come at the case from a different angle.

Karen quickly established that in Michigan, wills that had been granted probate were kept on record at the local courthouse. She knew O'Shaughnessy's grandfather had lived in Hamtramck, but she had no idea of his surname. She'd have to come at it by a circuitous route.

Shirley O'Shaughnessy had been born in Milwaukee, according to the magazine article. Karen soon discovered there were full records available digitally but she couldn't access them without ID that proved she had a right to see that particular birth certificate. She'd have to call them and persuade some clerk to give her what she needed. Once she had O'Shaughnessy's birth certificate, she could work backwards through her mother to her maternal grandfather. And from there to the will.

But it would be hours before she could set the ball rolling. Hours of sitting around waiting for the next person who felt like giving her a kicking. Karen wasn't in the mood for that. She pulled on her coat and left Gayfield Square by the car park door. At least the sun was shining now. She cut through the back lanes, doglegging her way past the prosaic backsides of elegant Georgian terraces as far as Dundas Street. Then it was up and over to Princes Street, and another climb up the Playfair Steps to the top of the Mound, blind to the spectacular views on all sides.

While she waited for the traffic lights at the Royal Mile to change, Karen took a couple of sidesteps, bringing herself alongside the statue of David Hume. Like the great philosopher himself, she was a rationalist. But it didn't hurt to follow the thousands of students and children who'd rubbed his bronze big toe to a bright shine in the superstition it would bring them knowledge and understanding. A quick glance around to make sure nobody she knew was in sight, and Karen indulged her childish whim. *God knows I need all the help I can get right now.*

And then she was across the street and on George IV Bridge. She marched on past the National Library of Scotland, where Jason was making new friends. Then she slowed. What was she doing here? This was the sort of nonsense

381

teenagers went in for, not grown women who should know better. She drew to a halt about twenty metres shy of Perk.

But why not? She was no teenager. She was a grown-up who could assert her own inclinations. She'd come this far, she might as well get a cup of coffee out of it. After all, she'd told him she occasionally popped in. Arranging her face in what she hoped was a neutral expression, Karen strolled in to the narrow coffee shop. There were half a dozen tables, most of them occupied by young people with laptops taking advantage of the free Wi-Fi. The gleaming coffee machine was behind a counter halfway along. Karen joined a short queue then ordered a flat white from a cheery barista with a tousled mop of black curls. He called her order to his colleague and as she paid him, she asked casually, 'Is Hamish about?'

The barista looked at her more carefully. 'Sorry, you missed him. He was in earlier.' He shrugged apologetically. Then he stopped and stared. 'You're the polis,' he said, laughing with delight.

'Sorry?'

'The earrings. I recognise the earrings. The big man had them sent here.'

'What do you mean, sent here?' Karen was confused.

'He had them sent here because he wasn't sure he'd be at home to sign for them. He said he was in a hurry to get them to you.'

'He bought them?'

Now it was the barista's turn to look confused. 'Well, yeah. How did you think he . . . ?'

Karen gave a breathy laugh. 'Sorry, of course, I didn't realise he'd got them mail order.'

His confusion over, the barista handed her the coffee. 'They look good. Not the kind of thing I'd expect a polis to wear, mind. I guess nobody expects you to have good taste, eh?'

'No. They really don't.'

The barista winked. 'Aye, well, you could do worse than Hamish.'

But she wasn't paying attention. She was trying to make sense of what had just been said. The barista had to have got hold of the wrong end of the stick. Maybe Hamish had bought a pair of earrings online for someone else, completely separate from her request that he try to find hers, and the barista had got mixed up.

But that made no sense, because he'd recognised the earrings and known that she was a polis. For him to have put those two things together, he had to have seen them when Hamish opened the package and also to have known they belonged specifically to her. Unless there was another police officer he was buying earrings for, which was, frankly, absurd.

Perhaps Hamish had been taken with her earrings and decided to buy them online for someone else. That almost made sense. Well, it made more sense than the notion that he'd failed to find her earring in the waste pipe so he'd tracked down another pair and bought them.

Now that really was absurd.

56

2018 — Edinburgh

Jason was learning all sorts of things about caravan sites. They didn't seem to change hands very often, for one thing. Which theoretically should have helped his cause. Except that one of the other things he learned was that they didn't always keep very accurate records. He suspected that failure might have something to do with not being entirely candid with the taxman. But even the ones that did keep reasonably thorough records didn't go as far back as 1995.

'See if you get a tax or a VAT investigation,' one motherly woman had told him gently on her family's site near Berwick Law, 'they can only go back seven years. So anything past that, we shred it at the end of every tax year.'

'Do you not remember people, though?' he'd asked.

'If they come back and rent a static year after year, we get to know them,' she conceded. 'But folk with their own van? Not really.'

'This van would have been here for maybe as much as three months. From September to December. I expect that's a quiet time for you?' Jason said. This was his fifth site; he was growing comfortable with his spiel. 'This is a picture of it.' He showed her the blown-up printout from the photograph they'd been sent and also a manufacturer's advertising shot of the van. Jason had painstakingly scanned in the ad and changed the colourways of the paintwork.

The woman was definite. 'Nice van. Doesn't ring any bells with me, though, son.'

'The driver was a young American woman. Shirley, her name was.'

'I wish I could help you.' She smiled regretfully. 'Wherever she was, I'm pretty sure it wasn't here.' She handed back the printouts. 'Good luck. You'll be needing it.'

By early afternoon he was close to the end of the list he'd extracted from the library's old guidebooks. And then, driving round the City Bypass, he saw a sign that nearly made him drive off the road. CAMPSIE'S CARAVANS AND CAMPER VANS it proclaimed. NEXT EXIT.

Jason duly turned off and followed the signs down a country lane to a site the size of a football pitch. It was a sea of camper vans, caravans and trailers. Technically, it wasn't a caravan site. But bearing in mind Karen's comment about hiding a needle, he wondered if this might be the answer. If O'Shaughnessy hadn't been living in her van, she wouldn't have needed the amenities of a site. She might have done a deal to stash it here. Like garaging a car if you were going abroad for a while.

He pulled up on the forecourt and went inside a static caravan that served as the sales office. He explained who he was and what he was looking for. He brandished the photos again. The well-upholstered man behind the metal desk didn't even bother looking.

'We dinnae do that,' he said, scratching his armpit. 'Too much hassle. I like to keep it simple. Sell a van, buy a van. Tell you what, though. There's a couple of places near the airport. They rent vans as well as buying and selling. They might be up for garaging somebody's rig.' He leaned across the desk to a pile of used envelopes and scribbled a couple of names. 'There you go, son. Don't tell them I sent you.' He cackled. 'Nobody likes a visit from the polis.'

'Unless they've nothing to hide.' Jason said sanctimoniously.

'We've all got something to hide, son. Even you.' He leered at Jason then winked. 'Shut the door on the way out.'

Jason drew a blank at the first name on the list. He could barely summon up the energy to hit the next one. He was hungry and he hadn't had sugar for at least three hours. The only thing that kept him going was the thought of how he'd get the crap ripped out of him by every other polis in Gayfield Square if he went back to the office.

So he parked up, noticing that Bellfield Mobile Homes was several rungs further up the image ladder than Campsie's Caravans. Their show-room was a proper building with big windows and leather sofas and a guy in monogrammed overalls behind a curved counter. Low tables were covered in brochures for the kind of monstrous vans that blocked Highland roads for six months of the year. Jason pushed the heavy door open and sketched a wave at the salesman.

He walked across to the counter and

introduced himself. The man in the overalls was in his fifties, his salt-and-pepper hair trimmed in an anachronistic crew cut. With his tan overalls, he looked like a leftover from the US Air Force in the Second World War. The illusion vanished as soon as he said, 'What can I do for you?' in a dense Doric accent. It took Jason a few seconds to process the words.

Wearily, he explained his mission. 'So I was wondering, do you ever garage vans for customers?'

To his astonishment, the man nodded. 'Not often, like. But we do sometimes. Particularly if we sold them the van in the first place.'

Jason whipped out the pictures. 'What about this van? In 1995?'

The man laughed. 'I wasnae here then, son. I was still in Buckie. But wait a minute, I'll get Donny.' He walked briskly through a door behind the counter. When he returned a few minutes later, he was followed by a bulky man whose puffy face and bruised-looking eyes made guessing his age a challenge. His overall was faded and stained with oil and his thick sandy hair looked as if it had been slicked back with the same grease. His skin had the rosy blemishes of a man who no longer drinks because it's a pleasure but because it's a necessity. 'Jos says you're a polis,' he said, extending a grubby hand. The nails were bitten down and stained black with oil.

Jason was used to men like Donny. They reminded him of his brother Ronan and his pals. He returned his grip and explained yet again why he was there.

Donny blew out a stream of onion-scented air. 'That's a long time ago, 1995. We'd not been going that long. See's a look at the van.' Jason handed over the photos. 'It rings a bell, right enough,' he said slowly, his heavy brows drawn together in a caterpillar frown.

'We think it might have been an American lassie driving it.'

The frown cleared, replaced by a lascivious smirk. 'How did you not say that right up front? I mind her, right enough.' He dug his colleague in the ribs. 'She was a looker, right enough.' He cupped his hands in front of his chest. 'You dinnae often see a rack like that driving a rig like yon.' He nodded enthusiastically. 'Now it's all coming back to me. She came in with the van, said she'd just bought it but she didn't have anywhere to garage it yet. In the end, we must have had it three or four months, if I remember right.'

Jason couldn't quite believe it. This was a pick-up as good as a Mars Bar. 'I don't suppose you've got a record of it? Like, in the books?'

Donny sucked his teeth. 'That would be before we got the computer,' he said slowly. 'Everything was still on paper back then.' He rubbed his chin, his thought processes obvious. 'Shelley used to keep them all in box files. They must be in the old Portakabin. Come on, we'll have a wee look and see what we can find.' He gestured with his head for Jason to follow.

They navigated a maze of narrow pathways between mobile homes and finally emerged opposite a Portakabin that had clearly seen better days. The olive-green paintwork was flaky as a patch of eczema and the windows were filthy. 'This used to be the office when we started up,' Donny said, unlocking the door with a screech of metal on metal. 'All we use it for nowadays is storage.'

The interior was furnished with industrial shelving and dust. It smelled faintly of ammonia and decay, and there were little pots of rodent poison at frequent intervals. It wasn't a place Jason wanted to spend time.

Donny wandered down the shelves, checking what had been scrawled on the archive boxes in black marker pen. 'It looks like they're kind of in order. See?' He pointed at one that read *VAT: 2, 3, 4 — 04*. 'That'll be all the paperwork for the VAT return for that quarter. You take that lot over there — ' He pointed to the opposite end. 'You'll be looking for one that says *8, 9, 10 — 95.*'

Jason did as he was told. Everything was grey with dust, and the further back he went the dimmer it became. He actually had to rub the ends of the boxes with his sleeve to make out what was written on them. The swirls of dust made him sneeze, causing fresh clouds to rise around him. But his persistence paid off and he finally found the right box on the bottom shelf. He crouched down and eased it out. 'I think I've got it,' he said. He lifted the lid and looked down at a stack of box files.

Donny loomed up beside him. 'That's what you need,' he said. 'Come on, we'll take them back to the showroom, you can look through them there. I'll get Woody to make you a cup of tea.'

It was a weary task, even fuelled by Woody's cups of tea and a plate of individually wrapped butterscotch shortbread biscuits. The accounts were clearly laid out, but because Jason had been taught by Karen to take nothing at face value, he felt obliged to match each entry to the corresponding invoice. To make absolutely sure. And even though he knew there was no point in looking at anything before the middle of September, he started with August anyway, in case a filing mistake had been made.

Predictably, August came up empty. There were plenty of rentals and a few sales, but nothing about storage. He ploughed on into September and finally, there it was. The third Monday in September. 'Storage rental,' followed by the registration number, make and model of Joey Sutherland's van. Jason felt like jumping up and down and punching the air but he settled for a deep sigh of satisfaction.

He turned over the next page in the pile of invoices, and there it was. Shirley O'Shaughnessy, the same address on the DVLA registration, and an invoice for a month's storage for a van she hadn't officially owned for another three months. He stood up and grinned at Woody behind the counter. 'I need copies of these,' he said. It was too late to go back to the office now. But at least he'd guaranteed Karen would have a better start to the day tomorrow than she'd had today.

57

2018 — Edinburgh

While Jason was exploring the VAT returns of Bellfield Caravans, Karen was pursuing a different but equally tedious document search, though hers was at one remove. She had no recollection of the route she'd taken back to Gayfield Square, so bemused was she by the conversation with the barista in Perk. She considered calling Hamish and asking him what he thought he was playing at. But when she ran through the possible outcomes of that conversation, she found none that she was comfortable with. The trouble was, she liked him. And she didn't want to have to stop liking him. She didn't want to push him into a corner where nothing good could be found.

It was almost a relief to be back in the office. There, she felt the obligation to concentrate on work. It was, she reckoned, already after eight in the morning in Milwaukee. On her way down the hill, she'd decided she'd have more luck soliciting help from fellow cops than a faceless clerk in a county courthouse. She knew that Americans tended to start their working days earlier than in Scotland so she called the Milwaukee Police Department's non-emergency number. Of course the line was busy but instead of the usual terrible holding muzak, she was treated to a series of public service announcements dressed up as mini-playlets. She learned about the dangers of leaving her keys in the car while it warmed up on a cold morning. And the importance of not leaving spare house keys where a burglar could find them. At last, a live human picked up the call. 'Milwaukee Police Department, how may I help you?'

Karen explained who she was and that she needed to talk to someone in the detective bureau. The operator sounded uncertain. 'Can you provide any proof that you really are a police officer, ma'am?' he asked.

They finally settled on having a detective call the main Gayfield Square number to confirm the HCU's direct line with them. 'I'll have someone get back to you as soon as possible, ma'am,' he confirmed.

The seven minutes it took for the phone to ring felt much longer. Karen grabbed it on the first ring. 'DCI Pirie. Historic Cases Unit,' she gabbled.

'I guess you really are who you said,' an amused Midwestern woman's voice said. 'This is Detective Amy Shulman. I have to say I'm very curious as to why a detective from Edinburgh' — pronounced Edinboro — 'is calling MPD for help. You got somebody on the run?'

'Nothing so glamorous, I'm afraid, Detective Shulman. I need to find out some background information for a case I'm working on. It's a bit of a long story. But the bottom line is that we've got a suspect in a twenty-three-year-old murder who is an American citizen. We think she acquired a substantial amount of money as a result of the crime. But she claims the money she used to set up her business back at the end of 1995 was an inheritance from her grandfather. I hoped you could help me find out whether that's true or not.'

'OK. So I guess you're looking to see a copy of the grandfather's will?'

'That's right.'

'What's his name? I'm assuming he was a Milwaukee resident, and you're not just calling us at random.' She chuckled.

'It's not quite that straightforward. Our suspect was born in Milwaukee, but her father died shortly before her third birthday. She and her mother ended up in Hamtramck in Michigan with her grandfather. He was apparently head of security at the Dodge plant there. But I don't know his name.'

'You don't know much, huh?' There was a little less humour in Shulman's voice now.

'I thought if you could access the suspect's birth certificate, it should be possible to track down her mother's documentation and come at the grandfather that way?' Karen remained businesslike, resisting the impulse to wheedle. She knew how much that pissed her off when people tried it on her.

'I guess. It shouldn't be too big of a deal. All that information's digitised these days. They might not be keen to hand it over to you, but I'm pretty sure I can get authorisation. I might have to ask a judge for some paperwork, but it's not like it's a state secret. If you email me all you've got, I'll see what I can do.'

'Thanks.' They exchanged email addresses. 'How soon can you get back to me, do you think?'

'I'm guessing it's not too urgent, with you being a cold case cop.'

Karen grimaced at the phone. 'I'm eager to wrap this up as soon as I can. The victim's family have only recently learned that their son is dead.'

'I get that. You don't want to leave them twisting in the wind. Leave it with me, I'll get to it quick as I can.'

'I appreciate it.'

'That's OK. When I come visit Scotland, I fully expect a personalised tour, Detective Pirie.'

Karen replaced the phone. She'd done all she could. Now it was in someone else's hands. There were few situations she found more frustrating. With typical swift efficiency, she compiled the scant information she possessed on Shirley O'Shaughnessy and pinged it across to Amy Shulman.

In the moment after she'd sent the email, she found herself wondering what was happening to Billy McAfee. He'd have appeared before a sheriff that morning and been remanded in custody. She imagined he'd be shell-shocked and disorientated in the terrifying world of prison. It would be as bad, if not worse, for his wife. In her shoes, Karen thought she'd be feeling twice-bereaved. Their daughter's death after thirty years of dependency must have felt like a release as well as a loss. But before the McAfees had had any chance to make something of their new freedom, while they'd still been out of balance and off-kilter, Gerry McCartney had thrown an irresistible temptation in Billy McAfee's path.

That seemed to be the hallmark of all her cases right now. Temptation laid out before people who either could not or would not resist. Willow Henderson had been greedy enough for her family home and the life insurance payout on her husband to sacrifice her best friend's life. Billy McAfee had been tempted to extract vengeance for the torment his daughter — and the whole family — had been forced to endure at Barry Plummer's hands. And Shirley O'Shaughnessy was tempted by the prospect of a shortcut to realising her business ambitions. If they'd all had the inner steel to turn their back on the seductions of what seemed the easy way out, at least three people would still be alive.

It was a chilling thought.

But before she could sink into it too deeply, her phone rang. The screen said *Hamish Mackenzie*. She hesitated for a moment. Knowing what she did now had compromised what she'd felt for him after their evening together. But curiosity got the better of her. She took the call with a brisk, 'Hi, Hamish.'

'Karen, I'm sorry I missed you earlier. Anders, the barista at George IV Bridge, said you'd been in, asking for me.'

'I was passing and I needed a coffee. I wasn't looking for you as such. Just being polite, in case you were around.' Her tone was cool.

'Right,' he said easily. 'Next time, it's on the house. And speaking of next time — when are you free for dinner?'

She was torn. She wanted to see him again but she was wary, both as a woman and as a cop. 'When did you have in mind?' she stalled.

'No time like the present. What about tonight?'

'I can't do tonight. I'm at a crucial stage of an investigation. I can't concentrate on anything else.'

'Some time over the weekend? Not tomorrow, but I can do the night after, if you think your case might have resolved itself?'

'They don't resolve themselves, unfortunately. They need to be wrangled into submission. Can I get back to you? If I can make it, I'll give you a call.'

'OK, I'll look forward to hearing from you. I really enjoyed spending time with you the other evening. I don't often relax with someone so soon after meeting them.'

Karen made a rueful face at the phone. She'd felt the same. But what she'd learned about the earrings had undermined that. 'I know what you mean,' she said, deliberately evasive. 'Leave it with me, Hamish.'

'I'll keep my fingers crossed, Karen. By the way, are you making progress with the Joey Sutherland case?'

He'd left it to the last possible moment if that had been the main purpose of his call. 'Slowly,' she said. 'These things always take time. It's not easy, having to rely on people's distant memories. But we'll get there. Trust me on that, Hamish. We'll get there.'

'Good to hear. I'll let you get on, Karen. I look forward to hearing from you.'

She felt sure he meant it. But she was less certain of his motives.

58

2018 — Edinburgh

After Hamish's call, Karen couldn't settle. The forced inactivity of waiting for the next break in a case always drove her stir crazy, but to her frustration, she couldn't stop turning over her conversation with Hamish. Why was she letting him get under her skin like this? She wasn't looking for any emotional complications in her life and she certainly didn't need a man to make her feel complete. She might not be skipping through her life in a state of ditzy happiness, but she was doing fine.

Grumbling under her breath, she pulled on her coat and left the office, running the gauntlet of dark looks and darker mutterings from those she passed on the way out. The sun was losing its battle with the thin grey clouds rolling in from the Forth, but there was still a bit of warmth in the air. She turned down Leith Walk and set off at a brisk pace. Time to find a quiet corner where she'd be safe from the disparagement of officers quick to blame her for Barry Plummer's death.

It was a busy time of day in Aleppo. Parents stopping by for a coffee on the way to picking up the kids from school; the self-employed sneaking out for a break from their own four walls; a quartet of pensioners who met every day to while away an hour playing dominos; and the Syrian refugees who had nowhere else to go that had the feel of home. There wasn't a free table, and Karen ended up on a stool at the counter. She wasn't in the mood for more coffee, so she ordered a sparkling water and a couple of ma'amoul. Amena served her, gesturing to the star-shaped pastries studded with almonds and sesame seeds. 'Fresh baked this afternoon,' she said.

'Dates or figs?'

Amena smiled. 'Dates, how you like them.'

Karen bit into the pastry and savoured the burst of flavour that filled her mouth. 'Oh, that's the business,' she said, feeling her tetchy mood soothed by the sweetness.

'Makes you smile.' Amena turned away to serve someone else. The rush soon died down and she returned to refill Karen's glass.

'You're busy today,' Karen said.

'Is good. Maybe we open another café, Miran says.' She patted Karen's hand. 'Thank you.'

Karen felt awkward, as she always did when the Syrians insisted on holding her responsible for their enterprise. 'I opened the door. You guys did all the hard work.'

'Miran has a cousin in London. People there are not kind like here. We are lucky we are not there.'

Karen smiled. 'It doesn't make up for what you went through in Syria, but I'm glad you feel that way.'

Amena nodded. 'Last time you were here, the women you talked to?'

'You remember them?'

She pointed to the wooden rack by the door that held copies of a free daily newspaper. 'I see photo of the one who paid. It says she's dead?' Amena shook her head in bewilderment.

'That's right. She was murdered.'

Amena's distress was obvious. Karen imagined it must have shaken her, to be confronted with violence again, after she thought she'd reached a place of safety. 'This is terrible. Who has killed her?'

'We're not sure yet. It's complicated.'

Amena picked up a cloth and started wiping down the counter. 'She was upset after you spoke to her.'

Karen, who hadn't waited to see the effect of her warning, was intrigued. 'Did she say something?'

'Not to me. But after you go, her friend comes back in. She was angry. She was loud. She ask the other one what you said.'

Karen's attention quickened still further. 'Did you hear her friend's answer.'

Amena nodded doubtfully. 'I'm not sure I understand. She sort of laughed and said, 'That detective thinks you're planning to murder him. And you're setting me up as a witness for the defence.''

Karen couldn't quite believe it. Testimony that proved Dandy Muir had made Willow Henderson aware that she'd not be able to carry out her plans without suspicion attaching to her. Testimony that gave Willow a motive for double murder. But how had Amena remembered something so precisely when her English was far from fluent? 'Are you sure?' Karen asked, cautious.

Amena gave one sharp nod. 'I understand better than I speak.' Then a shy smile. 'We watch a lot of cop shows, me and Miran's mother. Maybe it seems strange to you, because of all that happen to us. But we like when bad people get what they deserve.'

'And you're sure that's what the woman said?'

'I am sure. I remember because it's a strange thing to say. Scottish people don't talk about murder in here.' She pulled a wry face. 'Only us. The Syrians.'

It was significant, Karen knew. But was it enough? 'Did you hear them say anything else?'

Amena shook her head. 'The one who comes back in, she looks worried. She goes quiet. She puts a hand on her friend's arm and says something in her ear. Then her friend asks to pay. I take her money and they go. They are talking to each other, but quiet.'

'What you heard? It could be important, Amena. I have to tell what you heard to the detective who is investigating the case.' Karen spoke gently, but still Amena's eyes widened in alarm.

'I don't want to talk to police.'

'You talk to me all the time. This detective, he's a good man. Nobody is going to threaten you, Amena. Nobody. I promise.'

'I need to talk to Miran.' She looked around, wildly seeking her husband.

'Of course. Talk to Miran. He can be with you

401

when you speak to us. There's nothing to be afraid of, Amena.' Already her mind was racing ahead. She needed to talk to Jimmy. This might be what he needed to persuade the fiscal's office to charge Willow Henderson. If it came to court, the prosecution could claim Amena was a vulnerable witness and try to spare her the full weight of a hostile cross-examination. Karen leaned across the counter and took Amena's hand. 'This is a good thing you can do, Amena. Nobody knows better than you that people shouldn't get away with murder.'

★ ★ ★

They'd left it that Karen would speak to Jimmy, then talk again to Miran and Amena. Miran was as anxious as his wife about a close encounter with the police, but his hesitancy was tempered by the trust Karen had built up with him and his community in the struggle to get the café off the ground. Her commitment to helping them create a place where they could meet and support each other had won her credit. That hadn't been why she'd weighed in; she'd sensed their grief and isolation at a time when she'd been going through the same emotions. Helping them had helped her. 'No such thing as altruism,' she'd told River in a typically brusque brush-off when her friend had attempted to praise her for what she'd done. 'I got a lot more than I gave. Plus a constant source of good coffee.'

Later that evening, Karen met Jimmy Hutton in a bar a few streets away from the house where

Dandy Muir had lived with her husband and two teenage children. 'How's it going?' she asked, placing a glass of tonic water in front of him.

He grimaced as the naked tonic hit his tastebuds. 'Not great. We've been canvassing the neighbours, to see whether any of them had any significant conversation with Dandy. But we've drawn a blank. I'm going back with Jacqui in a wee while to talk again to the husband and the kids. I can't believe she said nothing to anybody.'

'I might have a wee bit of help for you,' Karen said, and repeated her conversation with Amena.

Jimmy listened keenly, his brow creased. 'It backs up what we're thinking, you're right on that score. The big question is whether it's enough to get us over the line.'

'She heard Dandy tell Willow that I'd warned her. If Willow went ahead and killed Logan, Dandy would remember that conversation.'

'No doubt about that. But would that be enough to persuade Willow to kill her?'

Karen shrugged. 'If she was cold enough and determined enough to be planning to kill her husband, I'd say so.'

'Having seen her in action, I wouldn't argue with you.' Jimmy fiddled with his wedding ring, as he often did when he was considering a problem. 'I'm worried about Amena as a witness, though. She could get hammered on the cross. They'll go for her connection to you. How they're so grateful, they'd do anything to help you out.'

'I hadn't thought about that.' Karen was disappointed in herself. She'd been so busy weighing the value of Amena's testimony she'd forgotten to include herself in the balance. 'You're right, of course. So what do you think?'

Jimmy shook his head. 'I think that's a last resort. If we get to the end of the road and we've nothing better, I'll talk to Amena and see whether I think we can make it stand up. That's the best I can do.'

As she waited for a bus to take her back across town, Karen tried not to give in to despair. No wonder the Dog Biscuit kept going for her. Everything she'd touched lately had turned to shit. The Joey Sutherland case was hanging by a thread. Barry Plummer was lying in the morgue. Her best efforts at preventing a murder had probably laid a death sentence on Dandy Muir, and Karen had completely failed in her attempts to resolve an innocent woman's murder. Maybe Markie was right. Maybe she wasn't up to the job after all.

59

2018 — Gartcosh

Although it was almost nine o'clock when Karen and Jimmy arrived at the forensics unit at Gartcosh, she'd had no hesitation in responding to the phone call that had cut through her despondency. The rain was sheeting down, but by that time of night, Jimmy found a parking space close to the entrance. 'See in future?' he said as they strode down the corridor to Tamsin's lab. 'I'm always going to come here at this time of night. Save myself the fifteen-minute drive around to find a parking space. Followed by the half-mile walk from the road after I've given up.'

'We're supposed to save the planet and get the bus.'

Jimmy snorted. 'What bus?'

'Exactly.'

Tamsin was waiting for them in her little cubbyhole off the main lab. 'You guys got lucky,' she said. 'See this little beaut?' She pointed to a wide screen on a table by her desk. The only thing that distinguished it from every other screen in the place was that it sat on a lumpy black plastic plinth with a USB slot on the front of it.

'It looks like a screen,' Jimmy said.

'I see how you got to be a DCI,' Tamsin said. She clicked a switch and the screen sprang to life. She quickly entered the details demanded by the system — her ID, the case number and when it asked for the investigating officer, she typed in 'DCI James Hutton'. Then she took a phone in an evidence bag out of the drawer and through a hole in the bottom of the bag, she plugged in a cable which she attached to the USB port.

'This lovely bit of kit arrived a couple of days ago. If it does what it says on the tin, there'll be another forty on order. They're so simple to use, you don't even need a digital forensics tech. Plug in the phone and this monster busts right through the password protection and strips out every last bit of data on the phone.' She tapped the screen and a list of all the items on the phone appeared on the screen. Contacts, calls made and received, text messages, emails, apps and more.

'Just like that?' Karen could hardly believe it. 'You didn't download this already?'

'I did, but that's on a separate back-up. I wanted to show you, this is how it works in real time, and this is Dandy Muir's phone. This is going to transform our work here in digital forensics. It's going to go through the queue like a knife through butter. No more waiting six months to get the data off a phone. And like I said, there's going to be forty of them spread round the country. It's a fucking bonanza.' Tamsin grinned gleefully.

'We'll have to make sure you don't do a Facebook and let the data slip out the back door,' Karen said.

Tamsin poked her tongue out at Karen. 'It's

not networked. It's a standalone. You have to take the data off it on a memory stick or burn it to a disk.'

'So what has Dandy's phone got for us?' Jimmy asked.

'I checked everything after the timing you gave me for Karen's mighty intervention. Jeez, did she write some boring emails. But nothing about the Hendersons. Not a cheep. She didn't even tell anybody she was going round there. The nearest she came to that was a text to her son telling him there was a pizza in the fridge for his dinner, that she wouldn't be back late and he should do his homework.' She pulled a face. 'Not exactly the last words you'd like from your mother.'

'So why are we here? If she didn't tell anybody what Karen said and she didn't tell anybody where she was going or why?'

Tamsin grinned and shook her head. 'Oh ye of little faith. I didn't stop with her emails and texts and entirely minimalist social media. I'm better than that, Jimmy.' She tapped the icon for 'audio/music'. 'Wherever she listens to music, it's not here. We've got some audio books, a couple of playlists that my grandmother would be ashamed of. And this lovely little gem.'

She gently placed her finger beside a file identified only by a string of numbers. 'Are you ready for this?'

'You're such a tease,' Karen said.

'If I'd said that, you'd be making a complaint,' Jimmy grumbled. 'Come on then, Tamsin, let's hear it.'

She activated the file. A few seconds of silence,

then a scuffling, then a muffled, 'Yes, I'm coming, Willow.' Then a rhythmic swishing. Tamsin pressed pause.

'So, Dandy turns on the voice recording function on her phone. She puts it in her pocket, speaks to Willow and walks to catch her up. I'm guessing this is them arriving at the Henderson house and Dandy hanging back to set up the phone.' Tamsin set it running again.

More swishing, then they could barely make out Dandy saying, 'Is that his car?'

Then Willow, her voice sounding as if it was coming from under water. 'Yes, he had to trade in the Beamer for a Seat. A bit of a come-down.' A rattle of keys.

Something indistinguishable from Dandy, then, ' . . . let yourself in?'

'It's my house, Dandy.' More unidentifiable noises, then a change in the acoustic. The sound of brisk heels on parquet times two.

Then a man's voice: 'What the fuck are you doing here?' Loud and clear.

'I've come to get my house back,' Willow said. Next, a clatter. Then the sound quality changed. It became much harder to make out the words.

Dandy's voice said something, then she shouted ' . . . put the knives down.'

Now Logan Henderson again. Muffled. More than one voice at a time. Something like, 'Put the fucking knives down.'

A confusion of shouts and screams, a roar of anger, the thud of a body hitting the floor in the midst of it, then Dandy's voice rising above the melee in a keening wail. There were words

408

but they were gibberish.

Then a definite shout from Dandy. 'Oh no! No!' A shout from Dandy. Women's voices, indistinct. A confusion of heels on tiles. Dandy screaming something incomprehensible. Swishing and a sudden thump then silence.

'That's the end of it,' Tamsin said. 'I think she hit the ground and the impact turned the recording off. Is that helpful?'

'She definitely said 'knives', didn't she?' Karen said. 'Dandy definitely said 'knives', plural.'

'Hard to be sure,' said Jimmy, his face sombre. 'But I think so.'

'We've got people who can clean it up,' Tamsin said. 'I betcha they'll be able to give you a script of what went down in that kitchen. But I'm with Karen: I heard 'knives'.'

Jimmy nodded. 'Well, hopefully the experts will settle Willow Henderson's hash. Then there'll be no need to put Amena through the wringer. Thanks, Tamsin.'

'No worries. We'd have got to it eventually on the old system. But this little bit of magic is going to make one helluva difference. Instantaneous and comprehensive.' She patted the top of the screen as if it was a favourite pet. 'What we always crave in here.'

Jimmy copied Tamsin, gently stroking the machine. 'Can you send me the file?'

'I already did,' she said, managing cheeky and smug at the same time.

The rain had eased off and Karen and Jimmy walked back to the car. 'It looks pretty certain you're going to get her. I'm glad about that,'

Karen said. 'But it doesn't make me feel any less guilty. If I hadn't stuck my nose in, Dandy Muir would still be alive.'

'You can't think like that, Karen. It'll paralyse you. Look at it this way: Logan Henderson is going to live. If you hadn't stepped in, he might well be dead right now.'

'It's not a trade-off, Jimmy. I can't help feeling I could have handled it better. Phil would have found a way.'

'I think Phil would have done exactly what you did. I certainly would have. Don't put him on a pedestal, Karen. He was a good cop, but not even the best of us get the right result every time. You're a hell of a cop. Phil was so proud of you, and he'd be proud of you still.'

Karen shook her head. 'You think? I've got two bodies on my conscience this week. I should have kept McCartney on a tighter rein, I should have spoken to Logan Henderson, not Dandy Muir.'

'And I should have paid more attention when you told me what Willow Henderson had said. I should have seen the signs and warned Logan myself. This is not just about you, Karen. Like I said, we all end up on the wrong side of history sooner or later in this job. All you can do is put it behind you and get on with the next case.'

Karen sighed. 'The next case has a whole different set of problems,' she said, thinking about Hamish Mackenzie.

'Aye, but they can wait for tomorrow morning. You never know what'll be waiting for you.'

Karen gave a dry laugh. 'The way my luck's going? I'm not sure I want to find out.'

60

2018 — Edinburgh

It had been one of those nights when sleep eluded Karen. It had started auspiciously enough. She'd been bone weary by the time Jimmy had dropped her off at home, and she'd crashed out like a felled tree as soon as she hit the mattress. But it didn't last. Just after three, an alarm bell sounded in her dream and she surfaced, groggy and disorientated. She rolled over and tried to drift back into sleep but her brain whirred and raced, disobedient to all her attempts to lull it into unconsciousness. In spite of her best intentions, Hamish Mackenzie kept insinuating himself into her thoughts.

She gave up around quarter to four and pulled on a pair of jeans and yesterday's shirt. A cup of rhubarb and ginger tea, then she was out on the streets. Not so long ago, she'd have found a group of Syrian men huddled round a brazier under a railway bridge. But they had the café now, and the denizens of the night were either furtively avoiding any eye contact or too tired, travelling to or from work, to care. That was fine, though. There was nothing to disturb her mental review of the Joey Sutherland case. Slowly, a strategy was taking shape.

She zigzagged through back lanes and side streets up from the shore to the broad artery of

411

Queen Street then walked back towards the office, the private gardens raucous with birdsong on one side, imposing Georgian buildings on the other. The first tram of the day was leaving the terminus on York Place as she passed, carrying a handful of bleary-eyed workers out towards the airport. She stopped on the corner of Picardy Place, considering. She could go home, shower and have breakfast. Or she could sneak into work before the station properly woke up and get the jump on the day. Amy Shulman might have turned up some information for her overnight. The downside of that was there was nowhere open for coffee. Even Starbucks wouldn't open its doors for another hour.

'I am not an addict,' Karen said out loud. 'I don't need coffee to think.' She almost convinced herself, and turned down the hill. As she rounded the corner into Gayfield Square, a car nipped out of the police station and down the hill away from her. It nudged her with its familiarity, but she couldn't place it. At least if it was the Dog Biscuit, she was heading in the right direction, as far as Karen was concerned.

She walked down the echoing main corridor. This was the dead hour in a police station. The night shift were skulking out of sight, trying not to catch any new jobs this close to closing time, and the day shift teams hadn't wandered in with their bacon rolls and tabloids yet. Nobody around to bother her or give her the hard stare over what had happened on their doorstep.

Karen logged on to her email, trying to keep optimism at bay. The way things had been

412

running lately, she'd be surprised if Amy Shulman had even started looking, never mind come up with any results.

She was gratifyingly wrong. The first item in her inbox was an email from the Milwaukee detective. With attachments. Karen snapped it open and read the message.

Hi Detective Pirie

Well, your inquiry really intrigued me. We don't really get the opportunity in my squad to do cold case investigations so it's interesting to me to see how an expert goes about it.

First, your Shirley O'Shaughnessy. She was real easy to find. I attach a copy of her birth certificate. You'll see from it that her mother was born Clare Gerardine Burke. She was unmarried but Shirley's father is named as James O'Shaughnessy and the baby took his name. Given that the grandfather took Clare and Shirley to Hamtramck after James's death, I thought it might be worth checking with my colleagues in Michigan to see if we could get a lead on Clare or her father.

So, turns out Clare was born in 1951 in Hamtramck. (Scan attached of birth certificate.) Her father's name was Arnold Burke. You told me the granddaughter supposedly started her business with a legacy from him, which kind of necessitates him being dead. So I checked that out too and he died in November 1994. (Scan of death certificate attached.)

I was starting to get interested by this point. So I called the courthouse in Hamtramck and asked if they had a probate copy of Arnold Burke's will. And hallelujah, they did. (Scan attached.) As you'll see, he left his house and his car to his daughter, Clare. And he left his beloved granddaughter $20,000 to support her through her studies. And there was a weird line in the will: 'If the aforementioned Shirley O'Shaughnessy finds the Indians, I bequeath them to her too.' Now, I have no idea what that means, and if you do, I would be obliged if you would put my curiosity to rest!

Like I said, you got me intrigued and so did that bequest. So I called the local library and found me a friendly librarian who checked the newspaper files to see whether Arnold Burke had merited any kind of obituary or death notice. Lo and behold, there's the connection to your jurisdiction. They sent me a copy and I've attached that too.

I hope this helps you on your way. I'd sure like to hear how it all turns out.

Best regards
Amy Shulman (Detective)

Karen had to read it twice to make sure she wasn't dreaming. Amy Shulman had come up trumps and she dashed off a quick email to tell her so, promising to keep her abreast of developments. Then she downloaded and printed out the attachments and settled down to work her way through them.

The birth and death certificates offered no more insights than Amy had already noted. But the obituary was a different matter.

414

ARNOLD BURKE (September 7, 1920 — November 7, 1994)

Arnie Burke, whose death was announced this week, was a familiar figure to anyone who worked at the old Dodge plant in Hamtramck. Arnie was head of security at the plant from 1948 until he retired in 1980, and he was known for running a tight ship. He was a keen target pistol competitor, winning many trophies throughout the state.

In later years, he developed an interest in the history of Michigan's automobile industry and he ran a local group in Hamtramck who collected materials about the factories and recorded oral accounts of people who had worked there over the years. Mr Burke was a regular on WDTK radio where he would take listeners on a trip down memory lane to the early days of automobile construction.

He was born in Saginaw, the middle son of Agnes and Patrick Burke. He was working as a car mechanic when war broke out in 1941 and he volunteered for the US Army. He shipped out to Europe as soon as he'd completed his training. He never spoke in detail about his war service, except to say that he'd been deployed behind enemy lines. His mother was French and she taught him to speak the language fluently as a boy. His family have since revealed that Mr Burke was in fact recruited by the OSS

415

and worked undercover in Antwerp, Belgium, where he was a key operative in combating the Nazi occupation. He was later decorated for his wartime activities.

After the Canadian Army liberated the city, Mr Burke was exfiltrated to Scotland, where he was stationed briefly in the Highlands in a training role before shipping home in 1945. His daughter Clare, who survives him, said, 'He wasn't a boastful man, but from the little he did say about his war service, we all understood he'd done some pretty scary things. I was very proud of him.'

Mr Burke is also survived by his granddaughter Shirley, who is studying in Scotland in a tribute to her grandfather's love of the country.

The obituary finished with details of the memorial service. The details were scant, it was true, but they filled a vital hole in the jigsaw of the case that Karen was slowly assembling. Arnie Burke had brought something back from Europe, something that had ended up in the panniers of one of the Indians that Austin Hinde and his friend had buried in a Highland peat bog. For some reason, he'd never recovered it. But he'd left enough clues for his granddaughter to identify the hiding place.

She'd got that far in her reasoning when Jason walked in. He nearly dropped his bacon roll at the sight of her. 'How come you're here?' he blurted out.

She gave him a mock-severe look. 'I work here.'

'I know, but it's barely the back of seven. You're not usually here this early.'

'Neither are you,' she pointed out, not unreasonably.

'I wanted to write up my report properly. It was going to be a nice surprise. To cheer you up.' He looked down at the floor, disappointed.

Karen's attention quickened. 'You got something?'

Jason nodded. 'I did. You were right. She did garage it for the three months between the last sighting of Joey and her officially taking ownership of it.'

'I want to hear all about it. And then you need to hear all about what's come in from America. We're cooking, Jason.' She glanced at her watch. 'We deserve a proper breakfast. Fuck the expense, let's go across to the Glasshouse and pillage their buffet.'

'What? A hotel breakfast? And we're not even out of town?'

'This has been such a shit week, Jason, I feel like we deserve a wee treat. We'll swap stories and then we've got plotting to do.'

61

2018 — Edinburgh

The dining room was practically empty when Karen and Jason arrived, so they were given a table with a grandstand view of Calton Hill. Jason looked around in undisguised delight. 'I've never been here before,' he said.

'I stayed here with Phil one time. It was his cousin's wedding and we didn't want to try to get back to Fife afterwards.' The memory gave Karen pause, but she realised all at once that the sharp pain of early grief had been finally blunted by time. She could enjoy the sweetness of memories now as well as the bitterness.

Jason scoured the menu. 'Can I get kippers?' he demanded, reduced by excitement to a child on an outing.

Seeing the array of food, Karen remembered she hadn't eaten a proper meal for at least two days. Snacking on the run was all very well, but she was going to make the most of this opportunity. 'Have what you like. I'm going to hit the buffet first, then I'm having a full Scottish. We'll eat and then talk,' she said decisively, pushing her chair back and making for the continental side of the buffet.

Sometime later, they both acknowledged they'd hit their limit. Jason eyed with regret the remaining half of a Scotch morning roll filled with Austrian smoked cheese and hardboiled egg. 'I don't think I can manage that. Do you think they'd notice if I wrapped it in a napkin and stuck it in my pocket for later?'

Karen rolled her eyes. 'Really?'

'My mum always says, 'Waste not, want not, pick it up,'' he said defensively.

'I thought that was The Pretenders? So, tell me what you found out.'

Jason looked around as surreptitiously as a two-year-old and shoved the roll and napkin in his jacket pocket. 'I had a brainwave,' he said. 'I thought maybe instead of looking at caravan sites, where you'd notice if somebody wasn't around at their van, maybe it would make more sense to garage it someplace that sells them and rents them out.'

'That was a brainwave.' She almost meant it. 'And was that where you found something to cheer me up?'

'Ta-da,' Jason said, producing an envelope. He handed it to Karen with a flourish.

She opened it to find the invoice he'd brought back from Bellfield Mobile Homes, carefully encased in a plastic sleeve. She read it attentively, noting the date. 'Ya dancer,' she said softly. 'At the very least, she's got some serious questions to answer. But not quite yet, I think. We need more ammo before we pull in someone with her connections.'

'If you say so, boss. So what did you find out?'

She filled him in on what she'd learned from Amy Shulman. 'I don't know what or why, but I think Arnie Burke put something in those bike panniers for safekeeping. Maybe he thought they were going to be shipped back to America like so much of their material. But somehow, Alice Somerville's granddad and his pal got their hands on the bikes and buried them. I'm presuming they didn't know there was anything hidden in them. And for whatever reason, Arnie couldn't get his hands on them at the time.'

'So why did he not come back for them later?' Jason asked.

'Maybe he tried. Tried and failed. Alice and Will couldn't find them last summer when they went searching, don't forget.'

'But if Arnie couldn't find them, how come Shirley did?'

It was a good point. 'I don't know, Jason. Maybe Arnie got better information later on, when he was too old to go digging in West Highland peat bogs. So he passed it on to Shirley and told her to go and claim her inheritance.'

He nodded. 'That makes sense.'

'Arnie was in Antwerp,' Karen said thoughtfully. 'What do we know about Antwerp?'

Jason looked blank. Then his face cleared. 'Royal Antwerp FC were the first registered Belgian football club,' he said. 'They've got a loan partnership with Manchester United.'

Karen groaned. 'For fuck's sake, Jason. How is that anything to do with our case?'

He flushed. 'Well, it isnae, boss, but you asked what I know about Antwerp and that's all I know about Antwerp.'

She sighed. 'Fair enough.'

'So what do you know about Antwerp?'

'I know one thing, and one thing only, and it's not about football. Think about something you get in Belgium that's very small and portable but very valuable.'

An expression of panic crossed Jason's face. 'It's not chocolate, is it?'

She laughed. 'No, it's not chocolate. Diamonds, Jason. Diamonds. Antwerp is one of the major diamond-dealing centres in the world.'

He frowned. 'OK. But how does that fit in with the bikes and Joey Sutherland and all that?'

'We know now that Arnie Burke was an undercover operative for the American Army in the Second World War in Belgium. The diamond dealers were mostly Jewish, back then. Probably the majority of them ended up dead in the camps and I bet the Nazis helped themselves to as many of their stones as they could get their hands on. Is it not possible that when the city fell to the Allies, Arnie was well enough in with the Germans to get his hands on some of the diamonds they'd looted?' Karen spoke slowly, feeling her way as she went.

Jason hesitated, working through her theory till he reached understanding. 'It makes sense. So you think that he told his granddaughter where to find the goods?'

'That's something we might never know, Jason. But however she found out, I think Shirley O'Shaughnessy used Joey Sutherland's muscle to get her hands on the diamonds. And then she killed him.'

Jason took a gulp of tea and scratched his head. 'How do we know she got the diamonds? If there were any diamonds.'

'Two things,' Karen said. 'By that December, she had enough money to buy a house in Leith for cash at an auction.' Jason was about to speak but she raised a hand to forestall him. 'She must have had cash because no bank would have loaned that kind of money to a more or less penniless overseas student. So she got the money from somewhere.'

'That's one thing,' he acknowledged. 'What's the other?'

'She only dug up one bike. If she'd not got the diamonds, she'd have dug up both bikes in the search.'

Light dawned. 'And if she'd dug them both up and not got the diamonds, she wouldn't have been able to start her business.'

'Correct.'

Jason poured more tea and stirred two teaspoonfuls of sugar into it, looking pensive. 'But we don't know for sure that there really were diamonds. That's you guessing, right?'

Karen sighed. 'Aye, it's me guessing. But there must have been something. And diamonds are what makes most sense.'

'But how are we going to find out?'

'I don't know. I need to talk to somebody who knows about diamonds.'

'What do you want me to do?' Jason sounded wary.

'Two things. I want you to find out where Hamish Mackenzie lived when he was in America. And talk to Ruari Macaulay again, see if you can get a list of names of heavy athletes who were around in 1995 and talk to them. Find out if any of them saw Joey Sutherland after the Invercharron Games in 1995.'

His face grew more cheerful. This was the kind of routine grafting that Jason had learned to do well. 'What's the deal with Hamish Mackenzie? I thought we decided he was one of the good guys?'

Karen sighed, her eyes troubled. 'We have to cover all the bases. So's we don't get fooled again. I had a fleeting thought that in spite of what he told us, maybe his grandparents did know about the bikes being buried on their land. For all we know, Arnie Burke could have written to every possible landowner in the area, trying to find out where the bikes were. What if Hamish found out about this and was near enough to make contact? He'd have had to be nearby, I think. He was only a teenager at the time, he wouldn't have had many resources for long-distance travel. But what if he was the missing link? What if he got a share of Shirley O'Shaughnessy's loot, and that's how he funded his first coffee shop all those years later?'

Jason's mouth fell open and his eyes widened. 'You think he's involved? I thought you liked him?'

'I did. I do. But that doesn't mean he's not in this up to his oxters. He said they moved to America when his dad got a job at Stanford. But maybe he didn't go to school in California. Just check it out, Jason. Set my mind at rest.' Because she knew he'd already told her one lie. She needed to be sure that wasn't a distraction from other, deeper untruths.

62

1995 — Edinburgh

Shirley O'Shaughnessy studied the map and the sheets of paper that littered her desk and gave a soft chuckle. 'I got you,' she said with quiet satisfaction. It was a moment she'd been waiting for since the day she'd left Hamtramck for Edinburgh. She remembered how she'd hauled her case through to the living room where her grandfather lay on his recliner, absorbed in a replay of some historic ball game.

He'd looked up. 'You sure you got everything you need in there?'

'Yeah, I think so.'

'I have no idea how we're going to manage without a sink in the kitchen,' he sighed.

'Very droll,' she said, her sarcasm gentle. 'I'm going to miss that sense of humour.'

'The Scots have their own kind of humour, Shirley. You'll spend the first two weeks taking offence and thinking they're mean sons of bitches, then it's going to hit you that they're making a joke.'

'I'll keep that in mind, Pops.'

'Now come here and sit down. There's something I need to talk to you about.' He turned off the TV and pointed to the sofa.

'Pops, I know all about boys,' Shirley teased, but sat down nevertheless. She'd learned over

424

the years that her grandfather didn't waste her time with stupid homilies.

'I know I've spoken a lot over the years about my time in Scotland. Training and being trained for going behind enemy lines. But there's one story I haven't told you. And you need to hear it now.'

'That sounds serious.' She could see from his face that he meant it.

'You know this cancer's going to get me, right?'

'You're going to fight it. And you're going to win.' She said it to convince herself as much as him.

'We both know that's not true. I've got a year at the outside — '

'It's not too late for me to postpone going to Edinburgh,' she protested. Not for the first time.

'I don't want you to do that. I don't want you here at the end. I've got your mom, and that's fine. But this might be the last chance I have to pass this on to you.'

'OK. What is it?'

And he told her about the diamonds. How he'd found them in an office safe after the Nazis had cleared out. How he'd hidden them in a bike pannier, and what Kenny Pascoe and his buddy had done with the bikes. How Kenny had passed the map on to him when he knew the TB was coming for him. She suspected her expression had told him how improbable the whole thing sounded.

'Why didn't you go back for them?' Puzzled, she stared at him.

'I went back three times in the fifties,' he said wearily. 'I drove all round the terrain we trained on. And beyond. I couldn't find the place. I'd find three things that lined up but then a fourth was in the wrong place. When Kenny sent me the map, he omitted to mention exactly where it was.' He reached for an envelope on the table next to him. 'Here's the map. And there's a letter with a grid of numbers on the back. I don't know what they mean, or even if they're anything to do with the map. But you're a smart young lady. Maybe you can succeed where I failed.'

She'd taken the envelope with a heavy heart. She knew it would be the last thing he ever gave her and it had felt like he was laying a quest on her, like some medieval knight in a *Dungeons and Dragons* game. She'd promised to do her best, but until now she'd failed.

She'd read books about cryptography. She'd hung out with mathematicians. She'd tried making sense of the numbers as grid references on Ordnance Survey maps. As a last resort, she'd even joined the rambling society because they were going on a walking trip to Wester Ross. And that had been the unlikely place where she'd found the answer. A few of them had gone to the pub after a Sunday afternoon walk in the Pentlands and she'd noticed one of the men scribbling down two sets of numbers for another. Two sets of seven digits.

'What's that?' She'd spoken so sharply that they'd straightened up, startled and guilty as schoolboys caught looking at dirty photos.

'It's longitude and latitude,' one said. 'We're

426

trying to work something out for a competition entry.'

'Explain it to me,' she demanded.

'Conventionally, you give longitude then latitude. Degrees, minutes and seconds to one decimal point. This here is forty-three degrees, two minutes, five point three seconds.'

She frowned intently at the numbers. 'How do you know if it's north or south?'

'Usually there would be an N or an S at the end. An E or a W for the latitude. That's part of the competition. You have to decide which spot it's referring to.'

She'd jumped up, leaned across the table and planted a kiss on his lips. Then she was gone, leaving a half-finished drink and an open-mouthed student behind her.

It had taken her every spare minute for a week to work out which were the real coordinates and which the red herrings. But now at last she was looking at the answer. It had come too late for her grandfather. Not for her, though. Shirley had dreams, and now the means to pursue them was almost within her grasp. She was going to leave something behind more lasting than anyone in her entire family had ever managed.

All she had to do was figure out how to get the damn bikes out of the ground. And she had an idea about that too. Over the summer, one of her fellow students had invited her to visit her home in Braemar. The family had taken her to the Gathering, where the Queen herself had presided over the Highland games. Which was pretty amazing on its own. It was as if the

President would have shown up at Tiger Stadium to watch a ball game.

What caught Shirley's eye — apart from the royal party with their tartan rugs spread over their knees the same as all the ordinary folks watching the action — were the heavy athletes. They were like a gift from the gods. These guys weren't only strong enough to do what she needed done. She gleaned from her friend's brother that they were guns for hire, going from town to town to ply their strongman trade. How much would it take to persuade one of them to do a job for her?

And did she have the nerve to make sure he'd keep his mouth shut afterwards?

63

2018 — Glasgow

Michael Moss had suggested meeting Karen in the Centre for Contemporary Arts on Sauchiehall Street. 'I've got to be at the Garnethill Synagogue till three o'clock,' he'd explained on the phone. 'So that would suit me best. They've got a nice café.'

Karen hadn't been at that end of Glasgow city centre for years. The art school had always left its mark on the area, but now the streets seemed to have been entirely colonised by students. She imagined Sauchiehall Street would come alive at night when the student flats and residences emptied, and the bars and kebab shops filled with a clientele determined to make the most of their last chance at irresponsibility.

But at this time in the afternoon, the populace were scuttling past, hoods up against the rain. She couldn't blame them; it was a day for getting indoors as fast as possible. Karen was a firm subscriber to the East Coast view that it always rained in Glasgow. She couldn't understand why a local dialect that had about forty words for being intoxicated didn't have the same number for types and conditions of rain. Maybe they were all too pissed to notice.

The café was half-empty, and Karen chose a table for two to one side. She sat facing the door, waiting to spot Michael Moss. 'I'll be wearing a black raincoat and a black porkpie hat,' he'd told her. She'd had to check on the internet what precisely a porkpie hat looked like.

She'd found Moss via the same route. Her researches into UK diamond merchants had brought her to the London Diamond Index, which claimed to be the association to which the overwhelming majority of diamond dealers was affiliated. These were the people who bought and sold stones, both cut and uncut, supplying the jewellery trade. The list of their members included Michael Moss in Glasgow, so she'd called him. 'I'm semi-retired now,' he'd told her. 'But I'm happy to help you if I can.' And so they'd arranged to meet.

Karen smothered a yawn with the back of her hand. The night was catching up with her. She had no confidence that this encounter would take her a single step closer to nailing Shirley O'Shaughnessy, but right now it was the only road she had to go down. As she fretted over what Jason might uncover about Hamish Mackenzie, an elderly man swept into the room. His black raincoat looked as if it had been tailored for his tall, spare frame by a costume designer from the heyday of film noir. It swept around him in elegant drapes and folds shaped by his every step. The hat was indeed a porkpie, but it was made of black leather that seemed to suck in the light, turning the top of his head into a kind of negative space. He was dashing. There was no other word for it.

Karen raised a hand and gave a wonky wave,

standing up to greet him. 'Mr Moss?'

'And you must be Detective Chief Inspector Pirie.' He gave her title full weight, taking her hand and bowing over it. 'I hope I haven't kept you waiting?' His face was an angular arrangement of planes as pale as the vellum in a medieval manuscript. His eyes were hazel, magnified through large horn-rimmed glasses. Karen liked him on sight.

'You're very prompt,' she said. 'Let me get you a coffee.'

'Just a glass of sparkling water,' he said. 'I can no longer indulge in coffee after the clock has struck noon.'

She went to the counter and by the time she'd returned, he'd removed his coat and hat. His hair was a fine silver, cut close to his head like the pelt of a chinchilla. He wore a pale grey suit, a charcoal shirt and a flamboyant tie with extravagant swirls of pink and purple. On his pinkie, a diamond sparkled in a gold signet ring. She'd been expecting an orthodox Jew in traditional garb, like she'd seen in photographs of the Antwerp diamond district, but Karen was willing to acknowledge she'd been the victim of her own prejudices.

She opened the conversational bidding. 'Thanks for agreeing to talk to me.'

'I'm intrigued. You say you think I may be able to help you with one of your historic cases?'

She nodded. 'It's a long shot, I know. But sometimes that's the only one we have. I believe that in the autumn of 1995 a young American woman sold a quantity of diamonds. I don't even know for sure if the sale happened in the UK, but I suspect it did.'

'Cut or uncut?' he interrupted.

'I don't know that either. I believe the stones were stolen in Antwerp at the end of the Second World War and they remained hidden until 1995. I suspect they were stolen from the Nazi officers who had in turn looted them from the Jewish diamond dealers they sent to the concentration camps.'

'Very interesting,' he said. 'Nobody wants to collude in someone getting rich from stones with that provenance. And what do you think I can do to help you?' He sipped his water, scrutinising her over the rim of his glass, unblinking as a cautious lizard.

Karen understood the delicacy of the ground she stood on. Anyone who had bought stones from Shirley O'Shaughnessy would themselves have made a profit on the deal in the longer term. Even if they'd known nothing of their provenance, they were still tainted by their very handling of them. 'This must have been a pretty unusual transaction. I don't imagine many young blonde Americans walk into the offices of diamond merchants with a bag of stones. I know it was a long time ago, but surely it's possible that one of your colleagues might remember such a thing?'

An elegant shrug. 'It's possible. As you say, it's not the kind of thing that happens every day. I can tell you with absolute certainty that I wasn't the dealer who bought those stones. And I never heard of such a deal. But there are a lot of us and we don't confide much in each other about the details of our business. What are you hoping for from me?'

'I don't know how your organisation works. Can you ask around? See whether anyone remembers such a deal?'

Elbow on the table, he leaned his chin on his fist. 'We do have a system for communicating with each other. It's important to be able to pass information among ourselves quickly in the event of robbery or some kind of scam.'

'Do you think you could access it on my behalf?' He was, she thought, making her work for it.

'I don't see why not. It's been used from time to time to circulate information from the police.' He took a small Moleskine notebook and a silver mechanical pencil from his pocket. 'Can you go through the details again?'

'Between September and Christmas 1995,' Karen said. He turned to a fresh page and scribbled a note. 'A young blonde American woman selling a parcel of stones.'

He wrote, muttering, 'Cut or uncut,' under his breath. He looked up and met her eyes. 'Are you going to tell me her name?'

'No. I don't want to prejudice any information that might come from this inquiry.'

'Sensible. And one should also bear in mind the law of libel.' His smile was crooked and quirky. 'And there is nothing more you can tell me?'

Karen shook her head. 'It's clutching at straws, I know.'

'But when straws are all you have, what else can you do?' He took a long swallow of his water. 'How will this information help you? What are you investigating?'

Karen didn't really want to discuss the case, but sometimes you had to give a little to get a lot. 'It's a murder. A man was shot dead twenty-three years ago. We suspect the diamonds were the motive.'

'A diamond robbery?'

Her smile was rueful. 'Not exactly. More a recovery than a robbery. I'm sorry, I can't really say any more.'

'That's tantalising, Chief Inspector.'

'I don't mean to be. But if something comes of it, I promise I'll give you the full story.'

He inclined his head politely. 'I'll hold you to that. And now . . . ' He pushed his chair back and stood up. 'I'm going home to send out a message to my colleagues. I will be in touch as soon as I hear anything. If I hear anything.' He replaced his hat, slipped into his coat and strode off in an eddy of black.

★   ★   ★

Much later that evening, Gerry McCartney huddled under the shelter of a dripping tree by the shore of Airthrey Loch, waiting for Ann Markie and her fox terrier. He'd tried to make an appointment with her that afternoon but her secretary had given him the brush-off. 'Until your disciplinary procedure has been resolved, the ACC believes it would be inappropriate to

434

have a meeting with you. If you want to communicate with her, she suggests you put it in writing.'

He was furious. He'd done everything she'd asked of him, and now she was cutting him loose at the first sign of trouble. She'd left him twisting in the wind because that was the better PR option for dealing with Billy McAfee's stupid over-reaction to the news that Barry Plummer was being released. McCartney had only intended McAfee to kick up a stink with the papers, to make Karen Pirie look bad. He hadn't thought the man would go completely mental and kill Plummer. Who could have predicted that? It wasn't the sort of thing that happened round here. This was Scotland, not bloody Texas.

But Markie hadn't even given him a chance to explain what he'd been trying to achieve. All she'd cared about was keeping her own hands clean. Throwing him to the wolves had been a shit thing to do.

Still, he thought he could turn things around. Whatever Markie's reason for dumping him in the HCU, it had to be as valid now as then. He didn't know or care why she wanted enough dirt on KP Nuts to pull her off cold cases and stick her into the kind of desk job that shouted loud and clear that her career was going nowhere. But want it she did, and maybe he could buy his way back into his job with the hard currency of information.

He'd sneaked into Gayfield Square in the small hours, waiting for the changeover of the traffic patrol to slip in while they were leaving.

He still had the door code for the HCU office. Between the obscure notes on Karen's corkboard and the bits of paper on the ginger ninja's desk, he managed to work out that they were looking at a woman called Shirley O'Shaughnessy for the Joey Sutherland murder. And that Shirley O'Shaughnessy was the poster girl for the Scottish government's housing initiative.

Arresting her for murder was, he reckoned, something Ann Markie would want to stop in its tracks. The last thing she'd want would be to piss off the politicians.

Now he had something to bargain with. All he needed now was the woman herself. Time was trickling by and there was no sign of her. Twenty minutes crawled by. His feet were wet and his nose was so cold he couldn't tell if it was rain or snot dripping from it. Bloody woman and her dog.

Enough was enough. McCartney trudged back to his car, a walking lump of misery. He'd get through the weekend somehow then find Markie and make her listen to him. He'd be back in harness before his wife had even noticed he'd been suspended. He'd show Karen Pirie what it took to be a cop.

64

2018 — Edinburgh

The weekend had dragged interminably. With nothing to pursue, Karen had been restless and grumpy. She'd put Hamish off till the beginning of the week and devoted herself to a long overdue deep-cleaning of her flat. So by the time Monday morning rolled round, she was raring to go. She arrived at Aleppo a few minutes before eight and settled at her favourite table at the back of the room. Miran brought her coffee as usual, a tiny shortbread disc on the saucer instead of the customary pistachio crescent. Karen picked it up, her eyebrows questioning. 'This is new,' she said.

Miran chuckled. 'We are assimilating.'

'As long as you don't stop making your own pastries,' she grumbled. She glanced around, checking that she'd not been remiss. 'Is Amena not in this morning?'

'My mother has an appointment at the hospital so Amena has to take the children to school. Do you need to speak to her again?'

'No, quite the opposite. I wanted to tell her that DCI Hutton has a new line of evidence which means he probably won't need Amena to be a witness in court. But we're very grateful for her helping us out.'

Miran's shoulders relaxed. 'This is good. She

is worrying, you know?'

'I know. And I'm sorry about that.'

He patted her shoulder. 'But it is important to speak. We know that too.' Then he was gone, off to serve the next customers.

Karen flipped open her laptop and jumped on board the Wi-Fi. Her automatic first stop was her email and the morning's bulletin from Police Scotland. She skimmed the reports and requests for information, then her eye was caught by the Dog Biscuit's name. *ACC Markie to deliver keynote speech*, the catchline read. Karen clicked on the link and read:

ACC Markie is at Europol HQ in the Hague today to deliver a keynote speech about the ongoing cooperation between Police Scotland and Europol in a post-Brexit world. She will highlight the importance of a continuing close relationship with our European colleagues in the fight against transnational crime.

She didn't bother with the rest of the flannel. The main thing was that Markie was out of the country for at least one day. Knowing she couldn't be blindsided was a bonus. She returned to her email and was pleasantly surprised to see the next message was from Michael Moss with an empty subject line. Nevertheless her heart quickened with hope as she clicked it open.

Good morning, DCI Pirie, she read.

It was a pleasure to meet you last week and fascinating to obtain some small insight into the work that you do in historic cases, an area I have always found particularly gripping. Following our conversation, I sent a communication to the members of the LDI with little hope of providing you with assistance. However, I was happily proved wrong. And this is the response I received late last night from one of our members:

--------Forwarded message--------
From: David Cohn: dcohn86@gmail.com
To: Michael Moss: giffnock73856@gmail.com
Re: help re unusual sale in 1995

Hello, Michael. Good to hear from you, even with such a strange request. I don't know if this is what your policewoman is looking for, but your inquiry stirred something in my memory. You probably don't remember — why should you? — but back in 1995, my father was still running the business though I was doing a lot more of the 'front of house' work. I was the face of Cohn Diamonds, if you like. So when anyone came in to sell stones, I was the person who dealt with them in the first instance.

Relying on memory alone, I can't be precise about the date but I do recall a young blonde American woman bringing in a parcel of uncut stones around that time. They were of a uniformly high gem quality, which is mostly why I remember them. Most of them were clear or very faintly tinted, and they were low in flaws. If I'm right, we bought them for something like £150k.

You will of course be wanting more detail than these vague recollections. We will have full records of the sale. As you doubtless practise yourself, we insist on proper ID — passport or driving licence — and bank details when we make a sale, as well as provenance. Also, back in 1995, before we had full CCTV in all the showrooms and offices, we had a concealed stills camera that photographed all potential vendors. I'm sending this email from home, but I will check our records when I get in tomorrow morning.

Can you let me have the contact details for the police officer concerned and if my partial recollection turns out to be accurate, I could get in touch with her directly?

Best wishes to you and your family,
David Cohn

I took the liberty of passing on your email address and mobile number to David. He's a very reliable chap — he took over the family business about ten years ago and he's been on the board of the LDI for some years. Cohn's have a solid reputation for integrity and discretion. Really, you could not have been more fortunate in terms of who you are dealing with.

I wish you the very best of luck in solving your historic murder.

Yours sincerely
Michael Moss

It was almost too good to be true. Surely there couldn't have been more than one young blonde

American selling diamonds in London in 1995? Karen checked the time on her screen. It wasn't even quarter past eight yet. She was going to have to possess her soul in patience for a bit longer. She swallowed the rest of her coffee in a single gulp and headed for the door. All the frustrations of the last few days fell away when she emerged on to Duke Street as a 25 bus lumbered into sight. She broke into a run and made it to the next stop with seconds to spare. She wanted to be sure she was in the office if David Cohn called, not halfway up Leith Walk with the noise of traffic to distract her.

By the time the Mint arrived a few minutes before nine, she was pacing. She felt electric with nervous energy, desperate to hear what the diamond dealer might have to tell her. 'What's up?' Jason asked, an edge of panic in his voice. She gave him the thirty-second version. Even that was enough for his jaw to drop. 'Jings,' was all he could say.

'Let's not get over-excited yet.' Karen was cautioning herself as much as him. 'How did you get on with your homework?'

Jason pulled out his notebook. 'I managed to track down six other heavy athletes who were competing on the circuit in 1995.' He looked up, pulling a face. 'None of them was much good on detail. They're all obsessed with their own performances. They don't pay that much attention to who else is competing on the day unless they get beaten by them. But they all said that Joey did disappear from the scene, and four of them were able to pin it down to 1995. And that fits with what the Scottish Highland Games Association told me. They've got no trace of Joey Sutherland being placed in any event after the Invercharron Games, and he never renewed his registration. It's possible he may have been competing abroad, but even so, the guys I spoke to said they thought somebody would have run into him along the way and got the story behind his disappearing act.'

'Good work. It doesn't definitively prove the window of death, but it gives us more circumstantial support.' And now for the more tricky question. Casually, she said, 'And what about Mackenzie? Any luck there?'

He flushed. 'I was a bit devious. He said he went to Edinburgh University, yeah? So I rang up their admin department and I said I was from the Home Office, checking on the immigration status of overseas students. I mean, I know Mackenzie is Scottish and not American, obviously, but I thought with him being at school in America, it might be the sort of thing somebody in immigration might have wanted to clarify?'

Karen was amazed. It was a deception worthy of her own deviousness. 'And what did they tell you?'

'According to his university application, he went to Palo Alto High School. Never went anywhere near Michigan as far as his education went. There's no reason to believe he ever met Shirley O'Shaughnessy. You google their names together, there's not even a photo of them at a charity gala. None of his coffee shops is in any of her company's properties. I think he's clean, boss.'

The extent of her relief surprised her. She would be able to sit across a table from Hamish Mackenzie tonight at dinner without having to worry whether he was a co-conspirator in murder. *No,* the carping little voice in her head said, *just a different sort of devious liar.*

Before she could reply, her mobile rang. They both started and looked at each other, anticipation on their faces. Karen snatched up her phone. 'DCI Pirie,' she said, more peremptorily than she'd planned.

'Good morning, Chief Inspector. This is David Cohn from Cohn Diamonds. I believe Michael Moss may have mentioned to you that I might call?' The voice was a very precise light tenor. To Karen's ear, he sounded like a Londoner, but she was no expert on the nuances of southern accents.

'Yes, thank you, Mr Cohn. I appreciate your help. And your time, of course.'

'You're very welcome. We've had occasion to help the police before. It's an occupational hazard in our line of work, I'm afraid.'

'I suppose so. With diamonds being so valuable and so portable.'

'Indeed. And in their uncut stage, not always easy to differentiate. Michael tells me you are interested in a purchase we made in 1995, is that correct?'

'It is. Sometime between mid-September and mid-December, to be precise.'

'And the seller was a young blonde American woman?'

'We believe so,' Karen said, matching his caution.

'I vaguely remembered a transaction that matched that description so I came in a little early this morning to check our records. We keep very comprehensive records, Chief Inspector. It's very important to us that no taint of suspicion attaches to our business. We don't approve of money laundering and we try very hard to be scrupulous in our dealings.' He sounded almost prim now.

'Very commendable. I wish everyone was like you, Mr Cohn.' Karen rolled her eyes at Jason. She was trying to keep her urgency in check. The last thing she wanted to do was to make him nervous. 'And did you find something in your records that matched your recollection?'

'I'm pleased to say that I did.' There was the sound of paper rustling. 'Wednesday the twenty-seventh of September 1995. We purchased a quantity of uncut diamonds of an unusually high gem quality for the sum of a hundred and seventy thousand pounds. The vendor was a walk-in, which is a circumstance where we take particular care. She produced an American passport, a Michigan driver's licence and an Edinburgh University student card. And of course, her bank details so we could transfer the payment to her.' He paused, milking the moment. 'Does that match your expectations, Chief Inspector?

Karen could hardly speak. 'Yes,' she squeezed out. 'Oh yes. And the name?'

'Shirley O'Shaughnessy.'

65

2018 — Edinburgh

It was the name she'd wanted to hear, but still Karen could barely believe her ears. 'Shirley O'Shaughnessy?' she repeated. Jason grinned and gave her two thumbs up.

'That's right,' Cohn confirmed. 'Is that what you were expecting to hear?'

'Hoping,' Karen said. 'Can you remember, did you ask her how she came by the diamonds?'

'I did. To be honest, I didn't recall her response until I looked at the file this morning. She said she'd been left the diamonds by her grandfather who had worked in Antwerp some years before. He had invested his earnings in stones, she said. I assumed, to avoid the taxman.'

'We believe the diamonds did come from Antwerp,' Karen said. 'But not as the result of an investment. We think they were looted by O'Shaughnessy's grandfather when the city was liberated. He was working as a double agent for American intelligence. We're still a bit hazy on all the details.'

'Obviously, if she had mentioned it had been during the war, I'd have been disinclined to buy the stones.' Cohn was clearly offended at having been conned in that particular way. 'So many dealers were dispossessed by the Nazis before they became victims of the Holocaust. We're always very careful about stones that might have been looted. But her story seemed plausible and she was a very self-assured young woman. Now my memory has been well and truly jogged, I can picture her quite clearly.'

'Speaking of pictures . . . In your email to Mr Moss, you said you had a concealed camera that photographed people who came in to sell diamonds. Did you take a photograph of this woman?'

'Oh yes, of course. It's attached to the file along with the photocopies of her ID. That's what triggered my recollection.'

It was almost too good to be true. 'Is there any chance you can scan the file and send it to me?'

'We're always happy to help the police. I'll have my secretary do it right away.'

'You've already been incredibly helpful but I need to ask one more thing of you,' Karen said. 'We're going to need a formal statement of what you've told me. I'm going to speak to a colleague in the Met and ask them to make an appointment with you to go through your recollection of your encounter with Shirley O'Shaughnessy. They'll also need to take with them the originals of your file. You'll get it back in due course, but you might want to make a copy of it for your own sake.'

'I see no problem with that. I'll expect their call. One thing you haven't explained, Chief Inspector, is your interest in this particular matter. You seem to be going to a lot of trouble over some possible Nazi war loot. We usually struggle to get the authorities to pursue cases like this.'

'I'm sorry to say that although the diamonds are a significant part of my case, that's not what this is about. We believe a man was murdered in the course of Shirley O'Shaughnessy getting her hands on the stones and that's what I'm pursuing. I know one murder doesn't sound like much compared to six million, but in my unit we try to treat each life as equally valuable.' She was aware of sounding both sanctimonious and defensive but she didn't know how else to explain without possibly offending this stranger.

When he replied, there was warmth in his voice. 'I'm glad to hear that. When we stop believing that, the road to six million becomes much easier.'

'I'm glad you see it that way, sir. I'll try to get someone from the Met to contact you today, if that's OK?'

'I've nothing in my diary I can't rearrange. I presume that if your case goes as you hope, there will be a trial?'

'That's the plan.'

'In which case, I look forward to meeting you when I come to give my evidence. It will be a pleasure. Till then, Chief Inspector.'

As soon as she'd said her farewells, Karen let out a whoop of joy. 'I think we've got a case, Jason! We need to brainstorm what we've got and where it takes us, but first I've got to arrange for the Met to do the interview with David Cohn. Go and get us some coffee while I make a list of questions for them to put to him on the record.' She waved her fingers in dismissal and turned to her screen. Step by step she constructed a set of questions that would lead detectives unfamiliar with the case through all the key points. She needed them to get this right. It was the keystone of the argument she'd be making to the Procurator Fiscal. She needed that approval before she went in all guns blazing to arrest Shirley O'Shaughnessy. When it came to taking on those with friends in influential places, you had to be very sure of your ground. And Karen was determined that Joey Sutherland's killer would pay for his death.

By the time Jason returned, she'd finished her questions and she was embroiled in a conversation with a Scotland Yard detective whose own mother couldn't have described him as helpful. 'This is a murder inquiry,' she said, lips tight across her teeth.

'Yeah, but by your own admission, it's not exactly current,' he complained.

'That doesn't mean you stick it on the back burner. I'm asking for two officers for a maximum of two hours to take a statement — '

'And that's another thing,' he butted in. 'Why do you need two of my officers? You think they need their hands held to do something that simple?'

'It's not about the competence of your team.' She wanted to add, 'you fuckwit', but restrained herself. 'It's about Scots law. We require corroboration for any evidence that's going to be presented in court. That's why we do things in pairs up here. It's supposed to mitigate the whole 'he said, she said' element of testimony.'

'Oh, for God's sake,' he grumbled. 'I don't see

why you have to have a different bloody legal system. We're all part of the same country.'

For now, Karen thought. 'I know it's inconvenient, but that's the way it is. I've told the witness you'll be in touch with him today. This is the crucial interview I need to move to an arrest, so I would really appreciate it if you could see your way to making it happen. I hoped we could get this done DCI to DCI. I really don't want to take it up the line . . . ' The words were emollient but her tone didn't leave room for discussion.

'Look, I'll see what I can do. I've got a couple of lads giving evidence at the High Court on the Strand this morning. That's just down the road from your man. If they get out of there in decent time I'll get them to swing by and talk to this . . . this David Cohn. Send your questions over to me and I'll see how the day goes. Don't hold your breath, though.'

'I'll expect to hear from you,' she said, ending the call. She shook her head at Jason. 'Talk about masters of the universe! Those wankers down there think they're the only proper polis in the country. Nobody could have a case as important as the most trivial job on their books.'

'At least we've got your notes to work with, boss.' Jason placed a flat white in front of her with a smile that was intended to be placatory but which would have made dogs howl.

'Aye. So let's go through this brick by brick and see if we've got a wall or a pile of rubble.' Karen took a pad of lined A4 paper from her drawer and sharpened her pencils. 'Let's start with 1944. Arnie Burke is in Antwerp where he's been working undercover for US intelligence. Antwerp is liberated by the Canadian Army and Arnie is posted to Scotland. I'm going to assume that he either stole his parcel of diamonds from the Nazis or he took them as payment for services rendered to a dealer. Either way, he's ended up in Scotland with something he needs to get back safely to America. Agreed so far?'

Jason nodded. 'Makes sense, boss.'

'We know from Alice Somerville that her grandfather and his mate Kenny Pascoe were stationed in Wester Ross and when the war was over, they were charged with getting rid of anything the military weren't taking back with them. That included a pair of brand-new motorbikes that they decided were too good to destroy. So they basically nicked them. Crated them, and buried them. I'm guessing — and this is reaching, but it makes sense — that Arnie had stashed the diamonds in one of the bike panniers because he thought they were going to be shipped back to the States on the same boat as him, and they'd be safer there than in his kitbag. Which for all I know was liable to be searched at various points. Then the plans must have changed at the last minute. And Arnie discovered the bikes weren't going back at all. There's his plans, going up in smoke and nothing he can do about it.'

'I know you said that's a bit of guesswork, but it's the only thing that makes sense to me.'

'Me too. The next bit's more hazy. I think Arnie tried to find out what had happened to his diamonds. With his contacts, he could probably have found out who was responsible for dealing with the bikes. Remember the mysterious American who showed up in Warkworth right before Kenny Pascoe died? I'd put money on that being Arnie Burke. Maybe Kenny's death wasn't all it appeared to be. Maybe Arnie was a bit too persuasive? And maybe that's how he got his hands on the map. But for whatever reason, he can't get his hands on the loot.

'Fast forward to Arnie telling his granddaughter the story of the diamonds and his failure to find the family fortune. He's saved up enough to send her to study in Scotland and he tells her it's up to her to find the diamonds. He gives her whatever information he has. And somehow, Shirley, who is a smart lassie, cracks it. But there's a problem, right, Jason?'

He nodded. 'It's buried in a peat bog on the Mackenzie family croft. And no way is she going to be able to get it herself.'

'So she fixes on the bright idea of persuading a heavy athlete to do the job for her. They're strong and they live the kind of peripatetic life where it will take a wee while before anybody notices they've disappeared for sure. Shirley's a good-looking woman and she'll likely be dangling a share of the loot in front of him as well as fluttering her eyelashes. We can put her with Joey at Invercharron, thanks to Ruari Macaulay's evidence.

'Whatever the deal she strikes with Joey at Invercharron, they end up in Wester Ross. Joey digs a hole and opens the panniers and hallelujah, there's the diamonds. But Shirley doesn't want to share and she doesn't want him talking about their wee adventure so she shoots him and fills in the hole.'

'And drives off in his camper van,' Jason chipped in.

'Exactly. She's got big plans, has Shirley. But she can't get started till she liberates the liquidity in the diamonds — '

'You mean, sells them?' Jason was puzzled.

'Uh huh. Who doesn't like to show off sometimes, Jason? She needs cash, and she needs the right property to renovate and sell on at a profit. She can't be seen with Joey's van in case anybody comes looking for him, and she needs time to set up a paper trail that lets her have legitimate ownership of the van. So she sells the diamonds — and now we can prove that — and puts an advert in the *Evening News* to make it look like she's bought the van fair and square. She pays cash for the property in Leith and she's off on the road to a property empire, clean as a whistle. And I bet she's never put a foot wrong since.' She drew in a deep breath. 'What do you think, Jason? Is it enough?'

'Where did she get the gun?'

'Good point. According to his obituary, Arnie Burke was a champion target shooter. Shirley grew up around guns. She could easily have brought one over in her suitcase back then. I know it's hard to believe now, Jason, but back before 9/11, it never occurred to airlines to X-ray hold baggage. And even if she didn't bring it with her, this was before Dunblane. She could have joined a shooting club. Back then, if you had a lockbox in your car, you could take your gun out of the club for competitions.'

He gave her a look that said he wasn't sure if she was at the wind-up. 'Really?'

'Really. It wasn't too hard to get your hands on illegal guns back then either. Between the end of the Soviet Union and the handgun ban, there was a lot of dodgy gun dealing going on. My dad said there was a pub in Lochgelly where you could buy Czech police pistols for fifty quid in the early eighties. But Shirley probably wouldn't have had to go to Lochgelly.'

Jason laughed. 'She'd have stuck out like a sore thumb trying to buy a drink in Lochgelly, never mind a gun.'

'True enough. I wonder whether Napier had a student gun club back then? Make a note to check it out, Jason. There's a few ranges near Edinburgh as well. One out Livingston way, I think, and another one over at Balerno. It's worth checking them out, see whether they've got any record of Shirley O'Shaughnessy being a member. She's got no idea we're looking at her, so we've a bit of time to play with to line up all our ducks in a row. While we're waiting for the Met to do us a favour, we can try to beef up the circumstantial. I don't want this one to slip away from us, Jason. Shirley O'Shaughnessy's done well out of Joey Sutherland's murder. That needs to stop.'

66

2018 — Edinburgh

Karen hadn't deliberately kept Hamish waiting. But the audio file of the Met detectives' interview with David Cohn had landed in her inbox as she was preparing to leave the office. She'd planned to go home and change for their dinner date but that wasn't going to happen now. She could have left the interview till morning; nothing was going to happen overnight that would have any impact on the case, she knew that. But she couldn't resist it.

There was nothing on the recording that contradicted what Cohn had said earlier, but nothing that amplified it either. That was fine, however. The very consistency of Cohn's account was reassuring. It spoke of a witness who wouldn't readily be shaken from his version of events.

By the time she'd done with the recording, she was already late. She forced herself to take the time to apply fresh lipstick and attempt to arrange her hair in the ladies' loo before she dashed out and fretted on the pavement, waiting for the chance to cross to the taxi rank without dying under a bus. She collapsed into the cab, cursing under her breath. Why was she letting herself get so wound up about keeping a man waiting for ten minutes at a restaurant table? Yes, it was bad manners, but not even her mother could give her a hard time for being late because she was trying to solve a murder.

The roadworks on Leith Street seemed even slower than usual, and beyond them, the traffic was clotted on the Bridges and congealed on Chambers Street. She'd have been quicker walking, Karen thought. But then she'd have turned up out of breath and sweating because she wouldn't have been able to stop herself from hurrying.

Finally the cab pulled up on George IV Bridge, almost directly opposite Perk. Karen walked into The Outsider and quickly scanned the room before any of the waiting staff reached her. She saw Hamish at once. He was sitting with his back to the door at one of the window tables that commanded an uninterrupted view of the castle rock and the brooding silhouette of its fortifications. In spite of her best intentions, her spirits lifted at the sight.

She quickly crossed the room and lightly touched him on the shoulder, continuing on without pause to sit opposite him. He half-rose, clearly moving to greet her with an embrace. But something in her face stopped him and he sat again. 'I'm sorry I'm late, and I'm sorry I'm still in my work clothes,' she said. 'Something came in at the last minute that I had to deal with.'

He shook his head. 'No need to apologise. I know your job isn't predictable. And I figured if it was something major you'd let me know, not leave me sitting here so long everybody in the room would know I'd been stood up.'

She couldn't help smiling. She caught his eye and knew there was something flickering between them. Then she reminded herself that he'd played her and the smile died on her lips. 'Had a good day?' she asked, her voice carefully neutral.

'Busy. And far too boring to share with anybody else. How about you? How is the Joey Sutherland case going? Are you making progress?'

'Slowly.' She was cautious. 'Did your grandparents ever mention an American called Arnie Burke?'

'No. Is he a suspect?'

She chuckled. 'Hardly. He died in 1994. But he might have had something to do with the bikes back when they were first buried.'

'Intriguing. What else have you found out?'

'I can't tell you anything,' she said. 'I shouldn't even have said what I did. Never let anything out in the wild that you wouldn't want ending up in the papers.'

'Do you think I'm here because I'm trying to winkle information out of you to sell to the papers?' His face crinkled in an incredulous half-smile.

'It's nothing personal. I don't talk about ongoing cases with anybody outside the tent.' And because it was preying on her mind and because she couldn't stay silent about so important a thing, she said, 'But even if that wasn't the case, I couldn't talk to you about it because I can't trust you.'

He recoiled as far as the chair would allow. But before he could respond, the waiter was upon them, delivering menus and drinks lists and reciting the specials. Karen ordered a glass of Prosecco. Not because she felt she had anything to celebrate but because it required less thought than a choice of gin. Hamish pointed to his half-empty glass of beer and said, 'Same again.' The waiter picked up on his brusque tone and backed off.

'What do you mean, you can't trust me?' He seemed genuinely upset.

'You're a liar.'

The words hung in the air between them. His eyes narrowed and a band of dark pink spread along his cheekbones like a swatch of blusher. 'That's a pretty harsh thing to say.'

'It's a pretty harsh thing to discover about somebody you've taken a liking to.' Karen's chin came up, challenging him.

'I really don't know what you're talking about.' He leaned forward, forearms on the table, his expression earnest.

'Come on, Hamish.' She was giving him one last chance. But he wasn't taking it. He said nothing, nor did he flinch under her stare. She fiddled with an earring, as if it were a nervous gesture. His lips twitched. 'I know about the earrings,' she said, her voice soft with regret.

Now he reacted. He sat up straight, one hand gripping the side of his beard. 'Oh fuck,' he groaned. 'How did you find out?'

'I'm a detective, Hamish. Finding things out is how I make a living. Your barista recognised me from my fucking earrings. Because you'd had them delivered across the road.'

457

He had the pained look that in a child would precede tears. But he was too old and too self-conscious for anything so revelatory. 'I couldn't find your earring in the U-bend. And I wanted to see you again.'

'You could have called me and told me the truth.'

'I was afraid that would be the end of that. I didn't think you'd want to go out with me because I was connected to your case. So I thought I needed an excuse. And the earring would be a great excuse. You wouldn't be able to say no to a drink, at least. You can't blame me for trying.'

Again the waiter's arrival forced them into silence. He placed their glasses on the table wordlessly, clearly picking up on the atmosphere. Then he stepped back, saying, 'I'll give you a wee minute to decide, eh?'

'It was devious,' Karen said.

'OK, it was maybe the wrong thing, but it was for the right reason.' He creased his brows, pleading. 'Karen, I spend three hundred and forty-five pounds doing the wrong thing for the right reason. That's how much I was prepared to gamble on seeing you again.'

'Well, lucky you, having three hundred and forty-five pounds to spend on a whim. Hamish, my working life consists of unravelling the lies people tell to cover the things they've done wrong. Sometimes they're trivial things, sometimes they're truly terrible. But all the lies are the same. They're reasons not to trust anything they say.' She sighed. 'I like you, Hamish. I really do.

458

But you couldn't have got off on a worse foot with me if you'd really worked at it.'

He shifted in his seat and hung his head, fixing his gaze on the table, apparently seeking answers there. Karen made herself stay silent, waiting.

At length, he mumbled, 'Do you want me to leave?'

Despite everything, she really didn't. 'What? And let you off the hook?'

He flicked a quick glance upwards and registered the wry smile. 'I'm really sorry. I only wanted to make you happy. I didn't think you'd find out.'

She shook her head and scoffed at him. 'Like I said, Hamish. I'm a detective. Even if Anders hadn't spilled the beans, I'd have noticed as soon as I looked at them closely side by side. The one you gave me looks split new. Mine has got the odd scuff and scratch and the back isn't nearly as shiny. It was a good try but really, you'd have done better to save your money and tell the truth.'

'I realise that now.' He let out a deep breath. 'I'm a fixer, Karen. I'm good at solving problems. Most people are content to let me fix things. They don't pay much attention to how, they just accept I've sorted whatever it is that needed sorting.' He gave a dry laugh. 'I should have thought it through. Realised that the very thing that's attractive about you is that you're different. So the same old, same old isn't the way to be with you.' He took a long gulp of his beer. 'Would you like me to go out and come in again so we can start over?'

'You could try it.' She watched as he stood up and wove through the tables to the door. He walked along the street towards Greyfriars Bobby till he was out of sight. For a moment, she thought he wasn't coming back and she felt a lurch of disappointment. But then he reappeared and hustled across the room to their table.

He put one hand on the back of the chair and raised his eyebrows. 'Is this seat taken?'

She inclined her head, a playful smile escaping against her will. 'It is now.'

67

2018 — Stirling

McCartney had called in a favour from a guy who'd been on the Strathclyde MIT with him back in the day. Now he was one of the HQ gophers. One of the ones who'd given up the ghost on being real coppers. Happy to settle for staring at screens and totting up performance indicators. But handy to have in your back pocket every now and again. Like when you wanted to know if the Dog Biscuit was back on UK soil after her jolly in Holland.

He wasn't about to make the same mistake twice, though. Tonight he'd wait till he saw Markie set off with the dog before he got out of the car. Then he'd circle the loch in the opposite direction and meet her halfway round. He parked in the gloom in the furthest corner of the car park and settled down with a podcast of his favourite football preview show, a slice of anarchy, gossip and surrealism. He'd shouted at the opinionated presenters for the third time when Markie's car cruised into a space near the start of the lakeside path. He watched her emerge and let the dog out of the tailgate. He gave her five minutes then he set off.

It was a clear dry night, a nip in the air but no sign of rain. McCartney walked briskly along the path, rehearsing what he was about to say. He passed half a dozen students, cheerful and noisy with drink. They paid no attention to him. Nor did the elderly man walking his golden retriever or the two middle-aged women deep in discussion about a research application.

He rounded a curving bank of rhododendrons and caught sight of Markie in the distance. He slowed to a halt and waited in the shadows till she was a few metres away. He stepped forward and announced his presence with, 'How was Holland?'

Ann Markie misstepped and staggered slightly. 'You should not be here,' she said, her voice low and angry.

'I need to talk to you.'

'Didn't you get the message? It's not appropriate for us to meet until the disciplinary procedure is over.'

The dog bounded up to them, tongue hanging out in what looked like a smile. McCartney wasn't fooled. She'd set the wee beast on him in a heartbeat if it came to it. 'You don't get it, do you? I want my job back. Fuck the disciplinary process. I want all that shit to go away. And you're the one who can make that happen. You put me in the firing line for this, you owe me.'

'I don't owe you a thing, Gerry. Yes, I moved you to the HCU to report back to me on how it was being run, but that's all. You make it sound like there was some special deal between us. Believe me, Gerry, you could not be more wrong. You blew it in a major way. A man's dead, and you're dead to me.' She tried to sidestep him and continue on her way but he blocked her with a sidestep of his own.

'Not so fast, Ann. If I've learned one thing from you, it's that information is currency under your regime. Now I've got a juicy piece of information that I think you'd repay with interest.'

'If you have information about a crime, you are obliged to hand it over. You know that. Don't make things worse for yourself than they are already. Don't make me add that to the complaints against you.'

He shook his head. 'This isn't information about a crime. It's the sort of thing you want to know about because not knowing about it means you'll get covered from your shiny hair to your shiny shoes when the shit hits the fan. Ma'am.' He leaned forward, almost spitting the final word in her face.

'And you think you can bargain with this information?' She looked as scornful as she sounded.

'I know I can.'

Markie sized him up. He suspected that under her surface she was as twitchy as any of them. 'You want me to make the disciplinary charges disappear, is that your price?'

'Aye.'

She shook her head. 'I can't do that. It's too high profile. The best I can do is reinstate you pending an inquiry. And then make the inquiry so long-drawn-out that everybody forgets about it and eventually it all goes away.'

He shook his head. It wasn't enough. The very idea of telling his wife and girls that he was suspended made his heart hurt in his chest. How could he lay claim to their respect if he was disgraced in the eyes of the world? 'I need more than that.'

She pushed his chest, taking him by surprise, making him stumble enough for her to get past him. 'Say goodbye to the best offer you're going to get, then.'

'Wait.' He snatched at her arm, grasping her sleeve. The dog growled deep in its throat. Markie shook herself free.

'Changed your mind?' Her lip curled in a sneer. She clearly thought she had the upper hand. 'How do I know that there's any value in what you say you've got?'

'Because I'm not stupid,' he said, his voice rising in frustration. 'You wouldn't have set me on Karen Pirie in the first place if you thought I didn't know shite from Shinola.' He took a deep breath and tried to calm down. 'Look, I'm not going to deny I'm looking after number one here, but I'm trying to do you a favour in the process.'

Markie assessed him, head cocked to one side. He wondered whether she sensed his desperation. 'Let's hear it, then.'

'Do I get to come back to work?'

'That depends on what you've got.'

There was a long moment of Mexican stand-off. Then his shoulders slumped and he conceded. 'The body in the peat bog?'

'The strongman?'

'Heavy athlete,' he corrected her.

'Whatever.' The dog sensed her impatience,

giving a soft whimper and leaning into her leg to show subservience.

'She's got somebody in the frame for it.'

'That's a good thing, isn't it? Why is that a bargaining chip?' Cautious now, Markie took a step away from him.

'The bargaining chip is the name of the person she's poised to arrest.' He paused, stretching the suspense.

'This isn't an episode of *Line of Duty*, Sergeant. Spit it out.'

'Have you heard of Shirley O'Shaughnessy?'

Markie's eyebrows rose in perfect arcs. 'Are you serious? Heard of her? I've met her. One of those party conference receptions where everybody stands around with their best smiles and promises. She was full of her plans for addressing the housing crisis and the politicians were treating her like she was the Messiah. And you say Pirie wants to arrest her for murder?'

'She's the only suspect they've got.'

'What makes Pirie think Shirley O'Shaughnessy shot a caber-tosser in a Highland ditch?'

'Peat bog,' he corrected her automatically.

'I don't care if it was a bloody pigsty. Why does Karen Pirie want her for a murder? Has she taken leave of her senses?' He detected a note of hope in her voice.

'I don't know all the details. She pretty much shut me out of the investigation. But I do know that she's put her and Joey Sutherland together at the Invercharron Games, which is the last recorded sighting of him. And O'Shaughnessy ended up buying his van a few months later.'

'And that's it?'

'Obviously there's more. But I don't know how much. They were getting pretty frustrated. She had that ginger idiot running all over the place trying to track down where the van was parked in 1995.'

Markie frowned. 'Sounds like she's clutching at straws.'

'Which you don't want to do around somebody like Shirley O'Shaughnessy,' McCartney said. 'Friends in high places, and all that.'

He could almost see the wheels going round as she processed the implications of what he'd told her. 'No,' she said pensively.

'So do I get my job back?'

'You get a job back,' she said, distracted. 'Kilmarnock CID is short-handed. Their sergeant's gone on maternity leave and one of their DCs broke his leg a couple of nights ago. Report there in the morning.'

'Kilmarnock? Are you kidding me? What about one of the MITs?'

She laughed in his face. 'You have got to be joking. Now fuck off to Kilmarnock and try to keep a low profile. You're drinking in the last-chance saloon, Gerry, and don't forget it.' She turned on her heel and stalked off, head high, shoulders straight, dog at her heels.

Kilmarnock? All that for bloody Kilmarnock? He took a vicious kick at a stone. Maybe there would be something better down the line if his information gave the Dog Biscuit what she wanted. But at least now he wouldn't have to confess his disgrace to his wife and see the look

466

of disappointment and contempt in her eyes.

McCartney walked back to his car, wishing he'd never crossed the paths of Ann Markie and Karen Pirie.

68

2018 — Edinburgh

Bewilderingly, the Hamish Mackenzie magic worked a second time. Karen slept straight through the night, surfacing from sleep in happy disbelief. They'd somehow negotiated an awkward path past the uncomfortable start to the evening. By the time they got to dessert, they were almost relaxed. Not relaxed enough for Karen to accept his invitation to go for a drink at a late-night whisky bar, however. They'd walked down the Mound together, then Karen had hailed a cab to take her home. Hamish was sensible enough to let that mark the end of the evening.

He opened the door of the cab for her then leaned in to kiss her cheek. His soft beard tickled and she felt cross with herself for the tingle of desire that ran through her. 'Shall we do this again, then?' he asked as she climbed aboard.

'It would be a pity not to.'

'I'll call you, then.' He closed the door and raised his hand in a wave as the driver pulled away from the kerb. Hamish was very definitely contrite. He'd done his best to recover from his misjudgement and she thought he was sincere. Something was happening between them, there was no point in denying that. But she needed to take it slowly. She couldn't afford the emotional attrition of an involvement that didn't work out. Grieving for Phil was still an active part of her life. If Hamish could understand that, they might be able to work something out between them.

Always supposing he felt the same. That she hadn't snagged his attention only because she was a novelty in his world. She had no way of knowing if that was the case. Time alone would clarify that.

And she had plenty of time.

Her good mood didn't last long. She'd barely finished showering when her phone vibrated on the bathroom shelf. Karen rubbed her hair then wrapped a towel round her body before she picked up the phone. The message read simply: Fettes. Conference room 2, 9.30. ACC Markie. Karen groaned. 'What now? How can she not just leave me to get on with my work?'

For once, she wasn't going to let the Dog Biscuit put her on the back foot. She had no idea what this latest manoeuvre was about, but she was determined not to start the conversation feeling inferior. She dried her hair with care, manipulating it into neatness with a tub of product she'd bought three months before and hardly used. Then tinted moisturiser, a thin line of eye pencil, mascara and a light slick of dark red lipstick. It occurred to her that she was taking more trouble for the Dog Biscuit than she had for Hamish. What did that say about her priorities, she wondered.

Her favourite suit, a lightweight dark green tweed from the outlet mall at Livingston, was still in the dry cleaner's bag. She paired it with a plain grey layer and buttoned up the jacket to check that the look worked. She'd lost a couple of pounds since she'd bought it, but that only made the trousers sit better on her waist. This time, Ann Markie wasn't going to be the only one looking the part.

Karen left the car in the Waitrose car park down the street from Fettes. That way she could pick up a coffee on her way to the meeting. Keep it casual, look as if you haven't got a care in the world about how your unit is running. If running was the word for the way the HCU was operating right now.

She was five minutes early, but the ACC was already installed at the head of the conference table. Markie was in full dress uniform, looking every inch the tailored professional. But for once, Karen felt she matched her boss. 'You wanted to see me,' she said, walking in and closing the door behind her. She moved to the chair at the opposite end from Markie.

'Phone on the table,' Markie said.

'Sorry?'

'Phone on the table. I want to be sure you're not recording this.'

Karen did as she was told, but said, 'Last time we met, you were the one wanting a record of what was said. Can I see your phone too, ma'am?'

Markie held up her phone. 'As you can see, DCI Pirie, it's turned off.'

'Is this more fallout from Gerry McCartney's stupidity? Because I'm not carrying the can for that.'

'Is it true that you're building a case against Shirley O'Shaughnessy?'

Karen was momentarily stunned into silence. How did Markie know about that? And why did she care? 'She's a person of interest in the Joey Sutherland murder,' she said cautiously. And then she remembered the car she'd seen driving away from Gayfield Square. McCartney, of course. If she hadn't been so distracted she'd have recognised his car right away. He must have weaselled his way back into the building and had a bloody good look round her office. It was the only explanation. But right now, she needed all her attention on Markie.

'A person of interest? On what basis?'

'She was with him at the Invercharron Highland Games, which is the last reported sighting of him. Three months later, she became the registered keeper of Sutherland's camper van, supposedly after seeing an advert in the *Evening News*. Whoever was responsible for Sutherland's murder had a reason for excavating that site. And within a couple of weeks of the last sighting of Sutherland, Shirley O'Shaughnessy was selling a parcel of uncut diamonds in London. Allegedly an inheritance from her grandfather, except there's no record of him ever having possessed such a thing. That was the seed corn for financing her property development business.'

'And how is she supposed to have known where to dig for the bikes?' Sarcasm, not interest in her voice.

'Her grandfather was around in Wester Ross at the end of the war. When the bikes were buried.

One of the men who was involved died in 1946, a couple of days after a mysterious American turned up in his village looking for him. I believe that was O'Shaughnessy's grandfather and that's when he got the map that showed the burial site.'

'You believe a lot, DCI Pirie. If the grandfather got the map in 1946, why did it take till 1995 for anyone to excavate the bikes? Isn't that the crucial question?'

Karen knew she should be grateful for the Dog Biscuit's scepticism. She'd have to make these same arguments to a fiscal to get a prosecution under way. But anyone from the fiscal's office would give her more leeway to explain her conclusions. Still, she had to keep plugging away. 'I've seen one of the two maps. If you know where to look, it's clear where to dig. But if you don't know the wider location, you could drive around for a long time before you'd pin down the site. I suspect Arnie Burke stumbled at that hurdle.'

'So how did his granddaughter succeed where he had failed?'

'I don't know the answer to that. It's the missing link in the chain. But we can finesse that in the interview, we can — '

'A chain with a missing link isn't a chain, it's a pile of scrap metal.' Markie didn't look like a woman delighted at the thought of wrapping up a cold case.

'I think she's got a case to answer. I can make the argument to the fiscal.'

Thin-lipped, Markie enunciated very clearly. 'You're not going anywhere near the fiscal with this.'

'At the very least, I need to interview Shirley O'Shaughnessy.' Karen's stomach hurt from a mixture of anger and fear that this was all going wrong.

'No. You will not go near Shirley O'Shaughnessy. That's an order, DCI Pirie. Leave her alone.'

'What? I'm supposed to just let this go? Forget about it? A man was murdered and she has justifiable questions to answer. We don't ignore material evidence.' Despite her determination to stay cool, Karen heard her voice rise.

Markie leaned back in her chair, a condescending smile on her face. 'You really don't see the bigger picture, do you, Pirie? You're a small-minded woman from a small town. But some of us don't suffer from tunnel vision. Shirley O'Shaughnessy is a major player in the future of this country. She's making government housing policy a reality. She's courted by our political masters. How do you think the government's going to react to you dragging one of their darlings into an interview room to answer questions on a case from the past that has more holes than a box of doughnuts? Without the goodwill of the politicians, Police Scotland is screwed. Not to mention what the media will make of it. Everybody loves Shirley. She's the one going to make their dreams come true. But you?' A contemptuous wave of the hand. 'You're only as good as your last front page. And your last front page was Barry Plummer. Your next one's probably going to be Willow Henderson. You're on course to being kicked out the door for bringing the force into disrepute.'

473

Karen swallowed hard. Markie's tirade hit all her sensitive spots, shrivelling her confidence to a husk. But still, she couldn't let it pass. 'So that's how it is now, is it? If you're pals with the politicians, if you're the darling of the rag, tag and bobtail of the Scottish media, you do what you like? Really? Is that our new policy?'

Markie sighed. 'Don't be even more naive than I took you for. And don't think about defying me. I'm going to have a quiet word with Shirley O'Shaughnessy in case your clumsy raking about has got back to her. I'll reassure her that your inquiries were purely routine and she has no cause for concern.'

'And what about Joey Sutherland? What about justice for him? What am I supposed to tell his family?'

'Tell them your investigation has dead-ended. That there are no viable lines of inquiry. I'm sure they won't have any difficulty believing you've failed. Now off you go and see whether you can find something useful to do in your wee back office that doesn't put all of our futures in jeopardy.' She stood up, indicating the meeting was over.

Karen sat and stared at her. She felt slightly dazed at what she'd been forced to listen to. She'd had her differences with senior officers before, but she'd never doubted their underlying determination to bring criminals to justice. This version of their priorities horrified her.

'Are you still here?' Markie said as she swept past on her way out.

You bet I'm still here. And this is not over.

474

69

2018 — Edinburgh

Karen's emotional response to Ann Markie's diatribe had distilled into seething rage by the time she arrived at the office. Jason took one look at her when she walked through the door and froze. 'What's happened?' he said.

'Apparently our job description's changed. According to the Dog Biscuit, we're not here to put criminals away any more. Our job is to keep everybody happy, especially politicians and media hacks.' She threw her bag on the desk and dropped like a stone into her chair.

'I don't understand.'

'That utter shitehawk Gerry McCartney must have managed to get back into the office after he was canned. He told Markie we're looking at Shirley O'Shaughnessy for Joey Sutherland. And she's losing her mind because Shirley is the Scottish government's best pal when it comes to putting roofs over people's heads. And obviously that's way more important than being held to account for murder.' Karen kicked her waste-paper bin, adding a new dent to its battered side.

'What? I don't get it.'

Karen rolled her eyes. She didn't have the patience for the Mint right now. 'Who pays for Police Scotland?' she demanded, each syllable clear and distinct.

With the air of a kicked dog wary of the next blow, he said, 'The Scottish government.'

'And who would we be pissing off if we arrest O'Shaughnessy?'

'I see what you're getting at,' he said. 'But I don't think the First Minister's like that.'

'I agree with you. I don't believe that's how she thinks either. But Markie does, and Markie's our boss. And she's basically told me to lay off O'Shaughnessy or collect my jotters on the way out the door.'

'She can't give you the sack,' he protested.

'She can do me for bringing the force into disrepute. It would drag on forever and if she won I'd lose my pension as well as my reputation. She's banking on me walking out the door in disgust, I think.' The white heat of Karen's anger was subsiding a little, leaving a cold coal of resentment in her heart.

There was a long silence, then Jason said, 'So is that it, then? We walk away from it?' For once, he sounded indignant as well as bewildered.

Karen clenched her fists. 'Fuck, no. I've spent years building the best HCU in the UK. I've been fighting the bullies ever since I put on my first uniform and I'm not about to start rolling over now. We're going to arrest Shirley O'Shaughnessy and we're going to do it now. Before our supposed superior officer marks her card.'

'We going to her office, then?'

'First we find out where she is.' Karen attacked her keyboard. 'Get on the phone.' She dictated a number. 'That's her office. Tell them

476

we need to speak to her about a break-in at her flat.'

Jason obeyed. Unlike Karen, insubordination never occurred to him. When the phone was answered, he put on his best official voice. 'This is Detective Constable Murray from Gayfield Square. I need to speak with Ms Shirley O'Shaughnessy. Is she in the office this morning . . . ' He paused. 'It's in connection with a break-in at her flat. I need to speak to her in person . . . ' He shook his head at Karen. 'So where will I find her? It is rather urgent, as I'm sure you'll appreciate.' Suddenly his eyes widened and he mimed, 'Help!'

'Aye, I've got that,' he said. 'Till half past eleven. I'll get over there right away.' He replaced the receiver and spread his hands in a disconcerted gesture. 'You're not going to believe this.'

'Try me. The morning I've had, my disbelief is well and truly suspended.'

'She's at a Scottish Government reception at Bute House.'

He'd been right. Karen could barely credit it. 'With . . . ?'

He nodded. 'Aye.'

Her mind raced through the options. They could stake out Bute House, the official residence of the First Minister of Scotland, and try to arrest Shirley O'Shaughnessy as she came out. About fifteen different things could go wrong with that, some of them involving an open-topped bus full of tourists. They could wait outside her office for her to return after the reception. But that left the possibility that

Markie could get to her first. If the ACC tried to call her or text her while she was still in the reception, the chances were that O'Shaughnessy would ignore it. But as soon as she left the room, Markie could get to her.

There was nothing else for it. They were going to have to arrest her in a room full of people, in front of the First Minister.

The one upside was that Markie might have a coronary.

'Let's get a Battenberg,' she said, leading the way to a squad car, whose nickname came from the chequered pattern of blue and yellow squares along their sides. 'If we're going to arrest her, we need to be able to stick her in something official. You drive,' she instructed him.

They were halfway along Queen Street when Jason suddenly said, 'It's pretty neat, this case ending up in Bute House.'

'How?'

'Do you not remember that story a couple of years ago about the chandelier in the drawing room?'

'No, it's fair to say I know nothing about the chandelier in the drawing room of Bute House.'

'They think it might be Nazi loot. It was sent back by some guy who was a pal of Lady Bute. He said he found it in the street. I don't know about you, but I've never found a massive great crystal chandelier in the street. Anyway, Lady Bute had it restored and hung up in the drawing room. Only, this all started with Nazi loot, right?'

'That's right.' She snorted with laughter and burst into song. '"The Nazi chandeliers light up

478

the paintings on your wall.''

The release of tension left them both giggling, and as they turned into Charlotte Square, Jason weighed in with, ''When the new wears off of your Nazi chandeliers.''

They were still chuckling when he drew up outside Bute House. Unlike 10 Downing Street, there were no barriers to keep the public at arm's length, and not even a police officer on the doorstep. They climbed the steps to the imposing Georgian townhouse in the centre of the blackened sandstone terrace that ran the length of the north side of the square. Jason rang the bell and the door was opened almost immediately. They both displayed their ID to the officer on security detail.

'We need to speak to someone in the reception that's going on right now,' Karen said. 'Is it upstairs in the drawing room?'

He nodded and Karen headed down the hallway to the elegantly curved staircase, Jason at her heels. 'Wait, you can't just breenge in,' he protested.

Karen swung round. 'We need to make an arrest, son. I don't need your permission to do that.'

He looked appalled. 'The First Minister's in there. You can't — Look, I'll get one of her people to come out and talk to you, OK?' He pushed past and took the stairs two at a time. Karen exchanged looks with Jason and followed.

When they reached the landing, they waited. The door into the grand drawing room was standing open and beyond it they could see people standing around in little groups, deep in conversation, coffee cups in hand. Waitresses circulated with plates of tiny pastries and tablet. 'Almost like being at home,' Karen muttered.

'Speak for yourself.'

The security officer reappeared, looking harried. A young woman followed close behind, apparently unperturbed. She smiled at them both. 'I'm Tabitha, I work for the First Minister. How can I help you, Officers?'

Karen introduced them, then said, 'I know this is really awkward, but we need to arrest one of your guests. For operational reasons, we can't wait to do it discreetly when she leaves. The last thing I want to do is to embarrass your boss, obviously. How do we do this?'

The only sign Tabitha gave that this was anything out of the ordinary was a momentary twitch of the eyebrows. 'Can you tell me who it is you need to . . . arrest?'

Karen took a deep breath. This might be the moment where her career disappeared. She found she didn't care. 'Shirley O'Shaughnessy. Of City SOS Construction.'

Now Tabitha was disconcerted. 'You want to arrest Shirley?'

'Is that a problem?'

'More a surprise.' She glanced over her shoulder, biting her lip. 'Give me a minute, would you?' She went back inside. Karen followed her to the threshold, peering round the edge of the door. Above the elaborate fireplace hung an ornate gilt mirror that would have covered all of Karen's living room wall. It reflected the controversial chandelier back at the room. The First Minister was over by one of the tall windows in a knot of intense conversation, unmistakable in vertiginous heels and one of her trademark brightly coloured suits. Karen watched Tabitha cross to her side and draw her away from the group. Her face showed nothing as she listened to her aide. Then she nodded and said something in reply. She returned to the people she'd been talking to, but her eyes kept moving back to the doorway.

When Tabitha returned, she said, 'The First Minister asked me if it would be possible for you to make your arrest outside the room? I'll fetch Shirley and you can speak to her here. Is that OK?'

Karen had some misgivings, but she knew she didn't have much choice. 'Just don't tell her it's the police who want to talk to her.'

She watched Tabitha scan the room and locate her target. She walked across and, without fuss, touched the elbow of a woman with her back to the door. When she turned. Karen recognised her at once. She looked momentarily perplexed, then let Tabitha lead her to the door.

Karen took a couple of steps back as O'Shaughnessy approached and waited till she was properly out of the room. Jason picked up Karen's nod towards the door, and he moved smartly past them all to close it. Abruptly the buzz of conversation diminished.

O'Shaughnessy turned to Tabitha. 'I thought you said — '

Karen stepped in front of her. 'Shirley

O'Shaughnessy, I am arresting you on suspicion of murder.'

It was hard to say who looked most astounded — Tabitha or O'Shaughnessy. 'This is a joke, right?' O'Shaughnessy said, the traces of her American accent still evident.

'No joke, I promise you.' Karen recited the rest of the caution while O'Shaughnessy stood shaking her head and reaching into her jacket pocket for her phone.

'This is crazy. I'm calling my lawyer right now.' She stabbed the phone with perfectly manicured burgundy fingernails.

'That's fine. Tell your lawyer to meet us at Gayfield Square police station.'

O'Shaughnessy gave a brittle laugh and stopped dialling. 'I'm going nowhere with you.' She swung round, making for the door. 'Wait till Nicola hears about this.' But Jason barred her way, standing impassive with his hands folded in front of him.

'We can do this the easy way, where you walk downstairs with us and get into the police car without a fuss,' Karen said, matter-of-factly. 'Or I can handcuff you and make a show of you for the photographers who will doubtless be outside waiting for their morning photo op.'

'Who am I supposed to have murdered? Is this some corporate manslaughter thing?' O'Shaughnessy was good at this. The blend of tough businesswoman and injured innocent was hard to pull off, but she was rocking the look, Karen thought.

'Joey Sutherland. Remember him?'

For a second her face froze. If Karen had blinked at the wrong moment, she'd have missed it. Then she recovered and said, 'Never heard of him. Did he work for us? Is somebody accusing us of negligence?'

'No. I'm accusing you of murder. Nothing corporate about it. Now, are you coming quietly, or are you going to make the kind of scene that'll guarantee you never get asked back here again?'

O'Shaughnessy looked at her with undisguised disgust. 'You're going to regret this for the rest of your career. Which probably is not going to be long.'

Karen smiled. 'You may be right. But at least I've had the satisfaction of this moment.'

70

2018 — Edinburgh

An arrest was never the end. It was merely the end of the beginning. Karen had been far from certain that her belief in Shirley O'Shaughnessy's guilt would be mirrored by the Procurator Fiscal's department, particularly since she'd made the arrest without consulting them. They weren't supposed to support any case unless it had more than a fifty per cent chance of success. But Karen had worked with Fiscal Depute Ruth Wardlaw in the past and the two women had learned to respect each other's judgement. Wardlaw agreed there was a missing chapter in the narrative of Shirley O'Shaughnessy's crime. 'But I think we can bury that under the weight of the rest of the evidence.'

'What about the jury? Is she not supposed to be the great white knight of housing development?'

Ruth grinned. 'Juries don't love the rich. And it looks like City SOS Construction's going to carry on with their programme regardless. That's the joy of a really big company. Nobody's indispensable.'

And so it was agreed. Shirley O'Shaughnessy would face trial for the murder of Joey Sutherland. It wasn't the only half-time result in Karen's favour. The audio experts had cleaned up Dandy Muir's phone recording enough to leave no doubt about the order of events in the Hendersons' kitchen. Willow Henderson had been charged with the murder of Dandy Muir and the attempted murder of her husband. True, Billy McAfee was awaiting trial for the culpable homicide of Barry Plummer, but his brief was confident they could plead that the balance of his mind was disturbed. And she'd had a note from the First Minister thanking her for her discretion at Bute House. 'We'll see what she says when we come for the Nazi chandelier,' she'd said, showing it to Jimmy Hutton.

It wasn't all glory and righteousness, however. Unsurprisingly, Markie had seized the credit for the HCU's work and had backed off. But Karen knew this was a truce, not a surrender. The Dog Biscuit would be back snapping at her ankles. And Gerry McCartney was still a police officer. Not in an elite unit, it was true. But Karen knew she'd made another enemy there. Time would tell how much damage he could do her.

And then there was Hamish. Even if Shirley O'Shaughnessy walked free at the end of her trial, Karen couldn't help thinking that something good might yet come from the case of the body in the bog. Like an arrest, this too was only the end of a beginning.

Epilogue

1995 — Invercharron, Sutherland

Joey Sutherland was no stranger to admiration. The adulation of small boys who wanted to know the secret to growing up like him; the hot curiosity of women who craved those hard muscles against their soft bodies; and the almost childlike need of grown men to be seen standing next to him at the bar, to be able to boast he was their friend. He'd learned to take it for granted. This was what came with being one of the world's top heavy athletes.

At Highland Games and strongman competitions on four continents, Joey and his colleagues wowed the audiences with their feats of strength. Tossing the caber, throwing the hammer, the stone, the light and the heavy weight, the sheaf — those were all impressive contests, and Joey had won plenty of them over the years. But the event where he still outshone the competition was the weight-for-height.

A hush always shivered through the crowd when it came to the most terrifying event of the games. Joey would make great play of rubbing his palms with the rosin bag to protect him from the nightmare injuries that slippage could cause. He would check the height the bar was set at, then he'd turn his back on the two slender uprights and the crossbar. He'd plant his feet firmly apart then bend his knees, taking a firm grasp of the fifty-six-pound weight with one hand. Then he'd swing it back and forth, up and down, to build momentum, his kilt swaying dramatically with each smooth movement. Three times, and then he would release the block of iron with a prayer.

If it went well — and so far, for Joey, it had always gone well — the weight would sail up over his head and high into the air. The crowd would gasp, the lump of iron would seem to freeze at the apex of its climb then it would descend on the far side of the bar, not even causing it to tremble. And then the crowd would roar. The world record stood an inch over nineteen feet. Joey was three inches behind.

Sometimes it did not go well and the bar came tumbling to the ground. And sometimes it went very badly indeed. Men had died on the field in front of families no longer having a good day out. But Joey refused even to consider that as a possibility. He threw with absolute faith in his command of fifty-six pounds of iron as aerodynamic as a breezeblock.

The afternoon at Invercharron had gone well. The sun had shone and there had been a good turnout. As well as his success in his trademark event, Joey had scored money places in four other events. Children had swarmed around him, demanding autographs, asking parents with cameras to take pictures of them being held high in the air by the champion of the day. He was a hero, not least because he was the nearest to handsome that the games circuit had to offer. He stood out in a world where most of his rivals looked like Saturday-night thugs.

Once the melee had died down, there was a gaggle of adults vying for his attention. As usual, he was focused on what was in front of him, so he didn't notice the watcher on the fringes, intent eyes never leaving him; assessing, considering, judging. Eventually, Joey extricated himself, and started towards the rather more luxurious camper van he inhabited these days.

He'd barely taken half a dozen strides when a light touch on his arm made him pause. He turned, the automatic smile on his face. 'I've got a proposition for you,' an attractive stranger with an American accent said.

So they'd travelled under cover of darkness, arriving at their destination close on midnight. The moon was a thin sickle in the star-studded sky, barely above the horizon. The camper van bumped down the narrow track, past a two-storey cottage with all the curtains drawn shut and no lights showing. 'I hope they're good sleepers,' Joey said. 'Otherwise we might have company. I bet they don't get a lot of late-night traffic on the road to nowhere.'

'We'll have to take our chances,' Shirley said. They crested a rise in the road and dropped down into a dip, invisible now apart from the cones of the headlights. 'See that tree on the right?' It was a stunted mountain ash, gnarled and twisted by the prevailing winds.

'Is that where you want me to stop?'

'Yeah, right there.'

They put on head torches and climbed out,

collecting a spade, a large battery-operated light and a crowbar from the tool locker on the back of the van. They picked their way across the rough ground with its covering of heather and coarse grasses, taking care to avoid the boggy pools of brackish water. About fifty yards from the road, Joey's torch beam picked out a small cairn of stones, no higher than the middle of his calf. 'This is what we're looking for, right?'

'That's it.' No note of excitement, just a calm acknowledgement that they'd found the spot. 'I put the marker there. I checked out the area with a metal detector, and that's where I got a hit. I think they're side by side, judging by the way the detector was beeping.'

'I better make a start, then.' Joey took off his padded lumberjack shirt and stuck the spade in the soft peaty soil.

'Careful with the top layer, we'll need to replace that.'

Joey looked up. 'Why? We'll be well on our way before anybody notices a big hole in the ground round here.'

'I don't want people asking questions. Better to be safe than sorry.'

'Fair enough.' Joey changed the angle of his spade so that he was taking off the top layer of turves and setting them to one side in a neat stack.

'I'll go and get the ladder.'

'And I'll keep digging.'

'It's what I'm paying you for.' A note of sharpness.

He gave her a long considering look. But what

she'd promised him was worth a bit of hard work. 'I know. I don't have to like it, though.'

★ ★ ★

Joey had stamina as well as strength but still it took the best part of two hours before his spade hit something that wasn't heavy wet peat. It was softer than he expected, but it was definitely something alien in the soil. 'I think this it,' he called up. 'That's about what you expected, right? Four feet down?'

'Exactly. They dug down about six feet and the crates would be a couple of feet deep at least.'

'I'll clear the top of it so we can pry off the top planks.' He set to work again, as the light from Shirley's torch played over the small section of wood he'd uncovered.

'Looks undisturbed.'

Joey nodded. 'No sign anybody's been messing with it.' He carried on, scraping the dark peat off wood that had been stained almost black by the tannins in the water. Twenty minutes later, he'd revealed a dozen four-inch planks, a shade over six feet long. 'I thought the wood would be rotten,' he said, leaning on the spade and breathing heavily, his naked torso gleaming with sweat. 'Better chuck me the crowbar.'

A few minutes and a lot of grunting later, two planks had been freed. In the light of the torches, they could both see what looked like a tarpaulin. 'Definitely something here,' Joey said.

'The tarpaulin's reassuring. Looks like we might be in with a fighting chance of salvaging the bikes.' It was the first time she'd smiled since Oykel Bridge, he thought.

'I hope so. One for me and one for you, like we agreed. Every biker I know will be green.' Joey returned to his task, piling the planks along the side of the hole. When he'd removed the last one, he carefully climbed down into the crate itself, his feet splashing as he went. There was barely room for him, but he was as eager as his employer to find out what lay inside the tarpaulin. He angled the light on the canvas, searching for a way in. 'Looks like they've sealed it up somehow.'

'All the better. Can you get into it?' She leaned over, the light gleaming on her blonde hair.

In answer, Joey dug into his pocket and brought out an impressive jackknife, waving it above his head. He opened a blade and sawed his way through the heavy tarp, letting it fall away as he opened the cut further. Whatever was inside the canvas was encased in another layer, this time of oilskin. He slit through it effortlessly. Even in the poor light, they could both see the motorbike was in amazing condition. Sealed inside the waterproofed layers, it had been protected for forty years from the bog that contained it. 'Ya beauty,' Joey breathed.

'See the panniers?' Now there was a note of anxiety in her voice.

'I see them.'

'Take a look inside.'

It wasn't a suggestion. But she was the one paying the piper; she got to call the tune. Joey shrugged, leaned over and struggled with the two straps. Time had hardened the leather to the shape of the buckle and Joey ended up using the spike tool from his knife to force them free. He lifted the lid. 'Empty,' he said.

'Try the other one.'

Joey repeated the process on the other side of the bike. This time, he struck lucky. He reached in and retrieved an oilskin packet about the size of a bag of sugar. 'Is this what you were hoping for?' He waved the package over his head.

'Perfect. Chuck it up here.'

Joey lobbed the packet up in a gentle underarm throw. The light from the other head torch followed its trajectory, which ended in a soft scrunch. 'Got it.'

'OK. Now we've got to get the bike.' Joey eyed the trophy carefully. 'I can lift it over my head. That'll take it above the edge of the hole,' he said, as if it were nothing. 'If you grab it when it comes level and pull it towards you, it'll fall to the ground. And I can take it from there. Can you manage that?' Now there was a faint note of anxiety. When it came to civilians, especially women, Joey had little faith in their strength or abilities.

'I think I can just about cope with letting a bike fall.' She gave a dark chuckle.

Joey braced himself, planting his feet apart. He'd checked out the bike's weight; it came in around 550 pounds. He'd never lifted more than 500 pounds, but he knew he was in peak condition after a summer of competition. He inhaled deeply, gripped the frame of the bike, closed his eyes and focused. The world contracted till he knew nothing but the intricate piece of metal in his hands.

He was oblivious to the differently intricate piece of metal that nestled in her hand.

Slowly, inch by inch, he raised the motorbike from the bottom of the crate. The veins of his neck and arms stood out and his muscles bulged with the effort as he strained every sinew to lift the bike high enough to topple it over the lip of the hole.

He'd almost succeeded when the first bullet crashed through his chest, just to the right of his heart. He stumbled momentarily but when the second bullet struck him in the throat, Joey crumpled backwards, the crushing weight of the bike forcing what air remained in his lungs out from his lips in a high-pitched wheeze.

By dawn, the only sign of what had taken place was an uneven patchwork of heather and grasses fifty yards from the road. By the following spring, even Shirley O'Shaughnessy would have struggled to spot where she'd replaced the peat to hide the last resting place of Joey Sutherland.

Acknowledgements

I know a lot less than people give me credit for. But luckily, I know people who can fill the gaps in my knowledge. The backroom team who lent me their expertise this time include:

Miranda Aldhouse-Green, for her encyclopaedic knowledge of what happens to bodies in peat bogs;

Lorna Dawson, the mistress of soil science, who explained the peat bogs of the Western Highlands of Scotland;

Judy Harvey of the Emporium Bookshop, Cromarty, whose anecdote set the wheels turning;

Jennifer Morag Henderson, whose biography of the great Josephine Tey reminded me, in passing, of what happened to the Highlands in WWII;

Jason Young, who generously shared his experiences of life on the Highland Games circuit for heavy athletes;

Sally Mackintosh for inviting me to be the Chieftain of the Invercharron Highland Games in 2016;

Jenny Brown for the earring and the Kolkata fun;

Tara Noonan at the National Library of Scotland for help with newspaper archive queries;

And Nicola Sturgeon for the use of her drawing room.

This is my thirty-second novel but still I need help to make it better. Those without whom I would struggle include Lucy Malagoni, David Shelley, Cath Burke and Thalia Proctor at Little, Brown; Jane Gregory and Stephanie Glencross at David Higham Associates; Amy Hundley at Grove Atlantic; my indefatigable copy-editor Anne O'Brien (any mistakes are mine, boss!); and Laura Sherlock who keeps the wheels on.

And last but not least, my brilliant, funny, adorable Professor and my smart, handsome lad, who both put a smile on my face when I feel least capable of good humour.

We do hope that you have enjoyed reading this large print book.

Did you know that all of our titles are available for purchase?

We publish a wide range of high quality large print books including:
Romances, Mysteries, Classics
General Fiction
Non Fiction and Westerns

Special interest titles available in large print are:
The Little Oxford Dictionary
Music Book
Song Book
Hymn Book
Service Book

Also available from us courtesy of Oxford University Press:
Young Readers' Dictionary
(large print edition)
Young Readers' Thesaurus
(large print edition)

For further information or a free brochure, please contact us at:
Ulverscroft Large Print Books Ltd.,
The Green, Bradgate Road, Anstey,
Leicester, LE7 7FU, England.
Tel: (00 44) **0116 236 4325**
Fax: (00 44) **0116 234 0205**

INSIDIOUS INTENT

Val McDermid

A quiet night on a country road. The stillness shattered by a car engulfed in flames, and a burned body discovered in the driver's seat. As the investigation unfolds, DCI Carol Jordan and psychological profiler Tony Hill quickly realise that this is more than just a tragic accident. And so begins the hunt for a truly terrifying killer, someone who believes he is invisible, untraceable and untouchable. As other victims are found to have met the same terrible fate, and with more women at risk, Tony and Carol are drawn into a dark and twisted web of fear and revenge that will force them to question their own ideas of justice . . .

OUT OF BOUNDS

Val McDermid

When a teenage joyrider crashes a stolen car, a routine DNA test could be the key to unlocking the mystery of a twenty-year-old murder inquiry. Detective Chief Inspector Karen Pirie is an expert at solving the unsolvable. With each cold case closed, justice is served. So, finding the answer should be straightforward — but it's as twisted as the DNA helix itself. Meanwhile, Karen finds herself irresistibly drawn to another case, one that she has no business investigating. And as she pieces together decades-old evidence, she discovers the most dangerous kind of secrets — secrets that someone is willing to kill for . . .

SPLINTER THE SILENCE

Val McDermid

Psychological profiler Tony Hill is trained to see patterns, to decode the mysteries of human behaviour. When he comes across a series of suicides among women tormented by vicious online predators, he begins to wonder if there is more to these tragedies than meets the eye. Similar circumstances, different deaths. Could it be murder? But what kind of serial killer wants his crimes to stay hidden? Former DCI Carol Jordan has her own demons to confront. But with lives at stake, she and Tony begin the hunt for the most dangerous and terrifying kind of killer — someone who has nothing to fear and nothing to lose . . .

THE SKELETON ROAD

Val McDermid

When a skeleton is discovered hidden at the top of a crumbling Gothic building in Edinburgh, Detective Chief Inspector Karen Pirie is faced with the unenviable task of identifying the bones. As Karen's investigation gathers momentum, she is drawn deeper into a world of intrigue and betrayal, spanning the dark days of the Balkan Wars. Karen's search for answers brings her to a small village in Croatia, a place scarred by fear, where people have endured unspeakable acts of violence. Meanwhile, someone is taking the law into their own hands in the name of justice and revenge — but when present resentment collides with secrets of the past, the truth is more shocking than anyone could have imagined . . .